GRIMM'S PUPPETS

TOM PRATER

TOM PRATER

Tom Prater asserts the moral right to be identified as the author of this work. He can be contacted at:
Tm_prater@icloud.com

First Paperback edition: October 2022

Cover art by Ollie Brunyate.

First edition.

ISBN 979 8 3583 6578 0

GRIMM'S PUPPETS

*For Mr. Elliott, who started my love of writing, and for
Mrs. Morgan, whose teaching remains with me.*

TOM PRATER

Acknowledgements

Firstly, thank you to Lizzie for all of your work on this book.

Thank you to my family for reading, editing, and helping with the plot.

Thank you to Ollie for the fantastic cover designs.

Thank you to Ellie and Maisie for being among the first to read this book.

Thank you to Jacob, Dan, Fergus, Harry, Matt, and Archie for always being there.

Thank you to the teachers at Harden for your support.

Thank you to 1855 for listening to me talk about Grimm's whilst I should have been working.

Thank you to Jacob, Ewan, Bradley and Sam—SL

Thank you to Phoebe R for her art, and to Phoebe T for her inspiration.

Thank you to Milli for her edits in the early chapters.

And thank you to whoever is reading this. I hope Will's story is one you'll enjoy.

Finally, thank you to Russell T Davies, Nick Cave, and Stephen King. These pages are echoes of you.

GRIMM'S PUPPETS

TOM PRATER

TOM PRATER

GRIMM'S PUPPETS

An extract from Hollyhead's Haunting by Will Metlocke (1974):

Allow me to introduce you to Hollyhead, a town famous for two reasons. The first being the burger that shares the same name. When a town is famous for a burger, you know the burger is either mouth-wateringly good or the town is fantastically dull. In this case, both are true.

Until 1968, Hollyhead was nothing more than a stop on a road-trip through Indiana. Somewhere tired drivers would grab a bite after a long day at the wheel. Stay any longer than that and you'd risk being sucked into the fading colors of the town. Until 1968, the burger was the only reason to go…

When a second reason for recognition comes along, most towns would snatch it up and squeeze the life out of it. Whether with tours, events, or t-shirts printed with phrases and logos that would fade after a single wash. At the time, Hollyhead would never have dreamed of marketing their tragedy, but a year later the first claws of capitalism started to scramble through the cracks—anything goes when you're trying to make a quick buck. Push on five years in the future and the town never lets you hear the end of it. As days go on, tragedy seems to evaporate into statistics and facts. This is what happened to Hollyhead.

The second reason for Hollyhead's fame is a photo. The photo in question was taken in front of the billboard located at the edge of the town, welcoming visitors to the area. The painted billboard featured a wide-grinned woman holding out a burger, emboldened by a background of red and green. There was something about the way she held that hamburger that reminded me of church, as if the burger were the next resurrection of Jesus Christ. To the people of Hollyhead it might well have been. In the years since, the poster has been removed, replaced with a dull white sign, HOLLYHEAD plastered in black letters across the horizon. It wasn't until 1972 that a bright spark decided to include: 'The location of the Billboard Murders' underneath.

The picture was taken by a detective named Eric Hatch and somehow leaked into the public only a few hours later, although anyone driving by wouldn't have had much trouble spotting what caught the cops' attention. Six bodies aren't easy to miss. I don't know how they got up there. Theories range from a collective suicide pact to a killer using a makeshift crane to hoist them up. I have never believed that suicide had anything to do with what happened. It's not really something that children think about. Personally, I believe Occam's Razor is in play here—the simplest answer is normally correct. Unfortunately, there is no straightforward answer. I doubt there ever will be.

All we know is that on the morning of October 15th, 1968, the six Spark brothers were found hanging from the Hollyhead billboard; the smaller boys on the side and the larger in the middle. Each dressed in a white gown. The hem of the fabric was sewn into their arms, presenting them in an almost angelic state. Their eyes were black, and their noses painted a dark orange. The youngest brother, Gus, was missing the entirety of his left arm. Six angels hanging from the Hollyhead billboard. When a town is famous for a burger and the murder of six boys, you know it's not a place to take the kids, much to the town's dismay.

Of course, I remember what it was like. It's not something you can easily forget. There was no escaping the ripple that commenced following their death. That ripple is still going. There's no way of knowing when it will end. Maybe it will be when the killer is caught—*if* they are ever caught. That is likely to be the answer as far as the police are concerned. Ask a friend of the family and they may reply that the ripple will end once the kid's mother and father have passed. As for me, I don't think that the water will ever be still again. Books will continue to be written about those murders. Newspaper headlines will still squeeze the last drops of juice from the story and if the killer is ever found, it will only exacerbate the tale.

That is as much as I will say about the Spark boys. I shall not add to the murmurs and speculation. If you want to know more, just head on down. You won't go a minute without hearing about them. The town will thank you for your interest. That's just Hollyhead's nature.

CHAPTER ONE:
A RUDE AWAKENING

11.28.80: Twelve years after the story began.

Will Metlocke wasn't sure whether it was the shrill ringing of the phone or the searing pain in his chest that woke him. Either way, the voice at the end of the line was enough to shake the last disjointed fragments of sleep from his body. Outside of his duvet, the air was thin with a chill that had seeped in throughout the night—the result of a broken window that he hadn't bothered to get fixed. It was only November—there were plenty of cold nights ahead of him. Holding the receiver to his ear, Will scrambled around his bedside drawer for a half-empty bottle of painkillers and tossed back a few, not bothering to check whether he had the correct dose. He sighed, already feeling the pain subside a little.

"Whoever this is, you'd better have a good reason for waking me up," he yawned.

"It's Frank," said the voice. It was a good thing he announced himself; the croak of his voice was a stark difference from the last time Will had heard him. He had gained a smoker's rasp—full of phlegm and sickness. Either that or his lungs had grown a couple of tumors.

"Sorry, I'm busy right now, but leave me your number and I'll *definitely* call you later," said Will, rubbing his eyes. He didn't put down the phone.

"Can you be serious for once?" Frank's voice was scathing. He followed up with a throaty cough. Will waited for the wheezing to cease, wondering whether a serious illness would warrant a call from his father. After all, Will hadn't told him about his own diagnosis.

"Started smoking, have you? Poor way to spend your golden years, Dad," said Will, testing the water. If Frank *was* sick, this was the perfect time to say so. Frank made a disgruntled noise on the other end. Will listened to his heavy breathing, waiting for the awkward silence to be broken by either party. Frank eventually spoke.

"I need to see you. Tonight."

Will's heart seemed to freeze mid-pump.

"I'm busy," he replied. In truth, he had spent most of the night wandering around the house, attempting to tire himself to sleep. When that hadn't worked, he'd sat down at his typewriter, but the incessant clicking of the keys had only added to his agitation. After an hour, having only typed a few measly lines he probably wouldn't use, he got back into bed and stared at the ceiling until the room faded around him.

"It's important," said Frank. Will didn't doubt it. The last time his father had contacted him was two years ago, and that was only to notify him that his uncle had died. The phone call lasted less than a minute.

"So is my beauty sleep. If I don't get my eight hours, I get cranky."

"You're a miserable kid anyway. You can catch up on sleep."

Sure I can, thought Will.

Every night for the past month had been disturbed by a dull ache in his upper body, followed by a bombardment of night sweats.

"When I say that this is important, I mean something life-changing. I wouldn't be calling if it wasn't. You know that."

Will considered slamming the phone down—a calmer solution than his urge to scream profanities down the receiver. Only someone insane would call up out of the blue with a sudden request.

"Have you replaced that car yet?" said Frank.

Will's eyes flickered to his driveway. The distinct absence of a vehicle was the only thing differentiating it from the rest of the street.

"It's in for repair," he lied, rubbing his chest with his hand. The pain was slowly subsiding, leaving a relieving numbness.

Frank was silent, leaving only the crackling of white noise in the receiver. "I'll call you a cab. I'm still at the old house."

Will shifted uncomfortably. He hadn't planned on returning to Hollyhead; the mere mention of its name unsettled him.

"Why now? It's three in the morning."

"Because I'm up."

"And everything must fit into your time frame. Can't you come here instead?"

"No, you need to come here, to Hollyhead... It *has* to be here. Be ready in twenty minutes. I'll see you soon."

With that, the phone line went silent, the dial tone burning into Will's skull as wild theories began forming in his head. He placed the phone back into its cradle, a red light flashing lazily on the monitor. Before falling back into bed, he jabbed the play button and a familiar, nasal voice droned into life.

"Mr. Metlocke, it's Doctor Christensen here. We want to see you again, just to talk through your options. I know I said it was treatable, and I would imagine it still is. However, time is of the essence. Give me a call when you get this," the voice said, followed by a lingering beep.

Will imagined the doctor putting down the phone and running a hand through his wisps of grey hair. Christensen probably still had that mustard stain beneath the left lapel of his doctor's coat. Knowing him, the doctor probably hadn't taken it off since their meeting two days prior. With each visit, his face grew an extra wrinkle.

Will tapped the erase button, just as he had done the last time, without thought or hesitation. The red light blinked out, leaving him lying in the few strands of moonlight that had crept through the slats in his blinds, frozen at the thought of returning home.

*

Will remained on his bed for a few minutes, staring at the shapes that danced on his ceiling each time a car rolled past the window. He had tried so hard to leave Hollyhead in the past. Hearing its name filled him with a deep sense of dread; the town had that effect on you. So many had told him they wanted to leave. They rarely did. Most of the inhabitants were born there and would end up six feet under its soil. He was one of the lucky ones. He'd managed to get out before its claws had dug in too deep. Still, it was deep enough to cause a wound. A part of him knew that in returning he would risk ending up there forever—or whatever time he had left.

It's one night. Just to see what Frank wants. You can survive one night…

Eventually, he sat up and hauled himself out of bed. His clothes from the day prior were thrown onto his chair and he put them on again. Pulling on his sneakers, he left the room, ignoring the duvet, which lay in a heap on the floor.

The house groaned in time with his footsteps as Will trudged down the stairs. He hadn't bothered decorating. When he had first moved in, he had only expected to stay for a few months—one-year tops. Two years later and there were still just as many boxes piled up as there had been on day one. All full of books and crap he had accumulated while living in Los Angeles. Reaching the bottom of the stairs, he kicked away a pile of letters that had spilled through the door. They had slowly been building up since the diagnosis; if it was important, they would call.

Before he could go, he needed something. He turned left into his study and flicked on the light, illuminating the room in a warm, electric glow. The study was the only room he had wanted to make his own. Most of the days consisted of settling down at his desk and rattling out another part of his latest novel. His typewriter had belonged to him since he was eighteen—a gift from an old friend. The keys were faded ivory, set around a base of crimson. If there was anything he was going to miss, it would be that. Crumpled paper surrounded the machine, representing his many failed attempts at writing something moving or original. Above, a shelf displayed a number of books, the first being a short, one-hundred-page trial and the last being nothing more than a glorified doorstop. His name was printed in golden letters down the spine. Over time, the shelf had become home to a thick blanket of dust.

A green sofa in the corner was purely for display. He had bought it several months prior and failed to recognize that it was too uncomfortable for anyone to occupy longer than a few minutes—not that he received many visitors anyway. Records were stacked against the wall, including his first pressing Glenn Miller, one of his most prized possessions.

Another book was displayed in a glass cabinet beside the door, sitting proudly on its metal stand. The front cover featured the view of a woman seen through a sniper scope with the title *The Death Clock* circled around it. Below, letters dripping with blood stated that the book was: *A Metlocke Novel.* The publisher's name lined the bottom of the cover: *Winston and Ricklowe.*

Will clicked the case open and picked the book up. He opened it to the first page and saw his face smiling back at him. In the three years since the photo had been taken, he had been stripped of the five-star meals cooked up for L.A.'s finest. The man in the photograph was a good twenty pounds heavier, with a shaven face and a long nose. Will was now skinnier than most people he met, and a patchy beard hid his gaunt cheeks. The nose had remained, of course.

"Five hundred pages of disaster," he sighed, snapping the book shut and replacing it. He returned to the desk and waited, his foot tapping rhythmically on the floor. It seemed most of his life consisted of waiting for taxis, whether it was to go to grand book signings near Central Park during his stints in New York or to race to his editor so that she could reveal quite how lacking his writing had become. For a while now, even the thought of driving caused his chest to tighten.

That was when the rewind called to him—a spark in his brain that filled him with warmth, a feeling that made him reach out for the object. It was a comfort that he had known for years. The small circular device buzzed alluringly in front of him. Purple lights positioned in concentric circles flashed one by one: it was waking, just as he was. Will picked it up, the metal warm in his hands. Heat radiated from the heart of the machine; sometimes he could swear that it had a pulse. Like so many times before, he gazed at it for a few moments. It sat perfectly in the palm of his hand as if it had been designed specifically for him. The muscles in his face twitched into a smile.

A harsh honk from a car outside brought him back to reality. Will slipped the rewind into his pocket, stepped out into the frosty night air, and closed the door firmly shut behind him.

Will hadn't been back to Hollyhead since his fourth book: *Hollyhead's Haunting*. Even while writing, he had refrained from staying in the town long, preferring to get a ride in from the neighboring town rather than stay in a local hotel. The only reason he had agreed to return was because his agent had told him that hometown murders sold. If it wasn't for the next commission he had received (*Spectres of Seattle*), he would never have agreed. Never return home if there isn't another stop on your horizon.

The route took the pair toward the billboard. Despite the time, there were a few cars dotted around the town, some bouncing rhythmically, causing the headlights to sway through the night, and others in complete darkness, only noticeable when lit by the cab's yellow glare. With a squeal of old brakes, the car came to a stop at a set of lights hanging in the air, allowing Will to look at the billboard that he hadn't seen in six years. A shop perched beneath it, a sign on the door displayed a card saying: 'BACK BRIGHT AND EARLY' inside a smiley face. Postcards and t-shirts were displayed in a large window in preparation for the next onslaught of visitors. It wasn't out of the ordinary to see photos of teenagers posing by the billboard, some even going as far as wearing long white gowns.

Will's attention turned to the billboard again. In most cases, a board as old as this would be in bad shape, but not here. Volunteers repainted it each year.

Hollyhead had started small. In the beginning, the town consisted of only a few houses, a shop, and a diner, scattered along the banks of the river. As the years went by, investors had seen it as a good opportunity from which to dispatch goods to the neighboring towns, leading to a fresh wave of residents. The town grew in size and a new family took over the diner. Immediately, they added their homemade sauce to the burgers, and word spread. Workmen told their families, who told their friends, and within weeks, the Hollyhead burger became the most talked about feature of the town—that is, until the deaths occurred.

At first, they had shied away from capitalizing on the Billboard Murders. A hush would shudder through the town at any mention of the Spark boys. That changed a year later when a man called Lopsided Bill, so named because of the way his face sagged on one side, a consequence of a stroke he'd suffered five years prior, started a group dedicated to conjuring up conspiracies surrounding the boys' murders. It wasn't long before the rest of the town saw the opportunity to exploit the tragedy. The theories stretched as far as the boys being abducted by the government to be used in experiments for the moon landing, complications causing their noses to turn orange and eyes to be blacked out. It was a testament to the standard of education in Hollyhead that this theory became one of the more sensible takes. Bill had been the first to start tours, his most expensive and popular commencing outside the Spark residence, a rotting old farmhouse barely big enough for a family of two, let alone eight. Melanie Spark had complained, even going as far as running at the tourists with a broom before being dragged back indoors by her husband, which was no easy feat; Melanie was at least six feet, five inches tall.

Many had told the couple to move away, though they knew they never would. A mother would rather hold on to a painful memory of her child than none at all. Benny Spark, although a weedy man and considerably smaller than his giant of a wife, remained convinced that whoever killed his children would be back at some point for bragging rights.

The sight of old Bill flying through Hollyhead in his gleaming new convertible Mustang catapulted the neighbors into action and before long, books featuring the Spark boys lined the shelves of every retailer in town, ranging from interviews with their schoolmates to debates concerning whether the supernatural had any involvement. At the memorial service to mark the anniversary of their deaths, arranged at the request of the mayor, there were more journalists than mourners. Whoever had killed the boys had done more than end their lives: they had turned them into cash grabs. Cash grabs and nightmare fuel. It was often said that parents would tuck their children into bed and tell them to be quiet and sleep, or the Spark boys would appear in their rooms and the kids would never see the light of day again.

Will tore his gaze away from the scene and noticed the taxi driver watching him through narrowed eyes in the rear-view mirror.

"You that book guy? The one who writes about aliens and shit?" he asked with a snort.

"Not aliens," breathed Will. "More like the supernatural."

"Well, you're in the right place for it," he said, jerking his thumb back towards the billboard, growing increasingly smaller behind them.

"I guess so," said Will, hoping to put an end to the conversation. He had already decided that the driver wasn't worth his time.

"Haven't read any of your stuff myself. More the kids who enjoy it. My wife reckons you've lost your touch over the years."

"Is that so?" Will replied, trying to sound as unbothered as possible.

"Yeah, all that psychic stuff you do. It's gotta be a trick, right?"

Will slid the rewind further into his pocket. "Well, if I told you, I'd have to kill you."

The driver looked at him for a second before breaking out into a deep roar of laughter. Will smiled weakly.

"Any plans on that other series you had going? The one about that detective who could taste all those colors."

Will felt a small stab of pain. After the success of his first few novels, he had tried his hand at detective fiction—the genre he had always wanted to write. The book ended up in bargain buckets within months of its release. He often saw it at garage sales, the owners just leaving it in a box labeled 'need gone'.

"No, it's just the one."

The driver scratched at the gray stubble around his chin. "I'll tell you what though. A book of that size is worth something, even if it is just for fire kindling."

"I'm sure," said Will.

*

Within five minutes, the taxi had reached the winding dirt roads leading to the southern area of the town. Hills surrounded Hollyhead as if the centre had been sucked in towards Hell before being spat out again. Will smiled. If there was any way to accurately describe Hollyhead then it was the place too rotten even for the Devil. Before he moved away, Will had often walked to the tops of the hills to look down upon the town, though it had always been covered in a haze of black smoke. He *could* say that the sight had grown on him, that the spire of the church was a knife cutting through into a better world, but he felt nothing. Perhaps the odd memory would squeeze through into his mind, but he had learned long ago that shutting them out was like extinguishing a match, harmless if done quickly, but painful if he held on too long.

The river crept through gaps in the rock, sometimes narrowing to fewer than ten feet wide. From Will's house, the quickest way into his hometown was to take secondary roads a short way after the billboard. After a short drive, the modern glass houses were swapped with windswept cottages and industrial buildings while wooden boats swayed indolently on the river. The water here was oily sludge, surrounded by docks nailed into the riverbank and stacks of crates ready to be shipped out on the next boat. The cab passed the jetty and traveled further into Hollyhead until Will started to recognize the streets that he had walked through as a child. Narrow sidewalks that had scorched his shoes when the sun was particularly harsh were now cracked and warped after years of neglect. Will didn't know why he had moved only a short car journey away from his hometown. Sometimes he had the feeling that there was a tether around his neck, binding him to the streets and vapors of Hollyhead.

It wasn't long before the number of houses slowly fell away and the car turned the final corner to their destination. Deadened hedges suddenly enclosed them. The cab trundled along, rocking slightly on the eroded remains of the path underneath. Soon, the foliage turned to stone as the wall leading to his childhood house came into view.

"Shame what happened here, used to be a nice piece of land," noted the driver, peering out of the frosty side window towards Will's old home. The paint, once white, had faded and plants had seized the opportunity to climb the brick and poke through the crevices where the cement had crumbled away. A single tree had broken through the soil in the front yard, bare of leaves at this time of year.

Will paid and stepped away before the engine coughed into life again and the taillights disappeared into the night. He opened the gate, careful not to pull it off its hinges. The sound of the creek crept towards him from the back of the house. It was a noise he had soon learned to tune out. Although the river was the playground of choice for many kids in the summer, Will had never been in.

Never will, he thought.

His bedroom had been at the front left of the house. The window, which he had spent most of his days staring out of, sat covered in grime and green moss. It wouldn't have surprised him if Frank hadn't set foot in that room since the day Will left for college. The only farewell being a handshake and a nod.

He arrived at the door and knocked, a part of him believing that the whole thing was some kind of joke. Through the black glass, he could make out a tall figure striding towards the door. Once opened, it took Will a moment to realize that the man standing before him was not his father, but Marty Goodall— his father's co-worker from his government years.

"It's been a while," he said, looking Will up and down before breaking into a toothy grin.

"Sorry I'm late. I didn't want to be here," Will replied. Despite his best efforts, his façade broke, and he gave Marty a hug.

He hadn't expected to see Marty after all these years. The last time they had met was on Christmas day, 1964. Frank had been too busy to drop off a gift for his son, so Marty, taking pity, had picked up a first-edition Christie novel. He'd been scrawny back then, dressed in an immaculate black suit, with a cigarette dangling from his mouth as if it had been permanently welded to his lip. Since then, his gaunt cheeks had filled in and were now covered in patches of bristle. Although balding, his hair stuck up with enough gel to cause splinters. They shared a quick handshake before Will stepped inside.

The hallway had long since been stripped of decoration. Only the clock adjacent to the kitchen door had survived the purge. The hands ticked dully as Will walked past; he had to take a second look to ensure they weren't going backward. Everything about the house screamed old and not in a fashionable kind of way. Long shadows chased away the shreds of light at the far end of the hall. The glow protruded from the lounge, situated at the back of the house. Will walked past the stairs, which had previously been home to a small gallery of family photos and approached the door.

"Knock first," instructed Marty.

Will hesitated but obliged. A muffled chair scrape was followed by footsteps approaching the door. The door opened to reveal his father, and Will couldn't help but feel like he was staring into a mirror. Frank Metlocke shared his son's height, though his military-like posture meant that he was always looking down on Will. It was as if he had fixed a string of wire into his skin that would pull him upright if he dropped his head for even a second. Round glasses, which he had a habit of pushing up his nose for no good reason, slightly magnified his penetrating eyes. Frank had dressed in a purple sweater, several sizes too big, which came across as very peculiar, considering Will was sure he had never seen his father wear anything other than a suit. The sweater itself was fraying in the arms, loose threads dangling from the elbows. It looked like something he had picked up from a trunk sale.

"Please come in," he said, opening the door wider.

"Fantastic to see you too, Dad," replied Will, showing a sarcastic smile.

"What's the matter with your face?" Frank asked. He seemed to blink slower than most people as if consciousness was a weight he had been carrying for too long.

Will smiled. Some things never changed and in regard to his father's observational skills, the saying was true. You either grow up admiring your father or go out of your way to be their complete opposite. Frank had never been abusive, nor had he ever smoked, though he seemed to have started since the last time they talked. Other than the way Frank spoke, as if everything he said was a fact under scrutiny, Will had no reason not to think of his father as a good man. Maybe he did think that, however, Will grew up neither admiring nor hating his father. For an emotion as strong as those, proximity was necessary, and proximity was something the pair had simply never shared.

"Charming as ever. I had an accident a few months ago. Existed on a diet of hospital food for a few weeks. I'm still in recovery. Plus, if I say I'm better, they stop giving me all the fun drugs."

Frank took a second to process the information. He seemed to accept it as he nodded and walked over to a trolley pushed against the far wall.

"Can I get you a drink?" he said, gesturing to the selection of bottles.

"Just water."

Marty sighed as he left for the kitchen. Will lowered himself into an armchair and looked around. "You know, as much as I love the minimalist lifestyle, it wouldn't hurt to have something in here that shows you have a family," he said.

Deep green paint coated the room, rather than the cozy red that Will remembered from his childhood. Just three armchairs and the drinks trolley made up the floor space. A marble fireplace stood in the center of the wall. A single large window was fixed into the wall furthest from the door, grey woolen curtains hanging on either side of the panes. Will could see the dust clinging to the threads of the curtains. A solid hit would produce enough filth to sideline an asthmatic kid for a few minutes. The house seemed strange. There was as much evidence that it was never used as there was to suggest Frank inhabited it every evening.

"I should accumulate more materialistic possessions, you mean? Like photographs? When did we ever have those?" said Frank, pouring himself a particularly large glass of whiskey.

So, now you drink as much as you smoke…

"Well, it was always difficult. We could never find your good side."

Before Frank could reply, Marty returned holding a glass and a beer bottle.

"Should I drink this? Or is this just an elaborate ruse to poison me?" he asked, taking the water.

Marty chuckled. "Well, if we wanted to kill you, we would already have done so."

Frank and Marty sat next to each other looking like something from an old comedy show. Their difference in size made Frank pale in comparison to Marty.

"We have a proposition for you," said Frank.

Will opened his arms to welcome their request. "What can I do for you?"

Frank and Marty shared a look. "We need you to solve a murder," said Frank.

CHAPTER TWO:
HIDDEN TRUTHS

Will let out a snort of laughter, but the look on his father's face quickly caused him to sit back in bewilderment.

"You know I'm an author, right? I throw words at a page and these days most people would say that I'm not even good at that. Give me a deerstalker and a pipe and I may look the part, but I'm afraid that's the best I can offer you."

"Let him finish," said Marty, attempting to mediate before leaning back into his armchair. The black leather of the seats could have been a part of his suit, right down to the stains on the material.

Frank nodded his thanks. "How much do you know about what your old man did?"

Will's ears pricked. He had known that Marty and his father had worked for the government, though the capacity of their role had always been a mystery. All Will remembered was the stretch of days that passed by between visits home and the occasional sighting of his colleagues, all men dressed in expensive business suits.

"Not much, but if you're about to tell me your meet-cute story, I would rather have it in writing—lasts longer that way."

"This is serious, Will," said Frank.

"Although we do have a good meet-cute story," added Marty to an unimpressed Frank. "We worked for the government investigating homicides."

Will frowned. "It sounds like you're exactly who you should be asking to solve a murder then," he said. To his surprise, Frank laughed. The climax of the laugh turned into a hacking cough and Marty passed over a handkerchief. Frank spat and folded it into his pocket.

"You would think so, looking at our record. We had the most solves for three years in a row back in the early sixties."

"Then congratulations are in order. You want a trophy?" asked Will.

"Already got one," smiled Marty.

"When you say government… you mean FBI?" said Will. Despite his best efforts, his curiosity had gotten the best of him.

"The very same. We spent years devoting our lives to the service. I've even had to change my last name. Goodall is fine, but boy I miss Daniels. All in the name of the cause," said Marty.

"Don't you have buddies back there who can help you?" asked Will. Frank's face reddened, and he threw another inch of whiskey down his throat.

"Frank hasn't been part of the squad for the last decade," said Marty, sneaking a pitiful glance at his old partner.

"And you have?" said Will.

"I have less of a role, but I am still employed by the bureau, yes."

Will risked a glance at his father, who was staring intensely at the floor as if everything above ankle-level had suddenly become very bright. As far as he knew, Frank had always been in a secure position, financially at least. Will had believed that the lack of furniture was due to Frank's austerity; he hadn't considered the fact that his father might be struggling.

"Why exactly do you need me?" said Will.

"It turns out you have something we need. Something we can't get anywhere else," said Frank.

"See, that's where you're wrong. We all have a brain; you just need to learn how to use it. Most people get the hang of it around the age of three, but for some, it does take a little longer," replied Will, tapping his head.

"Of all people, *you* would know what goes on in my head— the perks of being a psychic, I guess," said Frank. From behind his chair, he produced a large, leather book that Will recognized as his latest release: *Communicating with Spirits*. He slammed it down on the table. "We've stayed well clear of your work, of course. You think we haven't had run-ins with psychics before? Weirdos who come to us spouting nonsense about recent cases.", said Frank. "We had one woman approach us, saying she believed one of her clients had committed murder in the first-degree. Apparently, she'd 'seen it'. We looked into it, just in case."

"Fucker wasn't even in the country when it happened," laughed Marty, boisterously.

"Guess she didn't see that one coming," muttered Will.

"Then you took it on. Telling grieving people that you can help them connect with the dead. In *my* book, that's just as bad as pulling a trigger," said Frank.

Not a book worth reading then, thought Will. *At least mine have sold.*

"That being said, you must have quite the inner eye. Books on the paranormal, all backed up by your clients. I guess there must be a pretty substantial market for material like that. How much was your last book deal worth?"

If I got a dime every time you said something interesting, I might get the equivalent of what I earn from my books, thought Will.

It was the events his agent had told him to speak at that had provided him with the lifestyle he had since grown out of. As a young man, he had yearned for the glamour of New York or L.A. When the dreams had finally bled into reality, he realized that the countless drunken nights and hours of painful small talk hadn't filled the hole he had expected it to. Something inside him still desired to be heard. Being an only child usually means that attention is commonplace. What else are the parents meant to do if not dote on their child? Well, whoever thought of that theory hadn't taken Frank Metlocke into account. For most of Will's childhood, Frank left him with a nanny, Molly, a nice enough lady but lacking in the brains department. Despite spending most of his youth in her company, Will hadn't known her well. The one thing that stuck in his mind was her fondness for gambling each time there was a big race on. She can't have won much because she stayed with the Metlocke family until the end of her life. She hadn't learned to read well, and she often said that there was no point in starting once you get to her age. Still, she did a perfectly good job at her other tasks. Will could complain about her smell and lack of education, but the apple pie she made every Sunday was delicious, and he never went a day without ironed clothes and fresh underwear. Her death occurred a short while after his eighteenth birthday.

At the funeral he left her a betting slip. Maybe she would have better luck in the afterlife.

"It's none of your concern how much I make," he decided to say. He held onto his glass tighter, trying to hide the shaking that he felt sure would only encourage Frank to push the knife further.

"Anyway, then we started talking," said Frank, picking up the book and flicking through the pages. "We wondered how you seem to know exactly who they want to talk to without any error. We thought you might just do your research, but no, you're far too accurate for that. They report that you can conjure it up within seconds."

"You've read my books then?" said Will.

"We read enough. We decided we wanted more of a first-hand experience," said Marty. Will's palms started to sweat, and he wiped them on his jeans, trying his best to appear nonchalant.

"The name Terry Nightingale ring any bells?"

It did. Her case had stuck in his mind long after they had met. She had called him, hoping to talk to her recently deceased mother. Will had agreed—his publisher had stated that she wanted another 20,000 words for the next release. The client had to be focused—if the mind wandered then flashes of other memories broke through. It just so happened that Terry Nightingale's memory of walking through winter snow had been fractured by images of Will's father. Will had put it aside at the time—he could easily have been thinking of Frank himself. Now it was clear. She had been working with Frank the whole time.

"You set me up?" said Will, feeling his breathing becoming shallow.

Frank locked his fingers. "We needed our hypothesis tested."

"And what was it?"

"We wanted to know whether your ability is truly biological or whether there is something you're not talking about in those books of yours."

The rewind suddenly felt burning hot in his pocket. He knew he shouldn't have brought it, but after so long, he couldn't resist. At the beginning, he had been able to refrain; it would cross his mind on only a few occasions. Soon it had become something that he needed. Withdrawal caused him to shake. Just the feel of it calmed him down.

"We set up cameras to monitor you while you worked. Then we noticed something familiar. A piece of technology that we believed was destroyed a long time ago."

Will knew that there was no way out, but he resisted further. "What technology?"

"We called it a Memory Expansion Device or MED," said Frank, his tone serious. "It was made in the fifties under Eisenhower. It stemmed from the creation of a piece of tech called a Somniamatrix. The FBI used the MED to validate the reliability of witness statements. Ground-breaking tech like that, you would think we would be shouting about it from the rooftops. Ike didn't want that. He wanted it kept quiet. 'What the Russians don't know will hurt them,' he said. For about ten years, it worked without a hitch. Batches were produced and sent out to our agents to use in their assignments. Later, there were some issues… Apparently, there were some long-term effects they hadn't anticipated."

"For reasons unknown, the MED had to be scrapped. The government put out a squad to ensure that none were in circulation," said Marty.

"You stole one?" asked Will. Each time they spoke, he knew they had him at their mercy. They were just tiring him out first.

"No, that would be stupid. We stole two," said Marty, chuckling. "We knew we wouldn't be kicked out. Just a quick slap on the wrist and back to it. We handed one over. Let the big boys think they had tracked them all down."

"We kept it here. For two years we used it during cases," said Frank.

"You weren't caught?"

"How would they catch us? I don't know the ins and outs of how it works but the scientists who worked on the design knew what they were doing. I'm sure you know that the recipient doesn't recall being under its influence."

Will knew. As far as his clients were aware, he had psychic abilities, making him capable of communicating with their loved ones who had passed on. What they didn't know was that the rewind allowed him to view their memories. Will would put on a bit of a display—smoke and mirrors, the usual. In reality, the client need only think of who they wished to communicate with and, using the rewind, he would form a link.

"We know you have it, Will," said Frank, his voice sprinkled with sympathy. "I think you've had it since '71. You remember when we had that break-in?"

Will could remember. It was the only time he had seen his father cry. Molly had called him, wailing at him that the study had been ransacked. Within the hour, Frank rushed home and began searching through papers and files like a man possessed. Before long, he was hugging his knees and crying into his lap, rocking back and forth like a child.

"I think you took it that day."

Of course, he was right. Will had noticed the crack in the window the day prior. In twenty-one years, he had only stepped into the study once, before being ushered away by his father with a quick hand. His curiosity had grown wild and when he had found a crowbar hidden in the basement, a plan had quickly formed in his mind. That night, he had forced his way into the office. It had drawn him in like a moth to a flame.

"Show it to us," said Marty, his eyes widening.

Will's shoulders tensed. Before he knew it, his hand was reaching into his pocket. He didn't miss Frank's smile when he revealed the device.

"Put it on the table," said Marty, almost reaching out.

Anger surged through Will's fingertips and they clenched around the metal. "No. You tell me what you need from me and then I will decide if I'm going to help you."

"Last night, a young woman was killed, Abigail Finsbury. Only twenty-one years old. The police haven't released details yet, but we pulled a few strings. We have reason to believe that it is linked to the death of the Spark brothers," said Frank, still not taking his eyes from the rewind.

"Those boys died twelve years ago; it can't be linked."

At that moment, a heavy knock rang through the house and Marty raised a finger to indicate he'd return shortly. Will and Frank were left alone.

"Is this the only reason you wanted to see me?" said Will, breaking the silence.

"Is another reason needed?"

"No, but it would be appreciated. I haven't seen you in years."

"All you need to know is that I am trusting you with the most important task of my life."

Will couldn't come up with anything to say. When Marty reappeared, he was accompanied by a giant of a man. He crouched a little as he stepped through the doorway, the wooden frame flattening his tuft of dark hair. Ridges of old scars covered his gritty skin. Dark rings surrounded his eyes, and his breathing rang heavy throughout the room, it sounded as though he was breathing through a tube.

"Tell me what this is all about," ordered Will.

"We could tell you, but we think it would be better if we showed you," said Frank.

The expression on the visitor's face was one Will had seen many times before. It was common in war veterans. The only thing differentiating them from this man was the eyes. This man was far too young to have been in the war.

CHAPTER THREE:
THE GIRL

Frank stood up and shook the stranger's hand. "Will, this is Officer Bruce Fisher."

Bruce's eyes darted towards Will and the corners of his mouth adjusted into a smile. Of all things in the house, his smile was the most lifeless of all. They exchanged a few words before being directed from the lounge by Marty. Will noticed that the appearance of the cop had pushed the agent back into his shell a little. His confident strut had been replaced by a nervous slouch. Frank guided them into the study at the far end of the house. Will expected to see the desk that his father had been tied to whenever he came home, positioned by a globe close to the window, but the whole room had been restyled. Instead of the desk, a circular wooden table dominated most of the floor space, its base being a cheap rustic design that dug into the carpet. Books by a variety of authors lined the walls. Will couldn't help but notice that none of his books were on display. What looked like classic fairy tales made up the section closest to the window. *Snow White and the Seven Dwarfs* caught his eyes immediately. The red leather-bound edition poked out slightly further than the rest of the ensemble. Will noticed that, unlike his own, the shelves were spotless. Judging by the rest of the house, Frank was not too fond of cleaning, meaning he must be reading these regularly.

He spends his time reading fairy-tales? The man has lost it.

Frank pulled out a chair and Bruce thanked him as he settled into it. Instantly, his fingers began tapping on the table, his eyes indecisive as to where to focus. Trying to hide the pain that had started again, Will followed and took a chair to Bruce's right.

Marty poured himself a glass of a green liquid from another drinks trolley and sat on the other side of Bruce. He began scratching at his scraps of beard.

Frank lit up a cigarette, ignoring Will's displeased glare, and addressed Bruce. "Will is my son. He writes books about…" he cleared his throat— "the supernatural. He believes that he sees ghosts. It all stems from his psychic abilities."

Bruce nodded his head as if this was the most normal thing he had heard. Will hadn't experienced such a reaction before. Statements about his career were universally followed by a sniff of laughter or a scattering of intrigue. He wasn't sure which he preferred.

"Bruce is one of Hollyhead's finest. I know him from my day's working alongside the force. He was on patrol the night of Abigail Finsbury's death," said Frank.

"Did more than that. I found her," growled Bruce. Red blotches had accumulated around his pupils, and already a thin sheen of sweat hung from the top of his brow.

Frank nodded.

"He's agreed to speak with you," said Marty, turning to Will.

Ever since Bruce had arrived, Will had been waiting for the moment where he would have to 'prove' his psychic powers. At least this time, he didn't have to find excuses for others to leave the room.

"This ain't going to hurt or nothin'?" asked Bruce.

They had told him. To what extent, Will wasn't sure, but Bruce's body had become rigid at the sight of the rewind. Will pulled his chair closer.

"You won't feel any physical pain, though you may find you feel some emotional distress," said Will.

"I ain't experienced anything in life that's hurt more than this, and I've been stabbed twice."

Will nodded, one hand holding onto the rewind in his pocket. "I need you to close your eyes and think clearly about when you found the body." Bruce's lips twitched slightly as he listened. "Shut out everything else. Focus on that night. Was it raining? Where had you been? What did her body look like?"

Bruce closed his eyes, the crow's feet straining around his eyelids. Will took the rewind from his pocket and the purple lights flared dramatically. The metal was warm in his hand. It wanted to be used…

"When you are ready, hold out your finger." Bruce raised one shaking finger and hovered it above the table. Will slid the rewind beneath and gently placed Bruce's finger down.

"Be careful," said Frank, his voice attempting to hide the panic that his body language gave away. Marty's anxiety had intensified. He took in several deep breaths, but his gaze fixed solidly on the rewind. With a nod, Will placed his finger on the metal and smelt a familiar burning odor. It had only happened the night prior. The memory was still fresh—not yet infected with the decay from leading questions and other testimonies. At that moment, Frank and Marty's bodies morphed into a colorless mound and the room vanished altogether.

*

Why do I always get the beat when it's raining?

The thought dominated Bruce Fisher's mind as he turned his collar up, feeling a cold drizzle slide down his neck. The rain had been relentless for the last three days. As soon as it stopped, another cloud would roll in overhead and a fresh downpouring drenched the town. He looked down at his fingers. They were beginning to develop a sort of vapid blue tinge, though his nails remained yellow as always, a result of the many years of smoking. After flexing them, he shoved them into his pockets, welcoming a little warmth from the surprisingly dry fabric.

Puddles on the sidewalk reflected the streetlights overhead, the image continuously distorted by more rainfall. In the distance, the echoes of rock music rattled from a collection of houses. He strained his ears to pick out the song, but the harder he tried, the more it seemed like the wails of guitars were fading away.

Good thing too, he thought. *Give me jazz any day.*

He looked ahead and took in the vibrant blue lights of the Hollyhead theater. In a few more steps, he'd be able to smell the burnt popcorn and B.O.-ridden carpets. The crowds of movie buffs had all died away, and he got his first chance to take a look at the posters plastered across the wall. 'Star Wars' blazed in large, silver letters in front of him. A queue had formed for the final showing of the day, full of freaks in brown cloaks. Two had run across the streets, chasing each other with cardboard tubes colored in red marker. He had seen the film himself, nothing more than a few tin cans walking in the desert as far as he was concerned. That had been before the streets were cleared of window shoppers and teenagers looking for one last kick before bed. Since midnight, the only people he had seen were a couple of bums huddled under a bus stop and a man screaming up at a bedroom window where a woman stood, throwing down bundles of clothes and piles of books and papers.

"Eve, it was one night!" the man had shouted as a shoe flew past his head. Normally, Bruce would have had a word and tried to settle the dispute in a composed manner. Not today. His night had been ruined. It had been his first day off for weeks and he'd prepared a whole evening. Dinner and a show, he had told his wife. That had been before the phone had rung and he'd heard Clark's raspy breathing down the line telling him he was sick. Apparently, his throat was raw, and his ass felt like a miniature volcano. It was always Clark. Like an alarm clock, Bruce had quickly grown to wince at the sound of his voice.

I decline these shifts and I won't ever get that promotion, he thought, peering inside the theater. He should have been walking out of there, his arm around Carol's waist—maybe lower. A few more promotions and he would finally be able to get them out of Hollyhead. His father had told him 'stay here too long and you won't ever leave.' Bruce fully intended on leaving. Once the kids were old enough to move on to high school and he had a fat wad of cash in his pocket, they would all get as far away as possible.

Either way, he was here; though it didn't mean he had to be happy about it. Begrudgingly, he raised his hat and stepped back onto the street, continuing the circuit that Clark had set out for him. He didn't hear the low rumble behind him until too late. A blinding light seared across his vision. In a flash of red, a pickup roared by, only a few feet away, spraying him with a wave of icy water.

Before he could take a mental note of the license plate, the truck vanished, leaving him dripping and cold on the corner of Whitley Avenue. He shook the remainder of the rain from his hair.

God damn kids with their jeans and greasy hair.

His path was set to continue on the central route before twisting through the new housing estate. Half the town seemed to be stuck in the 50s and the rest wanted to move forward, causing a visible split in the layout of the town.

I'll head down the alley. Even a small win against Clark's regime felt satisfying. He turned down Whitley Avenue, a winding shortcut into the middle of town, choked by high-rise buildings on either side. Fire escapes zig-zagged up the crumbling brick, and droplets of shimmering rainwater clung to the rusting metal railings.

You'd be better off facing the fire—you'd break your neck climbing down that thing.

An array of graffiti stained the brick walls in a swirl of color. Cheap spray paints ensured that the rain had slowly bled the art into the gutter. Bruce had been tasked with chasing down so-called street artists in his early days on the job. Most of the perps were acne-ridden teens, but a handful were older—fools who believed that with each 'masterpiece' they imparted a piece of their soul. Bruce couldn't help but feel bad though, at least they still had dreams of success—something bigger than the interminable monotony of this town.

Whitley Avenue was a part of Hollyhead that Bruce believed reflected the real nature of the town—the part not seen by the tourists. A corner hemmed in by dumpsters was known as 'the pissing place' by drunks and tramps who passed through. It was typically littered with needles and heroin spoons. In summer, you could see the trails leaking into the drains, which were usually overflowing with sticky leaves and foliage. Sammy, his youngest, had once fallen in the very same alley and had his hand pricked by one of the needles. In what Bruce considered a miracle, Sammy hadn't picked up any infections. Even still, the family had never taken the cut again.

Bruce avoided the corner as he continued, feeling the backs of his rigid, black boots rubbing against his ankle. Three straight paths with sharp corners made up the shortcut. Turning on the inside risked colliding with someone shooting down the alley— normally kids on bikes that they had long grown out of. As he turned the first corner, he heard them.

"You've made me open it now, man. You can't get me to open it and then not pay. People get a bullet for less than that."

A light blossomed at the end of the street, glistening in the night for a second, then extinguishing to a dull glow. The guilty party was standing below a canvas propped out from one of the shops. Bruce trudged closer until he could hear the conversation of the small group.

"I only said I wanted to see it."

"You're fucking with me. This is the good shit, infused with oils and everything."

Bruce felt in his holster for his handcuffs. They clinked slightly as his fingers found the metal.

A night in a cell, perhaps a couple of good kicks in the stomach too— right where no one will see anything.

One of the boys gasped causing the other to spin around.

"What have we got here?" called Bruce, quickening his pace. In a flurry of swears, they scarpered leaving only a smoldering cigarette lying on the floor.

Bruce gave chase, already feeling his lungs straining from the exertion. His mouth twisted into a smile, if he could catch two birds with one stone, he would consider that a good night's work. As he took the corner, his body smashed into something. No, someone. Before they could fall, he gripped their wrist, pulling them towards him, ready to brandish the cuffs.

"Got you now, you crackhead piece of shit," he said. But it wasn't the boys. He had hold of a woman, about five and a half feet tall with straggly ginger hair. She ripped her wrist away from him and, for a moment, he thought she might strike him.

"I'm sorry, Miss," he said, looking her up and down. A green mac reached her knees, clearly picked up from somewhere. She was at least three sizes too small for it. Dirt and god knows what else covered the fabric. Her eyes were wild and panicked. She brushed her hair aside and Bruce saw a scar, slashed vertically from her eyebrow down to her mouth. Tracking his gaze, she whipped a hood over her head and carried on walking, her dark boots spitting water up behind her. Bruce watched as she took off again into the darkness.

Shaking his head, he continued. The final stretch of Whitley Avenue was almost completely dark, except for the end where the alley connected with the road. Here, one flickering streetlight lit up the entrance with an eerie glow. He grabbed his flashlight from his belt and flicked it on, sending the rest of the alley into a visible glare. Bruce felt like he was playing a game of hide-and-go-seek.

He almost missed her. If the light from an apartment opposite hadn't reflected on her costume, she would have been almost completely invisible. The light danced across green sequins, shooting up rainbows of color across his irises. Bruce stepped closer, his heart starting to beat a little faster. He aimed his flashlight a little higher and felt his heart drop, bile rising up in his chest.

A young woman lay forsaken on the floor. Her long, blonde hair, drenched by the night's rain, was splayed around her face like a halo, pretty curls clinging to the paving slabs, desperately maintaining any life they could. She was dressed in a tight coat, wrapped around a pretty green dress, embellished with shining sequins. The tights she wore were streaked with ladders, running up her legs, clinging to her damp skin. Mascara stained her cheeks like black tears and her mouth, smudged by a vibrant red lipstick, remained in a state of eternal horror. This wasn't the first thing Bruce had noticed, however. He had seen corpses before, but none quite like this. The girl had her very own hands wrapped around her mottled, purple throat, hard enough to draw blood from the flesh, and someone had disconnected them from the rest of her body.

*

This all happened very quickly as the memories flashed before Will's eyes. He tore his finger away from the rewind. Sweat, which hadn't been there a few moments before, dripped from his hair.

"That girl," he panted.

"Her name was Abigail Finsbury. Pretty young, had ambitions of becoming a teacher," said Marty.

"No. Not the dead one. The one you collided with," Will said, staring at Bruce.

"She was just some tramp," said Frank, flicking through a freshly printed police report. Bruce was displaying the familiar look of confusion. To them, it seemed as though nothing had happened. The rewind would leave his clients dazed, but they would have no reason to suspect he had ransacked their minds. Normally, Will had time to hide away the device before they could see it and ask questions.

"What about her?" said Marty.

Will swallowed. His whole body was numb. "She can't be alive—she died ten years ago."

CHAPTER FOUR:
FAIRY TALES

Will hadn't seen Lenora Brown in over ten years, but there was no denying that it had been her face behind the matted, ginger hair. Even with the scar, the eyes had given her away immediately. Lenora was born with heterochromia, a condition that caused one iris to contain two different colors. For the most part, her eyes were a bright green, but a small blotch of blue had snuck up on her right iris, causing the two to clash. This, plus the rarity of being ginger with green eyes, meant that Lenora Brown was quite an extraordinary figure—one that Will had never forgotten. Some dates stick in the mind long past their occurrence; for Will, November 4th, 1969, was one such date.

"She went missing," said Will, taking another sip of malt that Marty had poured for him following the shock. His liver would regret it in the morning. After four years of sobriety, he was sure that even a couple of glasses would render him useless.

Bruce had left, almost knocking over his chair as he stood up. The rewind left both parties a little disorientated. Will had managed to reduce it down to a few seconds of dizziness after such a long period of use; it was no longer an abnormal feeling. Sometimes he relished in the moment of confusion afterwards. Frank had poured him a glass of whiskey and Will didn't have the stomach to reject it. As soon as he saw Lenora, ten years of sleepless nights rushed back to him.

"I remember. There was nothing in it—sometimes people just leave. There's no rhyme nor reason for it," said Frank. Will could tell that he was getting agitated. He had invited his son to talk about the murder, not some girl that had left town over a decade before. His eyes shined with the kind of obsession that Will had only seen in dopeheads.

"She was pregnant, Frank. An expecting mother doesn't just get up and leave with no cause."

"Probably embarrassed," piped up Marty, who had regained some of his charisma once Bruce had left. "Knew she couldn't look after the kid, so got rid of it without anyone knowing." He lit up a cigarette and inhaled deeply.

"Don't say that. You didn't know her," said Will, glaring at him.

"I'm not saying I like it, but it's the reality. There are a lot of shitty men out there and a lot of mothers can't afford to keep their child healthy."

"What did you see in Bruce's memory?" asked Frank, changing the subject.

"Why don't you just have a look?" said Will, although a part of him refrained; the rewind was his.

Frank sighed. "We would if we had that option. Unfortunately, MEDs don't work like that. They function through DNA. The brain can store a limitless amount of information—it's not all available for recall, but it is there. The MED unlocks this recall potential and somewhere along the way it binds to the user, allowing them to experience the memory."

Will nodded. Although he had used it for so long, he had never known exactly how it worked. He wasn't sure that he fully understood now. "That doesn't explain why you can't use it."

"It's fused to your touch—your genetic code. You have been exposed to it for so long that it will need time to reset. That's why we were each given one for our cases. The more you use it, the stronger it becomes. It needs to have that genetic binding to be able to transfer memory to you. In time, I will be able to use it, but I don't know how long that will be. You've used it far longer than anyone else ever has."

"That's why you asked me? I'm just a middle-man to you," said Will.

"The way I see it, you have a responsibility to do this. After exploiting grieving people for so many years, why not help them instead?" said Frank.

"I tried helping people. For a while, it worked. So many people overcame their misery because of me. They would tell me it was the first time they had smiled in years. Is that so bad? I know I'm a fake. I know that I shouldn't have signed book deals and used them for my benefit, but I'll be damned if you think that is the only reason I did it because for years I was the only thing keeping those people alive. After all that, I think I deserve something."

Frank looked close to exploding in a cacophony of profanity and anger. Instead, he turned to Marty, asked him to give them a moment, and then returned to face his son. As soon as Marty had left the room, Frank spoke. "That's where you're wrong, Will. No one deserves anything in life. We get what we are dealt. You are in a position where your hand can make a difference to someone else. You won't gain anything from finding out who killed this young woman, but you need a purpose. Something that drives you. We all need that. And what about Alex Spark? Don't you want to know what happened to your friend?"

Will couldn't believe what he was hearing. After so many years away from his father, he had forgotten his manner, the way he needed everyone to agree with him—every opinion being a fact that others just hadn't learned yet. And then there was Alex, the eldest Spark brother. Death claimed him when he was eighteen—only slightly older than Will had been at the time. One of the reasons Will had tried to stay away from the speculation concerning the murders was because it was just too painful to picture his old friend's limp body and protruding eyes... He had seen those eyes in his nightmares.

"You're wrong. Look at you—you've wasted away searching for this guy. You don't even know whether it is the same killer. The house is falling apart, and you haven't had a job in years. I'm the only family you have left, and we only talk once every few years. Sometimes purpose is just an excuse for obsession," Will said. He paused for a moment before yielding. "I will look into the murder. Lenora was there moments before Bruce found the body—that can't be a coincidence. I'm going to find her. If she does know something about Alex, then perhaps we might stand a chance at finding out who is responsible for their murders."

A period of silence followed as Frank weighed Will's words carefully. "All my life, I have been trying to find this man. I don't care if the evil wretch is dead now, although, knowing the way God works, I bet he's at a good old age. Probably won the lottery and is now basking in the Californian sun as he trundles toward a painless death. It's me—I need to know, Will… I need to know if I've walked past him in the street. Maybe I interviewed him. Maybe he had a body packed into a suitcase that I didn't bother checking," said Frank, his knuckles almost white on the table. Will had never seen him quite so passionate about anything. It was like Frank wasn't even talking to him— just scolding himself for mistakes that he likely hadn't even made. "However, you are incorrect about one thing. I know it is the same person. It can be no one else."

At that moment, Marty returned holding a photograph, which he kept against his chest.

"What makes you think it's the same guy? It could have been an old boyfriend," said Will.

"Jesus, Will, how many jealous boyfriends do you think saw off a girl's arms?" questioned Frank.

"Remind me never to let my daughter near him," said Marty.

Frank stood from his seat and walked to the shelf of fairy tales behind him. His fingers hovered over the top row before carefully sliding out a well-thumbed blue book. An illustrated fiddler wearing a blue and yellow costume decorated the cracked spine. Frank placed the book on the table and slid it towards Will before switching on the overhead light.

Will leaned forward. "*Grimm's Fairy Tales?*" he said, holding back a laugh. The cover hosted the title in large yellow letters above a forest backdrop. Additional yellow and blue characters were drawn on the front. Will saw what looked like a goblin holding a satchel over his shoulder, along with a witch, complete with a pointed black hat and a long, crooked nose. "You're kidding me. You think that the killer is murdering in the style of fairy tales?"

Marty then handed over the photograph he had been clutching. It was the infamous picture of the six angels hovering against the Hollyhead billboard. Will avoided looking at the left-centered boy; he had seen Alex's body far too many times. Fred hung next to him. Positioned on either side were Nigel and Sam—identical twins. The youngest two were hung at the sides. Gus was only five when he died. His brother Petey was eight. Petey Spark had been a skinny kid—so skinny that if the wind had picked up, you wouldn't have been surprised if he had blown away. Although all six had soon become a tourist attraction, it was always Gus who the public would shy away from. Being only five years old, it seemed that his fate was the most tragic. Will disagreed. At age five, a kid's brain isn't quite wired yet. They wake up and see a pile of clothes at the end of the bed and mistake it for a monster; terrified, they call out for mommy. She whispers a few words in their ear and the panic dissipates. When you're older, you know that the monsters at the end of your bed aren't real and a part of you knows that mommy isn't going to come running when you're scared. That's why Will always felt the most pain for Petey. When his neck was snapped, he was just at the age where he knew no one would be coming to save him from the boogeyman.

"You know this happened twelve years ago, right? It's a pretty big leap to say it's connected to Abigail," said Will.

"Open the book. Look at the contents."

Will obliged and stared at the list of titles. There were over fifty stories. Will recognized some, of course. *Hansel and Gretel* and *Sleeping Beauty* were both stories he knew well, even if their adaptations were better known than the original story. Children don't want to read about a stepsister cutting off her toes so she could fit into some shoes. Whoever the Brothers Grimm were, they needed some deep psychological therapy.

"There's a story. *The Six Swans*. You know it?" said Marty.

Will shook his head, but he could see where the ex-partners were going.

"Everyone interprets the Spark boys as angels. They assume there is some religious connotation to it all. Quite understandably. White gowns and angelic positions would indicate that Christianity played a role in the murders. We think otherwise. Swans explain the state of their faces—black eyes and orange noses. Angels only tick the boxes for the dresses and wings," said Frank.

"Why would a killer choose to murder his victims based on children's bedtime stories?" asked Will. He had heard of serial killers following a pattern before: the seven deadly sins; something as trivial as hair color; hell, one of Christie's most famous villains even used the alphabet. There is always a reason for murder. What reason could anyone have to kill in the style of fairy tales?

"Fame? Psychoticism? It doesn't matter. Anyone who can kill in cold blood is messed up one way or the other. Having a pattern just gives us something to go off. If anything, it will help us catch him," said Marty.

"What happens in the story?"

"It's a classic *Grimm's* story. Evil stepmother and all," said Marty.

"A king marries a witch's daughter…" began Frank.

"You'll find there are a lot of witches in these," added Marty, giving him a slight wink.

Frank cleared his throat. "Yes. A king marries the daughter of a witch, but he already has six sons and a daughter from a previous marriage."

"Quite the frisky guy," muttered Will.

"He hides the boys away but visits them regularly. One day the witch finds out and instructs her daughter to make some 'magic shirts.' She visits the sons, and, somehow, the shirts turn the boys into swans. His daughter leaves the castle and finds the hut they had been hiding in. She finds the swans and they transform back into her brothers. Thing is, they can only become human for fifteen minutes a day."

"Who comes up with these rules?" said Marty, throwing back another shot of whiskey.

Frank shot his partner another annoyed glance. "They tell her that to become human permanently she must not speak for six years. If that wasn't enough, she also has to sew them new shirts made from a special plant. Being a good sister, she agrees to do so. Another king turns up and finds the princess. He takes her back to his castle, and they get married."

"The princess' new stepmom isn't too happy with the situation," chimes in Marty, "so she tries to frame her for eating her children. She takes the kids and wipes blood across the newly crowned Queen's mouth, leading to a murder trial. Now, being unable to talk is a pretty big disadvantage when trying to defend yourself from accusations of cannibalism."

"I can imagine," said Will.

"While in prison, the sister continues making the shirts. Eventually, the day of her execution arrives. Turns out, she has finished them just in time, all except for one sleeve. The swans arrive and put on the shirts, turning them back into their human form," he tapped on the youngest brother, Gus. "The only brother whose shirt was incomplete was the youngest. It had a sleeve missing. No sleeve; no arm. The queen can then talk and so she snitches on the stepmother. Overall, a happy ending."

"How does Abigail Finsbury fit into this?" asked Will.

Frank nodded and flipped the book through to another page. *The Girl with No Hands.* "Clear enough for you?"

"It's a nice theory, but I think you're clutching at straws. It's a fucked-up way to kill someone, maybe that's as far as it goes. How much do you know about Abigail? Was she popular? Did she have a boyfriend?"

"So far, all we know is that she's dead. Hollyhead is corrupt as a town can go, but murders like this don't just happen. There's a pattern here," said Frank.

"I've watched enough crime shows to know that nine times out of ten, it's the boyfriend. Find out who she was dating and I'm sure you'll have your killer."

"If it is, then we will let you know. For now, humor us. Help us look into the pattern. I'm sure that by this time tomorrow, it will all be sorted," said Marty.

Will stood up, feeling the eyes of Frank and Marty itching across his skin.

"You will look into it?" said Frank, a drop of concern in his voice.

"I gotta find Lenora. The only logical place to start is the alley—I doubt the yellow pages have anyone listed under 'street bum.'"

CHAPTER FIVE:
HOBOS AND HOMICIDES

The news of Abigail Finsbury's unfortunate and gruesome end spread through the town like wildfire. It seemed that every vendor on every corner wanted to inject a new sense of fear into the public—anything to sell papers. To Will, it felt like living through a Dickens novel with small urchins cannoning around the streets, desperately trying to find a vendor who would give them a dime to sell extra copies. On the front page, Abigail's face beamed out at customers. Interviews had been conducted in which her parents had described her as 'bubbly' and 'one of a kind.' If you read enough obituaries, the same words will keep cropping up over and over. Not everyone can be a nice person. By the end of the day, that same face was peering out of garbage cans. Local television networks had swarmed to Whitley Avenue, along with kids who hoped to see some grisly remains at the crime scene.

A detective had given a short statement on their investigation, with the suggestion that they had some leads already. There were no specific details on her death, only that she had been strangled. Will had no doubt the police were hoping that someone would slip up and give them a lead by knowing some obscure element of Abigail's demise; he had heard of other murders that had been solved by a slip of the tongue. The panic hadn't started yet. Perhaps some of the more paranoid members of the town were looking over their shoulders before entering a dark sideroad, but the pack mentality hadn't picked up.

"Probably some psycho ex-lover, he couldn't handle being rejected, so he figured he'd make sure she didn't have another chance with anyone else," Will heard a businessman say to a woman, whose attention was elsewhere. The man's chins wobbled as he sat back and took a large draw on his cigarette. No doubt he'd watch the future killings with a keen eye, conjuring up more and more theories until one of them proved right and professing he knew all along. Will had enough dealings with his kind to know that the deaths were nothing more than entertainment and gossip—it's easy when you don't feel threatened.

Over the next few days, the police presence in Hollyhead certainly increased. Unmarked patrol cars lined the streets and cops were assigned to close up the parks and keep an eye on the roads after dark. Bruce Fisher had been given time off to recover after his shock, despite his protestations.

After his meeting with Frank, Will returned home to pack a bag. In preparation for what was to come, he dug out his old high school yearbook. It was thick, with a double-page spread attributed to the few Spark boys who had made it to high school. He flicked through the pages, rows of faces smiling back at him. Some he remembered—others had thankfully washed away into obscurity. The page with Lenora's form group stuck out after years of quick glances. Although it had been over ten years, her features had largely stayed the same, except for the scar. Will cut out her picture and slipped it into his wallet. It was the most recent photo he had—better than nothing.

Will checked himself into a local motel and paid for a couple of weeks. It was a run-down establishment with peeling bronze numbers on each of the doors and an ancient wooden archway at the entrance. Frank had offered to let him stay in his old bedroom, but Will had declined, opting for a sleazy room with grime-encrusted windows, a bulb suspended from a fraying wire, and framed art that could have been drawn by a three-year-old. The girl at the front desk had been young, her nose so far into her magazine that it had taken multiple attempts at ringing the visitor's bell before she had taken the time to look up. She was a sight. Bright orange lipstick and hair streaked with pink caught Will so off-guard that his words seemed to clump together in his mouth. He signed in under a fake name. To his agent's annoyance, the name Charlie Steinbeck had been slashed across various covers of short story collections.

"What's the point of being famous if you're not going to have any fun with it?" she had said on multiple occasions.

Before finding his room, the manager, a skinny woman with curls of gray hair, approached him. "We hope you have a pleasant stay, sir. I must ask you to only occupy the front of the establishment. We got a lake out back—very deep and very dangerous; the Devil wouldn't touch it with a stick. Don't want you falling in and getting stuck, do we?" she said in a thick drawl. "We wouldn't be able to hear you all the way out there."

Will pressed her further, but she withdrew into herself, ushering him away with the keys and a token for the diner across the road, offering a free portion of chips if you ordered a family meal. The lake was tucked away behind a shroud of fir trees, which shut out the light that spilled from the motel windows. Will caught a glimpse as he shut his blinds. As far as the water went, he could see what the manager meant. It did emanate an unsettling air. It was devoid of any wildlife, happy to settle with the black reeds and sludge around it.

Will's head had been swirling with the images of Lenora the entire day. The scar on her face had looked old, definitely not a recent addition. His stomach seemed to tighten whenever he thought of her. He put it down to nerves. With only a few hours till he'd be awoken by the sound of children laughing on their way to school, Will fell onto the mattress and let the relief of sleep overcome him, managing to ignore the heavy, wheezing breaths that he had developed throughout the evening.

*

The next morning, Will woke up to find that Hollyhead had been choked by a thick fog that had settled throughout the night, sending the town into a deep slumber. He looked out of his window towards the lake. Less than six hours prior, he had been able to see the shoreline, now the entire horizon had been swallowed by the weather. He watched as the manager, Wendy, cut through the smog at the back of the motel, muttering to herself. Her arms were laden with firewood and she was being careful not to trip as she stepped onto the concrete path that wound through to the front entrance.

Will dressed in the same clothes that he had worn the night prior and tried to flatten down the tufts of hair that had been slept on. He stroked his stubble, inspecting the skin that lay stuck to his bones. The weight loss was cruel. He had always been in good shape, but his fat had been lost faster than he thought possible. He ran his fingers down his back, feeling the edges of stretchmarks that still hadn't faded from adolescence. He had told himself that he wasn't getting weaker—not yet; though, each day, it was harder to believe. After an unusually quick shower, the moldy ceiling and curly black hairs scattering the pan were particularly off-putting, he set off down the stairs. Whitley Avenue wasn't far away, a ten-minute walk if he didn't stop, but between the stabbing pain of the cold air filling his lungs and his general exhaustion, he decided to call a cab. What is the point of death if you can't have a little luxury beforehand?

*

Whitley Avenue was in the center of town. The further you spread from the middle, the more barren the area became—like a new infection invading nearby cells. Will's old school was only four blocks away. It had once been a hub of discipline and embarrassment until the building was deemed unsafe for the students. He wasn't sure whether that was due to the structural deficiencies or the fact that the teachers had relied on a strict code of beatings. In the years since the building had collapsed on its east side. A collection of rubble stood where the students had once been forced to vomit out French verbs. Police tape now crisscrossed the area, preventing anyone from accessing the remnants of Hollyhead High. The school hadn't been large enough to house every kid in Hollyhead. Some parents would do anything to ensure that their kids were let in; others decided to homeschool rather than have their children in classes of fifty or more. Admittance was a touchy subject for parents. The principal, Bob Kruger, wasn't an attractive man, but he always left parent-teacher meetings with an extra-wide grin—the kids weren't allowed in. Most partners knew, some didn't care. In Hollyhead, you do whatever you can to stop yourself from drowning in the ever-growing pile of bodies.

Before they left for summer, Will had spent most of his school days stretched out on the ball field below a large tree in the corner of the compound. Alex, Lenora, and her then-boyfriend, Nick, were common visitors, her nose normally embedded in a chemistry book while Alex and Nick watched the cheerleaders rehearse for the upcoming game. Will didn't care much for chemistry. The reaction between two chemicals was a fact; do it once and you'll know what's coming every time. He would tell Lenora as much, which normally resulted in a shush or a textbook being arrowed at his head. Nick was supposedly Will's best friend. Living on the same road, albeit with a good distance between them, meant that the two cycled in together. Nick had been popular, largely for being on the school football team. As captain, he had led the team out onto the field at every game, always met with a roar of support from the home crowd. Cheerleaders, whose outfits left little to the imagination, joined the team, waving pom-poms and performing flips. Nick was always their favorite, lapping up the attention with eager eyes. Lenora had never seemed to mind; she had laughed as he flexed in front of the school and was always first to cheer when he scored—then she went missing.

Over time, Will stopped asking Nick why she had gone. Each time, Nick would only reply with a dismissive grunt before returning to whatever task had captured his attention. The pair had only remained friends out of habit. After so many years spent together, drifting apart no longer seemed like an option. Then, when he had finally gotten his big break, Will had sent Nick a letter explaining that he had signed a book deal and was headed for New York. He received no reply. Will doubted that they would even acknowledge each other now. He did know that Nick had practically been made an outcast after Lenora's disappearance. Although it hadn't been officially stated, he had been followed by police for months, each officer hoping to catch him in some incriminating act. There had been a small amount of media attention on Will, but his alibi had passed police checks and the journalists had soon halted their interest. A small part of him feared that with each new book, the media would pull him back into his past. So far, he had managed to keep his home life away from the critical glare.

Each road he passed took him through old memories. The library, where he had gotten his first job, was currently limiting its hours to 10-4 on a weekday—weekends saw no sign of activity. Crumpled chip packets and beer bottles lay scattered on the sidewalks, the aftermath of a drunken night. As a child, he had never noticed these things. As he had crept into adolescence, Hollyhead had become a little darker.

Less than five minutes later, the cab pulled up to the Hollyhead movie theater. Will paid the driver and stepped onto the sidewalk, avoiding a puddle that had formed down a crack in the road. The alley was much the same as it had been in Bruce's memory, although fragments could sometimes be distorted due to the natural discrepancies between one's memory and reality. All that had changed was that police tape had been stamped into the floor; they had all they needed from the crime scene and clearing up had been one task too many. The news teams had reported all they could, and were probably outside Abigail's house, attempting to get a statement from her grieving parents. A few passersby glanced down the alley, as if hoping to see another body stretched out across the concrete.

Slipping his hand into his pocket, Will felt around for his wallet. He took it out and slid Lenora's photo from the inside. Even in the photo, her eyes seemed to be full of life. He was about to put his wallet away again when he realized—the rewind was missing. Panicking, he felt around in his coat for the device, but only found some loose change and a bus ticket. His throat started to clench, and he could already feel his palms sweating, despite the cold.

It's at the motel. It's safe. All you have to do is go back there.

His breathing started to steady again.

First, we need to find out what has happened to Lenora. It shouldn't take long. Ten minutes? Ten minutes, then we can go back. Just see it out for ten minutes.

For a second, he couldn't feel the cold anymore. His hands were twitching, and he pressed them hard against a wall.

"You looking for a fix, my friend?" came a voice from over his shoulder.

Will turned to find a man stumbling towards him, one hand clasped around a brown bottle and the other stuffed into a long trench coat. The brown fabric hung from his rake-like arms. Winter's frost hadn't been kind to the man; scabs dotted his face, and his teeth were a mess of yellow and black. Although he had never seen him before, there seemed to be a certain memory of this man at the back of Will's brain. The man's moth-eaten pants were damp, whether with piss or water, he wasn't sure. He doubted the bum knew that himself.

"A fix? No. I'm looking for an old friend," said Will, holding out the picture of Lenora.

The man staggered closer, almost colliding with the wall, and took the photo. His eyes were bloodshot, and his hands twitched outwards, as though swatting away a fly.

His lips twisted into a tight-lipped smile. "I've seen her."

Will's heart gave a small jolt. "Where? Was it here?"

The man held out his hand and rubbed his fingers together in a gesture showing that money came first. Will took out a crumpled twenty and handed it over. The man inspected it for a moment and, satisfied that it was indeed authentic, pushed it down into the depths of his coat pocket. "First saw her about a week ago. She didn't have a coat or anything. She walked down and sat under that canopy," he said, pointing toward the end of the alley. "It's a good spot, that. You get the heat from the theater coming out from a little vent above it," he said, pointing to a canopy hanging over a collection of trash cans.

"You talk to her?"

"I talk to everyone. Thought she might be looking to get off."

"Did she?"

"Nah, just went real tight-lipped."

Sounds like her, thought Will.

"Did anyone come and find her? Where did she go?"

The bum gave a small belch and took a swig from his bottle. "I haven't seen her since that girl was found. She left that night. Must be two days ago now."

"And she didn't tell you where she was going?" asked Will.

The man lifted his head in thought. "She said something about those Billboard Murders. Very interested in them, she was. Then she kept going on about the Spark farmhouse. Reckon she went there."

First, she's at the scene of a murder, and then she wants to go to the home of the dead brothers? Will thought.

"She give a name?" asked Will.

"Said she was called Chrissy Austen."

GRIMM'S PUPPETS

A fake name as well. She must not want to be found. Trust her to use the surname of her favorite author. Very subtle.

"Right, well, thanks. You've been a great help," said Will.

At that moment, the man rubbed his eyes and raised a shaking finger at Will. "I know you!" he exclaimed. "You're Will Metlocke! I remember you. Little weirdo you were back in high school. First Alex Spark, then Lenora Brown—you must be bad luck. You're some kind of bigshot author now. Do you remember me? After hanging out with all those Hollywood babes, I bet my name ain't even in your head no more."

Will thought back. There was something familiar about the man's face: the way his nose seemed to bend to the right. It reminded him of a boy in his class—the smallest in the year by far. The combination of his height and his terrible eczema made him the target of half the bullies in the year.

"It's Greg, right? Greg Lafferty?"

The man gulped down another swig and grinned. "You do remember! Why don't you help out an old friend? I reckon you have enough money to get me off the streets for a night or two."

Will took his wallet out again but paused. "What the hell happened to you? Your Dad used to own half the dock. You have no reason to be out here living like some kind of rat."

"He gave it all to my brother, didn't he," Greg bulged out his chest. "I shall not give my hard work over to a son who has spent more time in the drunk tank than in school," he said, in what was a very accurate impersonation of his father, from what Will could remember.

"Meaning it's your own fault that you're out here?" said Will, shutting his wallet.

"We don't all land on our feet like you did," said Greg, still eyeing the wallet stacked with cash. Will could just make out an emotion lurking beneath the booze—it was shame.

"I worked for what I got. You could have had everything, and you traded it in for alcohol."

Greg didn't reply. Instead, he took another gulp of beer. Will got the impression that it was a reflex, almost like a nervous tic.

"Wait a second. If you're Will Metlocke, then that girl must be the one you used to follow around like a puppy. Lenora something—that girl who went missing," he said, his eyes wide.

"No. It's someone else," said Will, but he had always been a lousy liar.

Greg almost skipped with joy. "I'll tell the papers! Think how much they'll pay me for that!"

Before Will could stop him, Greg stumbled back down the alley and into the street.

"Greg! Wait! There's another fifty in it for you if you keep your mouth shut!" Will shouted, but Greg didn't turn back.

"Fuck's sake," sighed Will as he started to run. He didn't know what he would do when he caught Greg—he'd figure it out later. Lucky for him, the years of substance abuse had made Greg slow. Will felt himself getting closer—only a few feet away. His chest roared in pain. His eyes began to lose focus, turning the stumbling figure of Greg into a blotch in front of him. All his breath had raced out of his body before he could grab onto the hobo's fraying jacket. Wheezing, Will fell against the wall, taking in great lungfuls of cold air.

The papers would plaster Lenora's name across the whole town and a manhunt would ensue. Lenora might not stick around. Clearly, she wanted to remain anonymous.

Prickling with anger, Will began to walk away, turning his collar up against the wind. His pocket felt unnaturally light due to the absence of the rewind. Already, the twitching had started again. Even an hour without the machine caused his mind to wander and his temper to spike. He passed the area where Lenora had supposedly resided only a couple of nights prior. There was nothing there except a few pages of newspaper and garbage bags. Beer bottles poked through the black plastic, which threatened to spill its whole contents onto the floor.

On his right, another tramp lay sleeping in a doorway. A cardboard sign by their feet stated that they had been part of the military. A flat cap perched beside him, littered with a couple of quarters.

Worth a try.

"Excuse me," said Will, walking over to the man. "I'm looking for a girl. She's about thirty, got a long scar down her face. I know that she's been around here."

The man responded with a single finger and promptly fell asleep again. The stench of alcohol was overwhelming.

Will felt his temper rise. "There's a reason you haven't got anywhere to live. Maybe give the alcohol a break. God knows it would make the smell more tolerable. People are more likely to give you money if you have some kind of talent. Give a musical instrument a go. I'm sure even *you* could play Three Blind Mice."

Sniffing in contempt, Will carried on down the alley. The absence of the rewind changed something inside him, and he despised it. A part of him wanted to go back and give the man a dollar—or find him a sandwich. He was so busy overthinking that the footsteps behind him didn't disturb him. The pace of the character would have been an instant indication that nothing good was about to happen.

He felt the metal smash into the back of his right leg first, sending him to the floor in an exasperated cry. The concrete met his mouth first as he felt his teeth crunch against the floor and a flash of red obscured his vision. Then the back of his head splintered inwards, followed by a searing white light. Whoever had hit him decided not to swipe but to stab, sending what he guessed was a bit of piping into the back of his skull. The blood congealing on the floor below him started to double, but he wasn't sure whether that was due to his visual cortex spiraling into disarray or because of the warm blood trickling down over his eyes. Static buzzed in his head. He felt a hand dip into his breast pocket and then an indistinguishable mumbling. They rolled him onto his side and tried the pockets of his jeans before taking hold of his wallet and flicking through. Another grunt came, and then the thundering of footsteps away from him. Will swore through strained breath and gritted teeth before giving in to the scarlet abyss.

CHAPTER SIX: HOSPITAL

The world had exploded. Stars had fallen from the sky and were bouncing around the landscape, surrounded by the blackness of space that leaked from every corner. A hand grasped Will's shoulder, gently pressing him forward. Though dazed and with no idea what to do next, his feet were headed in the direction of Hollyhead Hospital. He was on autopilot. Each step was painful and with every landing, a fresh wave of pain blazed through his leg. His eyes felt like they were forcing their way out of his skull, his vision pulsing and contorting into a blurry haze. Never before had he stared so intently at concrete, even if it was just to stop him from throwing up the contents of last night's dinner

"Keep going—not far now," said a voice. It sounded like the sort of voice that might narrate a children's book—soft and comforting. The tanned fingers around his arm were dainty; Will was sure that he was carrying the majority of his weight himself.

"Who are you?" he grunted, trying to force down the bile threatening to spill from his mouth.

"My name is Eve Pocock. You're in a right fine mess, mister."

As cars roared past, their headlights tore into Will's eyes, elongating into a psychedelic skein. It couldn't be late; he had arrived at the alley before midday, but the morning fog hadn't surrendered yet. Once or twice, he heard passersby ask him if he was alright. Eve pressed on, not stopping to reply to any nervous onlooker. Behind the scent of iron under his nostrils, the soft aroma of lavender drifted towards him from the side that Eve was struggling to hold up.

"You see who did it?" Will slurred.

"Looked like it was one of those homeless men, he tore past me as he ran off."

Will thought back to the sleeping veteran. *Well, he's certainly got more than a few quarters now.*

On a couple of occasions, he stumbled, once managing to land on his knee, instantly knowing that blood was slowly oozing from the area of impact. Eve kept them pressing forward—surely an ambulance was on-hand, but Will didn't question it. They crossed the intersection of Satchell Road and Bell, indicating that the hospital was less than a block away. Through his one good eye, Will watched as the gothic-style building drew nearer.

Hollyhead Hospital had been erected towards the end of the nineteenth century, although its original purpose was to house the clinically insane. During its conversion after the first world war, the bars were removed from the windows and the asylum became contained to the East Wing of the facility, the remainder of the building being reserved for physically sick individuals. The driveway towards the front entrance stretched into a loop. To the left of the building, a group of ambulances all huddled below a steel roof. New trees had been planted along the side of the road, cherry trees primarily—an attempt to make the hospital welcoming as opposed to the satanic perdition that it had been heavily rumored to be.

Eve dragged him further up the tracks before arriving at the pair of revolving doors at the entrance. She stopped; her face flushed as she glanced at her watch—a circular timepiece fitted around a pretty golden bracelet. "I'm so sorry, but I have to run. Just go through those doors and they'll take care of you."

Will had little energy left to protest, so he let out a choked thank you and pushed forwards through the doors.

*

The reaction from the nurses was enough to tell him he looked like shit. As soon as he entered, doctors threw him into a wheelchair, and he felt cold metal instruments against his skin. The doctors' mouths were bouncing up and down and Will couldn't help but think of those macabre puppets he had seen on the coast during his brief stint in England, with their long red noses and wooden batons. He laughed to himself before realizing that laughing caused his head to pound even harder. For the next few seconds, all he could hear was the crash of doors as more nurses ran to his aid. He managed to give his name before his sight gave out and he fell into the pit of unconsciousness.

*

For the next eight days, Will was confined to a hospital bed. He had come out of the incident with a few broken teeth, a knee that somehow hadn't shattered, and a brain injury, the extent of which had not yet been determined. The pain he could stand; he was hardly a stranger to it. It was the constant fever dreams that bothered him, which were often accompanied by The Boomtown Rats complaining about the days of the week. He would be a lucky man if he never had to listen to the song again.

His knee hurt too much to even consider standing; he could feel the layers of bandages wrapped all the way up to his thigh. The stench of disinfectant was a constant companion in the room. It was amusing to him that the whole room had been painted green, as it only served to remind him of the meals that he hadn't kept down in his first few days of recovery. He must have spoken to someone, though he couldn't remember it. A little sign at the end of his bed indicated his name, and doctors bustled in and out regularly to check his charts. Others came and blinded him with tiny lights, leaving dancing spots on his cornea. One doctor was particularly heavy-handed when checking his chest. As days passed, the black cloud lifted, instead being replaced with the harsh glare of hospital lights.

On the first day that his head felt vaguely normal, the doctor who had examined his chest visited him. She gave him a weak smile as she sat down by his bedside. Her dark hair was stretched into a strict ponytail and the bags beneath her brown eyes gave away the tiredness that her smile tried to conceal. A badge pinned to her white coat told him that her name was Highsmith.

"Lung cancer. You already knew that though," said the doctor, as she stuffed her hands into her coat. "I've been in contact with your doctor back in Saunton. He says you've been refusing treatment."

Will sighed. He knew it wouldn't take them long to find out. It had started with a harsh cough. It hadn't been until the pain started that he had gone to see old Dr. Christensen. Just the sight of the doctors rallying around the hospital equipment had been enough to tell Will everything he needed to know. Six rounds of chemotherapy were the agreed treatment; in the time Christensen had left to grab the forms, Will had gone.

"There's no point prolonging the inevitable," said Will, placing his head into a more comfortable position—only in sleep could he escape the nagging pain at the back of his skull.

"In the majority of cases where a patient is refusing treatment, they have come from a poor background. They can't afford enough food, let alone a medical bill. I disagree with it, but I can understand why they won't accept it. What I can't understand is why a famous author has decided that life isn't worth living."

"It would make a difference if I were just a rich *businessman*?"

The doctor sighed. "Now, I'm not so naïve as to think that fame solves everything, but you have something that you're good at. I personally don't see the merit in throwing that away."

"I don't understand you people. What is so wrong with me dying on my own terms? I could leave here and get hit by a car. At least this way I will know when it's coming."

"The longer you keep going, the worse it will get; the cancer will spread. Once that happens, it will be a lot harder to treat. In a fair number of cases, there's not even a point in starting treatment that late. It all depends on how aggressive the cancer is. So far, it doesn't seem to be too advanced."

"That reminds me of someone," said Will.

The doctor leaned forwards, close enough that Will could smell the faintest hint of coffee behind her overladen perfume—one thing he had found about doctors was that they overcompensated on their scent, undoubtedly, to mask the smell of all the fluids they had been in contact with that day.

"I don't think you want to die."

"No?"

"I think there's a part of you that you want dead, and I think the desire for that is clouding your judgment."

"I didn't realize you were a psychologist as well as a medical practitioner."

"Sometimes they are one and the same."

"Yes, but I imagine one involves far less sleeping with patients."

The doctor let out a small smile. "Doctors can cut away infection. It's the patient who has to do the healing. You think that you've left it too long. You think that everyone sees you as a miserable bastard, so that is what you are. A self-fulfilling prophecy."

"I think that's enough dissection on your part. Let me have a go."

The doctor reclined backward, crossing her legs as she did so as if to say, 'Come on then, do your worst.'

"You've obviously worked hard to get here. For most, it would be hard enough, but as a black woman, you've always felt the need to prove yourself. I just make you angry— someone who hasn't had to work for what they have— someone who doesn't even want what they have. Your brain can't comprehend it. Every cell in your body screams that I'm an abomination against nature. You're a doctor; you live in a world of facts and rules. I could name any illness and you would be able to name at least three ways to treat it. What you can't understand is that wanting to die is not being ill. There's nothing wrong with my head, so there is nothing for you to fix. So, you'll keep telling me to get treatment for this—just to prove that you are right. I'd be an equation that's finally been balanced. The world would finally be back to how it was meant to be, just because you'd mixed a few chemicals. All I want is a painless death." Will let out a puff of air. "All of that *and* I'm off my head on pain meds; that's not a bad run."

Yet, the doctor remained unfazed. "This won't be a painless death. The pain you feel now will only get worse."

"Which is why I have this," Will said, leaning over and increasing his morphine levels with a mock sigh of relief.

The doctor stood up and wheeled the equipment away before lowering the medication back down.

"Now, that's just denying me treatment," protested Will.

"Consider it a taste of the discomfort to come. I don't think you need to be fixed. Frankly, you are one of the only patients in this hospital for whom I have little concern, but believe it or not, Mr. Metlocke, there will be people out there who give a damn about you. You probably haven't met them, and I doubt you ever will, but the day you die will be a sad day for someone out there. Personally, I think you owe it to that person to stick around a little longer."

With that, the doctor walked away and slid the glass door shut behind her. Someone called her name, and she was instantly whisked away into the thronging halls of the hospital.

Will lowered his head onto his pillow and took a few deep breaths.

The day I die is the day my books get an extra few cents added to their value. That is all.

It had been several months since he had gone so long without the rewind. The twitching had increased. His fingers tapped the bedding like he was Beethoven in his prime, coming up with a new symphony. As soon as he could leave, he would go back to the motel and get the machine. Numerous nurses had asked him whether he smoked or drank more than a few a week in the hopes of finding a cause behind the withdrawal symptoms. He was hesitant to tell them it was due to a device that had mind-reading capabilities; he already had the feeling that Dr. Highsmith didn't like him.

*

"You've had no visitors. Is there anyone you want me to call?" A new nurse had come to sit with Will; her eyes were wide with concern behind large round glasses. Will racked his brains for a split second. His father would only care that precious days had been lost when he should have been focused on the case.

"The woman who brought me in. Did you get her number?"

"You came in alone, gave the nurses downstairs quite a shock," she replied, her eyes fluttering to the morphine levels. "We have a detective here if you wanted an investigation into who attacked you?" She gestured through the large window towards a bulky man, his shoulders almost as high as his head. He gave a small wave as Will looked over, the kind of wave that formed from a timid wiggling of the fingers.

"No, I'm fine," said Will, hoisting himself into a sitting position. The nurse nodded and left. Will watched as she wandered over to the detective and explained. The detective gave a knowing nod and a wink at Will, who sunk a few more inches down the bed.

When certain it was safe, he sat up again and looked around. On the table, set beneath a variety of medical equipment, a cheap dollar-store vase sat full to bursting with lavender. When he took a deep breath, his twitching subsided. That night, he fell into a peaceful sleep, dreaming of lavender fields and a woman dressed in red; his body felt weightless and his lungs gave him no hint of pain. They ran through the beating sun, Will never quite catching up to her. Every time he tried to reach out and touch her, her dark hair disappeared from view. He followed her further through the field until the lavender started to die, getting thinner and thinner until there was nothing left but the broken spindles on the floor. In the great empty spaces around him, she was nowhere to be seen. At that moment, the pain came back. Wincing, Will stumbled further before his foot connected with a root and he fell. The ground bit at his body and he kept rolling, falling deeper and deeper, plunging himself into the unknown. When he eventually stopped, he realized he had landed in a pit a good twenty feet down. He turned on his side and screamed. The six Spark boys were lying down flat next to him, all smiling up at the sun. Alex's mouth gaped open suddenly and bugs came spiraling from his mouth.

"You forgot about me, Will," he spluttered, as beetles and worms poured from cavities in his face. "You were supposed to be my friend."

"Alex... I'm sorry. For everything," Will replied, watching as his friend decomposed before his eyes. Flesh rotted and peeled away from the bone. The eyes vanished, leaving cavities in the skull. The pit then became overcast by a dark shadow. A man stood hunched above them, holding a shovel brimming with dirt. Before Will could move, the man threw the dirt into the pit, splattering the group in wet mud. Will's legs had gone numb; he couldn't move. The dirt kept piling up until his eyes were covered in soil. As the pit filled, the man's cackling laugh silenced, and the Spark boys began crawling closer to Will's useless body. He shut his eyes and gave in to the darkness.

*

The detective returned the following day. Will spotted him across the far side of the hospital reception, trying to end a one-sided conversation with an overly enthusiastic nurse. Every few seconds, the detective's eyes would turn toward Will. As soon as he could untangle himself from his admirer, he would make a beeline straight for Will's room. Deciding that his stay had come to an end, Will pulled out the various drips from his arms and grabbed his coat from the door. It had been scrubbed thoroughly, although it would take a lot more than soap to remove the bloodstains. He pulled it on and joined the crowd in the corridor, keeping low to avoid the detective's gaze. At the earliest opportunity, he opened an exit door and navigated down a few flights of stairs before coming out into another identical lounge. The hospital was a maze of corridors—enough to send anyone crazy. He checked the signs dotted on the walls and followed the orange letters indicating the exit. After a few curious glances from nurses, he hobbled down the final staircase and came into the hospital reception. Nurses were still rushing around, and telephones were ringing from every direction. He'd almost reached the door when he was stopped. With the door only steps away, a cold voice called his name.

"Mr. Metlocke. Are you going somewhere?"

Sighing, Will turned around to see Dr. Highsmith standing with one hand on her hips, the other clasping a blue folder to her chest.

"Just a stroll, doctor," Will replied, putting on his best innocent voice.

"You haven't been discharged yet. We need to ensure that your head injury won't cause any side effects for you."

"There's only one side effect I have noticed, and it's the fact that doctors seem to be following me around everywhere I go. I've been assured that this will stop in…" he glanced at his wrist as if checking a watch, "about five seconds!"

"I can't say that I'll miss you. I *can* say that you will be putting yourself at risk if you leave now."

Will took a step towards her. "Look, I get that you don't like me. Frankly, I don't care. What I do care about is doing what I want, when I want."

Highsmith tutted, "I can't stop you from leaving. I imagine you'll get some very odd looks if you go out looking like that, however," she said, nodding at Will's gown.

It had been so long that Will had almost forgotten about the flowery blue clothing. His old clothes had no doubt been bundled into a bag.

"We're in Hollyhead; they'll grab anything strange with both hands. I'll be the next local celebrity."

Will walked off, trying to hide the limp that had arrived as a result of the attack. "Let's just hope there's not a strong breeze," he called back as he exited the doors.

CHAPTER SEVEN:
ALL IS FAIR IN LOVE AND WAR

Though painful, the walk from the hospital back to the motel passed without incident. Wendy had asked if he wanted any frozen peas for his rather bruised face when he returned to the reception. After a few lines of protest, he had managed to shake her off and escaped to his room. The smell was still musty, and the bed unmade, yet it felt good to be back. As soon as the door closed behind him, he ran straight for the bedside table. The hospital had given him enough time to remember where he had left the rewind and there it was, obediently waiting for his return. He held onto it as a mother does to a newborn, feeling its warmth spread through his body. Anxious to get his next fix, he set out for the Spark farm.

*

Melanie and Benny Sparks' farmhouse could be found on the Western side of Hollyhead, nestled into a valley between two hills. At this time of day, the sun sat low in the sky, casting an orange glow over the house. A wooden fence surrounded the building, the gate at the front swinging on its hinges with a rhythmic clanging. Their livestock consisted of little more than a dozen chickens housed in a decaying coop. To the right of the house, a barn held a single combine harvester, which had one wheel missing entirely. Green paint flaked from the steel body and the grain platform had been neglected for so long that Will doubted the blades could cut through grass, let alone the acres of corn that the family owned. Alex had never wanted any of his friends to visit and now Will could see why.

He continued down the path, slipping occasionally on the mud that had been so well trodden by the countless tourists who came pestering. A cab had dropped him off by the gate at the end of the farm's road and left promptly. Will was gazing out at the empty land around the farm when something caught his attention. It was a red flyer, stabbed by a tangle of barbed wire separating the road from the overgrown grass. The flyer flapped in the wind and he plucked it from the metal teeth. 'BILL DINGLES' MURDER TOUR' it stated in bright yellow letters. The man himself was printed onto the sheet, his hands presenting the prices: $8 for an adult ticket, $5 for a kid. On the back, a map labeled the points on the tour, starting with the Spark farmhouse and ending with the billboard. The seven stops in between snaked through the town, even stopping off at Jack's Pizza, where Alex had worked, for a bite to eat. Will scrunched up the flyer and thrust it into his pocket.

He limped on towards the house, his knee aching in disagreement. The curtains of the farmhouse were drawn across, but he felt sure that an eye peered towards him through a gap in the red fabric. Three steps led up to a porch and Will took them slowly, using a rickety banister to hoist himself up. He stole another glance at the window and the eye vanished in a flash of blue. Before he could knock, the scrape of a heavy latch came from inside and the door opened, an iron chain holding the door a head's width from the frame. Through the gap, that familiar blue eye appeared, accompanied by a knot of graying ginger hair. The height gave them away, standing almost a foot taller than Will, it could only be Melanie Spark.

"Whaddya want? No more queshuns," she said, looking Will up and down.

"I'm not a tourist. I'm a writer."

She bared her teeth slightly. "Another journalist? Comin' to bring more people here?" she spat. "You people make me sick, laughing at us. Oh, you think we don't see you? We do. I hear all the things you say about us."

"I've come to help you. I'm looking into the murder of your boys," he said.

Melanie glanced at Will's forehead, taking in the extent of his injuries and he recognized the expression behind her eyes—*he's a cripple. There's no threat there.*

"There's nothing you can do. I've talked to authors, journalists, police—you're all useless," she said, pulling the door closed.

"I was friends with Alex!"

"Course you were."

Slightly embarrassed, Will stuck his foot inside the door. "Did I mention that I am a world-renowned psychic?"

Melanie stopped trying to slam the door. Her blue eyes raised to meet Will's. "You talk to the dead?" she asked, her voice cracking.

"I can, yes. More importantly, I can read minds."

"No chance," she said, before pausing. "What am I thinking 'bout right now?"

"You're wondering whether I can talk to your boys," Will said, slowly removing his foot from the doorway.

She sniffed and closed the door. Will heard the chain fall away, and the door creaked open to reveal a small entrance hall. Two corridors split in either direction to what Will assumed were the bedrooms. One rickety staircase led to the attic of the house; no doubt filled with the possessions of Melanie's boys. The bruised walls and cobwebbed ceiling gave no doubt that this was a house that stunk of melancholy. He took a step inside. Melanie Spark was the largest woman he had ever seen. He saw now that she had hunched over to answer the door; at her full height, she was at least half a foot taller than he had originally guessed. She was dressed in tattered work clothes; half of the original material missing, and random assortments of fabric had been sewn to cover the gaps. One piece seemed to be from the tablecloth currently strewn over the kitchen table. Liver spots colored her skin, and her electric blue eyes were underlined by dark circles, which stretched into crow's feet at the edges.

"I don't want you to talk to the kids. They deserve some rest after the lives they had," she said, leading Will into the kitchen. It was clearly the largest room in the house. Eight chairs were arranged around the rectangular table, six covered in layers of dust. Some of the cabinets had broken, their doors swinging open or broken off their hinges, revealing tins and cracked china bowls. Flies buzzed lazily around the room, coming through an open window by a sink stacked high with dirty cutlery.

This is a woman who has completely given up, he thought. Will remained standing, uncertain whether he should sit in one of the vacant seats.

Melanie walked past and threw a hand toward the table. "Just sit on any. It's a habit. We don't like to be in the boys' chairs. Don't feel right for us to sit in them." Will nodded and sat down on one of the chairs, feeling like he was lying on top of their grave somehow. "I know who you are. You're the son of Frank Metlocke," she said, pouring hot water into a mug that threatened to fall to pieces at any second.

"Is that a good thing?"

She let out a snort. "Frank Metlocke is a laughingstock. I'm guessing you're the same."

"You haven't heard of me?" said Will. He was used to people not recognising his face, but the name on the cover was usually identifiable enough.

"Should I have?" she said, throwing tea bags into the cups.

"No. I'm quite thankful you haven't, actually." Melanie sat down and pushed a cup toward Will. Brown scum laced the surface of the water. "There's something else I need to ask you before we start. Have you seen a girl around here? About thirty years old? A large scar down her face."

Melanie slammed down her cup. Will thought he heard it cracking even more. "You know something about that bitch? Snooping around here. Caught her twice out by the chicken coop, trying to dig it up! The nerve on her! When I caught her, she asked if she could question me about my boys. I told her to scram before I called the police. Was never going to, course— police are a bunch of pigs."

"She was digging?"

"Trying to. Late at night, it was."

"What did she want to know?"

"The only thing people ever want to ask me about. The day they went missin'."

What does she want to know about that for? Thought Will. Lenora's behavior was becoming more erratic by the second.

"Did you tell her?"

Melanie laughed, "course not. Told her to piss off. You're lucky I'm even letting you in."

"Why exactly *are* you talking to me?"

Melanie's face became stony, her eyes fixed on the table in front of her. "You say you're a psychic—someone who can read the minds of others? I think you're mad, but, after everything, maybe someone with a little madness is who I need right now."

Will could tell that she was opening a door that had been bolted for a long time. The police had evidently gotten on her bad side, but here was a real opportunity. For that second, all thoughts of Lenora subsided, leaving a feeling that Will hadn't experienced for a long time.

He leaned forward. "Mrs. Spark, I will find out what happened. I promise."

Melanie sniffed back her tears and smiled. "Alright, Mister. We'd better get started then."

*

The pair spent the next half hour discussing the events following the boys' disappearance. According to Melanie, the absence of evidence caused the police to lose interest after only a few months.

"Everyone here knows everyone else. I talked to the police and that ginger pathologist who poked around inside their bodies with all his metal tools. Alex wanted to train and become a doctor, ya know? He would have made a great doctor. Very caring, he was. We had some of those therapists 'round here, too. I didn't know your Daddy until later," she took a sip of tea before smacking her lips. "He nosed around here most days—asking queshuns and sticking papers through the door. Couldn't get rid of 'im."

Even the words made Will cringe. Had his father really been so desperate for answers that he hadn't left the poor family alone for years?

"When did he stop?"

"Only a few years ago. Guess he gave up." Melanie finished her next cup of tea; Will hadn't dared to touch his own. "He's a crackpot, old fool."

Will laughed. "Yeah, I think I figured that one out before I was out of diapers."

A silence followed. Will had been holding off on the part that came next. Despite Melanie's comportment, Will could tell that she just wanted someone to talk to.

"I need to ask you a few questions if that's ok?"

"You been askin' enough already. Few more can't hurt," she said, in a way that sounded like the years had drained any drips of emotion from her.

Will nodded. The rewind had begun heating up against his thigh; it knew its moment was coming.

"I need you to focus on that day. Focus on the day your sons disappeared. Where were you?"

"I was 'ere. Then we all went to the fair."

"Don't speak. Think."

She nodded; her eyes clamped shut. Will took the rewind from his pocket, feeling the metal grooves between his fingers. It emitted a soft whine as he placed it on the kitchen table. "I'm going to take your hand now."

Melanie twitched, pulling her hands away.

"No. No funny business. You 'ear me?"

"Trust me."

Her hands returned to the middle of the table and Will held them. He could feel the callouses on her skin and the bones making up her fingers tense with anxiety. The rewind flashed as he pressed her hand to its center, touching the side with his own hand. Her eyes shot open in a state of fear. The hairs on the back of Will's neck stood up. Her mind was his.

*

Melanie Spark was angry; she knew that much. She had been ever since she first laid her eyes upon Celine Drower. The sight of her husband stepping from her red sports car, followed by a flash of pearly white teeth, didn't help. With great resentment, she led her children into Hollyhead Fairground, an attraction full of rides that looked seconds from breaking down and toy guns that you needed to trigger twice to force a bullet out. The stands were squashed into a rented field, littered with a variety of multi-colored posters featuring a wide selection of clowns— enough to give even an adult nightmare fuel for a week. Tinny carnival music spluttered from speakers placed around the stands. Alex and Fred ran ahead, pushing each other on their way to the cotton candy vendor, which was sitting under a red canvas canopy just to the right of the entrance. Melanie was careful to keep an eye on them; after years of raising six boys, she had learned never to take her eyes off them. The boys ran between older teenagers, wearing hats that had been produced to look like burgers. She turned around, expecting to see her husband ashamedly lumbering towards her, his spine curved as he stared at his feet to avoid her gaze, but he wasn't there.

No doubt he's off with some other slut in a push-up bra and mini-skirt, she thought. Her youngest, Gus, was holding her hand, still wobbling on his feet. He'd thrown up twice that day: once over his schoolbooks and once over her. She could still smell the acidic stench of his insides on her skin, even after throwing away her clothes and scrubbing her chest raw. His face was pale, but a little color dripped in as he spotted his favorite attraction—the Ferris wheel. Melanie didn't like the look of it. It was an eye-sore that she was glad would be wheeled away in the morning. The carts, a vapid green, hung around the wheel, creaking slightly.

Gus tugged on her sleeve, looking up at her with a full display of yellowing teeth.

"Ma! The big wheel!"

Benny appeared by her side. The other three children traipsed along behind him, looking around in fascination at the flashing purple and green lights coming from the house of mirrors fronted by a man leaning back in a lawn chair, the brim of his hat drooping over his eyes.

"Honey, I really think we should get on home," said Benny anxiously. He looked towards the sky, which was threatening to unleash a week's worth of rain; ugly, dark clouds were rolling over Hollyhead making the air damp and thick.

It was at that moment that Melanie decided the fairground was exactly where they needed to be.

"The kids want a ride. Who are you to tell them no?" she said.

Benny tilted his head in disapproval but said nothing.

Melanie bent down to the four remaining kids. "Here's a dollar each. Alex can have two. Once they are gone, that's it, unless your pa wants to give you more."

There was an uproar of complaints. "Alex got the watch!" said Nigel, pointing towards his brother's wrist. "How come he gets more money, too?"

"Because he's the oldest," she replied beaming at her eldest son. He was something to be proud of, one shining example of parenting done right, she thought. Her strictness had dissipated with each child, her attention being pulled left and right. For some time, Alex had been her sole focus, and now he seemed to be the most likely source of salvation from the pit her life had fallen into ever since Benny's eyes had wandered to Celine Drower. With a shivering hand, Alex pulled his sleeve over his wrist. Melanie handed out the notes, and the pack divided, Nigel, Fred and Sam running towards the balloon vendor and Petey and Gus cannoning towards the wheel. Knowing them, their whole evening would be spent spotting town landmarks and pointing at the ant-like people as they returned home from work.

"You got any more money, Benny? Or you all out after buying a new purse for that bitch in that fancy red car you keep getting a ride in? What kinda ride, I wonder," Melanie hissed.

"I told you; she's interested in the farm. What would she want with a guy like me?" he replied glumly.

"I ask myself the same queshun." With that, she stuck her nose into the sky and walked away, leaving Benny alone at the entrance to the fair. When she turned back, half expecting him to be running along to catch up, he was gone. She couldn't help but feel a slight pinch of disappointment.

*

Lights from the fairground polluted the sky and the grumbling clouds swept over in flashes of neon lights. The popcorn vendor had marked his final servings down to less than 10 cents and Melanie heard a pigtailed girl complaining to her mother that her box consisted mostly of unpopped kernels.

The majority of the clowns had had enough of the jeers and boos from their audience and were now trudging towards their vehicles, red noses gone and paint dripping from their cheeks, revealing greying whiskers.

Benny had left; Melanie had told him that she would walk the kids home when they were ready, although he had insisted that he should take a few in the station wagon. She'd declined and even given the children an extra 50 cents each to spend, resulting in excited yells from the kids and a moan of exasperation from Benny. She watched as the blue wagon pulled away from the field, which was starting to become heavy with night-time dew. Benny didn't look back.

Alex offered to walk Gus home, who had turned green again, this time due to the enormous amount of sugar he had eaten, rather than his stomach bug. Melanie agreed, telling the boys to take the back lanes instead of the busy central street, which at this time was full of people leaving the fair. She watched as the lanky figure of Alex took Gus' hand and led him away from the lights before being swallowed by a cavern of dark trees in the distance.

Two down, four to go, she thought.

The remaining kids had blown their money within a half hour and came back to Melanie holding their hands out like street urchins.

"Please Ma, there's a big stuffed bear for sale. All I gotta do is shoot some cans over, just like shooting rabbits back home," pleaded Nigel, his curly hair sticking to his skull with sweat.

Melanie narrowed her eyes at him. "We both know you've never shot no rabbits. You struggle liftin' a water gun."

A flush of red spread across his face and he shrank away into the rest of his brothers, who began laughing and hitting him over the back of the head.

Melanie felt a surge of guilt. Normally, she would have given him an extra dollar to let him shoot away his dreams but seeing that blonde-haired whore had triggered a wave of anger in her. What right did she have flashing around her set of wheels in front of the kids and why did Benny always come home reeking of her perfume?

The clouds had silently stolen away the sun, and a few drops of rain began to splatter on the ground. Melanie took a deep breath and knelt down at Gus's level. "I'm going to give you two dollars. That's for y'all to share, but I want you to look after it, d'ya hear me? Don't let Petey blow it all on some of that hard candy crap. You got ten minutes before we make a run."

She winked as he took it, the redness of his face mellowed as he stared at the note. He leaned towards her ear.

"You're the best, Ma," he whispered. He presented her with a grin, dotted with the remaining teeth he had left. Then he ran, getting a head start on the other three, who tore off after him.

Melanie watched them leave, thinking about just how young they looked.

*

Less than three minutes later, Nigel, Sam, Greg, and Petey were waiting in queue for the final spin of the Ferris wheel. The man in the operating box sat tapping his foot, waiting for the passenger cabins to fill up. His eyes were set on a pair of brunette teenagers, their arms folded across their chests as their skirts whistled around their knees. His eyes raked across their bodies and Melanie wondered whether her own husband did the same: the man who stumbled over his words when they had first met until she had eventually asked him to go to the pictures; the man who had wept through his wedding vows.

Enough, she thought, *I'll catch them soon.* Another part of her didn't want to. The suspicion of his betrayal might be more comfortable than the reality of it.

The mechanical gasp of the wheel signaled that it was ready for motion and Melanie watched as her children waved down to her, edging closer to the night sky. She responded with a small wave, causing Petey to break into a grin.

Soon darkness swallowed their faces as Melanie waited on the muddied ground beneath them, surrounded by other parents and a few children, too scared to go on the ride. She kept her eyes on their cart until a flash of blonde hair caught her eye, illuminated in a jade glow by the fairground lights. The owner of the hair was walking arm in arm with a man, slightly taller, wearing a dark jacket. The blonde threw her head back in laughter—a fake laugh grown from desire. A red handbag hung from her shoulder, swaying from side to side as they walked towards the exit of the field. The lumbering movement of the man was a sight she had seen many times before.

Melanie felt a pain inside her as if her heart had dropped right into her stomach and the acid was already attacking the tissue. She pushed aside another parent, failing to turn back to face their exclamations of irritation.

"We could go to that little hotel just out of town; I'll make it worth your while," said the woman, looking up at the man. He grumbled in reply and it seemed to satisfy her as she let out a little squeak and quickened her pace towards the block of cars parked haphazardly at the entrance to the field.

Melanie pressed on further, feeling her feet becoming wet with dew as her shoes sunk into the grass. It wasn't until the woman reached to kiss the man's cheek that she let loose.

"Benny Gordon Spark! You'd better hope to God that I don't beat you!" she yelled; her face contorted in anger.

A dozen eyes fixed on her, but she was focused on the pair belonging to Benny; however, something wasn't right. She knew the soft hazel of Benny's eyes and the way that those eyes would widen and dart around in their sockets when he was caught out, like a deer in headlights. The eyes staring back at her were questioning and blue. As a wave of light lit up his face, she saw a mustache planted above his top lip and a nose that hooked down, not the clean-shaven, pudgy-nosed face of Benny.

Melanie felt her cheeks redden; her hands trembling with adrenaline at her side. The crowd, who had realized her mistake, had quickly dispersed, diverting their attention back to the Ferris wheel as it completed its final turn.

"I'm so sorry," she called out, but the man and woman had scurried away, his hand at her back to usher her towards their car.

It was stupid. Why would Benny and Celine come back to the fair when they knew she would be there? Looking at the pair now, they didn't look anything like her husband of eleven years and the woman who had been lurking around the farm for the last few weeks.

Melanie cursed to herself under her breath and returned to watch the swarm of people exiting their compartments.

One boy was crying, his sleeve soaked in a sticky concoction of tears and snot. He clutched his mother's hip as she glanced around nervously, hoping to avoid judgment from others. The operator slammed the final cabin door shut as the crowd trickled away.

The rain was falling harder, enough for Melanie to feel her clothes begin to stick to her skin. It was splattering over the rusting metal of the attractions, and the final stallholders were holding their jackets over their heads, packing away the stuffed toys and water guns. She stretched her neck over the final few people, but the boys were nowhere to be seen.

"You ain't seen four little kids?" she yelled to the Ferris wheel operator.

He stopped untangling a collection of wires and scrunched his eyes through the rain. "I seen a lot of kids, lady. Saying that, it's hard to see anything in this shit-storm."

Melanie swept her drowned hair from her eyes and scanned the last remaining areas of shelter. She heard the cough of an old van engine as it kicked into life, its headlights casting dazzling beams onto the various canopies, but the only people left were the operators.

The cars were slowly filtering away from the field, in a blare of car horns as they all scrambled to get out through the narrow gap in the hedge. A blue station wagon flashed its lights and Melanie saw her husband's face through the sweeping windscreen wipers.

They must be with Benny. They saw the car and are all waiting for me to join them.

She staggered towards the car; the field had started to swamp. As she approached, the driver's door swung open and Benny ran to help her.

"Get in the car, honey. They say a storm's coming," he yelled over a gust of wind.

"Benny, you got the kids? They're in the car?"

He wiped the rain from his eyes. "No? They must have found somewhere to hide."

His face seemed to swirl as a force kicked at Melanie's eyeballs. "They ain't here Benny! They're gone." Her temples were crying out like someone was hammering a nail into the side of her skull.

She didn't hear his reply. The wind stole his voice. It seemed to be laughing at her. And at that moment, she somehow knew she would never see Alex go to college. She would never see Fred win another basketball match. Nigel would never ride the Wheel. Sam wouldn't play with his kitten. Petey wouldn't get his adult teeth, and Gus wouldn't have the chance to smile again.

*

Will could feel the heat emanating from the rewind. Acrid smoke was pooling around his fingers from the pores of the machine.

"Melanie, I need you to come back now!" Will shouted.

Tears streaked down Melanie's face. "They were so young," she screamed.

The kitchen disappeared in a flash as the memories kept spinning and Will could see a pathologist's office—all white except for six steel beds lined up in the center of the room. The pathologist, a young man with fuzzy ginger hair, peeled back each of the white sheets covering the beds. There were the six boys. The makeup around their noses had been removed, but their heads still stuck out at odd angles, and their necks stretched beyond normal capacity. Benny collapsed by her side; his face scrunched into his hands. He was letting out a low weeping sound.

Melanie nodded, and the pathologist returned the sheet, covering the horrors from view.

Will forced his hand from the rewind, snatching Melanie's away as he did so. Her eyes snapped open as Will slipped the rewind back into his pocket. He wiped away a tear before she could see.

"The hell was that?" she said, her lip trembling. The rewind often had that effect. "It felt like you was roamin' through my head."

Will gave one of his signature smiles, a sympathetic attempt that more often than not lowered their defenses, almost a carbon copy of his old interview looks. "It's a new bit of tech. It rests your mind using a mixture of Valerian and Lavender— good for anxiety. Perfectly safe. I hope the memories didn't affect you too much."

Melanie's hand was raised to her mouth, one long, blackened nail being nibbled at by her even blacker teeth. "I don't often think of anything else."

*

Melanie led Will out of the kitchen. He was grateful—the smell had threatened to knock him down. He could sense that Melanie was close to tears. In one of his most recent sessions, an elderly man had broken down after Will used the rewind, only coming around when Will had given him a large brandy. It hadn't been long after that the man had died, having hanged himself from a tree in his backyard. At the time, Will had told himself that he had nothing to do with it; at the age of ninety, there's not a lot left for a guy to do. His heart knew better.

"And your husband? Is he still around?" asked Will, pushing all thoughts of the old man from his mind. Benny Spark had been a big figure in the town when the boys had first gone missing. His restraining of his wife from attacking tourists was a well-known story around Hollyhead. In the next decade, little had been heard of Mr. Spark.

Melanie turned away. "He don't come out too much now. He don't do so much on the farm either. I manage just fine on my own."

Will nodded, and the pair came to a door at the end of the corridor.

"He's just in there. I won't come in. He don't like visitors too much, so don't be put off if he throws you out."

Will thanked Melanie as she opened the door for him.

*

"Benny, I presume. I knew you were a big man about town, but I didn't realize that saying was quite so accurate."

Melanie's husband had changed, perhaps even more than her. He took up most of the double bed that he was sprawled across. Greasy tufts of dark hair grew unevenly around his head. The fat around his face had sprouted a few hairs, which he scratched now and again, leaving more grease on his skin.

"Got another man in her life, has she? Good. Maybe a bit of sinning will do her good," he said, his face stretching into a smile. The teeth were rotting, and flecks of blood had gathered around the base of his gums, surrounded by inflamed, white tissue.

As Will approached the bedside, the sour stench of body odor enveloped him. He rerouted to sit by the window, opening it as far as it would go. Hearing a creak, he glanced behind him to see a dark shadow creep along the bottom of the door.

"I'm looking into the death of your sons. I'm a writer."

"So go write me a bedtime story. Ain't any fucking point in telling you what I've been telling the cops every day for the past twelve years."

"And what have you been telling them?" asked Will, leaning forward.

Benny cleared his throat and raised his voice. "I've been telling them that my wife should be locked away for fucking neglect. Leaving our kids to fend for themselves was a crime."

"She couldn't have been gone for longer than a couple of minutes. Whoever killed your children wasn't an opportunist. They had been waiting for a while."

"Told you the whole bloody tale, has she? She tell you the only reason she left was to follow me?"

The shadow at the door jolted.

"We all make mistakes," said Will.

Benny sat up a little. "There's a difference between going the wrong way at a junction and losing your fucking kids."

"It may not be easy to accept this, Benny, but the truth is that a killer like that would have found a way. The fact it happened under your wife's watch is just bad luck on her part."

"You obviously don't have kids," replied Benny, taking a straggly-looking cigarette and popping it between his lips. He struck a match on the bedpost, which was graffitied in scratches of various sizes, and lit up before taking a long draw.

"No, and I don't plan to, but I've read up on these things, and believe me, when a madman wants someone dead, they often get their way.

"It's what happens when little kids are abandoned in the dark."

Will felt in his pocket for the rewind. He closed his fingers around the metal but hesitated. It wouldn't work. After use, it needed time to breathe—time to charge back up to its optimum capacity. It was too soon.

"You didn't see or hear anything that day?"

"All I saw was that bitch of a wife collapse to the floor when we should've been out looking for my boys."

"Why did you come back?"

Benny dragged a thick arm across his face, attempting to remove the ingrained sweat from his brow. "It was pissing it down. I had been telling them all night to get back home but oh no, the wife wanted them to stay till the end. Wouldn't surprise me if she was in league with whoever broke their necks and strung 'em up."

He looked away, but not before Will saw a tear slip down his bristling cheek. Benny sniffed. "Why you asking about it now? We ain't going to find out what happened; I gave up on that a long time ago."

You've given up on a lot of things—everything except food and booze, thought Will.

"Police want a fresh eye on the case."

"So they asked a fuckin' writer?" Benny snorted.

"I have a platform from my books. Those who haven't heard about the case soon will. Maybe some new evidence will show up."

"Will your scribbles give me my kids back?"

"Closure is worth something."

"I'll have closure when whoever did it is dead. If I don't know who it is then I can believe he stepped out in front of a train and had his head caved into the tracks. That's closure."

"You can't just give up on it," said Will, leaning closer despite the smell.

"If my wife had done her job, there would be nothing to give up *on*. People don't realize that giving up is sometimes the best option. When the boys were buried, Melanie threw in half their crap with them. 'Just in case they need them in the next life.'" Benny shook his head, defeated. "They're dead. What is Alex going to do with his old diary? What's Petey going to do with his stuffed bear? Fuck all, that's what."

A stifled cry came through the door. Benny's eyes flickered toward the hallway.

"That's it ain't it, love? You thought I was off with that skinny blonde supermodel, so you left the kids."

Will turned to see the shadow at the door turn away and there was an unmistakable sound of footsteps retreating down the hallway.

Benny let out a deep laugh. "She likes listening. I think she hopes that I'll tell someone I've forgiven her, but just won't admit it to her face." He raised his voice again, "not until the day I die." His laugh turned into a sickly, wheezing cough; his cheeks reddened.

"You should treat her better. She wouldn't have been looking for you if you hadn't already left her at the fairground."

"You fucker. You can't put any blame at my door," he gasped through a haggard breath. He tugged at the collar of his stained pajama shirt. A pudgy hand pointed to the side of the bed.

"I need my pills. They're for my heart. I got angina."

Will glanced at the small orange bottle on the bedside table. Beta-blockers. He took them and shook the bottle around in his hand, watching the pills clambering over one another, following the curve of the bottle.

"You torture that woman every day with your poison. Look at you. You lost your kids and found two hundred pounds. You disgust me. A cripple by choice."

"So why do you look like death is just around the corner?" His eyes sparkled with malice.

Does he know I have cancer? Some people can smell that kind of thing, thought Will.

In response, Will pocketed the bottle, enjoying the look on Benny's face.

"Beg me."

Benny was lying in a pool of his own sweat; so much that it was staining the mattress. "Please…" he croaked.

Will smiled as he took his jacket and pulled it over his shoulders. He reached into his pocket and placed the bottle on the dresser by the door.

"You want them? Get your ass out of bed." Benny crumpled over, a low groan coming from his suddenly very weak body. "Enjoy your heartburn, asshole."

Benny groaned. He clutched one hand to his heart and reached the other out towards Will, his eyes wide with panic. Will stepped out of the room, ensuring that the door clicked shut behind him.

CHAPTER EIGHT: DETECTIVES AND GHOSTS

Walking further away from the sickly groans coming from Benny's room, Will exited through the front door and walked down the steps leading back to the dirt path. Melanie was scattering corn to a flock of chickens which flapped their wings aggressively in competition for the scraps of food. She straightened up, giving Will a slight smile.

"You deserve better than him, Mrs Spark."

"We both failed our boys—we deserve each other," she replied, her eyes glassy.

Before Will could leave, he saw a lanky man walking towards them. The man clutched a large cooler to his chest, and his hair looked damp with sweat.

"I got your meat order, Mels," he said in a gruff voice.

Melanie let out the first real smile that Will had seen from her that afternoon. "Tony, you're a sweetheart, you know that?"

The butcher couldn't help but beam. Will recognized it immediately as a smile conjured by a deep, gripping love.

"Just doing my job."

"Your job don't require you doin' personal runs at this time of day!"

Tony blushed and started digging his shoe into the ground. "You know how it is. I gotta take care of my customers."

Melanie smiled again and walked over to him, putting one hand on his arm. "I really do appreciate what you've done for us. Every late visit. Taking Benny to his appointments. Let us repay you somehow," she said, taking the box. The pair looked like an ideal match: Tony managing to reach a couple more inches than her. Compared to the two of them, Will was dwarfish in structure.

Tony waved his hands. "No, no. You are valued customers. Happy to help out in any way possible."

"At least come in for some tea?" asked Melanie.

Will didn't hear Tony's answer; he had already slipped half-way down the path, anxious to get away before he could be offered another cup of what Melanie regarded as tea.

*

A single road meandered from the Spark farmhouse back into the centre of town. Originally, it had been a walking track with access only for the Spark's vehicles but, with the success of Bill's murder tours, tarmac had been put down, allowing easier access for cars. Trees lined the edges, their branches bare. In the summer, the road would be left in total darkness, even during the day due to the leaves that clogged up the sky. One vehicle accident prompted another wave of speculation. Bill took advantage of the occurrence, saying that the six boys haunted the road. Will didn't believe in ghosts, but there was something eerie about the place. Drivers had to be careful going around corners; anyone going too fast would risk colliding with the foliage and any recently fallen branches that were scattered along the road.

Will continued walking, hoping that the weather wouldn't worsen. It was only as he turned a corner that he saw a vehicle parked haphazardly by the side of the road on the grassy verge. It was a Ford Granada, a dark green in color with tinted windows and a large scratch running down the right side. A man sat behind the wheel, watching Will behind a pair of Aviator sunglasses. Knowing he had been spotted, the man unbuckled his seat belt and opened the door with a comically loud creak. The face felt familiar, and the posture reminded Will of someone he had met only briefly. It wasn't until the man removed his sunglasses that Will recognised him as the detective who had been waiting in the hospital to talk to him.

"You know, there are these things called crimes that are probably going on right now. The badge on your chest suggests you might want to be dealing with them," said Will.

The man laughed. "Right now, I got more pressing matters. I'm sure you've read in the papers about Abigail Finsbury. She died just over a week ago."

"I'm guessing you haven't found out who did it then?"

The detective scratched at his stubble. "Who? No chance. We don't even know why. To me, she seemed pretty *'armless,"* he said, waving his hands around, like a cartoon.

"A joke like that should put you in handcuffs," said Will.

"Just trying to relieve the tension," sighed the detective, thrusting his hands into his coat pockets. "I've been trying to get in touch for a while now. I was hoping for a little tête-à-tête."

"About what?"

The detective pulled a hand from his pocket and flipped open a small leather notebook. He licked one finger and swiped through the pages. "About whom, actually. Lenora Brown—a friend of yours I heard."

"You heard wrong."

"I don't think so."

"You're wearing sunglasses on a day like this," noted Will, pointing at the dark storm clouds that were rolling overhead. "I can tell thinking doesn't come easily."

The detective took the aviators off to reveal bright blue eyes. "These are my interview glasses: means you can't see my eyes. Eyes are very telling."

"Yeah, they're telling me that you're an idiot," said Will, moving forward to push past the detective.

"Hilarious. Well, this idiot's name is Teddy Ludlow," he said, sticking out a hand.

"Pleasure," replied Will, ignoring the attempt at an introduction.

Silence reigned for a second, interrupted only by a gust of cold winter wind.

"I can tell we got off on the wrong foot. I waited at the hospital for you, but Dr Highsmith told me that you had discharged yourself. You picked up a nasty injury, Will. I was just wondering whether you wanted me to look into what happened," inquired Teddy. The wind caught on the lapel of his coat, forcing it open to reveal a badge on his chest, which indicated that he served the HPD.

"I know what happened. One of those tramps hit me and stole my wallet."

"And you don't want us to find your wallet?"

"Money isn't an issue," said Will.

Teddy nodded. "What I would like to know is what you were doing down Whitley Avenue in the first place. You see, we had a journalist come and ask us about a recent sighting of a missing girl. They told me that a homeless man came to them saying that he had seen her. Being the good cop I am, I looked into it and your name popped up. Then I hear that you're back in Hollyhead days after a woman was killed in the very same place that you were attacked," he clapped his hands together, "and in the very same place that Miss Brown was seen. I'm not paid to believe in coincidence, so am I wrong to think that there's something here?"

"I'm just visiting family," said Will.

Teddy turned the words over. "Or maybe you were returning to the scene of the crime."

Before Will could reply, Teddy started laughing. "I'm just kidding. I just need to find out what's happened here, and you seem to be a good place to start. We've managed to keep Lenora's name out of the press, but her family are very worked up about this," he lowered his voice. "I know that you two were friends. Just help a guy out, would ya?"

"If you want to know what happened then I suggest that you ask her old boyfriend: Nick King. I have a feeling that he knows more about her disappearance than anyone."

Teddy noted down the name in his notebook and flipped his notebook shut. "It's a start," he said. He reached into his coat again and took out a card, passing it to Will.

Det. Teddy Ludlow was typed in red ink, followed by a phone number and his address. "My card. If you need to talk, just give me a ring, but no drunk midnight calls, alright?" he joked.

"Right, thanks," said Will, slipping the card into his pocket.

"Do you need a lift?" asked Teddy, glancing at Will's bad leg.

"I'll take my chances with the walk."

"As you wish," said Teddy, pushing his hat back onto his head. He gave Will a salute. "See you around."

With that, Teddy walked back over to the car, roared it into life and took off, skidding around the corner of the road with a sound like a jet engine.

Muttering about time wasters, Will started walking again. It was a two-hour journey back into the center of Hollyhead: enough for him to think over what he had seen at the Spark house. Four of the Spark boys had vanished from the Ferris-wheel, with the other two being lost at some point on their walk back home. It wouldn't have been hard to entice four kids, already hyped up on sugar, into an area where they could have been drugged, or even killed on the spot. Perhaps it was multiple people. If there was one person who knew the timeline of events that night the best, it was Frank. One step closer to the Spark boys also meant a step closer to finding Lenora, although he now wasn't sure which one was the priority. The look on Melanie's face triggered something inside of him. He shook off the feeling and focused on following the road, which was becoming harder to see with each passing second. The wind had picked up to the extent that it blew dust into Will's face, causing him to shield his eyes with his hand. His ears were already numb with the cold that bit and tore into his skin. A part of him wanted to head back to the Spark house and see out the inevitable storm that was coming in.

Then he saw it: a barn was situated just through a clearing of trees to his right. It was obviously old; parts of the wood were rotting away, and it looked as though it could crumble at any moment. Still, anywhere was better than the Spark house. He trudged through the undergrowth and approached the door. Praying it wasn't locked, he gave it a push. It took some effort, but he managed to create a gap big enough to fit through. With another shove, he closed out the wind, though he could still hear it battering the side of the building.

He collapsed on an upturned hay bale; his lungs grateful for the rest. From the deepest recesses of the barn, moans and rattling emanated. Will put it down to the ferocity of the storm striking the walls. Clumps of grass and weeds scattered around his feet, poking out from the dirt. In fact, there was no indication that anyone had been in the barn for a long time. The contents of the barn appeared to have been ransacked by a bunch of animals; strands of hay were tangled around frayed chicken wire. Nails stuck out from planks of wood that were propped against the walls and orange rust blistered across iron bars. Shafts of light penetrated through gaps in the rotting wood, illuminating the kicks of dust swirling in the air.

Will stretched out on the bale. Lenora had been digging around the Spark farm; there must be a reason why she had returned. The thoughts were colliding around inside his head, giving him a migraine. He took the bottle of painkillers from his coat and swallowed them dry. Lenora's face seemed to fill every inch of the darkness. Who gave her the scar?

Above his head, the strangled squawk of a raven erupted through the barn. An unkindness of ravens was crammed into a dark corner, all huddled together beneath a hole in the roof. The noisiest of the group flapped its wings and screamed again. Next to it, the largest had its beak locked around a fat worm, the worm's body twisting in an attempt to escape the clutches of its executioner.

Will had a good mind to leave and carry on following the road. He got to his feet and stepped forward, feeling a twinge at the back of his hamstring. A few days in hospital had helped reduce his pain, but at that moment, his leg felt like it was being beaten by that metal pipe. In front of him, the doors creaked, their hinges protesting as the wind picked up. Another gust of wind caused them to shudder open and crash against the side of the barn. Dirt blinded him instantly. Squinting through the debris, he staggered forward and managed to clasp his hands around the lock, which had been broken into pieces. He pushed the doors back together and fastened the latch again, dragging a couple of large bags up against the door.

It was then that he noticed the groaning again. This time, he knew it wasn't the sound of wood straining against the wind. Only a human could make this noise. A human on death's door, letting out the last wheezes squeezing through their struggling lungs. Will's muscles tensed in anticipation, his breathing becoming shallow and quick, fast enough to make his vision sway. He turned around. Six bodies floated in front of him, their necks stretched, and all twelve eyes fixed on his face. The

Spark boys… Their skin was mottled with small holes where the flesh had been eaten away.

One of the ravens flapped down from its nest and perched on the beam above Nigel. It nipped at his ear a few times before grabbing the lobe and ripping it away from his skull. After a second of gnashing, it took the prize and returned to its nest, where the rest of the ravens danced eagerly to grab as much of the ear as they could.

Alex's mouth cracked open; the back of his throat was so decayed that the barn was visible through the web of skin. "You forgot about me, Will. I was your friend. I needed you and you weren't there for me," the body croaked, the remains of his eyeballs rolling erratically in their sockets.

"I'm here now. I will find out what happened to you," cried Will, watching as the six boys began shaking, breaking away from their nooses.

He turned his back on the bodies and escaped the barn as fast as his leg would allow, not daring to turn back in case their lifeless corpses had decided to follow him into the night.

CHAPTER NINE:
THE KING'S RETURN

Was it some kind of projection? A side effect of the painkillers? Will's mind pulled explanations out like some kind of macabre lucky dip—anything to deny that what he had seen could only be explained by the supernatural. Ghosts sell, but only fools believe in them.

"The road is said to be haunted; you wouldn't be the first to claim a sighting of the Spark boys," the voice in his head whispered.

The sounds from the wind and trees vibrated through him, swarming him from every angle. He continued forwards, keeping his eyes on the road. The storm-darkened sky would play on anyone's mind, let alone someone pumped up on drugs; adrenaline was the only thing keeping him going. Images of the boys kept flashing through his mind, their faces twisting like the limbs of the trees that were around him. Birds conjured by shadows glared down at him from every branch. He tried the breathing techniques he had found in a self-help book. The height of his career had been accompanied by a spat of panic attacks—most usually concerning whether anyone would find out about the rewind.

"Get a hold of yourself. It's the cancer. It's messing with your head somehow," he told himself.

The sight of the Spark boys had roused a terror deep within him. He had seen his fair share of violence. Many of the people he interviewed couldn't help but let their mind wander. Will would often be confronted with disturbing images of death and abuse. He could cope with that. After all, it was just a memory. Still, the image of the boys haunted him—especially Alex.

Alex had always been the funniest in the class. His quick-wit and quirky physical features meant that he was popular without having to join any of the sports teams. Will, on the other hand, had always been seen as the class freak. Growing up on an impoverished farmstead, the brothers had never been able to afford the latest trends. Sometimes, they had arrived at school with their clothes still reeking of the shit they had been clearing up the night before. Being the favorite child saved Alex from most of the embarrassment, and his job meant that he could afford his own clothes. He had occasionally helped his brothers out when food ran low. The younger brothers hadn't even made it to middle school. The fact was that the Spark brothers were nobodies until they died.

Will's chest tightened. A part of himself wanted to make a bee-line for the hospital: possibly just for the drugs—he was happy to skip the conversation. Still, better not. He'd be a sitting duck for another of Highsmith's lectures. If he mentioned that he was seeing spectres, they would probably stick him in a straitjacket and wheel him away to the East Wing. Chances were, he wouldn't come out again. He continued walking with no concrete destination in mind. All he knew was that distance from the barn could only be a good thing. He could go back to the motel, although he hadn't seen Frank in over a week. How had his father not been in touch? Had he not noticed that his son hadn't been seen in nine days?

Will cursed. He should never have returned to Hollyhead. It changed a person, infecting everything about them until only malice remained. Now it was too late. Like a fool, he had made a promise. Melanie Spark was counting on him and the promise of finding Lenora was becoming stronger with each scrap of new information. He could face a few more weeks in Hell surrounded by ghosts and demons, if it meant he could find her. Only time would tell if his mind would survive the trip.

The next second passed in a blur. Just as he stepped onto the adjoining road, a large truck roared in front of him. The driver blared his horns in just enough time for Will to fall backwards, narrowly avoiding the vehicle. From his position sprawled on the ground, Will watched as the truck sped away, swerving from side to side as it went. It had been enough. His senses had returned. Groaning, he hauled his ass off the floor. There's nothing like a near-death experience to shake away obsessive thoughts.

"The fuck happened to you?" asked Marty, standing aside to let Will through, his face wrinkled with concern. Scrubbing off hadn't worked. After returning to the motel, Will had taken the chance to shower and dress in a clean shirt and jeans. The lump at the back of his head was still tender and his legs had been covered in red gashes where the concrete had torn his skin away. Other than that, he'd looked surprisingly well. The warmth of the room had enticed him to lie down; the sheets wrapping around his broken body until the pain had lessened. He hadn't meant to, but he'd dozed off, not returning from his slumber until early afternoon the following day. Then Frank had called.

"I want an update," he'd demanded. "You've been unresponsive for over a week. I was almost thinking that your heart isn't entirely in this job."

"I'll be there soon."

"You're not hungover again?"

"I haven't touched the stuff since I saw you last."

"Good. I'll see you soon. Same place as usual."

Now, the man himself was sitting in his chair again, filling his lungs with tobacco. The office reeked of frenzy. In the time that Will had been away, Frank and Marty had decorated the room with papers, notes, and newspaper clippings, all linked with red ribbon. Discarded chip packets and beer bottles took up the majority of the floor space.

"I was attacked. Some homeless guy took my wallet," said Will, lowering himself into a chair, his knee still twinging with pain at quick movements.

"Are you able to continue on the case?" asked Frank.

"Besides the bruised knee and the lump on my head, I'm dandy."

Frank obviously hadn't detected the sarcasm. "Good. In the time you've been gone, we have spoken to Abigail Finsbury's parents."

"Anything of worth?"

Marty shrugged. "Only some loose ends."

"Which we can tie together to get a picture here. You need to get your head straight, Marty. I know that you are close to the family, but frankly, you were useless back there," chastised

Frank, pulling a notebook towards him. Marty grunted and left the room, muttering something about grabbing another beer before he went mad.

"Abigail's parents last saw her in the early evening on the night of her murder. She was getting into a car with a man."

"No chance that they saw who she was with?"

"Of course not. That would be too easy."

"Easy? Easy would be the killer walking in right now. Easy would be the guy handing himself over to the police. Sometimes easy is good," said Will, rubbing his temples. It felt like he hadn't slept in days.

"Nothing of worth is ever easy. Now, the parents didn't know that she was meeting someone that night; however, just because she got in this man's car doesn't mean that he is the killer. Don't let that bias your thinking."

"He would have gone to the police if he were innocent."

"Or maybe he is scared. Fear is a bigger motivator than what is right and wrong."

Marty came back in and sat down, popping the cap off another beer with his nail. He took a long swig. "The details concerning who she was with were lacking."

"The parents suggested they were older than Abigail."

"They were looking through a window at a car across the street. It was dark outside. I've had better witness testimonies from crack addicts," said Marty.

"It gives us something to go on," Will pointed out.

"And how have you spent your time?" said Frank, turning to his son.

"I went to see the Spark family."

"And what did you learn?"

"Besides the fact that my father is a stalker, there wasn't much."

Frank's face reddened. He pushed his glasses further up his nose. "Did you use the MED?"

Will nodded. "Melanie had a strong memory. No doubt because she replays it in her head everyday thanks to those fucking tourists clamoring around her house. I saw what happened on the night of the boys' disappearance."

"Anything helpful?" asked Marty.

"Just what we already know. Alex took Gus back early; that was the last Melanie saw of them. The other four went missing in the time she had her back turned."

"How long was that?" asked Frank.

"It couldn't have been more than a minute. The killer only had a window of about 30 seconds."

"Someone they knew then?" said Marty.

Frank closed his eyes in thought, "or someone in a position of authority. Could they possibly have been drugged?"

"Perhaps," said Will. "The only food that Melanie saw them eat was cotton candy plus whatever else they picked up at the food stalls. Someone could have slipped them something."

"All they would have to do is cover it in sugar and the kids would have gone crazy," said Marty.

"Candy leading them into evil," pondered Frank. "Fits the stories."

"So we go and find the people manning the stands," suggested Will.

Marty shook his head in frustration. "No. It's too coincidental. It was a traveling fair. The killer knew there would be six brothers. It's the only way they could have told the story."

"It wouldn't have been difficult to work out that they were brothers. They look very similar. Either that or they knew the parents?" said Will.

Frank nodded in agreement. "After I was sent away from the Bureau, I tried talking to the Spark family. After a few attempts, I was no closer to getting a conversation going, let alone an interview. Of course, I gathered as much as I could from other sources. I've managed to develop timelines and sightings from others, but nothing that can lead me to any concrete propositions."

"It's strange that they wouldn't talk to you. I find that stalking is a perfectly normal way to talk to people," said Will.

"It wasn't stalking."

"It might as well have been," said Marty. "We had the notes from the police, even had a few agents on their tails for a few months after the murders. Nothing. They hardly left their house, let alone lead us to anything interesting."

"You had agents watching them?" said Will.

Marty shrugged. "Standard procedure. They had no idea. We can put agents on anyone."

"You had no right. You should have been helping them, not putting them down as suspects. Did you ever stop to think that the reason they didn't leave the house was because of grief? Or did you just suppose that's what guilty people do?"

"The agents were there to write them off, not to cement their position," Frank replied.

"Well, considering you two are still no closer to finding the killer, I assume that your actions were very beneficial."

"We're getting closer now. With your help, Will, we can find who did this," said Frank.

"I'm not going to turn into you two: stuck playing over the past. I'm here until I find Lenora and then I'm done," replied Will. A part of him knew that he didn't mean it. The promise to Melanie was a leash around his neck, getting tighter with every passing minute.

"Why do you have this obsession with finding Miss Brown?" asked Frank.

"Well, we started a game of hide-and-go-seek and I'm starting to think that she's winning."

"You're hiding something under your sarcasm. This mindset is not normal; she wasn't even your girlfriend," said Frank. "There is more to this than you are letting on."

Will's head dropped. The memories were still painful. "The night of her disappearance, I made a mistake. It's my fault that she's gone."

"If I remember correctly, you made a particularly big mistake that night. A mistake that very nearly cost your life."

"That was different. Lenora is gone because I was drunk. If I could only remember what happened, then I might have had some luck finding her."

"I really think you should be concentrating on the case. We have set a task for you and it would only be proper to see it through before continuing with your own venture," said Frank.

"I need to find Lenora. The day she went missing was the end of life as I knew it. After Alex died, she was all I had left besides Nick. She matters beyond anything else right now."

"She is more important than taking a violent murderer off the streets? Someone who has killed twice and will undoubtedly kill again?"

"She is to me."

Frank breathed out slowly. "She must be quite the character," he sighed. "Of course, we will help you find your friend. She evidently matters a great deal to you. What is your next move?"

"I think it's obvious," said Will, rising to his feet.

He had been putting it off since he'd seen Lenora in Bruce Fisher's memory: it was time to find the King.

*

It hadn't been difficult to find Nick King; his business cards were poked through the mailboxes of every house in Hollyhead. In recent years, he had become engrossed in the world of real estate. Fittingly, the card read: *The King of the Castle* plastered in royal purple letters, followed by his contact number.

Before dialing, Will's fingers had been filled with the shakes. The day he and Nick had parted ways was a distant memory and one that Will felt nothing but relief about. After a brief conversation with Nick's personal assistant and a minute of Clair de Lune on hold, Will had been put through to the man himself. Formalities were exchanged and Will suggested they meet at The Jazz Lounge—a small bar on the edge of town that they had frequented during their formative years. Nick had rejected the idea, offering the only high-class restaurant in town as an alternative. Will agreed. The meeting was important.

*

Nick King was as interesting as his name was original. His good looks had made up for his lack of brains and within a day of starting high school, he had been called up by the gym coach to try his hand at football. He quickly developed into the star of the team. He didn't look it, but his thick frame was surprisingly agile, allowing him to dodge his way through the defenses of most teams that came to visit Hollyhead. His speed let him bomb through flocks of players before catching a sixty-yard punt from one of the line-backs. That seemed to be the main tactic of the team, and Nick was happy to comply, if only for the roar of the crowd as he flexed after the final whistle.

"Nicking the hearts of every girl in the place," the coach would shout as the cheerleaders walked past, their eyes flickering over Nick's body before bursting into a fit of giggles. For a gym teacher, the play on words was rather clever. The truth was that Nick had never cared about football. There was no denying that he was good at it, but as a future endeavor, it had always been clear his heart wasn't in it. Will had thought that Nick might find luck working the docks with his father. One meeting with the pair had struck that from the list within minutes. Whatever respect had grown in childhood was scrapped once Nick had discovered fast cars and supermodels. Dock work was honest, but there was no way it could fit into the King's expectations. Will had gotten the feeling that Nick resented his father for not aspiring higher than stacking crates. The fierce temper had obviously been passed on from Nick's mother; his father had been no match for his son even when Nick was still stealing dago cigarettes from the drug store. After Will left for college, Nick ran away to New York. A few letters were exchanged before a period of silence settled in, which Will was happy to maintain.

As the meeting grew closer, Will felt his anxiety rise. On numerous occasions, he had been tempted to pick up the phone and call the whole thing off.

No. I need to do this. For Lenora.

When the time arrived, Will dressed in a smart jumper beneath his coat and shaved his face. He left the motel with a plan and a racing pulse.

*

Nick was an imposing figure. Since high school, he had gained a few inches. As Will entered, Nick downed his beer and clicked impatiently at the waiter to fetch him another. His peremptory manner remained. Will felt a pinch of satisfaction at seeing that his hair was already graying on the temples, the front swept back with gel to give him a distinguished businessman-like look.

He had done well for himself; his suit looked tailored, and he had accessorized with a pair of silver dice cufflinks.

"Will Metlocke as I live and breathe. What's a fella like you doing back in a shithole like this?" he said, rising from his chair and pulling Will in for a hug that had evidently been practiced on many occasions. It stank of PR. "You look like shit, by the way," he added, holding Will out as if inspecting him for fault.

"How you doing, Nick? I'm back to see Dad," said Will, taking a seat and smoothing down his hair. Nick had rented out a private booth located in the back parlor of the restaurant. As Will had entered, the man on the door whisked him away— apparently, they had been expecting him. He had been guided through the central part of the establishment, away from the fake chandeliers and the overly-polished handrails. They had entered a room filled with cigarette smoke and glamour, all bathed in a crimson haze.

"Never better brother. How is the old man? Not still going on about that murder business, is he? My god, I remember what he was like. Getting drunk out of his skin every night before fucking off home like some sort of tramp," said Nick, laughing at the memory.

Will poured himself a glass of water as the waiter arrived with Nick's drink. Nick cast an eye in Will's direction. "Don't be dumb, Will. Waiter, we'll have a bourbon. Double for my good friend here. Don't go soft on me now."

Despite Will's rejections, the waiter nodded and left. "I try not to drink anymore, Nick—not since Lenora went missing."

Nick didn't meet his eye. "Nonsense. All men must drink. How else are we meant to get by?" He slicked back his hair. "What is Frank up to these days?"

"Same old. Retired now."

"Got another woman? And what about you? Any females?"

Is this really what a few business meetings do to a man? Thought Will.

"No. Can't see Dad remarrying now. As for me, it's never really been my thing."

Nick grinned to reveal two rows of chemically whitened teeth. "Always thought you were a fag. You need to get yourself down to Lady Liberty's place. She'll sort you out. It's a bunny ranch like no other. I can confirm that."

Will felt himself redden. He raised his glass and drank slowly, hoping that his embarrassment would subside. "I can think of nothing worse. I just think there are more interesting things out there."

Nick clicked at another waiter and popped a cigarette into his mouth. The waiter flicked a bronze lighter and Nick took a deep drag. "Never did understand how that funny little brain of yours worked. Still, some people must tolerate you. Sold enough books, haven't you?"

"I've managed."

"Done more than that, I heard. Word gets around William. As for your drinking, I've heard a different story: turning up drunk to meetings, people finding you half-dead in the streets. No one can say you haven't lived, eh?"

"It's not a time that I remember fondly."

"Doubt you remember it at all!" said Nick, letting out a shrill laugh.

"You must have friends in far off places to hear about things like that," said Will.

Nick began turning his cufflinks. "I began networking as soon as you went off to college. Real estate gets you in the right places. Take last month for example, I sold a nice little penthouse apartment up in NYC. Now I can't tell you who, but let's just say he and 'best-seller' go hand in hand." He looked pleased with himself; his lips were almost meeting his ears.

"So, why are you back here? I'm guessing no A-listers want to hole up in Hollyhead."

"Never forget where you come from. Better to meet the past with open arms than to burn out trying to escape it. Plus, any business is good business, especially in a town like this where IQ is at an all-time low."

"I didn't realize that you had taken up philosophy as well," said Will.

"I'm a man of life. What more can I say?" Nick replied, holding out his hands. "Can I expect a mention in your next book? I was a bit surprised that you hadn't dedicated any of your work to me."

"If you can help me out with something, I'm sure your name will end up in my book somewhere," said Will.

Nick gestured for Will to shoot.

"There's been rumors: rumors concerning Lenora."

"You're not seriously writing about her? There's gotta be something else to keep the pages turning," groaned Nick, running a hand through his hair. His face had drained of color behind the neat stubble across his jaw.

"I've found witnesses. Both in the last couple of weeks. They say she's in Hollyhead. I want to know why she's back. It would clear your name completely if she has returned."

"As far as I'm concerned, the girl is dead," said Nick. His eyes were flicking around the room and one hand gripped tightly around his glass. Will noticed.

"You must want to know if there is truth to this. After everything you went through, there must be a part of you that wants to know why she left."

Nick leaned across the table with frightening speed. "I know exactly why she took off. She was a lying bitch who didn't believe that I could support my family," he hissed. A line of sweat had gathered on his brow.

"Then you do know! What did she tell you?"

"She told me nothing. The eyes did most of the talking."

Will pushed the dagger in further. "You remember the night she left then? You told everyone you were too drunk to remember."

"I can't remember what happened. I only remember the days leading up to it," said Nick, keeping his voice low. "I don't think anyone will ever know. It's a mystery that isn't worth solving."

Will had the urge to take out the rewind. Without even realizing he had done so, Will removed it from his coat pocket.

"The fuck is that?" said Nick, leaning back.

His head cleared and Will looked down. He couldn't get Nick to touch it—not in his current state.

"You did something to her that night. I don't know what, but I will find out. You can hide behind your tailored suits and your obnoxious quotes, but eventually, people will see you for what you are."

Nick pushed the table away, almost crushing it into Will's stomach. "I haven't seen her since she disappeared. Do you have any idea how hard it was? I fell asleep and she was gone when I woke up: no note, no indication of where she was going. She just vanished—along with my child," he said, his hands curled into fists on the table. "Of course, you don't know. I stuck up for you in high school. If you knew half the names people called you behind your back... You have no idea what it feels like. You've been alone half your life and you'll be alone for whatever is left of it," he finished, eyeing Will's pale face.

"I'll see you around," said Will, his breath raw.

"Let's hope not," Nick replied, before storming out into the main body of the restaurant, not bothering to look back. Will was left with only the bill for company.

CHAPTER TEN:
EVE

The outskirts of Hollyhead were no place to be during the day—let alone the night. It was a petri-dish for the vile and disturbed. The rain had stopped, leaving the paving coated in a thin layer of slime that threatened to send Will sprawling onto the sidewalk. Seeing Nick had left him shaking, though whether with anger or anxiety he wasn't sure. His old friend had an effect on Will that he had never experienced with anyone else. After years of reinvention, Nick was the only person, other than Frank, who treated Will exactly as he always had. Will shook his head, as if forcing the memory out of his mind. His breath caught in the air and coiled upwards. He remembered how he and Nick had used to pretend to smoke, like gangsters in an old movie. Before long, Nick had swapped imagination for reality and Will was left to catch up; a part of him felt like he never had.

Looking towards the busier parts of town, and the best place to get something close to edible, Will turned his collar up against the wind and set off. Nick knew more than he had told the police; Will was sure of that. Nick's street-wise artistry had always outweighed any academic talent he had and there wasn't a single trick in the book that he didn't know, especially where money was concerned.

After twenty minutes of walking, Will stopped and took out his pills. There were only two left. He changed direction and walked towards the pharmacy, checking his watch; it would shut in the next ten minutes. He stepped through the doors and scanned the shelves for whatever painkillers he could find. A noise from his right alerted him to another person's presence.

It was Melanie Spark. If she wasn't so tall, Will never would have given her a second glance. A number of paper bags, brimming with vegetables, were in her hands. The pharmacy was clearly her last stop before heading home. Boxes of medical supplies had fallen on the ground and she lowered down to pick them up. She had arranged her hair differently from the last time Will had seen her. It now fell across the left side of her face. As she knelt down, it parted to reveal her eye, which was now surrounded by a puffy, purple bruise.

Will walked over and helped her pick up the scattered boxes. "Mrs Spark, what happened?"

Melanie caught him looking and flattened the fringe back over her eye. "Just me bein' clumsy," she said, stacking the items back onto the shelves.

"I mean your eye."

She blushed. "Oh, it's nothin'. Just walked into a cupboard door."

"That's funny. I didn't realize cupboards left knuckle marks like that."

She sighed, "Benny lost his pills. It ain't his fault. He gets angry when his heart acts up. I found them for him. They had ended up on the other side of the room for God knows what reason."

"He didn't say how they got there?" Will's stomach clenched.

Melanie shook her head. "I must have put them there. Guess I deserved the beating. He used to be half my size, but now he's got one hell of a right hook."

"You can't let him do this."

"I stand by my vows. 'Sickness and health' we said."

"Did your vows include a round of bare-knuckle every week?"

Melanie shushed Will with her hands. "It ain't every week; I would never allow that. He calls it penance for my mistakes."

"I think the dictionary would call it abuse."

Before Melanie could reply, the pharmacy worker came to the pairs' side. "We are closing now," they said, in a monotone. They had probably been hoping to close up early. Will nodded and pulled his wallet out. He took out a fifty and handed it to Melanie.

"I forgot to give this to you. Consider it payment for our interview," he said, pressing it into her hand.

"I can't accept this," she said, pushing it back toward him.

Will moved back, resisting her attempts to return the money. "Just do me a favor and leave him. I hear the butcher around here thinks very highly of you," he said. He walked away, but not before seeing the solitary tear crawling down Melanie's cheek as she clutched the bill to her chest.

*

It had reached the time of night that kids retreated to their homes, gangly teenagers taking their place on the street corners. Businessmen, long finished with work, walked in the shadows, waiting for the girls of the night to skulk out from the alleyways. The increase in police presence that had followed Abigail's death had now diminished. They were back to their routine patrols, albeit far more nervously than usual; their fingers tapped the guns holstered by their sides. When a murder has taken place, smaller crimes are forgotten. Police won't bat an eye at prostitution or petty theft when they have the chance to catch a killer.

Then Will had a thought. He backtracked slightly and headed closer to the edge of town. At this time, the prostitutes remained inside in preparation for a night's work. Frank had said that Abigail had been with an older man. If anyone knew the type of man to go hounding young girls, it was sex workers.

Will wasn't sure where to start. Unlike seemingly half the boys in his school, he had always kept well away from Hollyhead's center at night. Hadn't Nick mentioned something about a Lady Liberty? He could have been talking about an institution in New York, but Hollyhead seemed more likely. Even if he managed to find it, there was no guarantee it would be useful; it was likely that every man in Hollyhead had visited at some time or another—it was just that kind of town.

He stuck to the streetlights, not out of fear of the thugs and dopeheads nesting in the darkened alleyways, but of the creations of his own mind. The darkness has ways of playing on your fear, and at that time, Will had plenty. For the majority of his life, Will had never believed in ghosts. Everything had a logical explanation. Now he wasn't so sure. The image of the boys had been branded onto his brain, only allowing him relief when he had forced his mind onto other things. It was time to focus on finding Lady Liberty. If only he had asked Nick what he meant. There wasn't much to go on, but if you want information, a bar is always a good place to start—drunks love to gossip. *Kennedy's* was only a block away and the pain in his knee from the beating was beginning to make walking more painful than it was worth.

*

Kennedy's was a popular blue-collar bar. The youth of Hollyhead stayed clear, only entering once they turned fifty, or their hands were so gnarled from manual labor that they could join in the conversations about compensation. Three men were smoking outside beneath a fire escape. Not even rain can stop an addict. Will had never been in before but he could imagine what the inside would be like: wallpaper stained with smoke, frequent fighting over nine-ball and so much testosterone that you could smell it. He approached the door, ignoring the suspicious glances from the smokers. Then he stopped. A glass phone booth stood on the right-hand side of the bar beneath a dripping gutter. Posters for a missing boy were plastered on the glass of the booth.

Ads, Will thought, *there may be one for Lady Liberty.*

He entered and immediately scanned the various flyers and stickers that decorated the area below the phone. There—a cartoon statue holding out the torch above her head. An address, printed in small, black letters, indicated that Liberty's was located a few streets away. Nothing on the ad signaled anything illegal, but even the cartoon smelt rotten. It was a familiar sensation. Will tore off the ad and pocketed it. Illegal prostitution—so much for freedom.

*

Lady Liberty's den was tucked away behind a sleazy hotel. It wouldn't take Sherlock Holmes to figure out why. A blinking red light advertised the entrance at the top of a creaking old fire escape that had certainly seen its fair share of first kisses, final kisses, and muggings. Will climbed the stairs and, at the top, found a heavily-stained, thick, iron door with a closed hatch at head height. He rapped on the door and within seconds, the slide opened, and he was confronted with a pair of green eyes that shone through thick layers of mascara.

"Lady Liberty, I assume?"

The eyes glistened. "Who wants to know?" she said in a far gruffer voice than Will had expected.

"I'm Will Metlocke. Is this where I can find a girl for the night?"

"My girls don't start working yet. Come back in a half hour and I'll see who I can get for you. Any preferences? Ginger? Brunette? Dirty blonde?" she joked, winking.

"Ideally not riddled with disease, but I feel like that's asking for a church without a vicar who is a little too handsy with the choir boys. What kind of ages are the women you employ?" asked Will.

Lady Liberty's eyes narrowed. "They're legal. We don't do any of that funny business around here. If it's older you're wanting, then it'll be cheaper but more of a risk."

"God no. No. I just need to talk to one. Preferably around twenty years old."

"Just to talk to? No way, son. I've had enough experience with jealous ex-boyfriends to last a lifetime." She looked him up and down. "You don't look like you could do much harm though," she said. The slide snapped shut, and she heaved the door open, with a grinding moan of hinges. A heavy aroma of perfume hit Will instantly, making his stomach lurch.

"I don't know any of your girls, I assure you. I'm a writer. I'm just looking for information about the girl who died a couple of weeks ago."

"She wasn't one of mine," said Liberty. She drew a cross over her chest and praised the sky. "Thank God. Nasty business."

"I can pay double. Well, whatever double is."

"I can give you five minutes with one for $25."

Will gave her a disgusted look. "$25? What kind of men do you see?"

"Men who can pay."

"Fine," said Will, handing her the cash. "Your best girl then."

Liberty took the money and stuffed it down her blouse. She wheeled on the spot and whistled, like a barmaid from an old

Western. "Destiny!" she barked. Her voice would have been enough to send Will running. "Come here, girl."

A powdered face appeared from a doorway. "Customer?"

"Something like that. He wants to talk to you."

Destiny visibly rolled her eyes. "We all know what that means."

"I think it's serious this time."

"He can do it while I get ready, then?"

Liberty faced Will. "That good with you?"

Will nodded and Liberty let him pass, closing the door behind him. As soon as he took one step into the premises, a small, but stocky woman, dressed in black, violently pushed him aside.

"Need to search you," she growled, pinning his arms against the wall and tapping him down. She took his wallet and his pill bottle. Then one hand dug inside his coat pocket and took out the rewind. "What is this?" she said, turning it over in her hands.

Will felt his temper spike. The rewind was whispering to him, pleading for him to take it back. Its tiny purple eyes were gazing at him morosely. She handled it like a piece of junk. "It's nothing. Give it back," he snapped, turning around.

The guard opened a lockbox and threw his belongings inside.

"You get it back when you're done. We gotta look out for our girls."

There was no point in arguing. Turning, Will found himself in a narrow red-brick corridor. Torn posters advertising old movies and circus visits were dotted along the walls, all losing their color. Heavy, wooden doors lined the corridor; Will hated to think what kind of business would go on behind them. Two girls ran past him in a flash of fishnet stockings, pushing Will aside into a doorway. The door behind him opened, allowing him a glimpse inside. A girl was sitting on a pink armchair, pulling a piece of ribbon around the top of her arm with fine precision. In her hand, she clutched a syringe, the needle blunt and brown. Liberty rushed in and slapped the syringe away from the girl.

"Ruby, what do you think you are doing?"

Ruby instantly started crying and spewing explanations. Liberty replied something about responsibility and looking good for clients. The woman was a mystery. Will couldn't tell if she cared about her girls or saw them only as easy money.

He continued forward until he got to Destiny's dressing table: a wooden writing desk covered in photographs of her with other girls. One included the billboard, with all six girls dressed in white, their tongues hanging from their mouths and eyes rolled up as if they had been hung themselves. Makeup brushes and cheap jewelry were scattered in front of the mirror. Destiny stared at her reflection, finalizing her look for the night.

"$25 jus' to talk? You're getting ripped off, mister."

"Well, it depends on whether you can enlighten me. Do I have to call you Destiny? What's your real name?" said Will.

"Destiny is the name I chose."

"Like it was your destiny?"

"It's better than Phylis."

"Your name is Phylis? Yeah, you're right, keep Destiny."

Destiny applied another layer of scarlet across her lips before pressing them together, spreading the color from one lip to the other. She stared into a mirror encrusted with lights that lit up her face in a harsh electric glare.

"How can I help? Don't be too long, mind. Friday's a busy night."

"Abigail Finsbury, did you know her?"

Destiny's face dropped and she went back to working over her skin with a fraying makeup brush. "I knew her at school. We were friends for a little while."

"But you lost contact?" pressed Will, pulling over a stool and sitting down. He had been on his feet for most of the day and he could already feel the blisters forming on the soles of his feet.

Destiny nodded. "That's what happens. Last day of school is all huggin' and cryin'. Then they all go off to college or get a job. She got real close to Katie Daniels and I'm left with the dirty men of Hollyhead payin' my bills."

"Did she often spend time with older guys?"

"Not really. She had a boyfriend in sophomore year—both sixteen—they got on pretty well until he ended it. Said he needed to focus on work or something. All he did was stack shelves." She turned to face Will. "Does this color suit me?" she asked, flapping her eyelids. They were covered in what looked like red glitter.

"I'm not really the right person to ask. I doubt your customers will be too focused on your eyes anyway."

"The eyes are the gateway to the heart! Heard that in some film."

"'The eyes are the windows to your soul.' It's Shakespeare."

Destiny gawped. "Well, look at me quoting Shakespeare!" she exclaimed. Will couldn't help but feel a fondness for her. She had a child-like energy, the kind that usually gets stripped away within a year of starting high school. He hated to think of what the evening would hold for her.

He shuddered. "Back to Abigail. She never came here? Not for some work on the side or to see you?"

"Now you mention it, I did see her not too long before she… ya know. She was with some guy."

Will felt his hairs prick up. "Some guy? What did he look like?"

Destiny shrugged. "Kinda tall. I don't know, I only saw him from behind. Didn't look like he wanted to be seen. He kinda kept to the shadows and had one of those wide-brimmed hats that he pulled over his eyes."

"Married maybe?"

"Most men I meet are."

Will wondered what drove such men to seek out young girls for an overpriced fifteen minutes. Could a man's family life be so dull that this was an escape? Like Saturday night bowling? Or maybe after twenty years of marriage, it was the only thing keeping them from slitting their wrists. Either way, Will despised them.

"You're sure that he wasn't paying Abigail?"

"I already told ya, she weren't that kind of girl."

"Suggesting that it was true love?" said Will, his voice sparking with sarcasm.

"Maybe. There ain't nothin' wrong with an older guy fallin' for a younger gal."

"True. However, strangling them with their own hands tends to fall on the wrong side of the spectrum."

Destiny dropped her hairbrush, causing Lady Liberty to poke her long neck around the corner. "You're not paying for anything more than a talk," she said, her eyes scanning the room for any hint of misbehavior.

"Is it true that Abbie was strangled with her own hands?" said Destiny, her voice trembling.

Lady Liberty seemed to grow a few inches. "What? Of course not," she said, turning to Will. "How dare you come in here and scare my girls. They have enough to worry about without you filling their minds with filth," she hissed.

"You think it's alright for them to go out there and work with a killer on the loose?" Will argued.

"My girls know how to protect themselves."

"No one can protect themselves against this guy. He has killed seven people now. Six in one evening."

"I have taught them everything I know."

"Yeah, I'm sure that five-minute pep-talk is all they're going to need."

Destiny yelped and covered her mouth in shock. Lady Liberty straightened up and snapped her fingers, a signal for the security woman to scamper toward them.

"Cathy, would you please escort Mr. Metlocke from the premises?"

Cathy smirked. "With pleasure."

*

Being kicked into the street by a tiny but very angry woman was not how Will had anticipated the night would go. He'd been thrown into the rain, along with his possessions and a promise that if she saw him again, he'd be looking at a night in hospital. Luckily, security hadn't bothered to look at the rewind properly. Will pocketed it and felt his breathing relax. Still, his meeting with Destiny had helped him learn one thing: Abigail had been courting the older man for weeks before she died.

His chest tightened. His throat clenched and he coughed long and violently enough to cause him to stagger against the wall. He felt as though pieces of his lungs were being forced up through his airway and out of his mouth as he fell to his knees. A long, congealed string of blood dripped from his mouth and he spat it onto the concrete. His breathing rang shallow, coming in quick bursts. The coughing fit had weakened him, and he groaned against the wet brick wall behind him. His body crept towards failure every day; the coughing would only get worse. The only relief was that it meant the end was closing in; sweet relief from life forever. He could go through the next months of pain for that.

He stood up carefully and took a few tentative steps closer to the main street again. On reaching the end, he saw a woman walking towards him, sheltering beneath an umbrella. It was only when she was a few steps away that he realized who it was.

"It's you!" he said, not believing his eyes. "Eve! You helped me a couple of weeks ago when I was attacked."

She stared at him. For an instant Will thought it was a different person, but then she broke into a smile. "You're looking much better," she said, pulling her coat tighter around her.

"I never got a chance to thank you. I probably would have died if you hadn't been there."

"Oh, I don't know about that," she said. Will couldn't pull his eyes away from her face. Her cheeks were rosy pink from the cold.

"You never did tell me your name," she said. "Will who?"

"I'm Will Metlocke."

Her mouth opened in shock. "You don't mean Will Metlocke, the author?"

Ah, brilliant, another weirdo who treats my book as gospel.

"I've read your book!"

Singular? Interesting.

"I loved your detective! Tyler Bowen. I could never create a character like that. I tried once but I gave up after a few pages. I just don't have the patience," she said. She talked very quickly as if each word was leapfrogging another to get in front.

"You read *The Death Clock?*" said Will.

"Oh yeah! Brilliant! You have such a wonderful way of writing. You had me hooked from the first line and didn't let me go! When will the next one be released?"

"I'm afraid that I won't be writing a sequel. It didn't do as well as I hoped."

Eve's face dropped. "Really? Maybe it didn't connect with everyone, but I'm sure there are lots of people who loved it."

"Yeah, maybe." A pause grew. Will felt the opportunity slowly fading into the rain. Eve gave a friendly smile as if to say *good talk, but you're creeping me out.*

"It was nice seeing you again. I'm glad you're feeling better," she said. Will replied with a sound that he wasn't sure he could make even if he tried, and she walked away.

"Listen, I was wondering, and you don't have to, of course, but if you wanted to then I thought we could go to the pictures. Or lunch? I'm even open to brunch. One of those? Or something completely different. I don't mind! Just something to say thank you for saving my life and everything," spilled Will. The cogs of his brain must have fallen to pieces.

Eve turned back and smiled. "The pictures would be good."

Will broke into a grin. "Alright, well there's a lot on. *Star Wars*? On me, of course."

"Well, who would I be if I said no to a film and a free popcorn?"

"You'd be someone with a lot more sense than to go out with me."

"Lucky for you I ain't got any sense then!"

"Great. I'll pick you up around seven? I don't have a car, but we could walk," said Will, the look on Eve's face suggested that walking was not the right way to go. "Or we could get a taxi. Or you could pick me up. Any one of those options, I guess."

Eve gave him a puzzled look. "For a writer, you really are terrible with words. Wednesday at seven? Meet at the bar on Barry?"

"Brilliant," said Will, just managing to remain upright. He was very aware that he had been repeating himself too much. "I'll see you then." Feeling happier than he had done in months, he waved Eve goodbye and continued walking.

He hadn't registered what he was saying. His brain had disconnected from his mouth and the words came spiraling out in a great waterfall of stupidity. Sooner or later, he would have to tell her and that would only see her leave forever. He had only met her twice, but Will was already sure that Eve Pocock was someone he didn't want to bid farewell to. For now, just the proposal of a movie was good enough for him. Will continued walking, knowing now where his feet were taking him.

*

The diner was a welcome sight: an open-armed, neon haven ushering him in through the acidic smoke of the streets. It sat proudly between a convenience store and a laundromat, all drenched in the electric glow of the streetlamps. Will was starving; the last thing he had eaten was a poptart at the motel and even that had left him with a gaping hole in his stomach. Red and white seats gleamed through the window at him. He looked up to see 'Ed's Diner', spelled in large fluorescent letters across the front. An example of a dying breed, soon to be replaced with fast-food chains that had seemingly sprung up from nowhere.

As he entered, a bell rang, and a small blonde head appeared from the kitchen door. "I'll be with you in just a second, hun," she said, showing sparkling white teeth. Will replied with a nod. The rich smell of bacon and beef overwhelmed his senses causing his stomach to let out a low growl. Apart from him and the waitress, the front of the diner was empty. Most of the truck drivers would have already been and continued on their way through the night, allowing them to avoid the heavy traffic of tourists. Will took a seat at the far table and sunk into the leather. The menu before him flaunted a selection of burgers, shakes, and variations of fries. Skinny, curly, and cheesy stole his attention immediately. Before he could decide, a door swung open and the waitress emerged, sporting a pinstriped dress. She beamed at him as she approached. Will could tell that it wasn't fake. It's easy to tell when someone is putting on an act for a job that they hate. The smile oozed contentment.

"What can I get for you today, darling? You look like you need a good meal," she said, glancing at Will's gaunt face.

"I'll have the Hollyhead burger with fries and a vanilla shake, please," Will replied, sliding the menu toward her. She couldn't have been older than twenty-one—her eyes showed the kind of optimism not yet crushed out by the nature of the world.

"Certainly, sir," she said. She walked away, humming a tune that Will recognized as The Stones.

Will closed his eyes, giving them some much-deserved rest as he heard the clatter of pans and the sizzle of fresh beef. If there was one good thing about Hollyhead, it was that damned burger.

*

He must have fallen asleep because the next thing he knew, the waitress was standing before him, his food piled high on the tray in her hand.

"Long day?" she asked, as she gently lowered the plate onto the table, trying not to spill the basket of fries covered in salt and sauce. The shake came next, the top covered in small bubbles, some clinging to a red-and-white-striped straw.

"Something like that," said Will, feeling drool filling his mouth at the prospect of the long-awaited meal. The bell at the front of the diner rang but the pair didn't turn around. The waitress seemed to be inspecting the grooves of Will's face: had he really grown that old?

"Always the way of it. You want a scoop of ice cream in that?" she said, nodding to the shake.

Will resisted the offer and she told him to let her know if he needed anything else.

The food tasted gorgeous. Full-fat cheese bubbled in his mouth and the shake was sweet—full of sugar that rippled through his veins.

The diner had changed considerably since Will had last been in. On the last day of high school, he joined Nick, Lenora, and Alex to celebrate the end of exams. Back then, the diner had been considerably busier—and cheaper. For less than 50 cents, you could get a burger stacked with as much as you could imagine with a side of fries. The whole interior had been refurbished, replacing the benches poked with holes with new leather that still squeaked when you moved. There had been a jukebox churning out 50s hits until one of the Hollyhead High quarterbacks had managed to stick his head through the glass, resulting in a visit from the fire department and a picture of him being strung up on the diner's wall-of-fame board. Now, a Space Invaders arcade game stood pride of place, covered in greasy fingerprints and chewing gum. Will finished off his burger and licked his fingers. The waitress was leaning on a gleaming countertop, twirling her hair around her fingers in one hand and absentmindedly wiping the surface with an old bit of tablecloth, still humming the same tune as she had been earlier in the night. Will took a few dollars from his pocket and handed them over.

"And that's for your service," he said, sliding another couple of notes onto the surface. The tip amounted to much more than the food, but it wasn't like he would be needing money where he was going in the next few years.

"That's very kind of you, sir!" she said, beaming once again. Will pulled on his coat, happy to be rid of the iron-like tang left behind by the blood. He watched as the waitress finished cleaning the counter before heading to the kitchen. As he pulled open the door, he didn't hear the bell; it was replaced by a blood-curdling scream. Not one long cry, but a collection of terrified gasps, each one shaking with fright. As quickly as he could, Will ran in the direction of the screams. He had just laid his hands on the kitchen door to push it open when the waitress came hurtling out, almost knocking Will to the ground. Her eyes were wide with fright and blood coated her neatly painted nails; her own bite marks stamped into the skin of her finger joints where she must have bitten down in terror.

"What's happened?" Will said, grabbing her by the shoulders.

"It's Eddie! H-he's dead!" she cried, pointing to the kitchen.

Will felt around in his coat and took out a pen. He pulled a napkin from its holder and scribbled down Frank's number before shoving it into the waitress' trembling hands.

"Call this number. He's FBI."

The waitress sniffed and nodded her head before running outside. Taking a deep breath in, Will pushed open the door.

The kitchen could have belonged to a completely different diner. Half-empty milk bottles lined the sides and molding buns spilled from a packet in the corner. An occasional drip echoed from the tap and an electric hum vibrated from the freezer. Will moved forwards apprehensively, his heart feeling as though it was forcing its way up his throat.

"Oh god…" he trembled.

Ed was slouched over in a chair in the middle of the room, his hat lopsided. His head had lolled onto his shoulder and thick clots of saliva dripped from his mouth onto his brown apron. Will clambered over towards him, knocking over a row of saucepans. First, he noticed the smell: drying urine and the scent of frying oil. The man was almost twice the size of Will, his stomach drooping over the side of the little plastic chair beneath him. His mouth seemed to be pulsing rhythmically as if he was pushing air into his cheeks before sucking it back down.

Will crept closer, his legs now numb. He crouched down. Poking out of the chef's mouth was what looked like a very small dragon wing. Will pinched the wing between his fingers and pulled. As the rest of the body popped from between the man's lips, Will jumped back in disgust, dropping the creature to the floor. It hopped away, leaving a slimy trail behind it. Will took another look at the chef. His mouth was now hanging open and Will could see more of the dragon wings inside. Only, they weren't wings; they were feet. At least ten frogs were crammed down Ed's throat, some still wriggling.

CHAPTER ELEVEN: STONE'S SURPRISE

Frank arrived within minutes, donning his disposable gloves with unnerving eagerness. Marty was hot on his heels, looking as though he hadn't slept in days. Will didn't know how long it had been since Frank had left the house on anything other than Spark business; yet here he was walking with the gait of a man twenty years younger. Will showed them through to the kitchen and Frank took out a polaroid camera.

"The police will make a fine mess of this place," he complained while he took photos of the tabletops, intermittently muttering into a small tape recorder, noting anything that he believed may be helpful. Frank maneuvered his way around the kitchen in such a way that Will was sure that each footstep was thoroughly planned; his movements were fine and precise. It was a brief insight into his father's FBI days: back to his prime of life. The look of raw focus on his face was enough to convince Will of the accolades he had heard; where Will saw only grease and puddles of water, it seemed that Frank saw the last few hours played out like a movie.

"You found him like this?" asked Marty, staring at the chef's corpse.

"No, he was fine when I got here," snapped Will. "Of course, I found him like this."

His stomach felt like someone had tied a large knot in the middle and his eyes demanded to look anywhere other than at the body. He had been trying hard not to throw up the burger and shake. The thought of his meal now made him queasy.

"I mean, did you move him?"

"I took one frog out of his mouth."

"The first is always difficult. It's not something you want to get used to," said Marty, resting one hand on Will's shoulder.

Frank didn't see. He took another few photos before the sirens started. Within seconds, flashing blue lights spilled into the kitchen, illuminating the chef's pale skin.

"We gotta go, Frankie," said Marty, looking out of the window. "I might get away with it, but they won't look kindly on you being here."

Frank waved a hand as if to tell his partner to shut up. "I'm almost done. I need a map of the room. Every detail may be crucial."

The entrance door opened, signaled by the shrill jangle of the bell. Marty grabbed Frank's arm and pulled him away, despite a round of protest. Will ducked down, avoiding the line of sight of the kitchen door, and followed Marty and Frank to a fire exit at the back of the building. It opened up into a dingy back alley crammed with garbage bags and cardboard boxes, all dampened by the rain. It was just wide enough for a van, with a loading bay area labeled next to the door they had just exited from. Frank motioned for them to keep close to the wall and they crept forwards. Sirens cried out through the streets and the police lights sent blood shadows rippling along the alley. The unmistakable voice of Teddy Ludlow instructed his workers to search the perimeter.

"Where are we going?" asked Will.

"We need to investigate Ed's house before the police get there."

"How do you know where he lives?"

Frank reached into his pocket and took out a large bronze key dangling from a green ring, marked with a 42. "Took them from his pocket. I used to know his dad."

"So... blind luck," said Will. Frank smiled and beckoned for Will and Marty to follow his path.

After vaulting a fence that Will was sure Frank wouldn't have been able to climb on any other occasion, they emerged onto Drummond Lane. The threesome straightened up and began to walk down the street, doing their best to avoid the streetlights.

"Our killer must have walked in while you were eating, Will. How did you not see them?" said Frank, scanning the house numbers as they went.

"I was eating. I didn't exactly expect the chef to be murdered in the next room," hissed Will.

"Never make it as a cop, would he Marty? Not got the attention for it."

Or the itchy trigger finger, thought Will, although he kept his mouth shut.

"It certainly would be helpful if you saw even a glimpse of them. Man? Woman? We could have had their posture, clothing, even their face pinned down," said Marty.

"The waitress might have seen them," said Frank. "I guess we'll see in the morning paper."

"Whoever it was walked right into the kitchen. The waitress was with me," said Will.

"They must have known the layout of the diner. Enough to walk in and go straight for the kitchen," noted Marty.

"Or maybe they just saw the big red letters plastered above the door," said Frank.

Marty gave Will a roll of the eyes and they both stepped up to keep in time with Frank's pace.

They arrived at 42 Drummond Lane just as the rain faltered. It had taken them a few minutes to locate the house. Each residence boasted a small front porch and was decorated with swings, trees, or the odd gnome. If anything, the street looked too perfect, as if any peculiarity was instantly swooped down on by the neighbors like a wake of vultures. The cars on the driveways were one of two colors: red or blue. Will wondered whether it was all just a show to prove who could be the most patriotic. They might as well have been waving a flag from their windows, belting out *Star Spangled Banner* with large Uncle Sam hats perched on their heads. The door of 42 was painted a bright white, so bright in fact that it seemed to glow ominously in the darkness.

"What if he's married? He might have kids at home," said Will, glancing through the kitchen window. Plates smudged with the remnants of previous dinners were piled high next to the sink. He could almost see the stench emanating from the room.

"We take our chances," said Frank, slipping the key into the lock. A heavy clunk sounded, and he tried the handle. The door swung open with an ugly creak as if to protest their attempts at silence.

Will's breath caught in his lungs; his body knew that he shouldn't be there. The man had died less than an hour ago and they were already preparing to search through his life. The door opened into a hallway with numerous rooms arranged on either side. On the left, unbroken moonlight bathed the kitchen in a silver mist. A calendar on the wall stated that the next day, Ed would be taking Hattie to the park, scribbled in what could only be a child's handwriting. Will tried not to think about her reaction to finding out her father wouldn't be there to push the swing. Maybe her mother wouldn't tell her the whole truth; it would be easier to tell Hattie that Ed had simply left town. Until word spread to the schools…

"Here, put these on," ordered Frank, passing the pair another set of gloves. Will slid them on—too small. "Time is of the essence. We must be quick and careful."

"What exactly are we looking for?" said Will, desperately trying not to step on any floorboards that looked prone to creaking. He didn't care that no one was home, it still felt like he was disturbing all the memories that the house had collected over the years.

"Names, meetings, anything unusual," said Marty.

"You think Ed was supposed to be meeting his killer?"

"Stranger things have happened," replied Frank, shining a narrow beam of torchlight onto a shelf full of Christmas cards. "If we are lucky then we might be about to find the lead that cracks this case open." He indicated for them to split up. Will was pointed to the backroom and kitchen, Marty to the front hallway and lounge. Frank would take the upstairs bedrooms.

Other than the stack of plates, the kitchen was derelict. The fridge contained a green jar of pickled onions and a crusty bottle of mustard, but nothing else. Will pulled his scarf into a bandana across his nose to save his smell receptors from the stench of the room. He edged into the backroom past a stack of boxes marked *Natasha*. He opened one; it was full of clothes, forcibly shoved in. A red dress, a white jumper with a dirt mark, unmatched socks, and underwear. He opened another box: more women's clothes. Nothing interesting. After a quick scout around the kitchen again, he reunited with Marty and Frank in the front room.

"What have we got?" said Frank, as he rifled through a pocket diary.

"The poor sod's mother died last week: car accident by the sound of it. He had to identify the body," said Marty, flicking through a collection of letters. His face cringed in disgust. "Jesus, I read about that one. Half her face was ripped off."

"He was divorced. There's a pile of boxes in the back room filled with women's clothing. Belonged to someone called Natasha by the look of it," said Will.

"An affair maybe?" said Marty.

"Perhaps. Would the killer care about adultery?" asked Frank.

"I doubt the Spark boys were known for their promiscuity," said Will. As far as he knew, Alex hadn't been seeing anyone at the time of his death.

"True. I believe I know the particular story," replied Frank, grinning.

"So it is a *Grimm's?*"

Frank nodded, "*The Ungrateful Son,* a son has a chicken but refuses to share it with his father. The chicken then turns into a frog and attaches itself onto the son's face, where it remains forever more. There can be no doubt now. The Spark boys, Abigail Finsbury and old Ed here were all killed by the same person," he beamed—another hypothesis proving true.

"You should stop smiling. These are murders and you're acting like you've just been invited to a private lapdance," said Will as he opened a cabinet—nothing but tacky paperbacks and records—mainly Springsteen. *At least he had good taste in music.*

"Each kill gives us new evidence: a step closer to apprehending the killer."

"It seems random. I mean, *The Six Swans* could only refer to six brothers. By chance, there happened to be six brothers here. There was nothing special about Abigail. Any girl could have been the victim that night. It's the same with Ed."

"Not quite. This was on his bedside table," said Frank, his eyes glued to a typed letter. He cleared his throat, "Dear Mr. McCain, I am writing in response to your decision to withhold supplies from the Hollyhead Homeless Shelter. The fact that you refuse to give your unwanted produce to Hollyhead's homeless community will be made public in next week's news. It is, after all, no secret how much food your diner wastes each night. The town shall not forget this action. We hope that you don't either. Sincerely, Jude Rogers."

"I didn't even know there was a homeless shelter," said Will. "That could be a motive."

"The shelter is part of the church. Jude is the caretaker. It proves that Ed here was just like the son from the story; he was unwilling to share his food too."

"Fine, Ed and the Spark brothers fit into the killer's pattern. What was special about Abigail?"

"That is yet to be known. This is a good step forward though, William," Frank said, slipping the letter into a small plastic wallet.

"We can't take it; it's evidence," said Will. "You are ensuring that we are a step ahead of the police."

"The police have failed for more than a decade on this case. We must be the ones to apprehend the killer. We've put in more time and effort than anyone else."

"It's not just the police who have failed; the pair of you have been clutching at straws too," criticized Will.

Frank took a visibly deep breath, even going as far as closing his eyes, and pocketed the letter. "That's enough time here. It won't be long until the cops come poking."

As if on cue, the front door swung open. Frank's face tensed with shock as they dropped to the floor. "You didn't lock the door?" he said, keeping his voice to a barely audible hiss. Will raised his middle finger in defense and shuffled backward.

Hushed voices came from the hallway—at least two, possibly a third. "Check upstairs. I got down here," one said. Frank crawled behind the sofa where Will had seen Marty seconds before the intruders came in. Will was in a far worse position; his back was pressed up to the window, and the curtain tugged around his body. For once, he was grateful for the weight he had lost over recent months. The sound of heavy boots came from the hallway and was quickly swallowed by the thickness of the carpet. A narrow beam of light panned across the room, reflecting off the television set and a glass table.

"Why would someone kill you, ey?" murmured the man. Will risked a look from behind the curtain. Teddy Ludlow was standing in front of the gas fireplace. He was holding a photo in his hand that showed Ed and his daughter at the Hollyhead fair. His analysis ended and he walked slowly towards Will, each step bringing him closer and closer to the curtains.

If Will was found, he would have a hard time explaining why he was hiding in the house of a murder victim. Best case scenario, he would only be held in a cell overnight. Beads of light filtered through the curtain, close enough to focus on Will's face. He shut his eyes. The light faltered.

I gotta move. Shit...

Breath held tight in his chest, Will sprung from the curtain and pushed hard into the back of Teddy, sending the detective crashing into the glass table. Teddy's hand pierced through the glass as it shattered onto the floor. Frank and Marty, moving surprisingly fast for their age, hurried into the kitchen, waiting for Will to join them before slamming the door.

"Sammy! We have suspects in the kitchen," shouted Teddy. Judging by his voice, the detective was now in the hallway. Will held his weight against the door as it shuddered from a kick.

"Out into the yard," he said through clenched teeth. Frank and Marty obeyed, and Will ran after them. They spilled out onto the grass and Marty gestured for them to climb a fence into the back yard adjacent. Frank shook his head and jerked his finger to the far end of the yard where a splintering wooden shed resided. Once the three were out of sight, Frank picked up a stone from the ground.

"Keep out of sight," he said, before hurling the stone into the neighbor's property. Just as the door to Ed's house was flung open, a light flashed on in the next yard—motion activated.

"They've jumped the fence," said Teddy, before following suit.

"Nice thinking," said Will, trying to get his breath back; it didn't take much anymore for him to lose it completely.

"You never forget it," said Marty, hitting his old partner on the back, his mouth twisted into an impressed grin. The men waited for all signs of life to disappear and then made their way back towards Marty's truck, all silently going over the events of the night.

*

Frank dropped Will at the motel just as the clocks struck one. For a long while, he sat in silence, staring out towards the lake through the frost-covered window. In the heavy mist, he wasn't even able to see it, but its presence pulled at him. As much as his body felt like giving up, his mind was racing. Insomnia was a silent companion that had walked beside him since his lungs had first shown signs of cancer. He was used to only catching a few hours of sleep each night. This was different. It was more than just the breathing difficulties. It felt like his mind was being condensed, pushed into a cell that was far too small. The more he told himself to sleep, the more awake he felt, and he knew that once his mind gave into exhaustion, his dreams would be full of ghosts. The thought terrified him. It wasn't until the first signs of dawn started appearing that he managed to fall into a shallow state of unconsciousness.

*

After a couple of restless hours of sleep, Will awoke to the sound of soft tapping at his door. A glance at his watch told him that it had just gone ten. He opened the door to reveal Wendy, the manager, holding a note that was made from paper far too lavish to have come from the motel's stationary set.

"Morning, Mr. Steinbeck. Or should I say… Mr. Metlocke," she said, her eyes sparkling with childish glee.

I'll have to move.

"Morning Wendy. How can I help?" said Will, his voice still thick with sleep. Wendy held out the note and Will rubbed his eyes to read it properly. The writing was in a tidy hand, etched across the paper in blue ink.

William,

I hope this finds you well. I am writing from city hall. It has come to my attention that you have been staying in Hollyhead for the past few weeks. You should have told us! I want to speak with you. I'll send a car over for eleven to bring you here. I expect that you must be writing your next book. If that's the case, then I have some truly exciting news for you.

Expecting to see you soon,
Mayor Stone.

The name was followed by a scrawled signature.

"What's someone like you staying here for?" said Wendy, eagerly waiting for Will to put down the letter.

"The privacy if nothing else," he replied, before closing the door in Wendy's face.

*

Hollyhead was not a city; yet the citizens' inflated self-view led everyone to call the mayoral building 'city hall'. Will had walked past it many times, never giving it a second thought. Its architecture set it apart from the rest of the town's buildings— a dusty white exterior crowned with a large clock tower. A parking lot adjoined the building, filled with a tiresome array of automobiles. A pink Beetle was the only splash of color in a world of grey and black. The car dropped Will off on the doorstep and he was met by an old man dressed all in royal blue. Heavy glass doors opened into a stretch of varnished wood shining such that Will could see his own tired face staring back at him. A receptionist sat in front of a spiraling staircase, a telephone cord twisting around her fingers.

"I told you, Janice. Another one. Young? No. This one was in his forties I heard. Rough way to go, but that diner was a real eye-sore. The Mayor is already talking about turning it into a museum, I heard," she paused and glanced at Will. The lift of one manicured finger signaled that she would be available in a moment. "A funeral? Not a public one. It's not the same, is it? That Abigail was pretty; people want to go and pay their respects. I think her funeral is tomorrow. Yep, the Mayor has already called them… Few dozen reporters. There's the Christmas lights parade in the evening. Well, it's good for the community isn't it? These are tough times, Janice. Let me know about the date. I've heard plenty of things about Tommy Law. My guess is you'll have a pretty wild night if nothing else," she said. After a dozen goodbyes, she put the phone down and smiled at Will.

"I'm Will Metlocke. Mayor Stone wanted to see me," he said.

"Upstairs," replied the receptionist before picking up a newspaper. Will narrowed his eyes to read her name tag, which read 'Bethany'.

He leaned forwards. "Oh, I was told to tell someone called Bethany that her car is getting towed. It's a pink Beetle."

Bethany gasped. "That's my car!"

With that, she ran from the hall, her high heels clicking on the floor. Will had never seen anyone run so fast.

"Always a pink Beetle," he muttered, smiling to himself.

He climbed the central staircase, gazing up at a chandelier that looked like something from a Hollywood movie. Was there anything in Hollyhead that wasn't a cheap knock-off? Mayor Stone's name was printed in yellow letters on the glass door at the top of the stairs. Will knocked sharply and was promptly invited in by a high-pitched, nasal-sounding voice.

The room was a circular propaganda den. Behind a large desk stood three flags arranged around a grand portrait of George Washington, lit up by a faint glow from lamps in front. Photos decorated the desk, including one of Mayor Stone in front of the billboard. Everyone had a picture in front of that damned billboard. The Mayor was sitting behind her desk, scribbling away on the same type of paper that Will had received his note on. She looked up as he entered.

"Will, so good to finally meet you," she said, rising from her seat and shaking his hand vigorously. "Metlocke: it's such an unusual name."

"Really? I hear it every day," replied Will.

Mayor Stone was at least forty, but she wouldn't let anyone see it. Her hair was an artificial red color, the ends straightened to reach past her shoulders. Will guessed that every time she found a gray hair, she attacked her whole head with a bottle of dye. Judging by the enthusiasm to call the meeting and her blouse unbuttoned one too far, she was early into her tenure as mayor. Will was shocked; it was quite progressive of Hollyhead to elect a woman mayor. She showed him to a seat and returned to sit behind her desk.

"I was surprised to get an invitation," said Will.

Stone nodded. "As soon as I found out we had one of our own celebrities in town, I knew I had to get in touch. Nice idea with the fake name but nothing stays secret here for long."

True. I wonder how long it will be until the press find the skeletons in your closet—if they haven't already.

"I'm not staying long."

"All the more reason to speak to you now."

"Then let's get around to why."

"It's winter. It's cold—some might even say gloomy—then out of the fog comes you: a knight in shining armor," she said before grinning widely. "We have forgiven you for what you wrote about us in your last book about the town. Times change and we are all sure that you have as well." She shuffled some of her desk ornaments around. "A man was found dead last night. His mouth was filled with frogs."

Will put on his best-surprised voice. "He was French, was he?"

Mayor Stone laughed heartily. "Such wit! No. He was murdered." Will had never heard anyone say that sentence with more glee. "It's terribly sad news, of course, but we would be doing a disservice if we didn't remember him in some way."

"Already got the t-shirts printed, I imagine."

"I wouldn't know. I'm sure the advertising fairies are busy as we speak. I've had a little think and have come up with an idea that I believe would benefit both of us. Even the town would reap the rewards. I want you to write a book about what's been going on. Think of it as a memorial for Abigail Finsbury and Ed McCain."

"As opposed to a soulless money-grabbing scheme?"

"Exactly." The sickly-sweet smile flashed again. "The truth is that they were nobodies. Sure, Ed could make a good burger, but half the town can now. Let something good come from their passing."

"The only good that can come from this is the police finding who killed them so that they can put an end to this."

"There is no one who wants the killer identified more than me," she leaned forward and placed heavily manicured hands upon Will's own, "believe me… but it would be wrong not to remember them in some way." She shifted back again. "Plus, let's face it, your career has had a teensy struggle of late. What was that detective book? *The Clock of Death?* This would be a certified best seller."

Cut-throat bitch.

Will smiled. "It was called *The Death Clock.* I don't need another best-seller," he said. He raised a hand to his mouth and coughed hard. Stone's eyebrows raised.

"Are you ill?"

"No. I'm fine," he said, resisting the urge to cough again. He could feel the blood at the back of his throat—a wet, slimy sludge that made it harder to breathe.

"Shame. Two murders and an author undergoing a debilitating illness would really go hand-in-hand. People love a sob story."

Will steadied his breathing. "Are we done here? I have a busy day."

"Not yet. There is someone I want you to meet first. Ah, here he is now," she said. There was a knock at the door and Stone gestured for them to enter. Will turned around to see Detective Teddy Ludlow walking in, confusion written across his face. His right hand was wrapped in a stained bandage.

"This was supposed to be an urgent meeting, Mayor," he said, eyeing Will. "What's this all about? I'm very busy this morning, as you can imagine."

"This won't take long, Detective. Please take a seat."

Teddy pulled a chair out beside Will and sat down on the very edge of the seat, not allowing his back to touch the frame.

"I'm sure you have read Will Metlocke's books," said the Mayor.

"I know of them," said Teddy.

"It's time to read up! He is back."

"Do I applaud now? Or do we have one scheduled?" said Teddy.

"That all depends," replied Stone, turning back to Will. "We were hoping you would agree to turn on the Christmas lights tomorrow evening. We think it would really bring out the crowds if you were to do it. We could do it along with the announcement of your new book."

"Tomorrow? You see I would love to, but I've got my jigsaw club tomorrow. A thousand pieces is a big dedication," said Will. Teddy stifled a cough that sounded like a hint of a laugh.

"I understand that it is daunting. Normally, I would do it myself, but I thought that you might appreciate a moment in the limelight."

"I'll think about it."

"With all respect, Mayor, I don't see why I am required for a discussion about PR," said Teddy, half standing up as if to leave.

Stone gestured for him to sit down again, "I have a proposal for you. What I want is for William to tail you. He'll stay out of your inquiries, but he can then write about our latest murder. You won't even notice he's there."

Teddy sounded offended, "I can't work with him; it's not professional. For all we know, he could be a key suspect."

The mayor waved a hand. "Suspect? He's famous!" she laughed. Her keen eyes turned to Will. "As for the killer, we already have a nickname for them: *The Grimm Reaper.* That was my idea. The journalists loved it. Detective Ludlow here worked out that all the deaths are connected to children's fairy tales. Unbelievable, don't you think? *The Grimm Reaper*—that's a name that sells."

"Very clever. Did that take you all night or was it a spur-of-the-moment thing?" said Will.

"You're a storyteller. All I am asking you to do is tell one more. You won't even have to use any imagination. I will need updates: once a day at least, preferably two or three visits."

"The force is overwhelmed as it is. They need me there at all times," said Teddy. "I can't afford to spend half my day reporting to you."

The Mayor smiled. "Hollyhead Police Department is a crucial part of this town. I want to work closely with you. The town wants updates on these murders. Speculation sells, Detective Ludlow. Unfortunately, I won't be able to guarantee police funding for the next few years if we don't have another push on publicity."

Teddy opened his mouth to reply but was cut off by a knock at the door. The receptionist was there, her face flushed with anger. "You have Mr. Sinclair for a meeting. He's downstairs," she said to Stone, flashing a look at Will that could sour milk.

The Mayor thanked her. Will and Teddy stood up.

"Thank you for your time, gentlemen. I'll see you tomorrow for your first report. You're going to light up Hollyhead, William: metaphorically and literally!" she said.

<u>CHAPTER TWELVE</u>: FAMILY

The idea of working with Teddy Ludlow didn't exactly fill Will with glee; yet it presented an opportunity to get first-hand experience on the case. He wouldn't forgive himself if he turned it down and he was pretty sure that Frank wouldn't either. They had left the hall and climbed into Teddy's car, where Will had needed to clear the seat of chip packets and cigarette cartons before he could sit down. He had agreed to go to Teddy's home before starting on the case. They would have to make it in one piece first; Teddy drove so erratically that Will forced his eyes close whenever they cannoned around a bend. For a few minutes, an awkward silence hung in the air, only interrupted by the harsh revving of the engine. Eventually, Teddy spoke: "Any news on your friend Lenora?" he said, as he turned the car down yet another suburban street lined with picket fences.

"Oh yeah. She calls me every evening for a catch-up."

"Sarcasm—the lowest form of wit."

"It will have to make do. I'm all out of knock-knock jokes."

Teddy lived in a small house detached from the rest of the street. The front was host to three small trees planted in heaps of frozen soil. It was a nice enough place, though perhaps trying too hard to fit in. Teddy swerved onto the driveway, stopping inches away from a white garage door.

"You going to sit in the car, or do you want to come in?" said Teddy.

Will peered out at the house. "I'm not much of a family man. I'll sit tight."

"That answer just convinces me to bring you with me," said Teddy, getting out of the car. Groaning, Will followed, and the pair climbed a few steps up to a newly painted white door. They entered. Teddy put his jacket on a stand next to the door and called out, "Gill? Grets? I'm back."

"Lounge!" shouted a voice from a room to their left. Teddy stepped through and Will followed, his joints aching. Toy horses and scraps of paper covered with wavy lines covered the lounge. A sofa sat by the wall, a blanket thrown over the seats— no doubt to cover a multitude of coffee stains and chocolate marks. Lying on the carpet was a small girl, her legs waving in the air as she hummed. Her eyes were glued to the television in front of her. *Sesame Street* was playing, the blue puppet chomped down cookies while counting how many he had eaten.

"Greta, we have a guest. This is Will Metlocke," said Teddy, placing his hat on the sofa. The girl turned around. She had the most circular eyes Will had ever seen, all centred around light-blue irises. Her hair stretched into neat blonde pigtails and she bounced her red, buckled shoes on the carpet as she spoke. Occasionally, she picked small sugar mice from a bowl next to her and wolfed them down in one.

"Good morning," she said, before turning back to the television.

"Daddy's just going to see your mother. Make our guest comfortable."

Will sat down in one of the pink armchairs. As soon as he hit the seat, he sank down several inches. Greta giggled at his surprised reaction.

"That's Daddy's chair," she said.

"I should've known Teddy would be a pink armchair kinda guy." He could feel her eyes scanning over him, maybe deciding whether he was worthy enough to sit in her father's chair. After a few moments, she must have decided he was, as she went back to watching Elmo count to twenty.

"Do you work together?" she asked, her eyes remaining fixed on the television set. "Are you here about the missing boy?"

"No. I write books. There's a missing boy?"

"He went to my school. I'm older than him though. Dad says that he just ran away. I tried that once. I hid behind a truck down the road. Then I got bored and came home. What do you write about? Are you writing about Daddy?"

"I write about ghosts."

"That's a silly thing to write about. They don't exist."

Says the girl watching a man stick his hand up a puppet's ass.

"We're not sure whether they exist. Some people say they have proof that they are real."

"Do you have proof?"

"I don't need to. If people want something to be real, the smallest amount of evidence will be enough to justify their belief."

"I think my mom reads your books. She didn't finish the last one."

"That's probably because the last one wasn't very good."

"I don't think she read the one before that, either."

Will nodded his head. *Doesn't surprise me.*

"Have you ever seen a ghost?" asked Greta.

Instantly, Will's mind flashed to the Spark's barn and the grotesque image of the boys dangling from the beams. "No. I just write about them, but don't go telling people that I don't believe they exist, ok?"

A mischievous grin spread across Greta's face and she tapped her nose in a 'now I know so you'd better do as I say' way. The door opened and Teddy walked in.

"Having fun?" he asked. He was accompanied by a woman slightly shorter than him. Her dark hair curled up just before the shoulders. "This is my wife, Gill. Gill, this is Will Metlocke," said Teddy. Gill walked forwards and shook Will's hand. She was dressed in a black jumper, covered in a bold sunflower print.

"It's lovely to meet you. I've read many of your books," she said, pulling off a passable fake smile. Greta sniggered before stuffing a pillow over her mouth.

"So I've been told. You have a very nice house, Mrs Ludlow."

"We're saving for an extension. We just have to hope that Ted gets a nice big Christmas bonus."

"Well, that relies on me catching whoever is killing these people," said Teddy, rubbing his temples and yawning. A sharp backhanded slap across his stomach by Gillian snapped him back to life. With clenched teeth, she nodded towards Greta, who had begun to draw what looked like a cross between a giraffe and a cat; it could have been either.

"She's worried enough already without you going on about it," hissed Gillian. "First that boy from school went missing and now death is on every corner!"

Teddy raised his hands in defense. "She should be scared! The Reaper has killed children before. She needs to keep an eye out. Everyone does right now."

Gillian nodded; her eyes low. "Do you really think he will kill again?"

That tends to be what serial killers are known for, thought Will.

"I do, which means that we need to be quick. Just stay home and keep safe. Always check out the window before you open the door to anyone. Got that?" said Teddy, holding his wife's hand.

"Of course—be safe," she said. Teddy responded with a soft smile, then turned to Greta.

"Daddy's going out for a little while. I'll see you later. We have the next *Disney* to watch, right? *Cinderella*, was it?"

"*The Aristocats,*" replied Greta, not taking her eyes from her drawing.

"Great American literature if ever there was," murmured Teddy.

*

After saying goodbye, Teddy and Will returned to the Granada. In the short time that they had been inside, the cold had caused the windscreen to freeze and Teddy had to clear the ice before they could leave. Will sat in the car silently, his thoughts fixed on Lenora. When the ice was gone, Teddy joined him.

"Opinion?" asked Teddy, turning in his seat.

"You need to get a new car," said Will, wiping crumbs from the seat onto the floor.

"About the family, I mean."

"Nice house. Nice wife. Nice kid. Looks like you're set."

"Can't get much better, right?" Teddy said, although his gaze at the house lasted a little too long. He had the expression of someone trying to convince themself that what they're saying is true.

Will felt the silence start to tingle on his skin. "Seriously though, of all names you chose Greta?"

For a moment, Will thought Teddy might hit him. Then he broke out into a laugh. "Gill's choice. Come on, who am I to tell a woman who has just gone through labour for seventeen hours that the name her heart is set on will trigger years of bullying down the line? I've arrested a few criminals in my time, but even I'm not that brave."

Will laughed. The pain in his chest seemed to subside a little.

Teddy switched on the ignition and the car purred into life. "There's someone you had better meet," he said, checking over his shoulder for the all clear. "Where there's a murder, there's a pathologist. If we want your *book* to sell, then you'll need all the details—even the most grotesque." As they pulled away, Will looked back at the house. Greta stood peering out of the downstairs window; her face squished up against the glass.

Weird kid.

*

"Busy day, George?" asked Teddy, as he pushed through a pair of black doors into the morgue. Will hadn't been sure what to think when Teddy pulled up to Hollyhead hospital. After a close encounter with Dr. Highsmith, they had walked down a flight of narrow stairs and entered the autopsy room. The cavernous room was painted a dull green, set around a tiled floor. Shelves were overflowing with papers and files jutted out at awkward angles from cluttered cabinets due to the lack of space. In the center of the room stood the autopsy table, silently awaiting its next visitor. Some objects just give off an unsettling vibe, at least in this case Will knew why. Teddy perched himself on a sideboard and looked towards an open cabinet. It creaked as it closed to reveal a thin, balding man, a clipboard clutched to his side. His eyes darted from Teddy to Will as if they were intruders into his home.

"Who is your friend, Ted?" he asked.

Teddy held out an arm. "This is Will Metlocke. He's an author. Will, this is George Upson, our resident pathologist."

Will walked forward and stuck out a hand. "Nice to meet you, George."

"I won't if you don't mind," said George, producing gloved hands from his pocket. Will nodded. George was short, with a scraggly mess of a beard like something a high schooler would grow to show off to the girls that his testosterone kicked into overdrive before the rest of the boys. For a man at least in his forties, the look wasn't so impressive. His social skills weren't up too much either, but Will guessed that came with the territory. Perhaps it would be worrying if someone who spent most of their days with a corpse was chatty…

"I don't think there is much need for you to be here, Ted. I think a child could work out the cause of death."

"Yeah, but if we hired a kid, then we'd be breaking a hell of a lot of laws. It would be cheaper though. We just want to have a look at the body."

Almost frustratedly, George left the room and returned less than a minute later pushing a spindly trolley. Ed's body lay on top, covered by a white sheet. Teddy hopped off the sideboard and stuffed his hands into his pockets.

"Put your hands in your pockets, Will. It means you're less likely to touch anything."

"It's a dead guy, not a puppy."

"Suit yourself."

After carefully positioning the trolley next to the table, George removed the sheet to reveal Ed's upper body. Dark hairs covered his chest, except for a shaved line where the autopsy had been performed.

"We have a forty-one-year-old male. Death by asphyxiation," said George. "The attack would have taken only minutes." The words obviously meant nothing to him, he spoke robotically. Will guessed that being a pathologist meant that everybody who came in amounted to nothing more than flesh and bone to them.

"What about that little mark on his neck? Looks like it could be an injection site," said Teddy, leaning close to the body. George followed his gaze.

"It's just a blemish. Tests signal nothing out of the ordinary in his blood, apart from a lot of booze. Still, you'll find the same in half of the people who live in Hollyhead."

"Is it possible he was already unconscious when strangled?"

"It's unlikely. A sedative would take too long to come into effect for a man of his size," said George.

"His mouth was filled to bursting with frogs," said Teddy, turning to Will. "It was a nasty way to go."

"You're kidding," said Will, trying his best to sound shocked. "Any leads?"

"We spoke to a waitress who was working last night. She didn't see who came in. Apparently, she was too busy talking to a customer. As of yet, this John Doe hasn't come forward. We'll track him down fast enough."

Shit.

"Do you think it's connected to Abigail Finsbury?" asked Will, trying to change the subject.

Teddy nodded. "There's no doubt. Similarities between the deaths are obvious."

"Similarities? She had her arms sawn off; he was choked."

"You heard what Stone said. *The Grimm Reaper.* Her head might be full of chalk, but mine isn't," said Teddy. "I know this is somehow linked to those damned fairy tales." He finished his inspection of the body and groaned. "Some sick fuckers in this town."

"Can I put him away now?" asked George. Teddy waved his compliance and George left the room. Teddy furrowed his brow in thought. Will could tell that he was unravelling what he had heard; trying to connect the pieces of the intricate puzzle that had fallen into his lap.

"I was reading a report into the murders back in '68. They said that Frank Metlocke was involved. I'm guessing that he's your father," said Teddy. George walked back in and started rummaging through a stack of files.

"Frank has been obsessed with this case since the billboard murders. He's getting on now. There isn't much else for him to do. It's not like he has a wife to go back to," said Will.

"Your dad never remarried?"

"I think that after she died, there was never anyone else. Apart from the Spark boys. They were a good enough obsession. Still, at least I missed out on the awkward stepmother part."

Teddy laughed. Behind Will, a pile of folders fell, causing a tray of surgical equipment to spill onto the floor. George jumped away, narrowly avoiding a particularly sharp scalpel from landing on his foot.

"You alright George?" said Teddy, bending down to pick up the fallen papers.

George wiped his brow. "Late night. I need to sort out these files. It's becoming a joke," he said. 'Is there anything else I can do for you?"

"Just keep us updated if you find anything else," said Teddy. He signalled to Will that they were leaving.

Will felt glad to be away. Even under the heavy bleach and disinfectant, the stench of death was pungent.

"Sorry about him. He doesn't get out much, but he's a good pathologist. I should know; I've been working with him for the entirety of my time here. Poor guy used to suffer from narcolepsy pretty badly. He was almost fired because of it. He's taking pills to get it under control. Everyone has got issues. I guess we would all become a little strange if we had his job," he said, before shivering at the thought. "I need to get some things from my house and then I'll drop you off anywhere you want."

*

Will had started to feel more comfortable in Teddy's company. Behind the macho exterior, he could tell that Teddy wanted this case solved just as much as he did—if only to bring a close to the town's speculation.

"Have you had any experience with serial killers before?" Will asked.

"Only one. We used to call him 'The Music Man.'"

"Did you catch him?"

They pulled up to an intersection and waited patiently for the light to turn green.

"Just about. It was a team effort. Too little, too late, though—he had already killed sixteen people by the time we got him."

"Why did you call him The Music Man?"

"He used to leave records playing at the crime scenes. They were never outside, you see. It's a strange one. Normally, these killers throw the bodies out somewhere. Ditches or scrap heaps usually—that's what my training told me, at least. If I'm being honest, I haven't got a lot of experience with this kind of thing.

He just left them exactly where he killed them. Only people with vinyls too. Opera and all that."

"Did he say why he left them like that?"

"Nope. We got to his apartment and he blew his brains out with a sawn-off." Teddy imitated the move, along with fake brains splatting onto the car roof. "Never seen such a mess. I've always wanted to know why he did it. His friends—I'll never understand how these people have friends—told us that he was a normal guy. Bloody music teacher, as well. I mean, we had a hunch that he would have a job like that, but the man worked with kids for twenty years. We only worked out his identity because his neighbor complained of a weird smell coming from his flat. Complete luck on our part."

"What was it?"

"Flesh. He kept it in his refrigerator. Didn't know there had been a power outage when he was out of town and he hadn't realized that the fuse had blown. We wouldn't have caught him if not for blind luck."

"What did he do with the flesh?"

"He fed it to his cats."

*

The conversation didn't last long after that. Following a short drive, they pulled up in front of Teddy's garage again and exited the car. They were about to enter the house when a cry sounded behind them. Greta was racing down the drive, her face now grubby and dress torn in numerous places. Teddy turned and took one look at his daughter before storming towards her.

"Where have you been?" he asked, his voice dashed with firmness.

Greta tried her best to lie; Teddy wasn't buying it. She kept one hand behind her back, hiding it from her father. Noticing this, Teddy took it and held it flat. A jagged shard of glass protruded from her skin, surrounded by crusting blood.

Teddy shouted for his wife and she came running from the house, not registering that she was still holding a brush. Seeing her husband and daughter hunched in the driveway, her first thought was surely an ugly one.

"I told you not to let her leave the house," said Teddy, pinching the skin around the glass.

"She said she was going to Chloe's house. I even checked with her mother," said Gillian, now at her husband's side.

"Chloe Gregson's mother has the personality of a horse and the brains to go with it. You've been to the landfill, haven't you?" Teddy asked Greta.

Greta nodded through a sniff of tears.

"Why were you there? You know that it's dangerous. What's wrong with the hollow?"

"We don't play there anymore," said Greta, digging her shoes into the ground.

Teddy crouched down to talk to his daughter on her level. "Why not? You used to run around there all day. You haven't already grown out of playing, have you? Not already."

Greta shook her head. "No. We play further up the river."

"All the kids used to play in the hollow when I was young," said Will.

Greta turned to face him, "did *you*?"

"No. I wasn't much of an outdoor kid. I went there a few times, but I wouldn't be able to tell you much about it. You know it better than I do."

"Did something happen there? If anyone picks on you, just remind them that your old man is in the police."

Greta locked her eyes with Will, "Mr Metlocke, did you ever see a witch?"

"Apart from my French teacher, I don't think so. Is there a witch in the hollow?"

Slowly, Greta nodded her head. "We saw her last week. She was covered in mud and her hair was all long and straggly."

"Probably just a homeless lady. God knows there are enough of them around here. Nothing to worry about," said Teddy, standing up again. "Just don't get too close to them."

"What made her a witch, Greta?" said Will.

Greta looked up at him, her features deadly serious. "It was her eye. It was made of two different colors."

138

CHAPTER THIRTEEN: THE WICKED WITCH

The Grimm Reaper. Every serial killer needs a good nickname. It transcends the perpetrator, making them more than a person. They become more like an entity. A supernatural creature like the Boogeyman.

Naturally, the town embraced its new cult hero with open arms. Cardboard Reaper masks filled the shops within days, and a startling number of children began playing with plastic scythes. Newspaper stands were empty within minutes of restocking, and the arcade had swapped out their metal ducks with a crude drawing of the Reaper wearing a Christmas hat, ready for another group of tourists to arrive. The alley where Abigail Finsbury had been murdered became the latest attraction for visitors, in part due to the memorial created by the entrance. Flowers and notes covered the ground where she had died.

It wasn't just the recent murders that had pulled the town out of hibernation, Christmas was forcing families back into the shops. The streets were crowded with fathers buying whatever was left in the sale section. Will learned quickly to ensure he had returned to the motel by six, or risk being swarmed by early evening shoppers taking advantage of the extended opening hours.

After Greta's alleged witch sighting, Will's mind was completely thrown off the Reaper. He woke at midday and stayed in bed for a few hours, unable to find the strength to leave. Eventually, he decided that it was just his anxiety, so he rolled out of the covers and dressed warm. Dark jeans, rolled into his boots, complemented a purple turtleneck underneath his jacket. The cold was bothering his lungs again, so he called for a cab and waited, this time deciding to stay in his room rather than face questions from Wendy at reception.

*

It wasn't a long journey. The hollow was located towards the east of the Hollyhead river, where the rocky banks caused the water to foam and writhe wildly. Will had never familiarized himself with its layout, although he knew most of the children in the town frequented it during the summer break. If you weren't spending the majority of the day running through the undergrowth, you were what the other kids would label as a freak. Then one day, someone decides that the innocence of youth has gone, and that booze and sex were the new highs. It was one of the only certainties in life. One day, the kids played. The next, they would never be seen in the hollow again.

Hillbillies had occupied it through most of the sixties, meaning Will had been forbidden to play there, especially after dark. Once he had managed to sneak from the house and run to the entrance. He could only remember standing perfectly still and watching the twitching of the trees, no doubt full of creatures and ghosts, at least to a kid with an overactive imagination. That provided enough fear to ensure that he didn't go in. Now, he walked in without a second thought. The fantastical illusion that he had held throughout his adolescence quickly proved to be wrong. Instead of forests straight out of Tolkien, the hollow transpired to be another decaying tomb of Hollyhead. Barbed wire had sunk into the ground due to being stomped down by the local children. However, some spikes still stuck out from the dirt. He wasn't sure where he was headed, but he followed the slosh of the river, allowing him to retrace his steps if he needed to. Bits of plastic littered the ground, but that was normal for Hollyhead.

Despite the cold, Will could feel himself sweating. He noticed a shallowly eroded path to his right and decided it was his best option. It led to a rusting iron fence, tied shut to a post with a shred of blue rope. He jumped it, satisfied that the cancer hadn't yet taken that from him. The gate led him into a clearing. Trees had been cut down, leaving huge wooden stumps across the area, allowing for caravans to occupy the site. Three wagons had been left. One had almost completely been cut in two, with jagged sheets of metal being the only thing keeping it together at all. The windows were smashed, with orange graffiti scribbled on the outside: 'GET OUT YOU HILLBILLY

SCUM'. Evidently, the message had sunk in. Nature was taking its land back; the caravans were being eaten by foliage and mold. Only one wagon remained relatively intact. No smashed windows, although the glass looked misted and covered in grime. The door even had its hinges. Will approached it and tentatively pushed it open. The wagon smelt like something had died within the walls; Will had to cover his nose with his sleeve to prevent himself from yacking all over the remains of the carpet. Mold infected the upper corners of the compartment and would undoubtedly be spread thickly across the back-ends of the cupboards. Empty bottles of water filled up a garbage bag, along with tins of corn and apricots. He took another step inside. At the far end was a wooden bed frame. Curled up in a squashed, purple, sleeping bag, someone lay sleeping. Coils of ginger hair rested on a folded-up jumper. He had finally found her. The sight of her summoned all the memories he had shut away. There were the long walks they had taken together, along with Nick and Alex, the hint of perfume that she had worn, and the way that his brain stopped working whenever he saw her.

"Lenora, it's me. It's Will," he said, gently resting his hand on her shoulder. Her body felt disturbingly cold. She turned; her movements still full of sleep. Her eyes opened. The blue and green pool of her iris hadn't lost its mesmeric effect.

He wasn't sure what to expect. A part of him wanted her to throw her arms around him and thank him for rescuing her from whatever pit her life had fallen into. He quickly suppressed the thought. He was no knight in shining armor.

"Just when I thought it couldn't get any worse," Lenora sighed, collapsing her head back into the makeshift pillow.

"That's a fine welcome," Will replied, his brow furrowed.

"I'm not welcoming you.

Had she really changed this much? Her looks had changed, but then so had his. The side of her face marked with the scar was hidden in shadow, only her green and blue eye broke through the darkness around her face.

"Really? After all this time, you don't even want to see your friend?"

She laughed. Not a soft giggle like he had grown so accustomed to back in school instead a harsh cackle. "Friend?

No. I don't want to see you. So kindly turn around and piss off," she ordered, twiddling her finger around to signal for Will to get out.

He hesitated. Perhaps all this wasn't worth it. *Fuck that. I want to know why. Then I can die happy.*

"No. I think I deserve an explanation."

"You don't deserve anything from me."

"Come on. I was your friend! I looked for you for years!"

"Sure, you must have had loads of time between writing your bargain bucket paperbacks and getting your head out of your ass," she snapped, standing up and pushing past Will. She must have been on the streets for a while—creases striped her shirt and dirt lined her jeans where she'd spent many a cold night in the backstreets of Hollyhead. Shivering, she pulled the sleeping bag around her like a pensioner creeping their way to a lonely death. He didn't want to mention the fact that she smelt like day-old vomit and sweat.

"You left me nothing to go on. Nick said that when he woke up, you had already packed a bag and gone."

Lenora snorted. "Yeah, Nick would say that. Easier than saying that he came at me with a knife," she said, opening a cupboard and producing a bottle of wine. Will didn't recognize the label—never a good sign.

Nick attacked her with a knife... Will wanted to believe that he was surprised. The majority of his brain had told him that Nick had nothing to do with Lenora's disappearance. The part left knew that every time he had seen Nick think of Lenora, his composure wavered. His hands began shaking like a dopehead out of relief.

"Why would he do that?"

"Does there need to be a reason?"

"To go after someone with a knife normally requires some form of motive."

Lenora looked towards the window, where thin rain was now skulking across the grimy panes of glass. Towards the back of the caravan, cracks in the exterior let in droplets that formed small puddles by the door.

"He thought that it was your baby." There was no awkward silence that followed. The rain filled the vacuum of quiet.

"Why?"

Lenora slammed the drawer shut. "Because you had that way! You followed me around like a puppy. Every time that Nick forgot to pick me up or didn't buy me a card for Valentines, there you were! My god, there was a part of me that thought maybe it *was* yours. Nick thought the same and Alex was too invested in his career to notice."

Will had nothing to say. Words were floating around in his head, but they wouldn't connect. It felt like being back in French class trying to conjugate verbs.

"I never loved you like that," was all he managed.

"Well, you could have fooled me. Do you really think that it's normal to stalk people?" she questioned, slamming another drawer. "Where the fuck is the corkscrew?" She leaned back and took deep breaths. Her ribs were so clear that Will could see them rise and fall.

Will walked to a sideboard and picked up the corkscrew before placing it into Lenora's hand. "Of course you know where it is," she said, falling back onto her heap of a bed and pulling the bottle of wine toward her. "Did it not occur to you that maybe I don't want to be found? This isn't my life now. It's just a pit-stop. Somewhere to end a sentence."

"Then tell me what you're doing here! Because this,"—he waved a hand around the cramped caravan— "is not a good look for you."

"It's none of your business."

"Why won't you tell me? I get you don't like me now, but there was a time when we were inseparable."

"No. There was a time when you and *Nick* were inseparable. You were the Robin to his Batman, always following him around when no one wanted you there. We would have shaken you off if Alex hadn't talked us out of it."

Will's eyes stung. "You tell me why you're back and I will leave you alone. You won't ever have to see me again."

Lenora narrowed her eyes, searching for a hint of a bluff. Eventually, she sighed. "I think Nick killed Alex and his brothers. He's back in town now. It can't be a coincidence that there have been two deaths since he's returned."

Will didn't know whether to laugh. "Or it could be exactly that."

"Nick was there that night. We both were."

"At the fair?"

Lenora nodded and pushed her hair out of her eyes.

"I didn't see you," said Will.

Lenora gave him a confused look. "Yeah you weren't there, dipshit. You were studying," she said.

Will felt himself flush. Stupidity was a look that he hated with a passion.

"We saw them there. Nick said that one of the brothers owed him money," Lenora continued.

"If you were with him, then there can't be a plausible way for Nick to have killed them," replied Will.

"He wasn't with me the entire time. I left him after a stupid argument. The last thing I saw that night was Alex walking home with one of the younger boys. Nick wasn't far behind."

"What? I can't believe that it's him, but that means Nick was possibly the last one to see them alive. Why didn't he come forward at the time?"

"Knowing Nick, he probably beat Alex to a pulp."

"They were friends. Nick would never have hurt him."

Lenora brushed her hair from her eyes. "I know you think you understand what Nick is like. People are different in private. I lost count of how many times that asshole beat me."

"Why didn't you leave him?"

"It's not that easy. I thought I loved him. The only advantage that it has given me now is that I know exactly what kind of man he is. There is no doubt in my mind that he could have killed those boys. If he beat the woman he supposedly loved, then I can't see why he wouldn't kill Abigail Finsbury. Maybe he got the taste for it."

Will rubbed his temples; a migraine was starting to form. "There must be more."

"When Nick came home that night, his pants were covered in dirt. I pretended to be asleep, so he didn't know that I saw him. No one has found the clothes the Spark boys were wearing that night. No sign of any of their possessions either. I think he buried them. I've tried everywhere, even the Spark farmhouse, just in case he planted them there."

"Let's say he did kill them. Why bury them? He could have burnt the clothes."

Lenora shook her head. "He likes to keep trophies. He'd keep anything; tickets from a game, the underwear of women he fucked… Teeth from people he'd beaten."

"Nick didn't go around beating people up. Sure, he was promiscuous, but there was never anything in his behavior to suggest that he was aggressive."

"He behaved differently in public. Everyone does. Trust me, Will, he was a monster and probably still is."

"No, it doesn't fit. Nick isn't the type of person to string up six boys. It was a display."

"I need to *know*. I need to look him in the eyes and *know* if he killed poor Alex."

Then there was silence. Lenora drank deeply from the bottle and Will watched his old friend. It was a lot of information to process and his brain was tired. He could only imagine what she had seen while sleeping rough. The years had whittled her down to a skeletal figure, and her mind had grown hostile. Beneath her hardened exterior, Will could sense a chasm of vulnerability.

"We'll draw him to us. You write a note saying that you're back and need to talk to him. I saw him two nights ago. He freaked at the mention of you. We'll get him to come here and then we'll get the truth from him."

"No. Not here. I need to break into his house. He had a box of his trophies when I lived with him. I would bet my life that he still has it somewhere. My guess is that he went somewhere desolate, buried them, and returned for them at a later date. I can do it on my own," said Lenora.

"I'm sure you can. It will be easier with both of us though," Will replied. He expected another outburst of protest, but Lenora shrugged and drank again. She wiped her mouth with her sleeve. Despite her coldness, the guilt Will felt still hadn't drained away.

"I drove him to your house the night you disappeared. I was so drunk," admitted Will.

"So was Nick."

"I wasn't using it as an excuse. Do you think I should have known? Perhaps if I had said something differently, none of this would have happened."

"You've been torturing yourself all these years because you dropped him off? If it wasn't you, it would have been someone else. God, that is just like you. It was always about mistakes you've made. You had nothing to do with my disappearance."

"Nothing at all?"

"You didn't drive me away, but you also weren't a reason for me to stay."

Will nodded, his head heavy. "What happened to your little girl? You didn't…" he tailed off. For a second a thought too terrible to consider had crawled out from his unconscious and wallowed in the front of his head. He pictured her giving birth alone. Maybe she wrapped her daughter in a coat and left her to freeze. Maybe it had taken longer for her to snap.

"I gave her away. It was obvious that I couldn't take care of her, so I left her at an orphanage. And don't look like that; you have no idea what a burden having a child is. You were alone throughout high school. You were alone during college, and you're alone now. The right to judge my decisions is one that you never had and never will."

"I don't think it takes a genius to realize that your decisions have been ill-informed. You're a drunk living in squalor. The only worse decision I can think of concerns the Greeks accepting a Trojan horse," Will replied. He gave himself a second to breathe. "Please just come back with me. I've got money; I'll set you up in a hotel for a night."

"I don't need your charity, Will. You can't offend me and then shower me with pity."

"Then go and stay with your parents. They're shells of the people they were before you left. At least tell them that you're alive."

"I can't. No parent wants their child to look like this," she said, tenderly running her fingers across her scar.

"Don't make excuses. You're just scared of the consequences. You can't run forever. It would be better to get it out of the way now."

"Sure, because you had such a good relationship with your dad."

"You're deflecting."

"Because I don't want to talk about me. I am back for Nick and I intend to follow through on my plan, with or without you," Lenora said. She held perfect eye contact; something Will found particularly off-putting.

"I'll meet you at the motel on Prowse Street on Monday night. We'll see what we can get from Nick's house. He must have seen something that night."

"Fine."

*

It wasn't long after their conversation that Will left the caravan and proceeded back towards the motel. His reunion with Lenora hadn't gone how he had imagined it for so many years. He had been stupid not to see that Lenora wanted nothing to do with him in school. It's funny how the people who mean so much to you often don't feel the same. Had he missed something? The most prominent hint of Lenora's true feelings towards him had been following Alex's death. The days ensuing the murder were scarred and fragmented. Therapists had been hired to talk to friends of the boys, but Will had avoided them, instead seeking his comfort from a bottle. Frank's attempts to help had all revolved around his own murder investigations and false promises that whoever had killed the Sparks would be brought to justice. Whilst he had wanted to find some kind of solace from talking to Lenora, she had always been busy with Nick and had never taken the time to return his calls. He had assumed that she was simply busy. Perhaps, that was the most obvious sign that his feelings had never been requited.

His thoughts were flying through his head with such ferocity that the rumble coming from town came as a slight relief. A good distraction from himself. He turned down a connecting alley and was met with a large crowd, all gazing toward a raised platform in the middle of the road.

Mayor Stone was standing front and center, a green Christmas hat fitted with elf ears perched on her head. To her right, there was a tree drowning in tinsel and shining baubles, reaching at least twenty feet. A glittery, sequined dress covered her slim figure—just like what Abigail Finsbury had worn on the night of her death. Will wanted to believe that it was just a coincidence. The dress split at the waist, revealing a long white leg.

She must be cold, thought Will. Then he remembered what was scheduled for that night. The Christmas lights were being switched on, with him as a special guest. He tried to turn back but froze in spot as Stone's voice blared down a microphone.

"Will Metlocke, ladies, and gentlemen!" she shouted, clapping her hands fiercely. The rest of the crowd roared, and a spotlight positioned on the stage turned on him, prickling his body with stifling heat. Noticing his hesitation, two men grabbed his arms and thrust him forward, despite his protests. Strong hands shoved him onto the stage. Journalists made up the majority of the front row, and all turned their cameras towards him. Some were yelling questions about his reasons for being in Hollyhead and whether he planned to write another detective novel after the 'general failure' of his last. Mayor Stone placed a firm hand on his shoulder. Will noticed that in her other hand was a large yellow box with a red button poking out the middle.

"One of our very own. Award-winning author: Will Metlocke!" she chanted, the microphone projecting her voice from at least ten different speakers. "He very kindly agreed to turn on the lights. I am also proud to announce that his next book will be focusing on the recent murders of Abigail Finsbury and Ed McCain!"

There was a cheer from the crowd and the stamping of heavy boots on concrete. It seemed to Will that the crowd was full of intense energy, in some ways reminding him of videos he had watched in history class—minus the arm salute and book burnings. Will tried to step away but Stone had his arm locked in a fierce grip. Noticing his intentions, she gripped him even tighter and pushed the yellow box into his hand.

"Three, two, one," she said in unison with the crowd.

Reluctantly, Will pressed the button. The town center exploded in a dizzying array of lights. From the dry cleaners, a star sprayed the town in yellow sparks before sucking them up again. The bar had six reindeer trotting along the side of the building, led by a smiling Rudolph. It all seemed very appropriate. Until he looked above his head.

Six angels hung down from a stretch of wire between the chemist and the butchers on either side of the street. The shorter on the sides and the largest in the middle.

"You put the Spark boys up there?" shouted Will, but his anger was drowned out by the clamorous audience in front of them. Parents were pointing out their favorite lights to their children, who jumped up and down to get a better look. Even the hot dog vendors recruited for the night had stopped to admire the festivities. Mayor Stone was smiling again, her arms held out as if all the applause were for her. Will forced his way over to her so that his mouth was inches away from her ear.

"Turn them off now." His hands closed into tight fists.

"Not a chance," Stone replied. Then she pointed towards a photographer at the edge of the stage. A hand clutched his side and Will realized that Stone was posing with him. "Smile," she said. The camera flashed before Will could move away.

Sometimes life slows down. Every detail is amplified by a hundred, and it feels like you can hear your heart drumming against your chest. You can feel the vibrations from the beating of a bee's wings and the whining of electricity running through the powerlines. That was what happened to Will Metlocke that night. A gargling, nightmare of a sound in front of him caught his attention and he turned.

A girl was pushing their way through the crowd, dressed in an emerald green dress. Her skin was covered with foundation, streaked with milky white tear marks. She limped forwards, her feet landing heavily to avoid falling over. If she had fallen, she wouldn't have been able to stand again. Her arms were missing. Abigail Finsbury was lurching through the crowd and she was heading straight for the stage.

CHAPTER FOURTEEN: REVELATIONS

The crowd hadn't noticed. Hundreds of arms were pointing at the lights as Abigail trudged towards the stage like a zombie from a cheap horror film. Even Mayor Stone hadn't spotted her. She was too busy lapping up the excitement of the crowd with animal hunger. Will couldn't take his eyes off the girl walking towards him. Abigail had been attractive at one time in her life; Will's understanding of beauty wasn't strong, but that much was obvious. Her cheekbones were high and slanted underneath her golden whispers of blonde hair. Even without good looks, a smile can make a world of difference. The Reaper had changed that; the woman before Will had pale, dead skin stretched across her face, causing her eyes to sink into the back of her head with pupils shot with blood. There was no smile now; the right side of her mouth sagged, allowing Will to see black gums underneath. Her dress dripped with dirty water and she staggered towards Will like a user looking for their next fix.

"Tell me you see her too," Will pleaded, his legs feeling like someone had just injected them with anaesthetic. The noise of the crowd had grown deafening, enclosing his head in a swarm of shouts and jeers. Mayor Stone followed his pointed finger.

"See who?"

"Abigail Finsbury," said Will. She had continued towards him, now reaching the front row of the crowd. Drool ran down from the side of her mouth and dribbled to the floor in thick threads. All the sustenance of life had clearly drained from her a while ago; she continually lost her balance and stumbled. The disruption had finally caused the crowd to turn their attention back to the stage. Their eyes were fixed on Will, some laughing and others desperately seeking to find his point of interest.

Mayor Stone clicked at a number of photographers and jerked her head towards Will. They eagerly turned their attention to him and started taking photos, barging each other out of the way so that they could get the shot for the morning paper. Through the flashes of the cameras, he lost sight of

Abigail. When his vision finally cleared of the blinding lights, she had gone.

"I gotta find whatever he's on," said someone in the crowd. "That's some heavy shit."

Will stepped forward, his eyes darting across the faces in search of the dead girl. She had been only feet away but had vanished as quickly as she had appeared.

A hand grasped his shoulder, and he wheeled around to see Stone staring at him. "Are you alright?" she asked. Feeling his body surge with adrenaline, he knocked her hand away and stumbled backward. His foot stepped into thin air. He fell from the stage, landing on the ground with a sickening thud and a roar of laughter from the people of Hollyhead. The lights above were sparkling with cruel malice and the pattern of the six boys transformed into their real bodies, once again hanging. They would hang forevermore. Will rolled over to escape the glare of the lights and crawled forwards until he felt the strength to stand. He was met with the first row of the crowd. Children were clutching their mother's hips in response to his antics and a few teenage boys laughed and threw popcorn in his face.

Jeers filling his ears, Will pushed his way through the crowd. Some pushed him back and twice he stumbled to the floor. The number of people in the audience had doubled since he had arrived, making it substantially harder to make any ground, but eventually, he found himself in an alleyway. He clutched his side and took shallow breaths—his lungs couldn't take any more than that. Then he bent double and threw up into the drain. It took him two hours to walk back to the motel. Hollyhead was making him sick. Perhaps even sicker than the cancer.

*

Early morning brought with it a fresh wave of newspapers. Another night of only a couple of hours of sleep had left Will feeling weaker than ever. After lying in bed until midday doing nothing other than replaying the events of the night before, Will had found a paper in the reception lounge and resisted the temptation to look. The streets of Hollyhead were an entirely different task. From the corner of his eye, he could see his terror-filled face gazing at him from every stack of papers, surrounded by various stories about town expenses and Cold

War speculation around the Communist movement in Europe. The Grimm Reaper was forgotten and Will Metlocke had transformed into the celebrity of the day. Three years ago, he would have been familiar with the sensation. A celebrity's life is often scrutinized—one wrong decision can haunt them for the rest of their life. Luckily for him, his fame didn't extend to more than a day on the front cover. His drunken antics were quickly forgotten replaced by affairs and conspiracies of Hollywood's greats. Still, the feeling made him uneasy. The eyes of Hollyhead had been following him since he arrived, and, because of the newspapers, now his own had joined the crowd.

Teddy had called at the motel and left a message with Wendy. He was hoping to discuss all things Grimm. "The way I see it, there's been two murders in the last month that have some kind of connection to these stories. Perhaps we can predict what comes next," he had said that afternoon.

They had driven to the station and entered Teddy's office—a cold, stark room with only a fake pot plant and a family photo breathing any life into it. Will had seen many office rooms before, but none so austere. Teddy had been hesitant to bring up what had happened the night prior, and Will, sensing his manner, had said that he was responding badly to medication. They had left it at that. At present, they were sitting behind Teddy's desk, poring over the case files of the Spark brothers, Abigail Finsbury and Ed McCain. Teddy handed Will the photos of the victims and Will placed them face down on the table—he had seen the bodies enough to last a lifetime.

"There's always a link, however weak," said Teddy. He had put on his glasses to analyze the files closer. "It's just a matter of finding it."

"You think? I would say the probability of there being a link is only present if you're dealing with a man at one with his sanity."

"We measure sanity by our own averages. I'm sure the killer believes that they are completely sane," said Teddy, slamming the Spark file closed and taking a sip of coffee. He promptly spat it out. "Fucking thing is cold," he said. "How long have we been at this?"

"A couple of hours. We just need to find out how *Grimm's* fairy tales fit into the motive."

"They have teachings, right? Like a kind of creepy Bible. Don't be greedy, women should be pure and the differences between classes in society. Maybe the Reaper has interpreted them in a certain way. Apart from his size, there was nothing to suggest that Ed McCain was greedy."

Will surged with guilt. He pictured the letter that Frank had taken from the chef's house. "Perhaps there was something you didn't pick up on. We all have secrets."

"A secret that cost him his life?"

"Potentially. What's normal procedure when searching for a killer?"

Teddy put his hands behind his head and groaned. "Psychological profile, map of the area. Serial killers tend to kill close to home at first and then spread out. Home is comfortable. It's probably something to do with evolution."

"It's different this time. Hollyhead is only so big. Are there any murders in other towns that may link? Saunton perhaps?"

"If there is, the link is minimal. Everything here points to *Grimm's*. We even checked other states. Nothing. The Reaper hasn't branched out yet."

"Maybe home isn't a comfort. We might find that Hollyhead acts as a trigger. The murders only work in the context of our town," said Will, flicking through the pages of Ed's file.

"You talk like you can understand their motives."

Will shrugged, "it's not difficult. Power, love, fear… in the end, it all just boils down to those. We just need to pinpoint which one causes the Reaper's behavior. Power could suggest a sexual agenda."

"Abigail Finsbury wasn't raped. Neither were the Spark boys."

"Maybe the pleasure of the kill is enough to get our man excited."

"Why fairy tales? They are what this whole thing boils down to."

"Lessons," Will said, closing Abigail Finsbury's folder. "And you can only teach a lesson if you know your content. Take *The Ungrateful Son*; it's a story all about greed. The Reaper feels like they know the consequences of greed. They can feel its ripple effects and they believe that makes them judge, jury, and executioner. The world has wronged them, and this is their way of ensuring someone else doesn't suffer the same tribulation. It's kind of noble in a way."

"Be careful, Will. It's a slippery slope once you try to empathize with these people. You know a fair amount of criminal psychology for an author."

Will shrugged. "It depends on how you see it. The Reaper is a little like a writer. They have their plot, and they are following it. We just need to work out the ending and work backward. We need to think of their next lesson."

"What we need is the man who Ed's waitress spoke with to come forward. He gave her a number to call, but she lost it. I've asked her to try to remember so we will see. The fact that he hasn't come forward, I interpret to be suspicious, to say the least."

"Perhaps he just doesn't want to become involved."

"Then he is a coward. His involvement may allow us to solve this case."

I wish, thought Will.

"I went to Ed McCain's house after the murder. That's when I got this," said Teddy, showing Will his still bandaged hand. Will's throat tightened. "I was with the killer that night. Why else would they be snooping around a dead man's residence?"

Will nodded and averted his gaze to the heating system behind Teddy's shoulder. Noticing the silence, Teddy swiped up his car keys from the desk. "Come on, let's go get something to eat."

"Just as long as it's not a burger."

*

They left the station and made the short walk back to Teddy's car. Will's mind ran so sluggishly that he didn't react to the step down from the curb. He lost his footing and fell hard, only just managing to pull his hands out to break his landing. Despite Will's assurance that he was fine, Teddy helped him up and asked whether he needed to sit down. Tiredness had crept up on him. Cold had run into his joints and it felt like he'd picked up thirty years overnight. He didn't notice the loss of weight in his pocket.

"Will, I think you dropped this," said Teddy, placing something cold into his hand.

Then the ground beneath Will gave way and water cascaded in from every direction. Teddy disappeared beneath the waves and Will felt the memories flood into his mind. There was a boy, scrambling towards him in the water, surrounded by coils of weeds. The light thinned and before long the boy had disappeared, eaten by the water. Then the scene cleared and was replaced by a new one. Will was standing behind a door, his fingers wrapped around the handle, staring through the crack. Gillian Ludlow lay curled up on a king-sized bed in the fetal position, the duvet clutched to her chest. It looked as though she was choking, but her eyes gave away that the forced jerking motions of her head were due to her attempting to contain her cries of sadness. Will wanted to help, only his hand wouldn't allow him to push the door open. Gillian let out a whimper and shoved her head into her pillow, stifling another round of pain. Her dark hair ran tangled, and her nightdress bore the signs of neglect. Smudged cosmetic marks circled the collar, and the bottom was wrinkled and threadbare. The hand on the door clutched the handle and gently pulled it to a close, ensuring no sound came when it clicked into place. With great difficulty, Will brought himself back to reality and found himself touching the rewind, now almost burning hot. Teddy was covered in sweat and his bottom lip trembled slightly. With a jolt, Will dropped the device where it nestled into the grass. Confusion had already stolen Teddy's thinking. He opened his mouth to speak, but the rewind had worked its magic. Will wasn't sure what he had seen in Teddy's mind. The only certain thing was that Teddy was harboring more secrets than Will had initially thought. Then again, who wasn't?

*

The pair didn't discuss the case over lunch. Teddy said that overthinking would lead them nowhere they hadn't been before. They had arrived at Jack's Pizza just before three and the food took less than ten minutes to arrive. As they ate, Teddy asked Will about his writing and whether he had started the book that Mayor Stone had asked him to create.

"I have no intention of writing another book," said Will, wiping his fingers on a napkin.

Teddy gave him a quizzical look. "I can understand not wanting to write about this shithole. None at all seems like a stretch."

"I told you I'm on heavy medication," said Will. Teddy replied with a nod. "It's because I have cancer."

"Shit," said Teddy, before taking a long sip of his chocolate soda. "Terminal?"

"It will be. My doctors say that I could survive if I began treatment now."

"But you don't want it?"

Will bit into another slice of his pizza, the cheese stretching as it came away from the base. "I don't see the point. I've played my hand in this life. Helping solve a string of serial killings is about the most interesting ending I could think of. It will make a good final chapter." Teddy opened his mouth to reply but Will stopped him. "Before you say anything, I don't want a lecture. My mind won't change on this."

Teddy chuckled. "It's not my place to make comments on another man's life. It's your decision. Personally, I'm just glad to have someone by my side on this case that doesn't think that these deaths are great for publicity. Have you told your family?"

"Mom died when I was a baby. Frank and I don't have that kind of relationship," said Will. Just the thought of telling Frank made his stomach churn.

"Even if you don't want treatment, you should tell him. You don't have to live with the guilt for as long as he will. Now," he said, picking up the menu again, "is it bad if I have another bowl of fries?"

Will told him that it was fine and they both ordered not only another bowl but also another pizza to share with more milkshakes. They left the pizzeria, laughing and feeling like they could hurl onto the sidewalk, in the best way possible.

*

It wasn't until that evening that Will returned to the motel. He entered the reception and came face to face with Wendy, who still hadn't wiped that smirk from her face that showed how pleased she was that Will had chosen her *establishment* over all others. "Good evening, Mr. Metlocke. You've had a good day, I hope," she said as she climbed a rickety stepladder and hung yet another bauble from the wooden beams overhead.

"I've spent the day looking at pictures of dead people. So yeah, a pretty great day," said Will. He enjoyed watching her scramble for words to make her reply.

"All in the name of your next book, I suppose," she said.

"Just a hobby. Any messages for me?"

"Do you mean Steinbeck or Metlocke?"

"Either."

"None," her tone became concerned, "are you not spending Christmas with your family?"

Will walked past her, careful not to step on the heap of baubles at the foot of the ladder. "I shall spend this Christmas in the company of Christie, Poe, and Hardy. No better way to go about it."

"I'll be alone if you would like to have some company," said Wendy, stepping down from the ladder to retrieve another decoration to join the plethora above their heads. "My husband died two years back and ever since, it's been such a lonely affair."

"I'll consider it," said Will, as genuinely as he could manage.

"Please do. It's nearly Christmas Eve, you know," she said, smiling weakly.

Will nodded, then his heart slipped into his stomach. The last few days had been such a mad rush that he had forgotten about Eve. Today was the day they had agreed to meet, and it had passed seven over a half hour ago. Will ran to his room, causing Wendy to exclaim and clutch a hand to her heart, pulled on the most crease-free shirt he could find, and ran from the motel, only just managing to avoid a collision with Wendy's ladder. He skidded into the street and made his way toward Eve; there was a chance she would still be waiting.

*

Luck was finally on his side. He turned the corner onto Barry Street and saw her standing beneath the neon sign of the bar, which cast a purple light over her body. She was dressed in a burgundy and white polka-dot blouse above a long, flowing skirt. The same red coat that she had worn the last time Will had seen her finished off the outfit, subtle but stylish. Her dark hair rested on her shoulders, and Will couldn't help but smile when he saw her. She smiled back, filling Will with a sense of calm.

"I'm so sorry. Today has been so busy, and I didn't have your number so I couldn't call you. I ran all the way here, which in hindsight was not a good idea," he said, trying his best not to sound out of breath.

"This film had better be worth it, that's all I'm saying," she replied. "We had better skip drinks. I like to watch the trailers before the film starts."

"That sounds like a good idea," said Will, clutching his side. His heart rate wasn't returning to normal quite as fast as it should have been. "I'll admit that this is the first date I've been on since high school," he said, not daring to look her in the eye. Some men walked past and broke into a rumble of jeers. "You must be mad, mate," one of them yelled.

"I'll give them that one," said Will. "I *must* be mad thinking I have a chance with you."

"Don't put me on a pedestal, Will. I've got just as many flaws as anyone else," replied Eve, absentmindedly pulling down the sleeve of her blouse.

"I'm sure that's true, but they don't have your looks," he replied. She shook her head, but Will knew it was in an effort to stop herself from smiling.

He wasn't sure if he felt more relaxed. Yes, his heart was beating at such a rate that relaxed is hardly the word he would have used, but she presented a certain energy. The sarcasm he so often used as a way of turning people away had gone. He couldn't have come up with a quick line if his life had depended on it. He guessed in that sense he felt more relaxed than he had been for years. Eve had the kind of face that you couldn't help but gaze at. Sure, she would never be a Hollywood star, but that didn't matter. If this was as far as it went, then he was happy that he even laid eyes on her.

"Did you grow up here?' he asked, as they turned the corner and saw the movie theater. He tried not to picture Abigail's rotting body down the alley beside it.

"Thankfully not. I'm a nurse; I trained in New Orleans and then came here when a space opened up at Hollyhead Hospital. Not been here long."

Will nodded. "What do you think of our little town?"

Eve grimaced. "I can't wait to get outta here. Once a new position opens up, I'd like to go to New Jersey. That's where my parents lived."

"Nice place, a bit dull though," said Will, trying to smooth the folds of his shirt. "The detective in my book came from Jersey."

"He moved to Brooklyn at the end though, after he caught *The Silver Nemesis*," said Eve. Will grinned, it wasn't often someone remembered the finer details of his critical failure.

"Have you got family there?"

"Just me now."

"My father lives here, but we don't particularly see eye to eye."

"He doesn't appreciate that you're an author?"

"Hasn't read any of my books," said Will as they reached the entrance to the theater. Will opened the door and Eve walked in, thanking him as she went.

"I can't believe you haven't seen *Empire Strikes Back* yet. You have watched the first one, surely," he said as they got in line. Eve sucked on her lip in a way that said *you're going to hate me for this*. "I've seen a lot of weird shit over the past few days and out of all of that, this is the most shocking revelation," said Will.

"I've never had the time!" she said, taking her purse from a little handbag across her hip.

"Don't worry, I got it."

"You get special celebrity-only offers?" she said, her voice slicked with sarcasm.

"The day I accept any special offers because of my work is the day I lose all self-respect." Will approached the concessions desk and put down his money. "Empire please," he said, before looking at the various snacks arranged behind the cashier, a spotty boy with braces.

With a puzzled expression, the boy slid Will's money back. "It's not playing today, issue with the film," he said. "We got *Flash Gordon* or *9 to 5*."

"Fine, we'll go for Flash."

"It started an hour ago."

"*9 to 5* it is then."

"Starts in an hour-twenty."

"Forget it," groaned Will, snatching up the money. He returned to Eve, who was absent-mindedly admiring the movie posters in the foyer and held his hands up. "Slight problem. Empire isn't on," he said, grimacing. "This whole thing's been a big disaster."

"Half an hour late, didn't get the movie right, and you arrive looking like you've just stepped out from a laundry machine," she replied, her eyes narrow. "You're a bigger disaster than me."

"I guess that means that a second chance is out of the question?"

"I think you're already on your third chance?"

"Exactly how many chances do you tend to give?"

Eve tilted her head. "Normally one. I'll make an exception here. I don't want anything fancy. Let's just go for a walk." She linked her arm through Will's and opened the door, this time leading him away. The date hadn't gone well, but perhaps the end would see improvement. They walked down the street, Will occasionally glancing over at Eve's flushed face and grateful that she hadn't taken her arm from his. Every so often, the cold made his body numb, and he had to keep glancing down to make sure that her fingers were still grasping his arm. Sometimes the earth wants you to succeed and Will was sure that it was on his side that night. The streetlights seemed to shine a little brighter, causing her eyes to sparkle as their gaze met. Rain became a stranger and even the puddles that never seemed to leave had finally dried up. The setting was tailored for a perfect evening. They walked through the town and Eve pointed to the lights, commenting on their cheapness and insensitivity.

"Whoever's idea it was to have the six boys up there deserves a good beating," she said, walking slightly faster now. "There's something sick about this town."

"The burger is pretty good though, right?"

"Yeah, the burger *is* pretty damn good. Is that the only reason you're back here? I wouldn't blame you if it was."

"Actually, I'm helping the police with their inquiries into the recent murders. Mayor Stone thinks it would make a best-seller."

"You wouldn't dream of marketing such a tragedy though, right?"

The question brought memories flooding into his mind. Widows talking to their late husbands, a parent grieving over their child. Then there was the man hanging from the tree in his yard, not found for over a day. He stuffed his hands into his pockets to stop Eve from seeing them shake.

"No. I declined her offer. My plan is to see this investigation to an end and then take a holiday," he said. Seeing a dash of disappointment on Eve's face, he added, "but my plans are flexible." Just in case.

"I bet it's hard having to sit around all day typing," she teased.

"It's hard on my ass, sure." Eve laughed and Will enjoyed seeing her nostrils flare. Making her laugh felt good.

"Stories with such creativity. I don't understand how anyone could sit and write a book from start to end. It appears to me to be such an eternal task."

"It certainly feels that way. Personally, my books don't feel creative. For many, I just found real people and told their stories. It doesn't require much talent for that."

"It takes heart to listen to their stories and want to tell others. That makes up for talent."

"It's a shame not everyone has that outlook."

"The world would be a lot better if they did," replied Eve.

They spent the rest of the walk talking about Will's writing. Eve must have read *The Death Clock* almost as many times as Will; she knew the intricacies of the plot as well as he did, even telling him parts he had forgotten. She understood the characters and her description of Tyler Bowen was pinpoint. If she hadn't been blessed with good looks, Will knew he would have found it almost scary. They reached a complex of apartments and walked into a damp entrance to the building.

"Which one are you?" said Will, pointing to the list of apartment numbers that allowed guests to ring up. There were over thirty different names, but none that said Eve. She pointed to one marked Louise Scott.

"I haven't had time to change it yet. My room is still a mess, as well. I'll get around to tidying at some point. There are so many things you have to sort out after moving into a new place," she said, pulling off her gloves. They stood in silence for a moment.

"Do you have any plans for Christmas?" blurted Will, praying that she would say no. His prayers were met. "We could see each other if you'd like to. I do have another offer, but I would rather spend it with you as opposed to the manager of my motel, who I am quite certain seems overly fond of me. It seems that neither of us has anyone in particular to spend it with."

Eve tugged on her coat sleeve, pulling it down to her fingertips, "I've signed on for the morning at the hospital, but we could meet in the afternoon," she said. Standing on tiptoe, she kissed his cheek, and he felt it redden at her touch; if he played it well, he could pretend it was just the cold. "Despite the disasters, I've had a good time. Until the next one." Then she disappeared up the stairs, leaving Will alone in the hallway.

*

Wendy had asked again whether he would be wanting company on Christmas day. Will managed to evade the question when another guest entered, a stocky man with greased-back hair, his arm draped across a skinny blonde, who was talking with such a loud voice that there was no doubt she had thrown back at least half a dozen shots of tequila. The man seemed perfectly sober. Will left the foyer and entered his room, the lock needing a good jolt before it retracted. After spending so long in Hollyhead, his suitcase was nearly empty, but he put on a woolen jumper to fight off the cold and then collapsed onto his bed, stretching. There wasn't any time to reminisce about the evening before there was a knock at the door.

I don't remember paying you to check on me all day, Wendy.

He opened the door, ready to give the manager a piece of his mind. Frank was standing in the doorway, holding a cheap bottle of wine and two glasses. He gave an awkward smile. "I thought we could talk about the case, and how you're getting on, of course," he said. Will wasn't in the mood. Then again, he rarely was, but stood aside and Frank walked in. "Only one chair?" he asked, looking around.

"One chair. One bed."

Frank nodded and smoothed out the crumpled duvet before settling down. "I heard that you are working closely with Detective Ludlow now?" Will replied with a nod. "He's a good man; fine detective, too."

"He seems to be on top of things, for sure," said Will. Groaning, he sat down on the harsh wooden seat.

"You can sit up here."

"I'd rather sit here. Far more comfortable," said Will. He was ashamed to feel a slight satisfaction from the hurt on Frank's face. "What have you been busy with?"

Frank cleared his throat. "Marty and I went to talk to Jude Rogers—the man who sent Ed the letter. He is the caretaker of the church."

"Do you think he is a suspect?"

"There is potential. However, his alibi seems airtight. Apparently, on the night of Ed's death, he was with a group organizing Christmas donations."

"At the Church?"

"No. There is a hall about a five-minute walk from the diner. They were there all night according to his statement."

"Meaning we are no closer to finding the Reaper?"

Frank raised his eyebrows. "You're using that nickname too? I thought better of you. It's disrespectful to the victims."

"Sure, I hear the Spark boys are suing the killer as we speak."

The look on Frank's face made it evident that he was in no mood for sarcasm. "I also heard about the lights. You're not one to sign up for that kind of thing? Maybe I don't know you quite as well as I thought," he said. "Corkscrew?"

"It's a motel, Dad; not a five-star hotel. I was asked by Mayor Stone and then I completely forgot. I was there purely by accident."

"Marty told me that you were manic on stage. You were described as having a psychotic episode."

Will took a deep breath in. "I have a lot of things happening to me right now. My body is failing me."

"Failing you? You're not even thirty; when you get to my age, you'll know what it feels like to have your body fall apart. I wake up aching and tired every day."

"I won't live till your age."

"You're confusing me, William. What exactly do you mean?"

"I've got cancer. My lungs are riddled with the damn stuff," said Will. At last, the weight inside him had lifted, though only slightly. Frank leaned forward, shaking his head. He took his tie in his hand and started smoothing it between his fingers—a habit that Will hadn't noticed before.

"How long?" he said, not looking up.

"I don't know exactly, but it's cancer. It could have been there a while."

"You're young. Doctors are very proficient at treating cancer now. You'll bounce right back," said Frank, convincing himself more than anything.

"Mom didn't."

Frank stood up, drew a cigarette from a carton inside his pocket, and rolled it across his lip before lighting it. "Your mother was an anomaly, and she wouldn't have had it any other way. Always had to stand out."

"Well, sometimes it's not so bad to blend in," said Will. "I've just told you I have lung cancer and you're still going to smoke that?"

Frank sniffed and snubbed out the cigarette. "I couldn't agree more. When is the first round of treatment?" he asked looking up, his eyes looking for an answer. Will couldn't bring himself to meet his gaze.

"I'm not having any treatment."

"You mean it's too late?" said Frank, a slight dash of fear shot through his eyes.

"No, they say I have a good chance of survival," said Will. Even as he said it, he felt his stomach plunge with guilt. Anger suddenly replaced the guilt. If Frank had tried to keep in touch, even a Christmas card once in a while, then he would have told him when he first received his diagnosis. Now it was too late for Frank's involvement. Will stood up and sat on the bed.

"Then why aren't you having any treatment?"

Will felt his arms tingle with frustration. "Because what would be the point?" he yelled, slamming his fist down onto the glass bedside table. A spiderweb crack formed at the point of impact. "I have spent the last ten years deceiving good men and women out of their money purely so that I could throw it all away on booze and fancy apartments. I deserve this illness and if you can't see that, then you are just as screwed up as I am."

"You told me that you made those people happy. You said that it was like therapy for them. And please calm down; you'll need to pay for that damage."

"At first it was therapy. How many do you think have phoned me up asking to have another meeting? One more opportunity to talk to their departed. It's worse than drugs. Drugs can make you do terrible things, but grief is a far more powerful brew."

"Yes. I think I know that as well as anyone. There isn't any action I would consider entirely selfless. Your outlook is far too cynical. Yes, I think you used the MED foolishly. However, there is a lot worse someone could do with a device such as that. I know you believe your actions were driven by greed, but if it were anyone else, they would find some positive in all this. You're using it for good now. We can find out who this killer is and offer closure to many."

"Don't pretend like you give a crap now. Do you know how long it has been since you last called me?"

"Two years."

"Two years and we spoke for less than a minute. You're not the first to try and convince me to have treatment. Multiple doctors have told me the same thing for the past two months. If there is one person whose opinion I couldn't care less about, then it's yours. It's too late now. I'm going to finish this case and take a holiday. I need somewhere I can die in peace," snapped Will as he wrapped his scarf around his neck.

Frank had become deathly silent. "All these mistakes you believe you have made. This is more than making up for those?" was all he said.

Will let out a snort and smiled.

"I didn't need penance. I needed you."

CHAPTER FIFTEEN: THE KING'S PALACE

Will got up, "I need some air," he said and left the room, slamming the door behind him.

By the time he returned, Frank had disappeared. The only evidence that he had been there at all was a note on the pillow, written on a cheap motel card in his hardly legible handwriting.

Will, I am sorry. I've left the wine as an indication of my apology.

Sure enough, the wine was standing on the table, untouched. Without hesitation, Will screwed up the card and threw it into the little wicker bin by the door. To someone unfamiliar with Frank, the card may have come across as sarcastic. Will knew that he meant it; Frank was talented at many things but putting his feelings into words was a skill he never developed. Looking at his bed, Will considered sleeping. Across the last week, he had managed to steal only a few hours each night, if that. Instead, he pulled out a copy of *Grimm's* and began reading. For the following two hours, he sat on his bed and immersed himself in tales of murder, trickery, and possession, only being disturbed from his reading by a loud and impatient knock at his door. He set down his book and checked out the window, a habit he had developed since the reappearance of Abigail Finsbury. It was Lenora, her arms crossed and her whole-body shivering. He let her in.

"All that money and you choose to stay in a motel?" was the first thing she said. "It makes the caravan look good."

"Luxury makes us complacent," Will replied. Lenora rolled her eyes. A brief silence followed, and then Will took a warm jumper from his case and threw it in her direction. "Put it on. You've seemingly died once already; I'd rather if it didn't happen again just because of the cold."

Lenora eyed it for a second but then pulled it over her head, covering the stained, black t-shirt she had been modeling for as long as she had been in Hollyhead. The jumper looked a couple of sizes too big, but Will didn't wear it anymore. Only a few months previously, he had managed to fit into it perfectly. She rolled up the sleeves to her elbows and flicked back her hair.

"Are we going then?" asked Lenora, looking out the window. Dark clouds had rolled in over the lake outside and it was threatening to rain. Will pulled on his jacket just in case.

"How do we know he's not there?" he asked.

"I made a fake invitation to a restaurant right across town. He should be leaving any second now. By the time he gets there and works out that he's been duped, we should be long gone."

Can't see any way that can go wrong...

"Fine. Let's go."

*

Nick had gained ownership of his childhood house after the death of his father only two years prior. The exterior was still kept neat despite him spending less than a month in the house each year. It wasn't spacious, but there was no need. Nick lived alone, other than the women he brought back almost every night. Like Will's, Nick's home was detached from the rest of the town. According to Frank, Nick checked out the house just before Christmas and then traveled back to whichever cesspit he was situated in at the time. Will scanned the house's surroundings. The absence of light and a car suggested that Lenora's ploy had worked. A faint hint of a smile on her lips told Will that she was pleased. There was more than justice here. Revenge seemed to be a far stronger motivation. The lack of neighbors allowed the pair to walk to the front of the house with relative ease; Will had to quicken his pace to keep up with Lenora. She reached the door first and began examining the lock mechanism.

"There must be a key or something around here," said Will, lifting up a stone from next to the door. He heard a loud smash and turned to see that Lenora had broken the glass of the lounge's window.

"Not very incognito."

"Not trying to be." Careful not to cut herself on the glass, Lenora hopped in and left Will alone outside. Grimacing, he followed. His feet landed on shards of glass on the lounge's carpet. Lenora had already started walking towards the door.

There were signs everywhere that the house wasn't often inhabited. It seemed that all the old memories had been choked by more recent ones. Nick was happy to display pictures of his deals. Half the photos in the house featured his wide-grinned face with some C-list celebrity outside a new apartment, their hands clasped in a done-deal fashion. The air inside smelled stagnant after being shut away for so long, yet Will could smell Nick's expensive aftershave mingling with the dust. There were many similarities to Will's own childhood house, except that Nick's had no reason to be purged of his past.

Will trailed Lenora upstairs and into a bedroom. The sheets were sprawled half off the bed and crumpled jeans and shirts made up most of the floor space. It didn't take much to see that not all the clothes belonged to Nick. Half-smoked cigarettes lay in an ashtray on the bedside table beside a bottle of pills and a pair of handcuffs. A strong stench of aftershave rippled throughout the air.

"He kept his treasures in a box. I wasn't looking for it, but I found it while cleaning. What are the odds that he never got rid of it?" said Lenora to no one in particular. She kicked aside some of the clothes and walked towards a sliding wardrobe door. She rummaged around inside for a few moments.

"Got it," she exclaimed. "Thank God, he's a man of habit." Lenora pulled out a shoebox. She placed it on the bed and removed the lid. Odd bits filled the space inside. Lenora had been right about Nick's past. Red, black and purple underwear were the most prominent attractions, evidence of Nick's triumphs. There were cut-out photos of men, women, and kids—some who Will knew. Lenora searched through the contents, careful to avoid the teeth that she had warned would be in there. She moved something that caught Will's attention. He pushed her hand away and took out a silver pen.

"The fucker took my pen. It was my mother's before she died. I thought I had lost it fifteen years ago," he said, slowly twisting it to reveal the tip.

"I told you. Anything that's not nailed down is his."

Will pocketed the pen and stepped back. "There's nothing to suggest he killed the Spark boys."

"What about this?" asked Lenora, holding up an old wristwatch. She flipped it over, "Alex, happy eighteenth, love from Mom and Dad," she read.

Will crouched to her level and took the watch. "Melanie said that the watch was missing from the body. It was a present." He ran the strap through his fingers, remembering what he had seen in Melanie's memories. Alex had been wearing it that night.

"Do you believe me now?" said Lenora.

Will didn't take his eyes off the watch. "I remember now. He hated this watch, said it was a clear sign of favoritism from his parents."

"When you compare it to what his brothers wore, you can see why."

Will sniffed and shook his eyes away from the watch. "It may be purely circumstantial."

"Come off it," said Lenora, snatching the watch back. "You just don't want to believe me because you know that we should have seen it. Had we been more attentive, these murders may not have happened."

"I'm looking at this with a logical mind. Don't try to bias my thinking," replied Will. Lenora had a way of getting into his head and manipulating his thoughts. In the past, he had let her, perhaps even *hoped* that she would. Not now. This was far more important than their relationship—or lack thereof.

"My situation allows me to know more about Nick than you ever have. It makes me the best person for this job. You were better friends with Alex than I was. Maybe you should have fucking asked him. He had issues, Will. You must have been blind if you didn't see it."

"A child could have better judgment than you right now," said Will. He lowered his voice, "Look, I understand that Nick hurt you and I want him to be punished for it, but this is more than a means to your revenge. There are families that will never be whole again and if we give this to the police, they will lock Nick up just so they can say that they have solved the crime. It would be a disservice to those families if we aren't sure. It would be a disservice to Alex."

"Then what do you propose?"

"We need to find Nick."

Lenora threw up her hands. "And then what? He's not going to confess to murder."

"I have other methods," said Will, feeling inside his pocket for the rewind; he hadn't used it in a while. The realization made him agitated.

"You know that makes you sound like a dominatrix, right?" asked Lenora.

"Come on," replied Will, turning to leave. He swore loudly. His movement had taken him within inches of a figure. Nick was standing in the doorway, dressed in a coat and scarf.

"What the fuck are you doing here?" he said. His shock was apparent from the deathly pallor of his cheeks and his hand clamped onto the door frame. Even with his position, Will could still see his arms vibrating with what he could only assume was a deep rage. He struggled to keep his eyes on Lenora, and Will could see that every time he looked at her, he was staring straight at her scar.

"Surprised to see me?" said Lenora. It struck Will that despite her height, she seemed to tower over her old fiancé. "You're in shit up to your head, Nick," she said, dangling the gold wristwatch in front of him in triumphant glee. Nick looked at the watch and then at the box, still open on the bed.

"You… You went through my things," he stuttered.

"Not your things. The possessions of half the inhabitants of Hollyhead and wherever else you have been," said Lenora, taking a handful of scrap from the box and slowly dropping it onto the floor. "I bet you thought I was dead."

"No. I knew you would be out there somewhere, skulking around like a diseased rat. I'm just surprised that you didn't return sooner," said Nick. Will felt like he had been absorbed into the furniture, watching a domestic argument taken from many years prior.

"Why do you have Alex's watch, Nick?" said Will.

Nick turned to face him. "That watch belongs to me."

"It has his name engraved on the face, you moron."

Nick rubbed the back of his head. "It belonged to him a long time ago. I took it long before he died."

"Bullshit," said Lenora.

"Lenora says that you followed Alex from the fairground. It is likely that you were the last person to see him alive," said Will. "And no more lies. We will go to the police if we don't believe your story."

"This is my house. I don't take orders in my own property," said Nick, in an almost animalistic snarl.

"You're going to start," replied Lenora, taking a step forward. Her stare was full of raw hatred that must have boiled away for the last decade.

"Why didn't you tell the police?" said Will.

Nick rubbed his forehead; his hands were constantly switching between his head and his neck. "There's nothing to tell. I found it."

"Found it where?" pressed Will.

"Come on Will, he didn't just find it," said Lenora. She turned back to Nick. "You ripped it from his mangled body after you stretched his neck and dressed him up in that fucking costume."

"Alex was a good friend to me until he went crazy. I never wanted him dead. I'm not a killer."

Lenora pointed to her scar, "you could have fooled me."

"I believe you, Nick. We need you to tell us what happened. The police will have a field day with this," said Will, nodding towards the watch. "If not, then I'm sure Lenora would love to spend a little time *reminiscing*."

Nick took one look at Lenora and broke down. "Fine. Yes, I followed him. It was just the two of them—Alex and the young kid. After Lenora left, I was angry. Alex owed me money. You know he was a user, well he got his stuff from me. He started off with marijuana; you can find it pretty easily so there were options and I had to lower my prices. Then he told me he wanted to try something with more of a kick. I had a contact who could get me acid, so I let him try it out. The fucker went and got hooked," he said. His eyes wouldn't meet theirs, instead darting around the room, most likely looking for a getaway route. "I had him coming to me every day trying to get another fix. Enough for me to be able to increase my prices. Course, then he can't pay on time. I let it slide the first couple of times, us being mates and all, but before long, the guy owed me a lot.

I'm talking hundreds, if not more. If I wasn't paying my supplier on time, I would have had my balls clamped. So I turned to assets. That's why I took that," he said, pointing to the watch. "I was planning to sell it, but after what happened, I knew I'd be an idiot to try and get money for it."

"When did you take it?"

Nick buried his face in his hands. "The night he died," he said in a whisper.

"You killed him, didn't you?" said Lenora. "You followed him from the fair and found him, probably saw red and beat him to the floor."

"I swear I didn't," protested Nick. Will almost felt bad for his old friend. The man who had been so composed and arrogant in their first reunion had crumbled into a suckling infant.

"He was with his little brother," added Will.

Nick nodded. "They must have been walking home. I'd had a drink that night and wanted to have it out with him about the money. It's not my fault. After I caught up with them Alex got violent with me. He said that what I'd supplied him with was some stepped-on crap. His kid brother didn't know what was going on, of course. He just watched me. Alex threw some punches but I pinned him and took his watch telling him that we were straight. He struggled and so I punched him in the face and gave him that bruise. That was all. I swear that when I left him, he was completely alive. Same goes for his brother. I admit that I have issues, but murder never crossed my mind that night."

"Did you see anyone or sense anything weird? Chances are that you were the last person to see them alive."

Will could see that Nick was trying hard to recall the events of that night. His eyes were darting across the room as if the memories were swimming in front of him and he was trying to pick out the correct one. "There was something," he eventually said. "I have never understood it. Alex's punches dropped like he was being weighed down by bricks and he was slurring his words. He was mumbling about seeing a doctor. I couldn't take him to a hospital, could I? His brother was the same, you know. As I walked away, Alex was on the ground trying to pull his face from the dirt and his little brother was kinda swaying. The acid had messed him up, but he should have been able to get in a punch or two. Looking back, I would say he was on something that fucked him up inside."

"They were drugged. It must have happened while they were all at the fair. That's why Alex didn't put up a fight."

"Right! That must be it," said Nick, clawing at his opportunity to step out of the limelight. "It wasn't me!"

Will twitched. There it was again, the itch at the back of his mind. He reached into his pocket. Nick was still reeling on the floor, and Will stuck out his hand to help him up. Although his face was contorted with anger, Nick accepted. The surprise on his face was clear when, instead of warm flesh, he felt smooth metal. Will gripped his hand tight. "I need to see what happened that night. Think of when you saw Alex Spark."

"Will, what are you doing?" said Lenora.

Nick turned his attention to her. He tried to pull his hand away, but it was too late. His pupils dilated and Will was thrust into the memories of his childhood friend. It felt different this time. The memory was distracted. Will could already tell that what he was about to see was not what he had intended.

*

"I would kill her," said Nick, knocking back the rest of his beer and wiping his mouth. "What kind of man would I be if I let her go wandering off with another guy?" he raised a finger at Will. "I'd be a coward. Plain and simple."

Will nodded drunkenly, his head balanced on his hand. Nick had never seen him drink so much; what had started out as a small catch-up had resulted in the pair being thrown out of the bar. The owner was a friend and had agreed to let them buy a few rounds, despite them being too young. What he didn't know was that the pair had been filling their glasses again when his back was turned. After stumbling around the streets of Hollyhead for what felt like a lifetime, they had found a shop, stolen a six pack, and fallen onto a bench. He didn't know why Will had suddenly embraced alcohol. For the last few years, he had refused to touch the stuff. Metlocke always had been a freak.

"I don't even want the fucking baby. Can you really see me as a father?"

Will tilted his head. "I don't know. Don't think it's something anyone is ready for. Just happens," he said in a thick, dull voice.

Nick thought of Lenora. Six months pregnant and it was showing. The only way he'd managed to get through the last half a year was his frequent visits to the red-light part of town. That and his meetings with the waitress from Ed's diner. What Lenora didn't know wouldn't hurt her. He thought of holding the baby. Lenora would be all proud and wave it around like a winning racing ticket. Sleepless nights and constant crying. It sent a wave of sickness over him. No. He had hardly started his own life yet. He wasn't going to be tied down by a woman and a kid. There was far more out there. He didn't want to end up like Will. He felt sure that Will would never leave Hollyhead. Apart from a knack for writing, Will was useless. His reciting of Poe and Hardy had grown old by ninth grade, and his business knowledge could be bettered by a five-year-old. If there was one thing that Nick was sure of, it was that Will would die here. One way or another.

"You've always had a thing for her," said Nick.

Will must have swallowed his drink wrong because he started spluttering. "No. She's your fiancé."

"She's the only girl you speak to. You haven't even had a girlfriend yet, right?"

"She's the only one worth speaking to and no, I'm just not into girls yet, it's not something I care about."

Nick laughed, "Ah, maybe you're right. She's never shown any interest in you. I think she finds you pretty boring actually."

Nick was pleased with the uncomfortable silence that followed. He had seen Will and Lenora together. The truth was that he wasn't certain that there wasn't chemistry between them. After leaving high school, Will had gone to Harvard. Lenora had the same ambition—in many ways she was more intelligent than Will, she just kept quiet about it. She didn't need to parade it around. That's what it felt like. Will and Alex would compare grades after every exam, not bothering to ask Nick what he had got since they knew he would be near the bottom of the class. Lenora would beat everyone else; she didn't need to compare. Nick had persuaded her to postpone college for a few years and then she told him that she was expecting. Maybe he should have just shipped her off with Will. He spat on the ground; just the idea caused a spike of hatred to rise within him. For both of them. How nice it must be for Will, living alone for long periods while his own mother watched him like a hawk.

"Anyhow, you wouldn't understand. A woman has gotta show respect. What kind of fiancé would I be if I let her go and talk to other guys?" said Nick.

"You sound like you've put some thought into this."

"I have to. Property is property. You keep a gun to protect your home; you keep a girl on a leash and she gives respect."

"Hmm, maybe. Well, we'd better get going. Busy day tomorrow," Will said, rising from the bench. Nick watched as Will stumbled a few steps from the bench, looking as though he might knock his teeth into the floor. Then Will clutched his stomach and bent double before unleashing a torrent of brown vomit onto the concrete.

"Can't even hack it. Guess that's another thing you have to learn—you won't find that out in a book," sniggered Nick, watching as Will wiped his mouth and rummaged in his pocket. He produced a set of keys.

"Need a lift?" he asked, still spitting remnants of his stomach lining onto the floor.

"Does the Pope like touching kids?" said Nick.

With that, the pair walked over to Will's car. A red Sedan parked almost diagonally to the curb. Will unlocked it and stepped in. Nick collapsed onto the seat. Scattered in the footwell were various paperbacks, mixed with what looked like Will's own writing. Poetry and the start of a story. And what was that smell?

"Do you miss him?"

Nick pulled his attention from the smell towards Will, who was glancing at him as he drove. "Who?"

"Alex."

"He was a good mate. Whatever waits for us at the end of all this can't be worse than Hollyhead anyway."

"I can't help but feel like we should be doing something. We haven't even met his parents. I mean, he was *murdered*. Shouldn't we be trying to find his killer? Bring him some justice?"

"If the police haven't found anything, then there's no chance that we will. Just drop it," ordered Nick, ending the conversation. His senses kept focusing on that smell again. Flowery. Some kind of lavender oil mixed with spices. Lenora's perfume... Was it?

Has she been here? Did you make a move on her in the back seat? You sick pervert.

The thought dominated Nick's mind for the ten-minute ride toward home. Towards Lenora.

*

Nick had often heard that a lover is a guiding light. A sanctuary in a rough sea. He could see a light now. It was the light from the bedroom that Lenora had recently turned into a nursery in preparation for the baby. Thank God for Lenora's parents getting them this place. It's only fair, he needed it to cope with her whinging all day.

Will veered the car onto the driveway, almost sending a trashcan flying. He had never been a good driver—God knows how he managed to pass the first time. Nick had taken multiple attempts, having been caught speeding twice.

"I'll see you in. I haven't seen Lenora for a while," slurred Will, practically falling out of the car. Nick exited the other side and walked towards the front door, trying his best to walk straight. Lenora had fixed a knocker on the wood, something from *Disney*. Nick hated it. Before he could open the door, it swung open to reveal his fiancé, hair tied up and draped in a flowery dressing gown.

"Thanks for driving him home," she said to Will, who was just behind Nick's shoulder. Where he always was.

Nick pushed past Lenora and hung his coat up. Their hushed conversation burrowed into his brain like a needle. He caught a glimpse of the climax of their talk.

Was that a wink when she thought his back was turned? She might as well have jumped him. Lenora thanked Will, not bothering to check how drunk the stumbling fool was and shut the door.

177

She turned around, her face pale. "Where have you been?" The words were loaded with worry. He could practically feel the leash tightening around *his* neck.

"I've been out. Will and I were at a bar downtown."

"You didn't think to tell me? A phone call would have been nice, Nick."

How could anyone be so interfering? He never asked her to tell him where she was. Nick had no doubt that she was often with Will. Talking until the sun fell low in the sky and the cold rolled in. He could imagine Will staring at her with his twitchy little eyes. Perhaps she enjoyed it... His eyes raking across her breasts when he thought she wasn't looking. She had always loved attention. Will would certainly give her that. Sometimes he was sure that the bastard wanted them to break up. Then he would snake his way between them, forcing them apart so that he could chastise her with words stolen from another writer. Impure words to go with his impure thoughts.

"Did Will not tell you? I assumed he would, judging by the amount of time you spend together—*talking*. What else do you get up to?"

"Why would he tell me? You know I find him a pain in the ass. He's your friend, Nick. I don't get one without the other," she said, gently pressing her stomach. "I need to get some rest and you need to sleep off the booze."

Lenora held out her hand for Nick to take. He took a step back.

"If you don't like Will, why don't you tell him?" he spat, walking over to the phone and dialing. "All you have to do is call. Prove it to me."

Lenora's face lowered in confusion. "I'm not going to do that. It won't be long until he goes off to college again and we'll be alone. I doubt he's home yet anyway."

Nick sneered. He pulled her closer with one hand. The fine tendons in her neck stretched as she flinched to his touch.

"Don't touch me! You're drunk. Sleep it off and we will talk about this in the morning," she said, pulling herself away from him. She was trying to sound authoritative; it was cute really. Nick grabbed her wrist with one hand in such a way that he was sure it would break if she moved the wrong way.

"We're going to talk about it now."

Lenora stopped struggling and met his eyes. "I am tired. Let go of me."

Nick pushed her away, causing her to stumble into the wall; she twisted to the side to avoid hitting it front-on with her pregnant belly. She shouted something in response, but Nick didn't listen. He could hear his breathing rattling around in his chest, like a coil of thick chains. It came out of his nose in bursts to go with the words still swimming about the room. He wiped his forehead. It came away wet, the stench of booze filling his nostrils. He raised one hand at Lenora.

"You and him! What has he got that I haven't? I'm going to make more money than that asshole could even imagine." A thought pushed through the membrane of alcohol in his mind and flashed in his head. "Is the baby even mine?"

Lenora was close to tears. "Of course it is! I want to have a future with you. Not with Will. Not with anyone else. I chose you a long time ago and I will always keep choosing you," she tried to hold his arm, but he pushed her away, letting her fall into a heap on the chocolate brown rug they had chosen together only the week before.

"You're lying. I've seen you!" said Nick.

"I don't know what you think you've seen, but I have never and will never be with Will Metlocke."

Nick shook his head, trying to push away the sentence before the words wormed into his head. It felt as though someone else was controlling his body. The surrounding walls were closing in, threatening to squeeze the life from him. Pushing Lenora out of the way, he staggered into the kitchen. Nick kicked over a chair and proceeded towards the cutlery drawer. There was a pounding sensation inside his head, and he put a hand to his temple.

Cheating whore, she'll do it again and again and again.

He didn't notice that he was holding a knife until he left the room. An ugly-looking blade welded to a wooden handle. Just the feel of it in his hands made him calm. His hands had stopped shaking and his mind seemed to clear of drink. How could something so small hold so much power?

He returned to the lounge to find Lenora sitting down, holding her bump. A bead of sweat was rolling down her face, mixing into the tears that were streaming from her puffy, reddened eyes. Her chest was rising and falling at an alarming rate and she made a noise like a terrified animal when she saw him.

Good, she should be scared.

Lenora held up her hands. "Nick, please put the knife down. Please. You're scaring the shit out of me."

"We can't keep going like this. I can't trust you. I knew you were a whore before we started dating, but I thought I had stamped that out of you."

"I have been nothing but faithful to you. Can you say the same?" she snapped. Did she really think that this was a situation where she could come out on top?

"As for the baby… I hope it kills you."

With that, Nick brought the knife slashing down, leaving a long scratch of crimson down the face of his fiancé. A mark of his ownership. Lenora's bloodied face twisted into a mess of swirling color and the scene seemed to compress inwards, elongating everything inside. It was ending; the memory was complete.

*

"Get your hands off me, you freak," spat Nick, pulling his hand away as if he had touched something foul. Will couldn't speak. It *had* been his fault. The scar on Lenora's cheek was a testament to *his* own actions. If he had stayed away, then it would never have happened.

Nick crawled backward, staring at the rewind in Will's hand. "The fuck is that?" he said, slowly getting to his feet. The effect of the rewind caused him to stumble.

"You hurt Lenora because you thought we were having an affair?" questioned Will.

"I told you that," said Lenora, grabbing his wrist. Will wrenched his arm away from her.

"Before we arrived at your house, I told you that my relationship with Lenora extended to nothing more than friendship. Did I have to spell it out to you?" he shouted, feeling his veins fill with a cocktail of confusion and hatred.

"Everyone saw you wanted her. Do you really think that I didn't notice how you looked at her? With your writing and poetry, how much of your work was created with her in mind? Nothing about you is original. You have stolen fragments from people you respected all through your life. I looked at you and I saw a weaker version of myself. An immature copy. You wanted Lenora to complete your latest character," said Nick, slowly getting to his feet as his confidence inched toward his old self.

Will swung his foot and caught the side of Nick's jaw, sending him back onto the floor into a bloody slump. So dazed that Will half expected stars to whirl around his head like in those children's cartoons, Nick tried to get to his feet once again. Before Will could stop her, Lenora pulled a knife from her pocket and pounced. She knocked Nick backward onto the bed and held his wrists in one hand. Buried under her weight, he was too stunned to think about getting her off.

"I've been looking forward to this since the day I left," she said. Will took a step forward, but his other foot didn't seem to get the message. He watched, a part of him almost pleased, as Lenora took the knife and pulled it down across Nick's cheek. The gash opened as she went, and after a couple of seconds, beads of blood were running down the side of his face. Lenora stood up, holding the knife in a way that said, '*come near me and I'll gut you.*'

"Come on, Will. Let's go," she ordered.

"I'll do you for assault," shouted Nick, touching his face and gawping when it came away slicked with crimson.

"That won't help you. I'm a ghost, remember?" said Lenora, with a smile that could curdle milk.

*

Will and Lenora exited the house the same way that they had entered. Hollyhead had finally grown silent, and they walked towards the motel without any interruption from other beings, except an encounter with a tortoise-shelled cat who scampered across the street in front of them, chasing one of the many mice that had plagued the town for years. When the microscope was removed, the last month had been little more than a chase between cat and mouse. All that was left to be seen was whether the mouse escaped and who was playing which role.

"I'm convinced that he's lying, but that doesn't matter anymore," said Lenora, pulling a golden chain from her pocket and showing it to Will. The end of the chain presented a large scarlet ruby, surrounded by a cluster of diamonds, each cut with expert precision. "A token from Nick's treasures."

"I think now is a good time to mention that I'm not a jeweler," said Will, although even with his lack of knowledge on the subject, he could tell that the necklace was expensive. He had seen plenty of Hollywood icons displaying them at award ceremonies.

"This belonged to the wife of Jacob Orchard — the famous movie director. Three years ago, this necklace was stolen from his home. Now, who do you think sold that residence to him?" said Lenora, walking with a newfound eagerness.

"You're kidding…"

"If I can't get him on a murder charge, I certainly can on theft."

CHAPTER SIXTEEN:
THE LAKE

It happened in the early hours of Christmas Eve. The cold had picked up, and a light dusting of snow had covered the ground, not enough to cause children to run outside in their masses, but enough to cause a satisfying crunch underfoot.

Over the past few days, the streets of Hollyhead had returned to their bustling highs. Exhausted mothers chased limited edition dolls while being halted at every shop window by over-enthusiastic workers trying to entice the crowd into their shops like sirens from a rock. The motel had put up a cheap tree in the lobby. Wendy claimed it was the most advanced creation of her time, praising its lack of needles or the need to replace it every year.

Will had spent the previous night with Eve. Her presence at the motel had increased and Will quickly grew to feel as though he had known her for years. Her warmth spread through his body and he would have been happy to bathe in it for years to come. They had found an old board of Monopoly in the motel reception and had played until early in the morning. It hadn't taken long for Will to forget all thoughts of Abigail Finsbury and the Spark boys. For a few blissful hours, it had just been them. She left just after eleven and the day consisted of readings of *Grimm's* and phone calls with Lenora. Apparently, she had left Nick's house with more than just the necklace and had finally moved out of the caravan and into a room on the other side of town. The hostility towards Will hadn't faltered, but her spirits were considerably higher after gaining the means to blackmail Nick into anything she could think of. The conversations were brief, and Frank hadn't called to fill in the empty spaces Will found during the days.

Then Christmas Eve arrived, creeping up the way it always does. Insomnia hadn't been an issue that night. Not until the early morning at least. Will woke to the sound of laughing. Not the deep chortle of drunken men returning to their wives after a round of drinking, but instead the laugh of a child. He groaned and dug his head into his pillow. A new kind of venom pulsed through his chest, splintering against his ribcage. The glowing clock on the bedside table told him it had just gone two.

What kind of kids play around this early?

The wind picked up slightly, carrying the sound of light footsteps away from his window. He strained his ears to hear them dying away. Before long, they had escaped into the night after the rustling of leaves and small branches subsided. Whoever it was, they were pushing their way through the undergrowth. Then he sat up. There was only one place a person could be going if they had to wade through the foliage to get there...

As if in reply, he heard a splash. His room was cold enough, even with the small electric heater propped up beside his door, but the lake would be at an entirely new level of freezing. Will jumped from his bed and hauled on his boots. His dressing gown was left sprawled on the floor and he pulled it on. Perhaps he could use it to keep the child warm. After tripping over an upturned piece of carpet at the top of the stairs, he made it to reception. It was deathly quiet, lit up only by an ethereal green glow coming from the neon sign above the desk. Flies buzzed lazily around it, sometimes bumping into the 'WELCOME' letters. Will hit the service bell, causing sharp dings to echo around the entrance. No reply. Wendy must be out for the moment, or maybe the Christmas preparation had sent her into a deep sleep. He ran to the back door and tried the handle—locked. Whoever had fallen into the lake would already be struggling, gulping down mouthfuls of icy water while their muscles screamed in agony.

He tried the window by the door. It opened a few inches, then stopped. Grunting in despair, Will took a chair from reception and swung it towards the glass, hearing a rewarding cracking sound from the pane. Another strike proved sufficient, and the window shattered. He snapped a leg from the bottom, poked out the more threatening shards of glass and clambered out, feeling some missed remains slice into his leg.

By this point, voices thick with sleep came wafting from the stairs. Will ignored them.

He ran out into the dark, praying for some sign of life, however weak. Freezing wind embraced him tightly so he quickened his pace, stumbling across the ice and weeds until he arrived at the mouth of the woodland. Frost had already melted into his socks, causing his feet to go numb with cold. Branches started to thicken as he continued through, a good sign that he was coming to the shore of the lake. The darkness meant that he wasn't prepared for when his foot dropped and was immediately met with a rush of cold water filling his boots. The other leg followed through and landed in the water.

"Kid! Where are you?" he shouted, wading forward, the mud grabbing at his ankles, sucking him down into the sludge. Each time he managed to wrench free, he became weighed down by even more of the lakebed.

No reply came. Despite his struggle, Will held his breath, listening for any sign of the child. A few yards in front, there was a ripple, just visible in the moonlight. He took a gulp of air and dove forwards, far enough into the water to avoid the mud. He thrashed blindly just under the surface, desperately trying to grab onto whatever he could. His lungs were already bursting; every inch of his body was injected with ice. He could just make out reeds and stones on the bottom of the lake, but nothing that he could interpret as human. Until he saw the face. The face of a young boy stretched into a look of horror as water filled his mouth, bubbles spiraling around him as his screams were swamped by mud-saturated water. Will swam towards him, his hand reaching out to pull the kid out, although he wasn't even certain that his minimal amount of strength would be enough to get himself out, let alone the pair of them. He closed his hands around the cloth of the boy's jumper and yanked. The boy ascended a little before Will felt a tug. Looking down, he saw a tangle of weeds snaking around the boy's ankle. The Devil wasn't about to lose this treasure so easily. Will's lungs gave another lurch as he forced his mouth to stay closed. Then the bubbles stopped. The kid's eyes rolled back into his head and his whole body went limp. It seemed that his soul had vacated its shell. Will gave another kick, causing his leg to scream, and felt the weeds tear. Allowing himself a small moment of triumph, Will kicked again, feeling both him and the boy rise further. The surface of the lake was hardly visible, and it was with an oxygen-starved prayer that Will swam upwards until his head broke through the seal of water and he could see shards of moonlight jumping around the ripples he made. Despite the bitter cold of the air, Will swallowed great mouthfuls of life, feeling the fog leave his brain with each inhale. Holding the boy's head above water, the pair swam to shore. With a final burst of effort, Will pushed him onto the bank. Their bodies sunk into the thick mud. Before he could check on the boy, a squabble of voices bounded towards him, accompanied by multiple flashlights blaring into his eyes.

"Mr. Metlocke, whatever have you been doing?" exclaimed Wendy, dressed in a pink spotted dressing gown, her hair assembled into a throng of curlers. Her eyes were full of motherly concern. There were a few murmurs of suspicion and Will pointed to the boy. However, where the boy should have been, there was just empty space. The mud was completely undisturbed. Whoever he had pulled from the lake was gone.

*

The following hour passed in a twisted nightmare. Will's mind had left his body, and he allowed himself to be dragged away from the lake like a lifeless puppet. Reflecting on the recent events, he couldn't shake the feeling that his strings hadn't been his own since he had returned to Hollyhead. Frank and Marty were controlling his movement, and Mayor Stone his focus. There were only two people who genuinely seemed to care. Three if he included Wendy, who had wrapped him almost to the point of suffocation in layers of blankets and settled him onto a cracked leather sofa. It wasn't long before the police came. Even with all the questions coming there was only one thing Will could think about: the boy's mouth being filled with water.

Teddy had arrived soon after the first police cruiser turned up. As soon as a lake had been mentioned, he had broken into a sweat and clasped his hands behind his back to stop them from shaking. His colleagues had gone to sweep the lake for a body, but Teddy had decided to keep Will company.

"Strange time for you to be awake," he said, pouring coffee into a mug and passing it to Will.

Will thanked him and relished in the warmth seeping through the china. "It's my chest. I struggle to sleep. How come you're not helping the others search the lake?"

"You said the boy vanished."

"It was dark. I'm surprised I could see him anyway," said Will, gulping down the coffee. Warmth enveloped his body, a sensation that not even the bundles of blankets had given him. His eyes had lost their sense of fatigue.

"Maybe, but these shoes are new. I'm not ruining them by traipsing through mud just to go and search a lake for someone who you have assured me is not there."

"You believe me then?"

"You've presented me with enough evidence to suggest that you aren't completely insane."

Then Will said what he had been thinking for a long time. "If there wasn't a boy at the bottom of that lake, then it means I'm seeing things. It means that I'm losing my mind."

"There are multiple explanations for what happened tonight. You look like you haven't slept in days and you said yourself that you're on heavy medication. Yes, maybe all you saw tonight was a hallucination, but until you start talking to trees, I'm going to trust your judgment." He smiled and looked at the floor. "I know what it means to lose yourself. Honestly, I am starting to see it in you, pal."

"What do you mean?"

Teddy took a silver flask from his jacket, worn and scratched from evident repeated use, and took a drink. "I'm sure you've noticed my reaction tonight," he said, his eyes brimming with concealed memory. "I do not like water. I'm sure someone has come up with a name for it, but I haven't looked. Drinking the damn stuff is about as far as I'll go with it."

"Have you always had this phobia?" asked Will, feeling conscious that his hair was still damp.

"Nah. I used to swim all the time. My Ma called me a dolphin. Dad reckoned it was just because I wanted to see girls in their swimsuits. Then something happened," Teddy sniffed, "I had a son called Nathan. He died."

"Recently?"

"He was born fifteen years ago. The start was a sign of things to come. Gill and I were basically outcasts. Pregnant at seventeen, not to mention she was from a very religious family. We left Boston and headed West, ending up way over in Oregon. Held out for a bit in Salem. Nathan stayed with a friend we had out there while we worked. Gillian managed to find some bar work, and I took my first step into the force."

"What year was this?"

"We first got to Oregon in '68. Left there in '74 and came over here."

"Your parents didn't support you?"

"My Mother sent us some money. I think she was just scared of Dad. He was a cop, too. Didn't quite have the same charm as I do. He was fired when I was twenty-one. Was a bit too heavy-handed with a suspect. The guy ended up in hospital, and Dad ended up back home."

"Have you seen them since?"

Teddy shrugged. "Mom died a few years after. Heart attack apparently. Dad's in the back end of the world somewhere, probably drinking himself into an early grave."

"I'm not close with my father either."

"You should try. We only get one, even if they are crappy. I regret many things, and my relationship with him is one of them," said Teddy. They were interrupted by a knock and Teddy called for them to enter as he hastily tucked his flask back into his pocket. A ragged-looking police officer came through the door, her clothes dripping with rain.

She shook her hands dry and turned to Teddy. "That's a preliminary search of the lake finished. If Mr. Metlocke did see someone in that lake, then they are gone now. We'll check again tomorrow, but it doesn't look likely that we'll find anything."

"No. It's not possible. The boy was almost dead. He must have run away," said Will.

The officer shook her head. "We've done a full search of the premises. No little boy would survive in weather like this."

Will's temper started to rise; his hands were shaking.

"Are you taking any drugs?" said the officer.

"No, I'm not fucking high! I heard the kid out of my window. I knew that he was going towards the lake, so I followed and then I saw him at the bottom. Do you think I jumped in for a quick dip? He was there!" shouted Will.

Before the officer could reply, Teddy gave her a signal, and she left the room, slamming the door behind her. "Cool off buddy. I believe you," he said. He checked over his shoulder to ensure that no one else was in earshot. "Listen, I heard about what happened at the Christmas light switch-on. You were screaming about Abigail Finsbury, right?"

"It's nothing. I'm on a lot of medication."

"Don't dismiss it. The way you're talking, I'm going to take a guess and say that it wasn't the first time you've seen ghosts. Christ, you write about them."

"Fake, all of it."

"I think you saw my boy," said Teddy, leaning so far forward that his ass was almost lifting from the chair.

"What I saw was either an invention of my mind or something supernatural. I've never believed in ghosts, but I cannot deny what I have seen recently. I saw the Spark boys hanging from a barn just after our first conversation and yes, Abigail Finsbury approached me when I switched on the Christmas lights. What makes you think it was your son?"

"Because your story is far too familiar to how he died. There was a lake. We were just there for the day; thought we might take a boat out. The edges of the lake were covered in all that green algae crap. Nathan ran out. I guess he must have thought it was grass or something. Last thing I see is him go under. If I hadn't seen him, then we wouldn't have known that he was in there. Within seconds, the algae covered back over, like it was filling in his grave. I guess we got unlucky—most other parts of the lake led up to some kind of shore, but we were at a section where the path around was higher up." Teddy took in a few ragged breaths.

"You can stop. I don't need to know this."

Teddy swallowed. "No. It feels good. I need to get it out there. I made the mistake of not watching him. As soon as it happened, I jumped in and managed to find him. He was too young to know how to swim. I don't think he saw me; he had his eyes all screwed up. Obviously, I tried getting him out. He must have struggled and twisted the lakebed around him because I couldn't tear out the weeds. People just went about their day. They didn't realize my son was under that water. I must have been splashing around in there for ten minutes before someone came and pulled me out. Took another three men just to stop me from running back in. When it happens, you expect the sky to snap. You think it will all go dark like it's the start of judgment day. The least you hope for is that someone will actually notice." He cleared his voice and took another swig of whatever liquor was in his hip flask. "They needed divers and equipment just to get him out. A month later, I carried his coffin. Tiny little thing it was. It's not right. During the entire funeral, my only thought was that it should have been me. A child should never die before their father. It's our job to see them through. After a death, some people go into overdrive. They shop, work, or focus on funeral arrangements. It wasn't like that for us. I can't remember much about the days that followed his death. It's almost embarrassing how much I have tried. My brain has deleted it. It had no right to do that. Trauma is mine and I have a right to hold on to it. I hate myself for having no recall of those days."

"It wasn't your fault, Ted," said Will, all of his own problems forgotten. "People have let kids wander off and the worst that happens is that they get lost for a few hours. It's not like you were letting him play in traffic. As for trauma, some things are just too much for the mind to carry."

Teddy shook his head. "It *was* my fault. For years I denied it, but if I want to heal, then I must accept the truth. It's the only way. The consequences of that day will follow me to the grave and it is all that I deserve. You never get over losing a child. After a while, you're so used to hiding it that it doesn't take effort anymore. We grow around our grief; it never lessens."

Will couldn't speak. He had never pictured himself having children. Disconnection was the only emotion he had ever attached to the idea. The emotions Teddy was displaying felt distinctly foreign and all Will could do was sit with his hands folded in his lap as Teddy poured his grief into the air for them both to breathe in like heavy fumes.

Will didn't want to tell him, but he was certain that the boy he had seen under the water *had* been Nathan Ludlow. The ghosts were getting closer. Soon they would be upon him.

*

Teddy had left the motel along with a troop of bedraggled officers, all muttering about how the trip had been a waste of time. A sharp retort from the detective shut them up. Wendy had offered to make Will a hot cocoa, but he had declined. After giving his apologies, he walked back to his room and put on his coat. His mind was telling him to see Frank. His lungs had returned to their aching state. The pain was manageable, and with the help of a few more pills from Wendy, low enough to ignore. He hauled himself into a cab and made the short journey back to his father.

*

Will traipsed towards the front door, but it opened before he could knock. Frank stood in the doorway, dressed in blue pinstripe pajamas beneath a black dressing gown. His hands fumbled around the cord that sat above his waist.

"What could be so urgent that you visit now? Is there a development on the case?" he croaked, squinting at his son.

"No. I just need someone to talk to," said Will. For a moment, Frank looked confused, as if his son had spoken a different language. Then again, Frank was fluent in over five.

"You had better come in then."

Within the following ten minutes, Frank had set a roaring fire and Will felt warmth like he hadn't experienced in weeks. The pair sat in silence. Will's mind still hadn't returned from the bottom of the lake.

"You're biting your nails again," said Frank.

Will hadn't noticed. He shoved his hands in his pockets. "There was an accident at the motel," he began, his throat dry.

"What kind of accident? No one was injured, I hope."

Will shook his head, "well I don't know. It was said that a boy fell into the lake."

Frank's posture faltered. "At this time of night? He must have frozen. Was he found?"

"No. When the police arrived, they couldn't find any sign of him anywhere. They searched the entire area."

"That puts it to rest then. Either the boy was fine and climbed out, probably managing to run back home and get into a hot bath, or he never fell in. Who came up with the story? Some drunk, I have no doubt."

"It was me. I heard him."

Frank sat back in his chair, his eyes narrowing towards his son. "You heard him?"

"I rescued him from the lake. He was tangled in reeds and I had to pull him out," Will's chest seemed to tighten. "Only… only when we got to the bank, he was gone."

"And no one else saw this?"

"No. I was alone, but for the boy."

Frank rose from his seat and walked slowly towards his son; he placed his hand on Will's shoulder. "I should never have asked you to take on such a case. I should have acknowledged that the material we cover is sensitive. My god, sometimes I feel I am so immune to death that I no longer understand what it is to be human. If you have started hallucinating, then I fear it has already gone on too long."

"I don't think I am hallucinating. I think I am seeing the paranormal."

Frank pulled his hand away as if he had touched a hot stove. "The paranormal? Pure fantasy from your books," he said with an uneasy laugh.

Will stood. "It's not fantasy, Dad. It's the only explanation."

"I think you will find that human psychology is a far more realistic and logical theory than ghosts and demons."

"The boy was Teddy Ludlow's son and only last week I saw the Spark boys hanging inside an abandoned barn on the edge of town."

Frank's face was tinged with blood. "Another hallucination! Nothing more. If you continue telling yourself these fantasies, then they shall only continue."

"They're not fantasies. They are real!" said Will.

Frank raised a hand as if to slap him but stopped mere inches from his face. Will's breathing had become panicked and he could see the anger in his old man's eyes. Anger that had been tucked away for many years.

"Get out. Get out and don't come back until you have some worthwhile news."

"What? I came here to talk to you… because I *need* you."

"*I said get out!*" roared Frank, slamming his fists down on either side of Will. He took a step back, the veins in his head throbbing and his hands curled. Will stood up, refusing to look his father in the eye. Having reached the door, he stopped and took a small parcel wrapped up in a bundle of brown paper packaging from his jacket pocket before placing it on the arm of the sofa.

"I got this for you. Merry Christmas," he said. Frank didn't turn around. His frame shook as he breathed composure back into his body. Will gave it a second and then left, slamming the door behind him. He turned his collar up against the wind and retreated down the path. How could his own father turn him away at such a time? And why had the mere mention of ghosts ignited an anger in Frank that Will had never seen before?

CHAPTER SEVENTEEN: DRIVING HOME FOR CHRISTMAS

Will had seen his fair share of shitty Christmases but waking up in a cheap motel to the sound of an argument turned violent had to be up there. Repeated thumping on the walls and the unmistakable sound of a slap on bare flesh was followed by the voice of the woman that Will had seen a few days prior, back then drunk as a teenager after prom. She flounced from the room, carrying skinny heels, and made her way down the stairs toward the lobby. Halfway down, the door opened again and the man she had accompanied followed, still doing up the fly on his jeans. They escaped from Will's gaze and he decided to get dressed.

He had spent Christmas Eve in isolation. The events of the night had left his body aching and it seemed he couldn't go more than a few minutes without letting out a hacking cough that left him weak and spitting into the wash basin. Wendy had knocked three times during the day, and he had tried his best to ignore her. He had never known a motel manager to be so interfering. Night had crept up faster than he had expected, and his body finally allowed him some rest.

Although the morning hadn't started well, the rest of the day looked bright. Eve didn't have any family in Hollyhead and hadn't yet made any real friends at the hospital. She had been given an early shift, allowing Will to see her after she finished. That gave him the morning to read through some more of *Grimm's*. A foolish thought had come to him when he opened the book; the idea that Frank would be open to host Christmas. He didn't even know if Frank celebrated it anymore; his house had shown no indication that festive cheer was on the cards. When Will was younger, he didn't have the thrill of a visit from Santa. Sure, Molly had sometimes left him a few new pairs of socks, but it was pretty obvious that she had taken some of her husbands the night before. Occasionally, he would find another gift under the tree from Frank (although he assumed it was really Marty who placed it there). Will still appreciated the thought. Then he went away, and the presents stopped. It always stops as you get older.

His melancholy dissipated throughout the morning. He took a brief walk towards the river and for once a crisp new light covered the town. A young boy whizzed around a parking lot on a gleaming red bicycle, his father holding a set of stabilizers and running to ensure the boy didn't stray too close to the road. Sat on a bench facing out onto the fields beyond, an old couple were reading dog-eared books. The wife's giggle seemed younger than her age and as she flicked through the pages, her husband put his arm around her, taking a break from his own novel and finding the time to smoke. The sight both raised and dampened Will's spirit. That's the thing about Christmas. Its joy is unmatched, and its warmth is infectious. As much as he tried to renounce it, Hollyhead on Christmas morning looked like something from a postcard. A perfect snapshot of a memory that allows you to ignore the bigger picture.

*

Will returned to the motel around midday and climbed the steps up to his room. He was surprised to see that Eve was waiting at the door, this time wearing a woolly hat and gloves. "I thought I wasn't seeing you until later," he said, feeling self-conscious. The walk had been cold, and he had forgotten to take a tissue. He tried not to sniff.

"It's been a quiet morning; they said I wasn't needed," said Eve, hugging him tightly. "Let's go in. It's freezing."

Will obliged and opened the door to platters of food stacked high on a small table that hadn't been there before he left, along with a new chair. Roasted potatoes were steaming on a china plate, a large roast turkey lay in the center accompanied by stuffing and every color of vegetable. By its side, a pot brimming with mashed potato was covered in butter, and a jug of gravy sat ready to be poured. Below the food was a tablecloth, decorated in golden stars across a burgundy fabric.

"Eve… You didn't have to do this," said Will, grinning from ear to ear.

She put her chin on his shoulder from behind. "It's Christmas! I figured we could spend it in a better way than watching crappy movies."

"We could have gone somewhere, this room is hardly the Ritz," said Will, entering the room and taking in a deep inhale, his senses jumping around from one smell to the next. He pulled out a chair for Eve before sitting down opposite.

After a comfortable absence of chat, filled only with comments on the quality of the food, the conversation quickly turned to high school antics and old flames. "When I was seventeen, I asked a girl named Amy Friedman to senior prom. I didn't even like her; I just figured that I would look like a freak if I turned up alone. Then she turned me down anyway. I ended up tagging along with my friends Lenora and Nick," said Will, helping himself to another roast potato.

"Why did she reject you?"

"I don't think she needed a reason. Throughout high school, I kept myself to myself and I think she received a better offer. Can't blame her really. Most of the guys came up with romantic ways to ask and I just passed her a note in English class. Still, I got the last laugh. I got her name wrong in one of my books."

Eve laughed. "On purpose?"

"On purpose. After eight years, I was still trying to get the last word in."

"Taking petty to extreme levels."

"The main reason I'm well known is because of my pettiness. It's one of few consistent parts of who I am. Everything else changed."

"How do you mean?"

"I was passionate about writing. Still am, I guess. Throughout my childhood, I wrote anything I could. Cowboys meeting Vikings, time travelers with long coats and wacky accessories. Sure, the stories started out as thousand-word crapheaps, but I got a taste for it and had a bit of success in some literary mags. I had no interest in becoming famous for years; as far as I was concerned, just getting published was success enough. Then I had some good luck," he said, patting his pocket to check that the rewind was still by his side. "Or bad luck, depending on how you see it. People believed I was psychic and I could write about their experiences talking to their deceased. I tried to incorporate ghost stories as well, just to really pump for every cent I could. Writing those fraudulent embarrassments didn't sustain me. Each one made me want to throw myself off a cliff."

"Why continue writing them?"

The lid had been screwed off and words spilled from his lips. He had fallen into a state of ease that he hadn't felt in a long time. There was no thought of the murders or the ghosts. Frank had completely left his mind. Now, it was him and Eve, and there was nothing else worth noting. "Even as a kid, I felt like I didn't deserve anything. If I did well on a test, then it was because the questions were easy. I passed my driving exam first time, but the roads must have been unusually quiet, and I got an easy route. A part of me believed that the only way people would find me interesting was if I was famous. I needed hundreds of stories, it didn't matter if they were true or not. If they weren't in awe of who I was, then I might as well have not been in the room.

"Then, when I got my book deal, I went straight to LA and spent a little time in London on the side. My name became recognizable, yet I couldn't shake the feeling. One night, I was sitting with a couple of actors and their agents and I realized that everything that was being said was fake. There were these big Hollywood stars dating and in the public eye, they were an iconic pair. Girls wanted to be with him, and guys wanted to be with her. We were in a penthouse apartment together and for the four hours I was there, they didn't say a word to one another. Her arm was practically attached to another author, despite him being twice her age, and he was in a side-room nose deep in snow. And that's OK. Their private lives aren't our business, but as soon as we left the apartment to drive to an uptown bar, they were back together. They were living a lie, and they didn't even care. Then there's me. It's like I only know who I am when I know who others want me to be."

"Did you not expect it to be like that? Celebrities are normal people. They have the same flaws and the same agendas. All that's different is that they have more photos in the papers."

He hadn't noticed his hand on top of Eve's, their fingers intertwined like vines around an infant tree. Her skin ran soft but blemished and he traced his fingertips across the bones that assembled into her fingers.

"I thought that something was wrong with me, like my brain's processing was faulty. Acceptance is something that I thought was earned, and it seemed that I hadn't done enough to warrant it from my peers."

"Perhaps you're just not a good enough actor to pretend to be someone you're not for so long," replied Eve.

A knock at the door pulled them from their conversation.

Wendy poked her head inside, her giraffe-like neck allowing her to do so. "Enjoying your food, Mr. Metlocke?" she asked, not even bothering to address Eve.

"Wendy, I don't think it's normal for a motel owner to keep checking up on their guests," said Will, trying his best not to tell her to buzz off back to reception.

"Just making sure you're not dropping food on my floor. I'll add it to your bill if I find anything," she said, pointing to the carpet that was already so stained that it was impossible to tell what the original color had been.

"We won't," said Will, now standing and gently pushing Wendy out of the doorway. She gave him a confused look as her face disappeared. "Sorry," he said, sitting down again, "I don't know how she still gets guests. She didn't even say hello to you."

"Maybe she's just jealous that you're eating with me rather than with her?" said Eve, pushing her plate away. "I don't know how you're still eating. There's nothing to you."

Will had a sudden urge to tell her about his cancer. The thought of her ending things kept his mouth shut. "It all goes to my thighs," he said. Eve nodded with an almost-knowing speed and smoothed down her skirt.

"When are you planning to tell me you're ill?" she asked, now giving Will no shelter from her stare.

A thousand lies and excuses flashed before him. He sighed—there was no point in being dishonest now. "It's not that bad," he said.

"I'm a nurse. I can tell when something is wrong. Hiding it suggests that it's either something embarrassing or life-threatening. The fact that you haven't been rushing to the toilet every five minutes suggests life-threatening. Your cough, painkillers, and weight suggest cancer," she said as if performing a full diagnosis in a doctor's office. "But hey, a medical degree doesn't mean so much anyway, right?"

"Lung cancer. Still stage one last time I checked."

"Not in your lymph nodes yet then."

"Not yet."

"And you're obviously not being treated with chemotherapy. Was radiotherapy an option?"

"Actually, I've decided not to have treatment."

"That's very common. I would say a little less than a quarter of the patients I have seen refused at first. Doctors have given you your options and you've chosen one of the various paths."

"No. Don't talk to me like I'm a patient."

"You want my emotion to bias my opinion?"

Will shrugged. "I'd rather just end the conversation and move on to something more interesting, like how many of these potatoes can I fit in my mouth without choking. You're not my wife, hell you're not even my girlfriend. Still, I think you're one of the few in my life whose feelings are something I will actually take into consideration."

"You should have treatment," said Eve, bluntly.

"Why?"

"I don't want you to die. I know that makes me selfish, but I don't care. Our futures may not be entwined. That's life. If you go down this path, it means that our fate is already decided. You could get older and have a wife, kids, or grandkids even. I may not have a role in your future, but someone else may not have had the pleasure of meeting you yet. Life is a lot more than Hollyhead."

"I wouldn't mind it if you *were* my future, Eve. In fact, I think that might make life worth it. And yes, I know we have only just met." He sighed. Eve's expression was enough to break his armor. "I'm willing to give that chance a go. I'm not saying that I will have treatment, just that I will consider it."

"Thank you," replied Eve. Then her eyes lost their normal sparkle, and she started playing with her food. "There's something I should tell you as well. We don't want to have secrets straight away."

Will turned to look out the window. "There's not a husband waiting for me, right?" he said, grinning.

Eve didn't laugh. "No, nothing like that," she said, one hand fluttering from the table to her wrists. "Don't freak out," she continued, rolling up the sleeves of her jumper. She presented her arms. Her wrists were covered in dozens of scars. Most were horizontal, but a few were slashed vertically down. The skin had tried its best to heal over, leaving her with ridges slightly darker than her complexion.

"It started when I was fourteen. Issues at school and with my family spurred it on. There was so much going on inside my head, I couldn't get out. Cutting helped. Although I know it couldn't have done, all the stuff inside my head seemed to lessen as if I were bleeding all of them out as well. Eventually, I became numb to it all," she breathed in and straightened up. "It was in my past and I have moved on. I promised myself that I wouldn't forget what it felt like. My past doesn't shame me. It's a part of me I embrace and carry with me," then she looked away. "Sometimes I see a knife and I want to feel it again. Nothing scares me as much as that thought."

Will reached out his hand and held her wrists gently. "They're a sign that the world tried to take you on, and you beat it. Think of them like little league trophies," he said, dragging one finger along a scar. It had taken her a lot to talk about her past, and her shaking hand steadied with his touch.

"Actually, don't think of them like that. It's not one of my best analogies." And at that moment, he made a decision. Having wiped his mouth with a napkin, he stood. "You've shared your fear with me. I want to share mine with you," he said. Eve unconsciously pulled down the sleeves of her jumper again. "Do you fancy a walk?"

*

Revelation wasn't on Will's mind as he walked down the derelict secondary road, the food still sloshing around in his stomach. Eve had questioned his motive as they progressed through the late evening shadows until he reached the familiar sight of the hanging gate and the moss-covered walls that echoed so much of his childhood.

"And here is *mi casa*," he said.

"It's a bit shit," commented Eve, scrunching her nose at the crumbling exterior. Will nodded his agreement. The house looked deserted; either that or Frank had drunk himself to sleep. Frank's car was outside the gate, the dry ground underneath telling that it hadn't been driven for a long time. Marty must cart him around Hollyhead, a taxi driver paid only in shared history.

"If I remember correctly…" said Will. He dislodged a brick from the right-hand side of the door and slid it out, along with years' worth of cobwebs and dust. Reaching in the gap, he groped around inside before pulling out the key he had kept there all those years ago. "Now let's just hope that he hasn't had the locks changed," he said, placing the brick back in its position. Sure enough, the lock clicked, and he crept inside. The house was a nest of darkness, and he walked in. Keys were hanging from hooks by the door and Will grabbed a pair that had a little tag showing a Mustang logo. He left the house and closed the door, pushing the handle down to make as little sound as possible. Eve hadn't followed and remained standing in the front yard.

"Are you going to tell me what's going on yet?" she asked, rubbing her arms to keep warm.

"I want to take you for a spin."

"You haven't driven in years," she said, nervously eyeing the rusting car.

She remembers more about me than I even remember telling her, thought Will. *She's a keeper.*

"I know, but I need to try again." He rammed the key into the door and twisted. With apprehension, Eve entered the other side. The car smelt like a book that hadn't been opened for years and Will saw dust spurt from the nylon as he sat down.

"Do you remember how to get it going?"

"I'm assuming you mean the car?" said Will. Eve rolled her eyes. "Yes, I think I can get that far."

Frank's car hadn't been driven recently. The spluttering before the kick was evidence of that. Will switched on the headlights, illuminating the bushes opposite with a dirty yellow haze.

"Your Dad drives stick?" said Eve, noticing the gearstick.

"Always has. He says automatic isn't proper driving," in response to Eve's confused face, Will added: "I don't know either; he's a weird guy."

"Let's get the bite…" said Eve, shivering. The heating was down.

Will pressed in the clutch and shifted the engine into first. "Getting the bite," he said, his teeth clamped down on his tongue. A small jolt indicated the car was raring to go.

"Now just go gentle. Don't go shooting off," said Eve, bracing slightly. Will nodded and slowly lifted his left foot. The car didn't stall, instead, it lurched, causing the pair to jump forward. Will managed to hit the brakes just before they went into the bushes.

Eve started laughing, "I said gently; just relax. Try again."

Will nodded, already feeling his collar sticking to his neck. He shoved the car into reverse and this time; the car rolled back without a hitch. When the car had room to turn, he put it back into first and trundled along the path, not yet daring to push the little dial past ten.

"How are you doing?" asked Eve, still not brave enough to keep her eyes off the road in front. One of her hands was gripped on her grab handle.

"Getting there," Will replied. He turned the car onto another secondary road, narrowly avoiding a grassy verge. It was coming back to him. The effortless changing of gears and the feel of the wheel beneath his fingers. He channeled his breaths with the rise and fall of the revolutions. Once his mind had settled, one thought was rolling around in his head.

I'm enjoying this…

The soft vibrations of the gas under his foot felt like the gentle purr of a kitten and he pressed further until he could hear the engine start to hum. He shifted into the next gear and listened for the falter of the engine.

"Are you going to tell me what this is all about?" asked Eve.

Will tightened his fingers around the wheel. "I haven't driven since I was a teenager. Part of why I spent so much time in cities was because I could hop on the subway or get a cab with no trouble."

"I'm guessing something bad happened."

"Almost. Something bad *almost* happened. Alcoholism is a word that is tossed around a lot these days. I guess it could apply to the younger me. That kid did a lot of dumb things. For most of my life, I've been a complete moron. One night I made three big mistakes. I listened to my friend tell me he would kill his wife and did nothing—mistake number one. I dropped that friend at his house where he proceeded to beat her—mistake number two. Then I was driving home completely blind drunk," said Will, taking a sharp breath between sentences. "I don't know exactly what happened. One minute I was driving fine and the next I had driven straight into a bus stop. Completely totaled my car."

"Was anyone hurt?"

"Thankfully, no. The difference between that and a yes was two minutes. Two minutes before I crashed, a group of teenage girls was waiting at the stop, coming back from a big party out in the Holmes house on the South side. The way I see it, those two minutes saved their lives. What if the bus was delayed? What if they left the party five minutes later and missed it? All I know for sure is that some asshole drank himself into oblivion and got in that car."

"But no one was hurt. Isn't that the point?"

"Because of sheer luck. There was a payphone not far away, so I called Frank. Within minutes, he arrived. He didn't say a word to me. One look told him I was out of it. He tidied up the best he could, and we called out a tow truck. Then he drove me home and left me in the recovery position. I didn't see him until the next morning. The car was on the scrapheap and he didn't mention it again. That was the last time I drove. I didn't manage to kick the liquor until years later."

"You can't continue to atone for something that didn't happen. You're buried so deep in your past that you can't even live in the present."

"The past is where we are taught our lessons; we would be foolish not to listen to them."

"Sometimes we misinterpret the teaching," said Eve. Will contemplated her ideas for a moment and smiled. He turned the wheel, and they glided around the corner, further away from the grip of Hollyhead.

*

Arguably, the greatest accomplishment of the trip came when Eve let go of the grip bar and switched on the radio to the sound of *Hotel California*. She began singing along to the words.

His mind knew better, but Will's heart could feel the cancer inching away as she grew around the lyrics. Perhaps this was what peace felt like.

*

The car shuddered over loose rocks as it rolled back to its resting place. Will straightened the wheel and popped it into park. After nearly ten years, he had done it. Cautious not to let Eve see, he let himself smile. He relaxed his shoulders and turned to face her. There was no opportunity to say anything because as soon as he opened his mouth, she kissed him. Soft and unlike anything he had ever felt before. His body relaxed, and he felt like his whole being was melting into her. He reached towards her waist and pulled her closer, desperate to dive further into ecstasy. Then it was over, and she pulled away, looking like a cat caught licking butter.

"I'm sorry," she said, "I don't know why I did that. It just…"

"Felt right."

"Yes. Exactly." They smiled at each other.

Should I kiss her now? Is she hinting that she wants me to? No. That would ruin the first. Second is never as good. Though, maybe it will be better. My god, this is difficult. Stop smiling Will, you look creepy.

His next action would never be known because before he could decide, they were startled by a light bursting into the car. Will turned and saw that someone had entered the study and switched on the desk lamp.

"Is it Frank?" whispered Eve, although there was no need to keep quiet. If the noise of the car pulling up hadn't grabbed Frank's attention, then hushed voices had no chance.

"It must be. It's unlike him not to notice his car is missing though."

"You need to return the key," said Eve.

"Return the key? I can't go in the house now he's awake," said Will, peering into the recesses of the house.

"Sure you can. Just be quiet."

"You go do it then," said Will, pushing the keys into her palm.

"I can't!" she said in a voice close to a squeal. "It will make a lot more sense if he opens the door and sees you there instead of a woman he's never met before."

"Fine," said Will. Squashing down his anxiety, he left the car, full of mutterings about the prospect of getting caught. He opened the gate silently and approached the front door, keeping himself out of the light spilling from the study. His curiosity got the better of him. Crouching down, he peered through the frosted glass. Frank was sitting alone at his desk; an untouched lump of Christmas cake was in front of him. In his hands was his wife's pen that Nick had stolen—the present that Will had given him the day before. Light from his desk lamp was reflecting off the gold, flashing Frank's brow in a shimmering bath. Continually, he twisted the casing around and stroked it with his fingers. Then he took a sip of wine and slumped forwards. Within seconds, the shell of Will's father was sobbing into his hands with an unbridled sadness. The stiff upper lip had broken.

I should go in. Christmas is the time for forgiveness, after all.

The thought almost took him to open the front door. Instead of turning the doorknob and entering, he pushed the keys through the mailbox. Then he walked away, leaving Frank alone once again.

CHAPTER EIGHTEEN: HIGH HOPES FALLING

It's a universally known truth that for every good day, there must be a bad one. For some, this day may be one and the same. One person's best day may just be the worst for someone else. The day of Mary Goldstein's wedding was certainly the happiest she had ever been. A few hours after the ceremony, Floyd Wilson's mother was buried. He was the only attendee. That's life. All we can be sure of is that the day is coming without discrimination. There's just no knowing when it might creep up on you. For Will, the end of 1980 was a string of bad days after what he stated to be the best day of his life.

After leaving Frank's house, Will had walked Eve back to her apartment and been rewarded with another kiss, leaving him with an extra spring in his step that he had been lacking in recent months. He was wrong. The second was better than the first.

The drive had taken a lot out of him and he crashed onto his bed without removing his coat, waking the next morning to bright sunlight bursting through his window. According to his watch, he had slept ten hours. Far longer than most in recent memory. Eve was working an all-day shift, and he was still in no mood to receive another yelling from Frank. Remaining in bed for the entirety of the day was a pleasant thought, and he was close to following it through until he looked at the book of fairy tales open on his floor, halfway into *The Six Swans*. Coughing, he rolled out of bed and stepped into the shower, meeting lukewarm spray and rock-hard soap. He avoided looking into the mirror as he dressed; the face looking back at him was peeling back to reveal more of the illness than ever and he had no desire to see it again.

His plan for the day was drawn up after placing *Grimm's* on the bedside table. He had a strong sense of responsibility to inform Melanie of the pattern of deaths. Knowing that her sons' murders may solve numerous others may lessen her grief, even if only a little.

*

Wendy called him another taxi and he arrived at the Spark residence shortly before midday. Although it was surely not possible, the farmhouse looked even more rundown than it had on his first visit. The weeks of cold temperatures had caused frost to burrow into the cracks that cobwebbed across the wood and Will was careful not to slip as he climbed the stairs leading to the front door. A window on his right had broken and visible wisps of heat were escaping through a gap in the glass. He knocked on the door and stepped back in preparation for Melanie to open up. Nothing, but he could swear that voices were penetrating through the house toward him. The unmistakable sound of Melanie and what resembled Benny's slurred accent. Will knocked again, a little louder this time, and listened intensely. The voices had stopped.

He was a second from turning away when there was a deep roar and a large crash from inside the house followed by a repeated thumping. Will pressed his ear to the door. "Melanie?" he shouted.

No reply. He tried the knob and found it to be unlocked. Pushing open the door, he clambered over shoes and boots into the hallway. The sight at the far end almost made him gag. Benny Spark lay crumpled at the bottom of the stairs. He was still wearing the grubby vest that he seemed to have spent the last twelve years stuck in. Only now the grease and sweat stains were being covered by crimson blood, which still glugged from the tear in his skin. His neck had snapped, with his head at the mercy of the rest of his body. Judging by the state of the stairs, now dotted with broken wood, he had fallen, landed on the lower steps, and crushed his neck underneath his body— snapping the apex of his spinal cord and causing it to protrude through the broken flesh.

"Jesus…" croaked Will, unable to take his eyes from Benny's body.

"He fell…" said a wavering voice. Will looked up to see Melanie at the top of the stairs, hunched against the banister. Tears streaked her face and her hands were shaking against her stomach with enough force that Will wouldn't have been surprised if smoke started spilling from her skin. Behind her, there was the faint sound of 'High Hopes' by Sinatra coming from the radio—what a way to go out. Will had the sudden urge to laugh. Melanie took a tentative step on the top stair.

"Don't! We have no idea how strong they are after that beating," warned Will. Melanie nodded and stepped back. "Are there any more stairs down?"

"No," she said, her voice trembling.

"Surprise, surprise. Alright, put as much weight as you can on the banister and keep to the edge of the stairs. It will be strongest on the sides," said Will. "Don't look at the body, just keep your eyes on me."

Melanie put a foot forward and tested the top stair. It held. After an agonizingly long time, she had reached the bottom and Will held out his hand. She took it and instantly broke down into his shoulder; Will managed to remain standing only by leaning back onto the fading wallpaper behind him.

*

With a steaming mug of coffee in her hands, mixed with a dash of whiskey that Will had found in a kitchen cabinet, Melanie sat at the kitchen table. She had changed out of the clothes he had found her in and hadn't muttered more than a word of thanks in twenty minutes. Will had taken the time to tidy the kitchen, scrubbing the stacks of plates with the cleanest rag he could find in the house. He wasn't sure what to do with Benny's body other than lay a bedsheet across him. Moving the body was out of the question. Even if he had wanted to, Will doubted that he could heave the body anywhere useful, especially with his lungs being particularly bad that day. When he had finally worked out how to get the phone working (Melanie had unplugged it due to a horrific amount of prank calls), Will called Teddy. While waiting, Will and Melanie sat in silence until it was too heavy to hold.

"All I have is your word on this," said Will. Melanie didn't look up, instead deciding to fixate on the swirling liquid in her mug. "If you say he fell, then I have no reason not to believe you. You need to think about this. If there was some kind of altercation before he fell, then they can put that on you. Benny was a violent man. There's plenty of proof to support that. Tell me, are there any signs on his body that you punched or kicked him? Hell, did you bite him? Anything like that?"

She slowly shook her head. "Nothin'."

Will relaxed slightly. "What was he doing out of bed?"

"After your visit, he started walkin' again. He only managed a couple of steps on the first day, but he got strong. By the end of the week, he was able to get to the kitchen and back. The more strength he got, the more he got his swagger. When he was bedridden, I could escape him, pretend I couldn't 'ear his shouts and groans. Walkin' meant that he could find me. I couldn't get far enough from his voice anymore; like a constant shadow."

I told him to get out of bed. Is this chain of events due to my involvement? thought Will.

"Was there no one you could talk to? What about the butcher I saw last time I was here?" he asked.

"Tony has always been a good friend of the family. He's a good man, down to his bones. Benny and 'im went way back. Childhood friends, they was."

"People change. I saw how he looked at you. He might have been friends with Benny, but I think he had stronger feelings for you."

"Maybe. Never know now, will we?" she finished.

There was a firm knock on the door and, after no indication that Melanie was going to answer, Will left the room and opened it. Teddy gave him a weak smile and entered, removing his hat as he did so, revealing that familiar quiff of blonde hair.

"How are you doing, Will?" he asked in a way removed from his police voice.

"I'm fine. It's Melanie I'm worried about."

"God, that woman has been through a lot. Let's just get through this quickly," said Teddy, calling his partner to follow. It was the same woman he had been with the night Will had taken a dip into the motel lake. She went to inspect the body as Teddy entered the kitchen.

"I'm sorry for your loss. I've called my coroner. He'll be here soon to examine the body. Then we can get your husband somewhere more *respectful,*" he said. Will could tell that he was doing his best. Talking to recent widows wasn't something that he seemed comfortable with. Although it would take a hard son of a bitch to not care. His partner entered and showed them her credentials—Felicity Williams HPD. She whispered something to Teddy, and he nodded before waving her into a corner of the room where she stood stony-faced for the entirety of the conversation.

"Mr. Spark fell down the stairs. Is that correct?"

"Yes."

"Before he fell, was there anything that I should know about?" he said, eyeing a bruise on Melanie's wrist. She pulled her hands from the table.

"No."

Teddy shot a glance at Will as if to say: *she's not exactly helping her case here.*

"I was here when it happened, Ted," said Will. Teddy responded with a raised eyebrow. There was another knock from the hallway and Williams left the room. "We were upstairs looking through some of the boys' belongings when Benny walked up. He was angry and started swearing at us. It was almost scary; him throwing his arms around. I thought he might go for us at one point."

"Why was he angry?" asked Teddy. Melanie didn't reply. She was too busy trying to untangle a string from her apron.

"I met him a couple of weeks ago. My impression was that anger is his base setting," said Will.

Teddy felt in his pocket and took out a pen. He jotted something down on his hand, needing a couple of scribbles before the pen gave ink. "Forgot my notebook," he said in response to Will's bemused look. "How did he fall?"

"He came storming up the stairs and started shouting at us about noise. I told him that we would quieten down and as he turned to leave, he must have missed a step. After he fell, I checked for a pulse and then called you."

"You didn't think to call for an ambulance?"

"My first thought was to call you."

"I'm flattered."

"We panicked. It's not every day someone dies right in front of you."

Teddy was about to reply when a familiar ginger head poked around the doorway, followed by the stick-thin body of George Upson.

"I've done all I can with the body. The autopsy will be completed later today. If it wasn't the fall, then it would have been his heart. I would have given him months at the most," he said, his voice flat. Long, spindly fingers tapped against his leg as if he was anxious to be away.

"Thanks, George. Can we move him?"

"The van is outside. I'll take him out. Might need a hand, though."

"Will, can you help George?" asked Teddy. "I think it would be good to talk to Mrs. Spark one on one. Williams, you can join them."

"Fine," said Will, standing up. Melanie's face remained stony and blank. They left the room. Benny's body had already been slid onto a stretcher; a new white sheet was placed over his corpse.

"On three," said Williams, squatting down and picking up one side of the stretcher. She was considerably stronger than both the men she was accompanied by. Will and George picked up the other side and heaved Benny out the door. A white van was parked a few steps away from the porch.

"You couldn't have got wheels for this?" groaned Will as George opened the backdoors with one hand. Neither person replied, and they pushed the body into the back before shutting him into the void. They trudged back to the house in silence and Will returned to the kitchen. Back into the mist of grief. Teddy remained seated, defeated by the lack of talk from Melanie. She had finally finished her coffee and was now fixated on pulling a thread that had come loose from her jumper.

"Mrs. Spark, the faster we can get through this, the less time I will need to spend asking you to recall the events of the past couple of hours," said Teddy, pleadingly.

"We was always saying we had to sort out those damned stairs. Too narrow. Too slippery. I have lost my husband and the last person in my family."

"And you say he just fell?" said Teddy, directing his head to Melanie.

"He just fell," said Will, sensing Melanie's conflicting emotions about to spill out. "That's all there is to this."

*

Teddy and his crew left after one final sweep of the house. Will changed the bedsheets and wiped down the bathroom, managing to scare a few dozen spiders back into their tiny slits in the walls. Perhaps it was the feeling that all this was his fault. Either way, tidying the house allowed him to leave with the knowledge that he had done some good in Melanie's life—even if the extent was minimal. He told Melanie that he was leaving to no reply, but as his hand reached for the doorknob, he felt a gentle tug on his coat. Melanie was standing behind him.

"Thank you," she said, squeezing his hand with the strength of a newborn.

"Don't mention it. And I mean that literally," replied Will. Melanie glanced at the spot where Benny had landed and nodded. "Get a hotel or something for tonight. Go and see your butcher friend. Just get out of this place. When this is all over, please get yourself out of this town before everything you are is leached from you." Melanie let go of his hand and allowed him to leave.

He walked out to Teddy leaning against his Granada. Williams was sitting inside, flipping pages of a notebook and muttering to herself frantically.

"You've got a visitor," said Teddy, jerking a thumb towards the gate behind them.

Will craned his neck to see Marty Goodall standing by his car. He beckoned Will over.

"Hold up a second," said Teddy, pulling Will aside. He lowered his voice and turned them away from Williams' shrewd glare. "I know what a guilty person looks like, Will. Assisting her will just mean that you end up in prison as well," warned Teddy. He exhaled and rubbed his eyes with his palms. "I also saw the bruises. I've seen enough domestic abuse cases to know the signs. Look, as far as I'm concerned, the man fell. You just make sure that your stories match."

"Don't you want justice?"

"Seems to me that this *was* justice."

"They'll match," assured Will.

"Good. Remember, it's not just your head that risks ending up on a spike here," replied Teddy, his face crinkling with stress. They said goodbye and Will walked towards Marty, who was now counting the hands on an imaginary watch.

"Frank needs to see you," he said, pointing to the car.

"I've got a girl back in my room. I think I know who I would rather see."

"Sarcasm only works if it's believable. Now get in."

Will followed Marty into the car and they sped off back into the middle of Hollyhead.

"How did you know I was here?" asked Will.

"Frank told me where you were staying. I used the ol' charm on the owner. Poor woman just wanted someone to have a chat with. She told me that you asked her to order a cab. Called up the cab company and they told me that you had come here. Easy when you have the means," said Marty, turning on the wipers. Rain had started falling like thick tears.

"What does he want?"

"What he always wants, I assume. Update on the case. What have you found out?"

"I think the Spark boys were drugged. Abigail was courting an older man, but that lead is too vague to get any real attention. As for Ed, we're no closer. The police aren't either."

Marty sighed. "You shouldn't be doing this. You're young, far too young to be getting caught up in all this business. Do you even want to be back in Hollyhead?"

"I don't know anymore," said Will. The thought of another death occurring in Hollyhead had grown like wildfire in his mind and had been slowly eating away at his conscience for the past few days. He was sure that he had most of the pieces. Only arranging them into a cohesive narrative was proving too much. All he knew was that if another person died, he would feel responsible.

"No one would blame you if you wanted to leave all this behind you. You don't owe this to anyone. Especially not to Frankie."

"I've spoken to him more in the past week than I have for years."

"And that's not on you. That's because of his failings as your father, not because of yours as his son."

"What was Frank like? Was he always like he is now?"

"Cold? Obsessive? Nope. We had a big case before your mother died. It changed him. He was a family man before the Nasarlis crap. Then Monica passed, and he lost it. I should've been there for him, but it was a rough time for all of us. I tried telling him that he'd regret it if he didn't bring you up properly. Hell, there were times when I considered taking you off his hands. He couldn't cope with it all."

"And Mom, did you know her well?"

"Sure. Frank and Monica were something special. It seems these days that two people stay together out of convenience. Your parents were the exception. She was headstrong and knew exactly how to handle him. As for Frank, he was happy. Before her cancer, he was a good father to you and a good husband to her. Taking her from the world was God's cruelest act."

Marty turned silent and Will had the feeling that he was replaying years of memories in his head.

"Thank you for taking care of him."

"It may not seem like it, but your father is the best friend a man could have."

Expecting Marty to turn towards Frank's home, Will was surprised when they took the opposite road, bending around towards the north of the town. "Are you not taking me home?" he asked.

Marty had lit up a cigarette and shook his head while it smoldered, dropping ash onto his pants. "A home, yes. Your home, no," he said through the corner of his mouth.

*

Will had always wondered about the big house with the sky-blue paint. He had wandered along the sidewalk outside it as a child, always trying to peer inside at the walls of books visible in the bottom left window. It wasn't often easy, as the blinds were shut for most of the year. He'd made up stories about the owner. Perhaps he was an adventurer, now paranoid that an ancient curse was out to get him. Or maybe a criminal, hiding from the law. One thing was for sure: Will's imagination had known no bounds. Without indication, Marty swerved the car to the side of the street. Frank was sitting on a bench, his weary eyes gazing up at the house in front of them.

"Are you not coming?" Will asked.

"He didn't ask for me. Just you," said Marty. "I don't know what he wants, but don't be scared to tell him where to stick it if you need to."

"Thanks, Marty," replied Will as he clambered out.

The car kicked up stones as the tires screeched away. Will walked towards the solitary figure of Frank, who made no indication that he was aware anyone was with him until Will sat down.

"I always liked this house," he said, without taking his eyes off the building in front of them. 'We had plans of moving here when we were old and decrepit. Before it all fell through…"

"It's far too jolly for you. It would be like putting a eunuch in a brothel."

Frank let slip a smile before returning to his reminiscence. "Your mother lived here. Her parents continued living here until they died five years ago. It now belongs to a Mr. and Mrs. Westbrook."

"Do they know you sit outside watching them?"

"This is the first time I have seen it since she died. Her bedroom was that one," he said, pointing to the top floor. Pink curtains were drawn across a window facing towards the street. "Completely different now, of course. New memories painted over the old. The story of life." He smiled weakly at Will. "I proposed to her on this very bench. Our initials are carved into that tree," he said, nodding towards a tall oak on the other side of the street."

"Not very extravagant," said Will, although the comment wasn't loaded. It was simply an observation.

"It didn't need to be. I had thought about asking her for so long that after a year I realized I still hadn't done it. Then here I was, and it was perfect. Perfect because she said yes," said Frank, running his fingers across the arm of the bench. He dug inside his jacket pocket and showed Will the gold-plated pen. "You have no idea what this pen represents. What it means to me. You believed it to be hers. It was for many years and then it was mine. I gave her the ring, and she said it was only fair that

I receive something in return. The pen was a family heirloom, passed down through generations. Giving me that pen was her way of telling me that she wanted to spend her life with me. Her answer was much more than a yes," said Frank. Even when talking of a memory that clearly rippled melancholy through him, his face remained impassive. The FBI hadn't purged him of emotion, but it had made him desensitized to it.

"I've left you with very few answers concerning your childhood," he continued, turning the pen in his hands. "I think you deserve to know a little more. It is no excuse for my behavior, but I would like you to see."

"What is it you want to tell me?"

Frank smiled but his eyes didn't receive the message. There was no excitement, no passion. "Once again, I think I would rather show you, son," he said, finally turning to face Will. "The rewind, if you please." He held out his hand and Will placed the device into his palm.

"I admit that this one particular memory is not an easy one for me to hold. It is one of those pieces of one's soul that you hope never to bring to the surface. If you could give me a second to think," he said. His brow furrowed as he tried to pull his thoughts into one comprehensible string. "Ready."

The rewind's call once sounded was hard to ignore, but even as Will edged nearer, he felt his body tense with apprehension. Whatever Frank wanted to show him was something that had been buried deep for decades. Will placed his finger on the rewind and felt himself melt into Frank's memories.

CHAPTER NINETEEN: TO BE FRANK

The woods were silent tonight, as if in anticipation. Dusk had fallen rapidly, and the sky was already shot full of dimly burning stars. Tree branches were swaying in the wind as if parting to allow Frank to navigate his way through. He appreciated the silence of the night. God wanted this to be done properly; he sensed it.

He hadn't been home in over a day, having spent the best part of twenty-four hours in Ed's diner, his head halfway into a pitcher of beer. Ed had been kind; he'd given free drinks until close, although the alcohol had turned to water by the evening. Before he left, he had even offered Frank the couch.

"It's the least I can do Frankie. You've certainly bought enough from me to warrant a night in the warm. That's if you don't want me to drive you home?" he had said, a look of deep concern on his face. Frank had declined. The house was nothing more than bricks now. Bricks with a few windows scattered across the exterior and cheap furniture decorating the inside. Once they are gone, you realize that your possessions are nothing more than bits of material strung together. Clumps of atoms in a dying wasteland. That's why he had thrown out all his records and books. They had no meaning now. It was all just chords and empty words. Maybe it always had been.

Ed had watched him walk away and waited in the car, possibly hoping for a change of heart. When it became clear that Frank had no intention of getting in, he drove away, until the red lights of his red Ford Fairlane just became blips in the dark. Maybe if he had waited one more second, then Frank would have joined him. Maybe one more second was all it took.

Everyone had been so generous over the past week, it almost made Frank sick. The wife of one of his FBI colleagues had cooked him a roast chicken and offered to take Will out for the day. Frank had given both the food and Will to his parents before driving to a local motel and drinking himself to sleep. Tonight, he had decided it was time.

His foot stumbled over a tree root sticking up through the dirt. The forest floor was so densely covered by leaves that he couldn't see where the path narrowed, and the towering Elms began. It didn't help that his flashlight wasn't working—his own fault. He hadn't bothered to check whether it had batteries. The matches in his bag weren't for now. He needed them later. Anyway, he knew the way to Blake's Point. He knew how the path curved and where the barbed wire fence started. The musty smell of the dampened leaves and the oaky hue that lingered relaxed his pulsing heart. Years ago, the forest had been where the earth ended. Twelve-year-old Frank knew nothing but Hollyhead. Tucked away in his mind were all the hiding places and burrows that he had discovered all those years ago. Isn't it funny how often things end in the same place that they begin?

For the last hour, he had walked, his muscles pumping with no conscious effort. His mind was fixed on the Point. Frank had never considered himself to indulge in obsessions. One should not become dependent on anything, for it can be taken away as easily as it comes. Yet this idea had snaked through his mind and for the last week, he had thought of little else. After a few minutes, he realized that he was nodding, as if his body was persuading his brain that this was still a good idea.

Luckily for him, the streets had been quiet tonight. As he staggered towards his destination, only a handful of cars had passed. Everything was falling into place. It was as if they knew. The whole town knew what he was going to do, and they were happy to let him. Thank you Hollyhead.

There was a full moon, although its beams weren't strong enough to break through the trees. The branches were still covered in leaves that soaked up the moonlight in spades. Frank continued forward, pushing his way through the undergrowth. The cold had bothered him at first, but it hadn't taken long for his body to become numb. Blake's Point was a popular third-date location, but not tonight. He could already see that it was deserted. The normal view of headlights and the sound of hushed whispers were absent. The scene was over, and the curtain was about to fall. From the cliff, you could see the whole of Hollyhead, stretching as far as the Spark farmhouse. It was here that he had brought Monica on their first date. She was new to the area, and he had spent hours pointing out the various buildings and land that made up his hometown. Although she'd laughed at his jokes and asked questions at all the right times, Frank wasn't sure whether she had enjoyed it, but it had been enough to warrant a second meeting. He knew that she *had* when she remembered every detail he had told her, down to the dates that the buildings were made and the name of each street. Frank prided himself on his keen retention of facts and figures; Monica had proved that he wasn't the only one in Hollyhead with a strong memory. It was that night he had decided that he wanted to marry her. The movies had got it wrong, he thought. There was no battle to win her love. There was no conflict. Isn't that how love should be? Tranquil.

There was a barbed fence blocking the edge of the cliff from visitors, which Frank stepped over with ease, his feet landing in the thick grass that overran the section of the point furthest from the edge. Further along, there was a part of the fence that had been cut away, allowing cars to glide in and out as they pleased. Back in '55, a car had fallen from the cliff in a game of chicken, resulting in signs being put up to try to discourage similar behavior. Only a few signs remained now. The rest could be found at the bottom of the cliff after Jimmy Morales decided to show his strength after a dozen beers. These were the thoughts catapulting around Frank's mind. He didn't want to think about what was coming, although it tried its best to tear through his stream of consciousness.

He shook the thoughts away and studied the view in front of him. Pinpricks of light dotted the horizon and he saw the house where Monica had lived in the far distance, a few blocks from the Hollyhead library. When meeting her parents, he had worn his prom suit, even adorned with a wonky bow tie that he had stolen from his father's wardrobe. Monica's mother had told him that he looked handsome; her father had sniffed rather dismissively. When Monica saw, she burst out laughing. Then everyone had seen the funny side, and it proved his anxiety wrong. Not that he had taken it off. Wearing a suit felt right to him. Even now, he was decked out in his finest Italian-made—the exact one he had worn on their wedding day. Frank hadn't been to see her parents since the death. Although he knew that there was nothing anyone could have done to prevent it, he feared the silence of the father. He feared that even more than the inevitable weeping of her mother.

The wind picked up to the extent he could hear it whistling in his ears and his untamed hair was flapping across his eyes to the extent that one hand was constantly brushing it away from his face. He could smell the booze on his breath, curling upwards in the cold of the night. And there it was, the point where the rock started clawing at the grass before ending in a jagged verge only a few feet wide.

His rucksack had started digging into his shoulders and he was relieved to take it off. He swung it off his back and placed it on the rock before opening it and taking out a box of matches. The wind had lessened now and Frank was grateful. The match scratched into life and for the first time in the last two hours, he could see properly. He wished he couldn't. His black pants had been torn by branches and long trickles of blood had stained through. In the light, he couldn't convince himself that his hands weren't shaking. The shadows of the trees were dancing as his hand wavered. Holding the match downwards, the fire grew larger, reaching for his hands. Before it could burn his fingers, Frank held it to a candle he took from his bag and the flame jumped across onto the wax. He blew out the match and tossed it over the cliff.

How easy it looks, he thought.

Stepping back to his bag, Frank took a wooden board from inside and placed it on the ground, where it basked in the flickering candlelight. He had stood stones around the candle, sheltering it from the wind. The board was decorated with two arches. Along the top arch, the letters A-M were written in black ink. The arch below ended the alphabet. At the bottom of the board were ten numbers, surrounded by an assortment of random symbols that Frank knew nothing about—they weren't what mattered. On either side of the arches, 'YES' and 'NO' were etched into the wood.

Frank rummaged around in his pocket. Out of the loose change and scraps of paper he took a stone object. It was triangular with a wide hole in the middle—the planchette. The idea had come to him as he had passed the church. Over the years, many stories concerning angels had accumulated. Farmer Derek Yates had claimed a winged spirit had stood by his wife's bed as she died, ready to take her into Heaven. Frank hadn't believed that story—if there was anyone who he was certain wouldn't be going there, it was Brenda Yates. He remembered how the hag had chased him through the cornfields, threatening to fill him full of buckshot. No angel was taking her to the pearly gates. Still, the stories had given him hope. That was all he needed.

He cleared his throat. "Mon, it's Frank," he said, his finger lightly brushing the planchette. He waited for a second, his eyes closed, straining his ears for any sound to indicate her presence. "I don't know if I'm doing this right. Perhaps I need to pray or something. I guess I'm looking for a sign. Anything really, just let me know you're out there."

Walking through the Autumn leaves and crunching them underfoot. Holding your hand. Sunlight sparkling down through the trees.

Nothing. Just the faraway sound of car engines cutting their way through the wind. "Things haven't been going so well since you've been gone. Work gave me some time off, but I wanted to go back in. I was worried that they would get it all wrong without me. They sent me home. You told me that everyone is replaceable except for family. As always, you were right." He paused. Again, his words were met with nothing but the various sounds of nature.

Will's birth. Holding him for the first time. A family. Together.

"Will took his first steps the day after you left. They didn't take him very far, and he fell over at the end, but he walked from the door to your chair. You should have seen him. You would have been so proud," he said. Then he looked to the floor and blinked back tears.

"He's getting older every day and you're missing it. We said that we would grow with him. His mistakes would show us where we've gone wrong, where we strayed from the path. Then when he got a little brother or sister, we could inevitably make those same mistakes again," he sighed. "The truth is, I'm not ready for this. I'm not ready to be a father. Not without you. I should have attended more of those child-care classes. I guess they weren't such a waste of time after all," he said. "I'm sorry for my stubbornness concerning all of that," he added, mentally scolding himself. Normally, he chose his words with such precision and now they were pouring out into the air like powder. If a reply was coming, then he would need to be clear and succinct. That was why she hadn't heard him. His words were being lost in the wind, the signal not strong enough to reach through and grab her up in the clouds. That was the only explanation.

Records playing crackly music as you get ready. That yellow jumper you wore even in the summer. Watching you brushing your hair until you catch my eye and start laughing.

"I want to say that I am sorry for not seeing your parents. The truth is that I am terrified. They know that I make a lousy father and perhaps I was worse as a husband. Your love was all I wanted, and I should have been there at the end. My work was a blanket that I wrapped around me until I suffocated. You were far more important. Excuses were made until the end and I shall spend the rest of my life repenting for that—however long that proves to be."

Your eyes. Your brilliant, overwhelming eyes… Just to see them once more in the flesh.

There was still no movement of the planchette, and Frank felt his heart sink even lower with each desperate attempt. "Please forgive me. Just talk to me. Help me through this…"

His body went still. All strength had run from his veins and evaporated into the melancholic sky. "Will is at my parent's house. They're moving out of state and I think it would be for the best if he went too. This cesspit is no place to bring up a child. You could have done it. I can't. Without you, there's nothing I can do."

Please. Please. Please. Talk to me. Show me you are here.

There was nothing. In a flash of unbridled rage, he threw the board over the cliff before following it up with the candle. The planchette he kept, pocketing it. It hadn't worked. His mind had always been rational and scientific; if something wasn't proven, then it simply didn't exist. He had betrayed himself by thinking there was a chance that he could speak with Monica. Something he would never try again. It was easier to believe that it was all a scam rather than face the truth that she might be ignoring him. What if his words were finding her, and she was simply swatting them away like an irritating fly? Even in the afterlife, forgiveness may be too much to ask.

Then he found himself at the edge of the rock. The entirety of Hollyhead stretched in front of him, shining their tiny spotlights over him as the finale began. They all wanted him to do it. The man who had left his wife alone when she needed him most.

His feet had never felt heavier as if they were loaded with stones. The fact that the drop below him was shrouded by the night relaxed him a little. At least he wouldn't be able to see the ground.

Count to three. Three seconds and you'll be back with her. If she'll have you...

He closed his eyes gently and felt the ripple of the wind through his clothes. One foot hovered over the pit of darkness below.

In the distance, a dog barked, a large one by the sounds of it, possibly a collie. A distraction. He hadn't expected to hear anything. It ruined the tranquility. Unless...

Frank snapped his eyes open and took a step backward. Will's birthday. He'd almost forgotten. The week before Monica had gotten really bad, the three of them had walked through Hollyhead high-street. They'd had ice cream and played in the park. It was the first time that Monica had felt like herself while wearing the wig. They had stopped on the way home. Will had seen a brightly colored toyshop fitted with stuffed animals and a bike already fitted with training wheels.

Monica had grabbed Frank's arm and pointed excitedly at a grey and white dog, fitted with a red bar sticking out from its back. Small black wheels were attached to a red frame, allowing a toddler to walk while balancing on the handlebar.

"Frankie, that's it! He'll love it," Monica squealed. They'd gone inside and Frank had asked the man on the till whether he could hold the dog so Frank could pick it up the following week. The cashier had agreed and placed a blue collar around its neck, fixed with a piece of paper stating that the Metlocke family would be back to pick it up the following week.

It was her final wish. That damned dog.

It's funny how thoughts form. A stimulus with seemingly no meaning could bring you to the highs of ecstasy or the lows of depression. It seemed to Frank that they could also save a life, if only for now.

*

Will felt it all. The depression. The slight relief Frank had felt as he had taken a step away from the edge. The memory had been stronger than any other he had encountered before. Frank said that the rewind worked through DNA, perhaps a match as strong as between father and son wielded a higher power than any other.

Frank's eyes were wet with tears. His chin was vibrating with the effort to stop himself from breaking down.

"You tried to kill yourself?" Will asked, still trying to stop his own head from spinning.

Frank nodded, gravely. "At the time, I saw no other option. When she was diagnosed with cancer, my brain started preparing itself for grief. It's hard to imagine, but I was not always the optimist I am now. God's cruelest trick was allowing her to recover. The doctors told us that she was doing better. When they said that, I was fooled into believing that the rest of our days would be together. Then she got bad again. All the preparation I had undergone was removed and I couldn't grasp it again. Everything piled up and I saw only one way to escape from my pain. As we grow up, we all search for someone to connect to in some way. We want someone who will pull us back from that ledge. That's not how it works. Sometimes the people who will pull us back are the reason that we find ourselves on that ledge anyway."

"When did you change your mind? I don't remember living with your parents."

"You didn't. The day before they left, I took you back."

"I could have had a home where someone cared for me. Proper parents who could give me their time. It was selfish of you to keep me if you knew that you didn't care."

"I always cared," Franked snapped. "Roof over your head; a nanny to watch over you. I know I wasn't there for you, but you were the only reason I didn't jump that night."

There was no denying it; Will had felt his father's emotion and replayed his thoughts. Frank wasn't lying.

"That's why you freaked when I mentioned ghosts. Your mind of logic and reason was opened to the supernatural for one night and nothing happened."

"I believe in many things. There has been evidence of aliens, creatures, and beings I thought only existed in fairy tales, but if ghosts really exist, then don't you think that Monica would have spoken to me? If any such paranormal beings endure, then it means that she believed me not to be worth talking to. That is one thought too far for this old man."

"I think she was there that night. Not in voice, but something else. Signs aren't always obvious. Perhaps a sign can be as small as a dog barking. That's all you needed to step away."

Frank didn't reply. His hand on Will's shoulder was enough.

*

Still not having her number, Will wasn't sure whether Eve would be present that evening. Their previous meetings had been arranged through chance and quick throwaway comments.

"I'm happy to wait. Eve sounds like the perfect woman for you," said Frank. Walking back to the motel, Will told Frank about Eve. Not everything. Just that she was a nurse and had read some of his books. Now inside Will's room, Frank insisted that he wait to meet her.

"I don't even know if she's coming over tonight. Planning isn't exactly our strong suit."

"Neither is cleanliness," commented Frank, glancing at the heaps of clothes and books scattered across the floor. He made his way toward the motel art and studied it for a moment. No one would need more than a moment. Whoever had painted it hadn't got to grips with a paintbrush and the house depicted was a mess of blue and green swirls. The thing about motel art is that it's either exactly what they saw or an abstract piece that makes sense to no one but them. All the time Will had been at the motel, he hadn't been able to work out which kind this was. Frank placed his hand on the side of the frame and pushed it a little to make it straight. He then bent down and picked up a loose pair of socks.

"You won't be able to think properly if your room looks like the aftermath of a blitz," he said. Will didn't see him put the socks away, but he heard the squeak of the drawer as it opened and closed. "I have a diary to help me organize everything in my head. You should try it."

"Yeah, then maybe we can swap and talk about boys," replied Will, in a passable impression of a teenage girl.

"When you mock everything that may help you, it just reinforces the notion that you don't want to be helped," said Frank. "I'll go for now, but I would like to meet this lady." Frank stepped towards the door.

"Enjoy writing your memoirs. I'll take a look at your diary one day," said Will, smirking.

"It's a diary, Will. Not a piece of my soul," said Frank. He gently shut the door behind him.

Souls… People use diaries to write down their inner monologues. Thoughts, feelings, darkest secrets. You're wrong, Frank. That diary is your soul…

Will scrambled to the floor and clawed his way through *Grimm's*. He had read something. The name of the story escaped him, but he would know it when he saw it.

"You're either a super-fast reader, or you're looking for something," said a familiar voice from his side. Will paused from searching to see Eve next to him. She must have walked straight past Frank as he left the motel.

"Found it! Look," he exclaimed, shoving the book into Eve's startled hands.

"*The Grave Mound?*" she read.

"It's a weird one. Well, they're all weird, but listen," said Will, almost breathless. The cogs in his brain were going into overdrive and a theory was snowballing in his head. "The Devil tries to collect the soul of a rich farmer following his death, but when he arrives at the grave, he meets a poor man and a soldier who have decided to watch over his final resting place. The Devil tries to make them leave by bribing them. The soldier tricks the Devil by cutting a hole in his boot and telling the Devil to fill it with gold. When the Devil tries to fill it up, the gold falls through and he has to go and get more. Eventually, they are out for so long dawn breaks. The Devil runs away."

"Why does he run away when morning comes?" asked Eve, reading the story herself, her dark eyes glossing over the pages.

"I don't know. Perhaps he burns easily. That's not the point," snapped Will. "The poor man and the soldier take the gold and live happily ever after."

"I'm assuming this links to the recent murders. You think that there is something that the killer wants in the grave of their victims?"

"Potentially. Benny Spark told me that all the boys were buried with a possession. Something that meant a lot to them. I think that those possessions represent a piece of their soul. What if the killer has dug the graves and taken what they believe to be rightfully theirs? He's killed them and now he wants their souls."

"They are not going to break into a grave just to pick up a stuffed toy."

"Wouldn't they? If you care about something enough, then it forms part of your persona. It bleeds into your very being. Why wouldn't the soul be made up of things that we love? We need to check. Alex was buried with his diary... What if something was in there that could lead us to the killer?"

"Then the police would have picked up on it?"

Will buried his face in his hands and groaned. "Apart from Teddy, they couldn't find their own asses. They didn't know about the *Grimm's* link. Not even Dad picked up on that until ages after they died. See, there are two reasons to find out. The Reaper could have left something. They wouldn't be careful once they broke in. Perhaps there is something there. Even if not, we still need to take a look at that diary."

"Do you really think the killer would do that? Ransack the grave of their own victim? If you are saying that they have taken something from each of their victims then the diary won't be there."

"Look, either the diary is there and it might give us another clue or it's gone and we not only chance finding something else, but we also find out something about the Reaper's psyche. We don't know how they think. Maybe they haven't just been a step ahead of us this whole time. Maybe they are on a completely different path. Even madmen possess logic. They see things in a different way than others, that's all."

"What do you propose?" asked Eve.

"I need to go dig up some graves."

*

Eve had work at the hospital that night, so Will decided to test their theory on Teddy.

"It's crazy, but maybe that's how we need to think," he had replied. They had arranged to meet later when the clock struck twelve.

By the time Teddy was ready, dark clouds had strangled the sun, and a breeze had begun to rifle through the trees. Will's chest was pulsing. The dull ache he had found so inconvenient had evolved into a throb.

They had parked Teddy's Granada in a nearby clearing, hidden behind a bramble hedge in case of any late-night wanderers. Teddy hadn't dared to move until all the houses surrounding the cemetery became dark. His confident persona had given way to paranoia. On their way towards the church, they had managed to evade the last drips of people returning home and had clambered over the low fence with ease. The gate had been locked a few hours prior. Will had watched as the bumbling old groundskeeper fumbled his keys into the padlock and shook the gates to ensure they stuck tight.

To stop people coming in, or to stop them getting out? he thought. A few weeks earlier, the thought would never have popped into his head, but after the ghosts, he wasn't sure anymore.

Teddy hadn't spoken a word; Will could see it on his face that the thought of breaking into a coffin went against everything he stood for. The only reason he had come along was because he agreed with Will's theory and their options were now becoming severely limited.

"I'll lose my job if we're found," he said, zipping his fleece up to his neck.

"More than that, we'll be chucked into a psychiatric ward."

"Small steps, Will."

They continued forwards; their torches low to avoid any notice from nosey passersby. The church sat in the middle of the cemetery, encircled by rows of headstones. It had been erected in 1899, although the wood had been preserved well. The gleaming white exterior was a popular print on postcards that would no doubt be thrown away immediately after reading. The interior was not so well maintained; the last time that Will had been in, the pews needed a good dusting and the Christ figurehead above the altar was cracking, adding to his gloomy look.

The stones closer to the church were the oldest; those that weren't half destroyed by erosion were still just about legible. Most were still surrounded by clumps of dead grass that made a ferocious rattling in the wind as if they were infested with snakes. As the graves spread out from the center, they became more diverse. They still had flowers; the generations hadn't reached the point where the ancestors had forgotten who was there. Will pictured the Spark boys hanging from the barn, their faces half eaten away. How many bodies below his feet were still hanging on to their flesh? Whose eyes had been the first to decay?

He pushed the thought from his mind and jolted the spade into a more comfortable position over his shoulder.

"It doesn't feel right. A person should have dignity even after death. We shouldn't be desecrating their resting place," said Teddy.

"If I'm correct, then we won't be the first to dig up their coffins. There's nothing wrong with witnessing the aftermath," replied Will, he hadn't yet told Teddy about his relation to Alex. It didn't seem so real that way.

"They were children. I don't think they ever knew peace in this life. I hope they have some in the next."

"Well, if you think being eaten by maggots and worms is peaceful... sure," replied Will, his fingers gliding over a shaven slate of gravestone.

"You can be an asshole, you know that?"

"It's been said," replied Will. He didn't mean to snap at Teddy. Out of everyone he had met recently, Teddy was one of the people Will didn't mind spending time with. Even *enjoyed* being with.

"What do you get out of it? Is the kick really worth it when it makes everyone around you miserable?"

"People just annoy me. They're all so caught up in pitiful arguments. You would think that they would realize that in the end we just end up in the ground somewhere. Then the choice of going to a Christmas party in a green or red dress isn't so important."

"We act to make ourselves happy. I think everyone deserves a little happiness. It's not pitiful if it means something to them."

"You think everyone deserves to be happy? Tell that to the Reaper."

"Real mature. You can't just take wild examples and apply them to a point about Christmas dresses."

"My argument stands. Happiness is defined differently by everyone. I'm pretty sure it doesn't make the killer miserable to squeeze the life from their victims."

Teddy opened his mouth to reply.

"Do you remember where they were buried?" Will asked. He knew already, having visited every time he walked past, but he wanted to change the conversation.

Teddy sighed. "They're over in the corner."

He was right. The six graves were laden with flowers and photographs. Close attention had been given to the boys; unlike some of the older graves, the surrounding grass was mowed short, and the headstones were scrubbed clean. Handwritten messages were scribbled on colored pieces of card and propped up against the stones. How many were just for show? Teddy took off his hat and lowered his head towards the graves.

"What are you doing?" said Will, preparing to stab into the dirt.

Teddy opened his eyes. "It's called respect. We're about to break into a grave just to check one of your *inspirational* ideas. The least you could do is let them know there is a reason."

"If they could still hear, then they wouldn't be six feet under me, would they?"

"I'll put you six feet under if you're not careful," replied Teddy, hoisting his own shovel off his shoulder. He took a thermos from his rucksack and twisted the lid off before pouring the contents onto the ground. Steam hissed as the water pooled onto the ground. Will followed suit.

"Digging up a twelve-year-old grave... didn't think I'd be doing this in my spare time," sighed Teddy.

"Let's just start digging," said Will, trying his best not to sound like his own conscience was eating away at him. He knew that by now Alex would have decomposed to the bone but seeing his old friend for the first time in over twelve years still terrified him. The visions were grotesque enough.

It was tough work. Even with the hot water, the ground was rock hard. Their shovels only dug a few inches, and they were required to use the pickaxe more than they had hoped. Will had known that the task would strain his already damaged lungs, and he tried hard not to let it show to Teddy, who was struggling himself. After what felt like hours of little progress, Will rested on the handle of his shovel and listened to the noises filling the gloom of the graveyard.

Was that the wind? Or was that whistling noise coming from something beyond life itself? Maybe the Devil had come for his reward. He was owed a soul, after all. Thinking about it, the lights in the distance seemed to be swinging. The Devil with a lantern, perhaps, snaking his way towards them. Teddy had stopped to think about what desecrating a grave would mean to the big man in the sky. Had he considered what it meant to the beast below?

Will was pulled from his internal monologue by a sharp prod in the ribs from Teddy.

"Are you going to dig? I'd get more help from my mother and she's been dead for years."

Will blinked his mind back into his body. "Yeah. Coming." Teddy gave him a concerned look, and they continued their mission. At last, Will's shovel hit something harder than dirt. Teddy was standing outside the grave, drinking deeply from his hip flask. Will brushed dirt from the bottom of the pit until his fingers connected with wood.

"Give me a hand with this," asked Will, wiping sweat from his brow. The cold was causing it to bind to his skin. He gripped his shovel to hide the trembling of his hands. Alex was close.

Teddy slid into the grave, causing a landslide of pebbles and shrubbery to collapse onto the wood. They cleared the rest of the dirt until the edges of the coffin were easily accessible. Nervous energy spread through Will's body, warming his fingertips. Teddy climbed out of the hole and passed down a crowbar before joining Will again. Will plunged the crowbar under a gap in the lid and they pressed down hard, grunting with the effort. Creaking signaled that they were almost through and then the lid popped off entirely. Teddy tipped it over.

"Well... that's certainly a surprise," said Teddy. The diary was the only item in the coffin. Where Alex Spark's body should have rested, there was nothing. Someone had already stolen the body from its slumber.

CHAPTER TWENTY: GRAVEROBBERS

"Either someone has been body snatching, or this really is the night of the living dead," said Teddy, reaching towards the grubby book resting on the bottom of the coffin. Creatures of the earth had found the corners, and the pages had turned stiff and yellow. A quick flick-through showed that most of the pages were blank. The ones covered in scribbles were just about clear enough to read. "Do you think it's just Alex that has been removed?" asked Teddy. "I checked the files earlier and none of the bodies have been exhumed."

Will couldn't think. White fog had filled his head. Why had the Reaper taken the body but left the diary? So far his theories had generally turned out to be backed up, but this revelation put him right back at square one.

"Only one way to find out," said Will. "You go and check one of the others. I'll go and look for Ed. Then we'll join up again and see if Abigail has been on a midnight wander." He paused. "What do we do about Alex? Melanie has a right to know that her son is missing."

"What she doesn't know can't hurt her. We'll be the ones in the shit if anyone finds out we did this," said Teddy, already replacing the lid of the coffin back over the empty shell.

"Can't you find some reason as to why we are here?"

"I'll need a warrant. Your theory was just a theory, not grounds to dig them up. I'll think of something and pull out my best acting when it's found to be empty again."

"Fine. Let's fill this one back in and then get started on the others," replied Will, starting to heap dirt back in the pit.

"No. You go and get started. It will take you long enough as it is. I'll finish here, go and take a look at Fred, and then find you when I'm done."

*

Ed was missing, too. There weren't even any possessions in the coffin. Just damp wood. Will had just finished filling his grave in again when Teddy joined him.

"He's been taken as well, right?" he said, cutting through the silence of the graveyard. "Fred is gone. By my reckoning, that will be all the boys taken. Ed too. Just Abigail. Should we bother?"

Will wiped the dirt from his hands onto his jeans and took a gulp of water from his bottle. "We need to. She might have left something as well."

Abigail had been buried in a white box, with two pink stripes lying vertically across the lid. According to Teddy, there had been an unusual amount of people at her burial. Her classmates were crying; only some managed to pull it off convincingly, and the press had been there to interview anyone who wanted their spot on the next day's headlines. He told Will where she had been buried and it didn't take long to find her grave. Despite their aching arms, the pair made quick progress, now having worked out a technique to break through the dirt faster. Abigail had been buried less than a week and the dirt hadn't had time to settle yet, adding to their speed. In less than forty minutes, they had made a large enough hole to drop into and find the box.

Six blackened nails bound the top down. Abigail's family had been wealthy enough to get her name plated in metal on the top.

Will took his crowbar and stuck it in the gap between the wood. Before he could apply any pressure, Teddy put an arm across his chest. "The grave is fairly new. We should be able to get this off with a hammer. Reduce the damage."

"I don't have a hammer. I must have left it with my magic tool kit!" hissed Will.

"There's a shed over there," said Teddy, pointing towards a corner of the cemetery. "See if it's got one." His tone was strict, and Will felt like one of his low-ranking officers.

Will pulled a little salute and said: "yes, sir!"

The shack sat abandoned; a part of the roof crumpled in by a gnarled tree that was infecting the surrounding ground. Berries hung from the branches not ensnared around the building. There was a familiarity about it. Something in his brain was trying to push through the layers of fatigue. They had been out for almost three hours and the temperature had dropped by a few degrees, enough to cause the grass to bristle with specks of ice. A wheelbarrow lay propped against the side of the shed, covered in rust. An abundance of apples spilled from the tray, those on the floor almost rotten, and large holes scattered the skin where various insects had fed from the fruit. Will walked closer, careful to avoid a wood axe standing next to a crumbling grave. Cracks in the wood of the door almost allowed him to see straight through into the darkness and he pushed it open without any resistance.

It was cramped—the shed was roughly six square feet. On one side, an array of gardening tools hung from the wall, the side not abused by the tree branch above. The shears were blunt, and a hammer hadn't been used in so long that moss had crawled from the wall to the handle. At the far side of the room sat a chest held together by bolts and leather straps. A padlock fastened the lid to the base, still shining.

"Better than nothing," muttered Will, taking the hammer from its place on the wall and brushing off the shrubbery that had found its home on the steel.

When he returned to the grave, he saw Teddy standing over the box, deep in prayer.

"Your prayers are answered," said Will, tossing the hammer towards the detective. Teddy opened his eyes just in time to grab the tool.

"Great. Let's just hope they don't crumble in my hands before I can use them," he said, holding the hammer out like it was covered in something foul. He bent down and started carefully removing the nails from the lid. It took some effort, but before long, the lid was gone. The pair heaved it from the box.

"Jesus," groaned Teddy, pulling his sleeve to his nose. What they don't tell you in the movies is how a coffin reeks after a few weeks underground. Abigail remained in her rest…

Her body was dehydrated, peeling back the skin around her nails. What was left of her hands lay across her chest, exactly how she had been positioned before the funeral. This grave hadn't been disturbed. Until now.

*

"They have the bodies of the Spark boys. They have Ed. Why not take Abigail?" said Will.

"Maybe they see women differently," replied Teddy, quickly stuffing the nails back into the lid again. "Women are often seen as untainted compared to men. Taking a body from its rest is arguably the most disrespectful act you can commit against a person—after killing them that is."

"Is it common for killers to treat the sexes differently?" Will asked, pulling himself out of the hole.

"Religious fanatics are often more careful with their treatment of women, in my experience."

"This killer certainly treats *Grimm's* as a kind of Bible. However, I doubt they are religious. Something about this all feels weird."

"Besides all these coffins missing their residents?"

"Yes. When I was looking for the hammer, I saw something in that shed. I just don't know what."

"It's a good thing you're not vague," said Teddy, using the shovel to throw dirt back onto Abigail's coffin. The white wood was now suffocated under a thickening layer of earth. "We'd better take a look then."

Will was filled with a warm sense of gratitude. "After everything I've *seen* recently, I'm surprised you don't think I am mad."

"I don't like the way you think. Far too close to the border of criminality in my opinion, but I can't deny that so far you've proved yourself to be right more than you have been wrong."

They finished returning the grave to its original state and went to return the hammer to its place on the wall of the shack.

"You religious?" Will asked, aiming his torch towards the shed. Winter hours meant that they still had time before the sun forced through the fog of grey clouds.

"Sure," said Teddy

"You don't strike me as a man of God. You've never mentioned it. If I hadn't seen you praying, then the thought wouldn't have even come to me."

Teddy scrunched his nose. "I'm a lot of things and most of them don't need mentioning. Just because I don't talk about God all the time doesn't mean I don't pray."

"Even after what happened with Nathan?"

Despite the darkness, Teddy's unease was clear. It wasn't as obvious as a shudder, but by now Will had learned to read Teddy's body language with relative ease. Any mention of Nathan and Teddy's voice wavered.

"I buy the story that God created life. Whether he wants anything to do with it now, I'm not so sure. I could blame God for what happened that day. I could blame the people in front of us. I could blame Gillian. If I blame anyone else, then it is only to take accountability away from me. It was me who took my eyes off him. It was my decision to take my family to the lake. No divine presence led me to that, just as no divine intervention stopped him from walking into the water." Teddy cleared his throat, a sign that his emotions were grasping at his voice.

"Have you been to church here before then?" asked Will, subtly trying to change the subject.

"Only a couple of times. I don't think that you can build a crapheap like this and say that it's the home of any deity. No, I don't think he's ever been here. I certainly haven't seen any evidence of the fella. Reckon he spends most of his time in the Sistine Chapel. Wouldn't blame him for that."

"God works in mysterious ways, though, right?" Will said, smiling slightly.

"If by mysterious you mean without any morals then, maybe. All I know is that before every case, I pray. Not for me, but for the people I'm helping. I don't interpret a lot of what the good book says as how the majority do. If everything it said was true, then surely we'll all end up in Hell."

Will had left the door to the shack open and Teddy stepped in first. "You're right," he said. "There is something odd about this shithole."

Still struggling to place what was attempting to catch his attention, Will placed the hammer back onto the wall and watched Teddy inspect their surroundings.

"This chest… It's not battered and neglected like everything else in here. The padlock looks shining new," said the detective, crouching down and turning the lock in his hands.

Is that what's been bothering me? No… It's something else.

"We ain't getting in there without a cutter," continued Teddy.

"Or an axe," said Will, nodding towards the grave outside. Teddy caught his eye and grinned.

*

Teddy swung the axe over his head and brought it crashing down into the top of the chest, causing fragments of wood to dent but continue to cling together. With his spare hand, he wiped a line of sweat from his brow, set himself and tried again, this time managing to create a crack in the wood.

"A couple more should do it."

Teddy straightened up.

"For you maybe." He hit the chest directly on the crack, causing the lid to fall in on itself. A tangy aroma rose from inside. Will crouched down and risked a look inside the box. It was full of apples, a collage of red and green. Most of the top layer was rotten, and the mold was slowly spreading to the rest, emanating a sour odor.

"Seems a little extreme putting a lock on a box of fruit," said Teddy, picking up an apple yet to be ruined and taking a large bite.

Will pounded the floor with his fist, feeling a strong ripple of pain through his arm. It had been for nothing. Whatever he noticed was just his wilting mind playing tricks again. Then Teddy gagged, showering Will in droplets of fruit-filled spittle. His hand was pointing toward where he had just taken the apple. In its place was an eye, staring towards them, bloodshot and sickly looking. With a silent nod, they continued pulling away apples, revealing the full picture: two bloodshot eyes, a small piggish nose, blue lips. They were left with a severed head, covered by wisps of grey hair. It looked to belong to a woman, but it was so brutally beaten that it was difficult to tell. Purple flesh remained where the neck should have been, whoever had done it had crushed the base of the head repeatedly with the lid of the chest. Flecks of dried blood and broken bones were stuck to her skin. This one felt different, almost more like it had been conducted by an animal.

"I think I know the story," said Will, his voice shaking.

Teddy shuffled back from the chest and met his eyes, his skin grimly pale. Now it made sense. It hadn't been the chest that was bothering him. Nor anything else in the shed. Will nodded towards the tree that crushed the shed. Above the box dangled a collection of fruit. Juniper berries hung from the branch, sparkling in the rays from the flashlight.

*

The New Year was set to be introduced by the end of a snowfall. In a few days, the pure, white frost would melt into dirty puddles. The rest would be used to make myriads of snowmen until Hollyhead's population was outnumbered. Although the month of December had been frosty, the snow didn't begin until the 29th. At first, it came down in thick swirls, blasting the town into hibernation. Will was awake to greet it. He watched from his motel room window as the grass outside was quickly covered in fresh layers of snow. His plan for the morning had been to grab a breakfast of waffles and syrup in town before heading to Frank's house to tell him what had occurred in the cemetery. Now, he didn't think he would be able to face outside. Each breath of cold air was painful. It filled his lungs, causing them to shudder as if being stabbed by tiny icicles. Both insomnia and the cancer were pulling his body apart. He shook his head, trying to push the thoughts from his mind. Thinking about his sleeplessness only made its presence stronger. There was nothing he could do about the cancer. He knew it had continued skulking through his cells and attacking his own immune system.

The trees outside were covered in a misty haze. Their pencil branches had been covered with snow and for a moment, he considered walking out into the morning cold and hanging himself from the branch. How long would it be until Wendy came out and found him? Maybe he would hang there so long that his body would freeze, and the snow would bind to his clothes, making him just another snowman. He laughed. Insomnia does funny things to a man's brain.

The head was quickly identified as belonging to Meredith Flax. Teddy confirmed that she was in her late seventies, but her records were incomplete. Her body was nowhere to be seen. Before the rest of the police had arrived at the scene, Will had told Teddy the story that Meredith's death seemed to relate to.

"It's called *The Juniper Tree*. A mother dies while giving birth to a baby boy. Her husband buries her beneath a juniper tree. Once he remarries, the new couple has a daughter named Marlinchen. The boy's new stepmother abuses him because he stands to inherit his father's wealth. We found Meredith's head in a chest filled with apples. In the story, the stepson is decapitated by the stepmother when she offers to give him an apple. She proceeds to chop up his body and put him into a soup. When the father arrives home, he eats his boy."

"These brothers were seriously fucked up," ranted Teddy.

"They just wrote them down. Fairy tales are folk stories collected all around the world. Anyway, the juniper tree becomes covered in a kind of mist, and out flies a bird. It visits the town and is given a set of gifts from a goldsmith, a shoemaker, and a miller. The bird kills the stepmother using a millstone given by the miller and then turns back into the boy. It seems the rest of the family live happily ever after."

"The boy just committed murder. He'd be hanged back in those days. It's not very realistic."

"I tell you a story about a boy who rises from the dead as a bird and you pick out the fact he wasn't executed as the most unrealistic part?"

"I'm a cop."

Will sighed. "There's a pattern to these killings. They are linked to the stories, sure, but it's not quite the same. The six boys were made to live as swans until their sister saved them. The ungrateful son didn't die either. His fate was to remain with the frog attached to him for eternity, but not death. As for this one, it was Meredith who was decapitated by the apple chest, not a boy. It's like they have been flipped. Except for Abigail, who really did lose her hands."

"The killer isn't recreating the stories; they're going a step further or changing the victim," said Teddy. "There's something personal about this kill. Meredith Flax wasn't put out for the world to see. It doesn't fit in with the rest. No one could miss the Spark boys; Abigail was found in one of the busiest alleys in town, and Ed would have been found by the next morning at the latest. Meredith could have gone weeks, even months, without ever being found."

"So what?" said Will.

"Serial killers can break a pattern and that is when they are at their most vulnerable," said Teddy, his eyes full of childlike excitement. He grasped Will's shoulder in an iron grip. "They have just made their first mistake. We are a step closer."

*

A certainty of any police investigation is that the lead detective will come under as much scrutiny as any potential suspects. Despite Teddy's initial hope that the case was coming together, his impression on the public was waning. He had been called in for news interviews and briefings and it was easy to tell that the process was getting to him. Rumour had it that the higher-ups were planning to bring in a detective from New York to take over the case. Three murders in a month were causing everyone to look nervously over their shoulders while walking home and it seemed that most of the town now owned a firearm, whether they admitted it or not. Old Stephen Hunter made a show of sitting on his front porch, whiskey bottle by his side, and a fat cigar between his lips, holding a shotgun and cocking it whenever he saw anyone he found suspicious—these people mainly consisting of black youths. While Teddy was busy answering questions from reporters about the manner in which Meredith was found, Will decided to follow up on what was proving to be the only solid evidence they had.

The diary: a black, leather-bound representation of a schoolboy's soul. Will didn't know what to expect when he opened the book. Family feuds? Girl trouble? His stomach clenched when he thought about what he might read about himself in his old friend's thoughts; finding out that Lenora hated him was bad enough. Knowing about Alex's dependency on drugs, it wasn't a total surprise when he found that many of the scribblings described fever dreams. Delusions and paranoia while being grasped by the claws of addiction. Apparently, in the weeks leading to his death, Alex had been tormented by visions of the dead. One entry detailed seeing a dead child on an iron slab.

I was not meant to see it. I know that much. The worst part is that I saw them before. Weeks ago. Dying. My mind has changed. I can't carry on following this path. Slowly, it's breaking me.

Whatever hallucination Alex had seen was powerful. However, the story didn't fit. The writing was dated only weeks before his death. If Alex had been talking about his addiction, then his cold-turkey attitude didn't last long. Nick had recounted that Alex was still desperate until his murder. Either Nick was lying, or Alex's willpower hadn't been enough, and the visions had slowly driven the young man into insanity. Unfortunately, there was no mention of a secret meeting or anything else that could lead them toward a new suspect. With each attempt of getting closer to the killer's identity, they seemed to get further away. Why had the killer taken the body and left the diary? It didn't fit.

There was a run-down television set in the motel lobby, and Will glanced its way as he entered. Teddy was being interviewed, this time standing outside the cemetery gates. Despite the weather, he was only wearing a shirt and his signature hat. Mayor Stone stood beside him, flaunting a mink coat. Her spindly fingers were hooked around Teddy's shoulder.

"Can you turn it up?" called Will towards the shadowy figure of Wendy in her office. She came out grumbling about her hip and unmuted the set.

"The simple fact is that I cannot assure you that it is safe to be out after dark. Three murders have taken place so far and all three have been identified as being committed after lights out. Parents, please keep your children inside. Walk with them to school and do not let them out of your sight until they have been signed in by their teacher. Ensure that you have a trusted friend with you if necessity causes you to leave your house. Until we find this killer, Hollyhead is not safe," Teddy warned, to a crowd of flashing cameras and scrabbling hands.

"Detective! You're no closer to finding the killer?" shouted a pudgy-nosed reporter.

Teddy wiped his brow. "We have multiple leads that we are following. There is talk of extra aid being brought in from out of state. Speed is of the essence here."

"What about the reports of your replacement as head of the investigation?" said the same reporter, followed by nods from the rest of the crowd.

"My duty is to protect this town and its people. If stepping aside will help that cause, then that is what I shall do."

"Mayor Stone, do you believe that Detective Ludlow is capable of finding the killer?" asked a blonde journalist.

"He has my full confidence," Stone replied. "I'd also like to remind everyone of the parade next week in memory of Abigail Finsbury. We would love to see as many out-of-towners as possible."

Teddy wasn't a good enough actor to hide his annoyance. He dropped down from the makeshift stage and was immediately surrounded by other officers.

"He doesn't fill *me* with confidence," said Wendy as she turned the volume down again. "I think I could do a better job than him."

"If not for your hip?" replied Will. Seeing Teddy's despondent interview had bothered him. This wasn't just about Alex anymore. Or Frank. He had grown fond of the detective.

"If not for my hip. Exactly."

*

That evening, Frank and Marty joined Will and looked over the diary. Despite knowing far more than Will about bootleg drugs, Marty couldn't make sense of Alex's ramblings.

"Attitude is a strong predictor of behavior change," he had said, reading the extract that Will had picked up on that morning. "If Alex was as traumatized by the vision as this suggests he was, then I would say that he wouldn't have been asking for stronger drugs. Addicts often try to wean off through less addictive substances such as marijuana. Either his addiction was too strong, or Nick was lying."

"Either could be true," said Will. Years of close contact with Nick had strengthened Will's ability to tell when his old friend was lying and there had been no signs of it the night he had told them his story. The thought was painful. If he was so sure now,

243

then why hadn't he been certain that Nick had attacked Lenora?

"Do you mind if we take this?" asked Frank. "I want to have a closer look. See if there are any connections to *Grimm's* concealed in the pages."

Will agreed, watched them leave, and decided to try to get an early night. He had just settled his mind down when there was a knock at the door. Prepared to give Wendy a piece of his mind, he flung the door open.

Teddy was standing in the doorway; he was a sorry sight. His hat drooped with water thanks to the onslaught of the rain. In his hand was a battered leather suitcase, streaked with creases. Bits of fabric stuck out of the cracks as if he had thrown in all he could before arriving.

"Can I come in?" he said bleakly. Will nodded and sheltered the broken detective from the world, if only for a little while.

*

After a brief attempt at small talk, which was equally painful for both of them, and multiple shots of straight whiskey. Teddy revealed why he was there.

"Gill and I have been having issues for a while now. At first, I thought it was because she had stopped smoking. She quit when she was pregnant with Grets, but I guess stress got to her. Stopped again earlier this year. I'm ashamed to say that I probably haven't been as attentive to my family as I should have been," he said, his hand rubbing his leg in a nervous tic.

"There's been three murders. Of course, you are going to be busy," said Will, still in his pajamas. He had kept the chair from Christmas and given it to Teddy, apologizing that one of the legs didn't reach the floor properly.

"A man should always make time for his family. It's the one constant in life. When I retire from the force, they'll be able to replace me within weeks. I've accepted that. It's different with family. You only get one."

Will nodded. "What do you think set it off this time?"

"These killings are getting to the whole town now. Greta's scared shitless, and I'm having to balance my duty as a father and catching this son of a bitch. So much death flying around right now, I think that it brought everything with Nathan back.

Gillian doesn't blame me for his death," he added. "Even if I do."

"She'll come around. We're close to catching this guy. I feel it," Will lied, and it was obvious that Teddy knew it.

"There's no fixing it this time. A big elephant has been sitting in the room and we've finally gotten around to acknowledging it. It was only a matter of time."

"What was it?" said Will, knowing that, despite their growing friendship, care was needed to ensure that Teddy didn't fall apart. There was no telling whether he would be able to pull himself together again.

"I'm a homosexual," he said. The man who oozed charisma was a shadow of his former self. His eyes were wide and fearful as if he expected Will to punch him straight in the teeth. Fear was so blatant that Teddy even leaned backward, trying to distance himself from the words he had just sent through the room.

"But you're married?" said Will. The logistics of the situation didn't make sense.

"I told you that I got involved way too young. Straight relationships were all around and I got mixed up in the culture. It didn't feel wrong, but it didn't feel right either. Like a gray middle. I loved Gill. I still do. My behavior was what I believed to be expected of me rather than what I felt most comfortable doing."

"And Greta? She's only seven."

Teddy's face was struck with regret, and he rubbed the back of his neck. "I didn't want a second kid. When Gill suggested it, I only agreed because of Nathan. Gill is a brilliant woman. She's stronger than me and a hell of a lot smarter. If anyone deserved a second chance at being a parent, it's her. What happened to Nathan was my fault and she shouldn't suffer because of it. Greta was only born because I was too much of a coward to say how I really felt," said Teddy. His voice sounded choked and detached. This was something he had been hiding for so long that the words were still chained. "You wouldn't understand how difficult it is. I've been faking who I am because society has decided that one way is the right way. Greta is my sunshine. She's bottled happiness and I love her to bits. Every time I look at her, I can't help but feel like she shouldn't be mine."

Maybe it was the lack of sleep. Maybe meeting Eve had changed something inside of him. Either way, Will's hand grasped Teddy's shoulder. "The only thing I care about is that you're a bloody good detective. A good man, too. Your preferences make no difference to me. As for Greta, she knows that you are there for her when she needs you. Your sexuality isn't going to stop her from wanting to watch *Disney* films with you. She loves you because you're her dad."

Teddy blinked away tears and gripped Will's hand. Trembling nods thanked him. "Gillian wanted to take Greta to her parents for a few days, but I managed to persuade her to stay. Greta doesn't need the disruption. I just don't know what to do."

"Stay here tonight. Tomorrow, we can figure out what you're going to do about Gillian. This isn't going to be easy, Ted. Nothing that is important ever is," said Will. He looked around the room. "Although, if you're staying the night then I should have booked a twin room," he added, smiling.

Teddy laughed and wiped his face. "You're not really my type, Will; zombies aren't really my thing."

They raised their glasses and drank deep into the night. There was no need to talk more about Teddy's situation. They would get to that in the morning.

CHAPTER TWENTY-ONE: THE REWIND

When daylight finally arrived, Teddy remained passed out on Will's bed, having drunk himself into a deep sleep. Will hadn't managed to follow him into dreams. For a few hours, Teddy had told him stories of previous cases, all ending with the successful capture of thieves and wife-beaters. It was easy to imagine Teddy's broad smile with an almost comical interpretation of a criminal crumpled beneath his feet in a stance of victory. His experience with murder was lacking, and he admitted that he felt completely out of his depth. Having a few stories of his own, Will recounted his time hanging with various actors and other authors, giving Teddy the rundown on the personas behind the public eye. The conversation slowly faded out and was replaced with light snoring, spurring Will's decision to read another story from *Grimm's*. The brothers told of a Pied Piper, who, after being conned by a greedy mayor, stole a town's children while their parents were busy at church. The book continued by specifying that several versions of the story had different endings. One said that the children were drowned, while others were more cheerful, with the children being returned after payment was made. He skimmed across the story of *Hansel and Gretel,* a story he knew well, and ended with *The Juniper Tree.* As the curtain fell, an overbearing sense of dread fell over him.

What kind of person decapitates a defenseless old woman? The thought sat at the front of his mind until Teddy woke with a series of grunts.

"I feel like I've been sat on by Benny Spark," he said, rubbing his head. "May he rest in peace…"

*

Following a cheap breakfast at another local diner, Will agreed to fetch a few of Teddy's belongings. It was only a short walk to his house, but Teddy let him drive the Granada. 'Every little helps' was a good philosophy and one that he thought was relevant to the situation. Teddy stayed at the motel and booked himself a room. Will parked around the corner, anxious not to be seen driving by Gillian, and knocked on the door. Still working on what he was going to say, he waited a few seconds. Gillian answered. Her eyes were puffy and red. Evidently, the situation had affected her just as much as it had done her husband.

"Teddy wanted me to collect some of his things," said Will, his hands scrambling into his pockets as far as they could go. The look on Gillian's face made him hope that the ground would open up and swallow him whole. She let him in all the same.

"What does he need?" she asked. "Greta doesn't know yet, and I would appreciate it if you didn't tell her."

"Of course," he replied. "I think he just needs some of his case notes. A change of clothes wouldn't be a bad idea either." Gillian ushered him in and went upstairs, leaving Will sitting in the same pink armchair that he had found himself in last time, albeit far more awkwardly.

*

Gillian returned carrying a satchel full of loose papers, a carton of unfiltered cigarettes stuffed down the side. When she caught Will looking, she pushed them further down into the bag.

"Did he say anything about what happened?" she asked, not managing to look him in the eye. Her voice was branded with embarrassment. All Will wanted to do was tell her that it wasn't her fault.

"Yes," he said, not able to add to his sentiment. "He says that you didn't know, but you don't seem surprised. I almost want to say that you knew all along."

Gillian sighed. "Yes, I knew. It's not easy. I'd go to bed and ask him to join me, but there would always be some excuse. We haven't been intimate for years and even then I could tell he wasn't into it. We had Greta and then he changed. It was like he was doing me a favor."

"Why not get a divorce?"

"Because I love him. If the town knew, do you think they would be easy on him? No one would trust a gay detective.

That's not how the world works. The police would fire him for a start. The papers would love it and then we would get letters and prank calls. They would turn to threats and we would have to leave town and find somewhere else to live. Someone would find out there and the cycle would start again. We will never find peace as long as people know," she said. Will took her hand and gave her a weak, but meaningful, smile.

"I'm getting on," she continued. "I won't be able to have another child. You can live with someone and have no idea who they are, but you are used to their company. Once they're gone it all feels a bit empty. I owe it to Greta to keep him in our lives. For her sake—and his."

"What about you? It's only fair that you have a chance to find someone again. This shouldn't mark the end of your life."

"I'm a mother. If my child is happy and doesn't end up dead or in prison, then I can say I did a good job. What happens to me doesn't matter."

"Teddy wants you to be happy."

"And I don't want him lynched."

There was no use. Gillian had made up her mind and there was nothing he could say that would change that. As noble as her intentions were, she would be living a lie. That lie would stop Teddy from going through traumatic, and possibly painful, conversion therapy. Will collected the rest of Teddy's papers and Gillian let him out, slightly happier than she had been when he first arrived, although Will suspected it was just a façade.

"Promise me something," she said before he reached the sidewalk. "Don't let him lose himself in this case. Just make sure he gets through this."

"I promise."

*

Teddy had booked a room a few doors down from Will and gratefully received his belongings. He had asked how Gillian was and Will replied that she was worried about him. Sheepishly, Teddy thanked him for his help. "If there's anything I can do then please tell me," he said, opening his door.

"Actually, there is," replied Will. Teddy had access to a myriad of archives. There was a particular one from a decade prior that Will was especially interested in. Teddy agreed to help.

A night of no sleep left Will exhausted, and his chest was more painful than ever before. There was time to steal a few hours before Teddy would inevitably knock on his door with his answer.

He was right. Teddy handed over a document four hours later, ordering Will to keep it quiet or his ass will be on the line. Everything was in order. He walked to the lobby and stuck a quarter in the payphone. He had two calls to make. Then, if everything went to plan, another chapter of his life would be over. The final day of 1980. A new year meant a new start.

*

The second call was to Lenora. With less protest than previously, she agreed to meet him at the park near Hollyhead High. Somewhere Will had often walked through as a kid, always alone. The park was nothing special, with just a swing set and jungle gym. That was all it needed—child imagination would fill in the rest.

Tense with nervous excitement, Will waited until she rounded the corner, now having found herself a stylish leather jacket and jeans. A far better look than her *Columbo* impersonation. Her pace was quicker and for the first time, her hair was arranged so as not to conceal her scar.

"What's up Will? What couldn't wait till later?" she said, shivering. Snow was gently falling onto the grass, bunching into clumps of white powder. She nuzzled her foot into the floor, enveloping it in a thin layer of ice.

"It wasn't Nick. His crimes don't extend to murder."

Rather than asking questions as Will had expected, Lenora smiled. "It doesn't matter to me anymore. An eye for an eye, right?" she said, pointing to her scar. "Plus, I still have the necklace. Let's just call it leverage until the time is right. I'm guessing you have found something."

"I broke into the graves belonging to the Reaper's victims. Unless Nick has a pile of bodies hidden away somewhere, I think it's safe to say that his role in events that night ceased after giving Alex a beating."

"Are you saying that the bodies weren't in their coffins?" asked Lenora.

"We checked two of the Spark boys. Gone. Ed McCain. Gone. Abigail Finsbury was the only one who hadn't been disturbed."

"That's weird. Why take them and leave Abigail?"

"I don't know, and it's driving me mad," said Will.

Lenora laughed. "You haven't changed one bit. I mean it," she said, "and for some people, that's a good thing. For others, I'm not so sure."

"Brilliant, so you're saying I'm still the same as I was at eighteen? That's great to hear."

"I don't know where the sarcasm came from. Other than that, you're exactly the same. You didn't quite fit in then and you still don't. You can try. You *have* tried. Even back then, you tried to be like Nick. Not in every way, but enough to make it obvious. Maybe that's what happens when you spend a long time with someone. I hated you following us around. I never knew why but now it's clear. It's because I liked you for you. The more you became like Nick, the more I couldn't stand being around you. One Nick King was enough for me."

There it was. Years of animosity condensed into one reason. It was true; he had been a cheap imitation of Nick in many ways. Not until Lenora's disappearance had he finally seen the darkness behind the mask.

"I believe a part of me loved you. You liked Nick and I guess I thought that my only chance was to emulate him."

"You know, if you had been yourself more often, then I…" She stopped. Her gaze was fixed at a point behind Will's shoulder. He followed her eyes and smiled. Two people had walked around the corner. One was a slightly plump lady with permed brunette hair who waddled slightly as she moved. By her side was a smaller girl with bright ginger hair. She was dressed in a yellow raincoat that was slightly too big for her. Her walk was apprehensive; she knew this was a big moment. It was. Meeting your birth mother for the first time always is.

"Lenora, this is Sarah," said Will, as the pair came closer. The first call had been to St Agnes' orphanage in Saunton. The documents that Teddy had given him contained names of orphanage entrees starting from the year that Lenora had disappeared. Although the list was larger than he had thought, Will had managed to identify a girl with ginger hair, given to Hollyhead orphanage three months after Lenora's disappearance. The most convincing evidence that she was Lenora's child was one of her eyes. Made of two different colors. Sarah had been transferred multiple times due to disruption in her home—like mother, like daughter. Even if Lenora had tried, it would have been difficult to find her.

Sarah stepped forwards. "We have the same eyes," she said, inspecting Lenora's pupils closely. "And the same color hair."

The woman with her, Jane, watched the girl carefully, ready to step in if there was an issue. Will wasn't completely relaxed himself; Lenora was unstable and still trying to glue the pieces of her life back together. A voice inside his head was telling him that this was a bad idea.

Lenora crouched low and put her hand out. "My name's Lenora. Lenora Brown." The girl took her hand, shook it gingerly, and said that it was nice to meet her.

"We thought it would be nice if you spent some time together. Get to know each other a little," said Jane. "I'll be just here if you need me, Sarah." But Sarah had already seen the swings, and it was clear her attention had been stolen. Lenora nodded, clearly scared shitless by the situation. Jane walked away and Lenora turned to Will.

"How did you find her?"

"I was owed a favor."

"I would have searched for her myself. It's terrifying… She looks just like me."

"Just a shame about the hair color," said Will. He then started laughing as Lenora nudged him in the ribs.

"Why did you do this? I've been horrible to you," she said with an inflection of guilt buried at the end.

"Even if everything I believed about our friendship was fake; you were one of the only reasons I made it into adulthood. I don't need to hear from you again. Maybe that would be for the best. This is just a thank you. Thank you for the years I believed there was love there," Will replied. He nodded towards Sarah, who had already found some height on the swings.

"You'd better make sure she doesn't go flying off or she might get a scar to match as well."

*

Still chewing over whether he made the right decision, Will unlocked his motel room door and walked in. As he shut it, a small voice caught his attention. Eve was walking towards him; her face clenched in distress.

"Steady on. What's the matter?" asked Will, taking her hand and leading her into his room.

Her voice was tight and she let out small gasps between words. "The hospital. I can't believe I did it. Never in a million years. I've got nothing. No plan. Nothing."

"Slow down," said Will, rubbing her arm. 'What happened?"

Eve took a deep breath. "I told you how much I despise this place. There was so much going on and I just snapped. Walked into my boss' office and quit on the spot. Told him that I was leaving town and then walked out."

"Shit… You're going then?" said Will, filled with disappointment. He should have known. The good things never lasted long. For years he had shut himself away from any chance of rejection, it always ended the same. Then he ran away until the hurt couldn't catch him anymore. The one time he thought that running wouldn't be needed now seemed to be the time he needed it most.

"Come away with me," she said, so quickly that the thought must have only just come to her. "We'll leave here together. Go and start somewhere new and forget about Hollyhead completely."

Will's brain stopped. Running together was an entirely new concept. Weeks ago, he would have accepted without hesitation. "I can't," he replied. "I promised that I would help find the Reaper. Teddy needs me for this."

"He's been a detective for years. I'm sure he can do it alone. Even if not, he has a whole group of police to work with."

"What about Frank?"

"He ignored you for years, then asked you to obsess over a case that he couldn't solve. Spreading your wings would be the biggest *fuck you* that you could give," she said, now holding Will's hand with her warm fingers. Her eyes appeared more rounded than normal, like something from a cartoon. "Thing is, I can't do this by myself. I tried it when I came here, and it hasn't worked. The only good part of this experience was meeting you and, honestly, I love you."

The words sounded like a different language. He had written them down before as part of his books. Characters he had conjured would say them effortlessly, while he hadn't heard them for years. There was a vague recollection of Molly saying it to him when he was young, but even that might have just been a dream. His throat tightened.

"Frankly, you've helped me to see color in a world that I believed to be completely black and white. I love you too."

Eve laughed and pulled Will into a hug that almost knocked the wind out of him.

"Come on! Pick out your favorite dress. I'm taking you dancing, then we're going to haul ass out of here," said Will, releasing himself from her grip. Ushering her towards the door, he kissed her again. "I'll pick you up at eight. Don't be late!" he said, catching a glimpse of Eve's smile before closing the door. He sat back on his bed. The hard and lumpy bed that he had detested so much when he first arrived now didn't bother him. He had Eve. They could leave now. Perhaps his last years were looking up. Perhaps they didn't *need* to be his last years.

*

It didn't take long to pack. Will threw his few belongings into his case and put it on the bed. He dressed in a smart shirt and pants and waited, his foot tapping impatiently on the floor. The Reaper's identity would be revealed at some point; maybe he would still be alive to hear it. Teddy was a good enough detective to work it out on his own, and if not then maybe Frank and Marty would have a breakthrough. There hadn't been many positives about Hollyhead. Eve mattered. For maybe the first time in his life, something mattered. Then the phone rang.

"Will," said Frank, his voice unusually raw. "I need to talk to you. Can you come to the house?"

Will checked his watch. Two hours until he had agreed to meet Eve; he had time. "I can stop by, but only for a short while."

"Thank you," Frank replied, before abruptly hanging up. Assuming that there was an update concerning the case, Will stood up buttoning his coat while doing so. An opportunity had presented itself to tell Frank of his intentions and possibly even get his blessing. If anything, the return to Hollyhead had shown that his father was a romantic. Then there was the matter of Teddy. He wrote a note telling the detective that he was leaving town with a girl. Rounding off with a message of thanks and good luck with the case, Will folded it over and pushed it under Teddy's door, before setting off to see Frank.

*

Less than twenty minutes later, Will was sitting where he had been a month earlier, only this time, Frank was alone. He hadn't stopped pacing since Will had arrived and on more than one occasion, he had needed to leave the room, each time returning with another finger of whiskey.

"I'm meeting Eve soon; whatever you have to say, can you get on with it?" said Will.

Frank smoothed his tie and ran a hand through his hair. "It's not an easy conversation to instigate," he said, draining his glass again.

"I'll leave and come back tonight then," replied Will; Frank didn't need to know that he wasn't planning on being in Hollyhead come morning.

"No. No, it must be done now," he paused, swallowed, and said: "It's the rewind. There was a reason the government had to destroy them."

"I'm all ears, Dad," said Will.

Frank sighed. His mouth twitched erratically like the words were trying to wriggle out but not quite making it. "It started off perfectly. We could check witness testimony and have a lie-detection system that was waterproof. At its inception, the MED was deemed a total success. The higher-ups wanted it distributed to all agents as quickly as possible. I told you that Jackson Cole was let go. I didn't tell you why."

"Well, we are talking about the FBI, so I'm guessing he got in trouble. Maybe he was doing a little white dust on the side," said Will, raising his eyebrows. "It wouldn't be the first time."

Frank wiped the back of his neck. "He was sent to a psychiatric ward. He kept having horrific visions. Dead bodies, crying women," he paused, "he saw the same woman commit suicide at least three times a day. He couldn't escape her; he saw her in every corridor and reflection. Her name was Anne Gillepsie. She had died a few years prior. Abusive husband, parents lost in a car crash, that kind of thing. In '62 she had slit her wrists in front of the mirror. I guess she did a good job of it because when the ambulance arrived, she had been dead for at least two hours. Cole was haunted by that woman as long as he had the MED—as long as he was using it."

Will had been following the words with care. Any mention of Frank's FBI days and his ears were pricked. It was starting to make sense now. "You mean the visions that I have been seeing are because of the rewind?"

Frank held out his hand. "Please let me finish." He cleared his throat. "We found out that he had been taking an MED home and using it in his own time. He tried it out on his wife and discovered that she had been sleeping with her boss. That night, he cracked her skull open."

Will could picture it. Jackson Cole standing over the broken remains of his wife, his own face speckled with blood. He blinked back into the room.

"A neighbor heard the commotion and rang it through. As soon as the cops discovered that Cole was in the FBI, they called us to deal with it. When we arrived, he was hunched in a corner, clutching the MED to his chest. I have never seen a crime scene like it since. His wife was on the floor in the dining room. A fire-poker was sticking from her head where he had impaled her. Blood covered the entire room. So much that forensics had a hard time distinguishing whose was whose. Marty tried taking the MED and Cole stuck him with a knife. I managed to restrain him long enough for a team to sedate him and send him packing to Hollyhead Asylum. The MED is like a drug, Will. I know what it feels like to use it. I also know how it feels to be without it."

Will's head felt like it was splitting. "You mean, the Spark boys and Abigail were just hallucinations from withdrawal?" He had a spark of relief. After allowing himself to believe it was his mind wilting, knowing that there was a reason reassured him.

Frank shook his head. "No. Every time you use the rewind, your neurons are being wired information from the victim. You see what they think, correct? You feel what they feel. It leaves imprints. Pictures in your mind that you have only seen in their head. Teddy tells me you saw his boy in the lake. You saw what Teddy saw on that terrible day."

"I've used it for years. I think I would have noticed if I were seeing dead people everywhere."

Frank shrugged, "I don't think the brain is picky. I doubt you saw many murdered children in your career. Perhaps you walked past them in the street, no reason to suspect that they are not really there."

"I've seen people dying before. When I was interviewing for my book, I spoke to many widows and widowers."

"I daresay that your pain medication for your cancer may have strengthened their effects. They started in your dreams. Perhaps you put them down to nightmares without realizing why it was happening. Now, your brain signals are all over the place and it is likely that these imprints bled through into reality. You've had so much on your plate recently: the case, Miss Brown, your diagnosis… A mind can only take so much. I've seen you take enough pills to knock out a small animal. It all adds up."

Will looked at his father. "Why didn't you tell me?"

"The rewind was helping us in this case. I thought that if we came to a conclusion, then these hauntings would cease. We could wean you off the device and destroy it. I didn't want you leaving before we had a conclusion."

"It's too late. I'm leaving with Eve tonight," he said, taking the rewind from his pocket and placing it on the table. It seemed to watch him as he pulled away, and he had a strong urge to take it back. "I don't need it anymore. I'll go cold turkey for a few weeks." He put on his jacket and made for the door. Frank's hand gripped his arm.

"There is more." Frank picked up a tape recorder from the fireplace and placed it in front of Will.

"What's this? If it's your karaoke, then I think I'll pass."

"Please, just listen. All the evidence you need is on there," Frank said, pressing the play button. The wheels spun and through the crackling, a voice emerged, Frank's voice. The real Frank spoke up: "I put it in your room after our talk on the bench. Inconsistencies filled your recollections, and I thought history might be repeating itself."

"You were recording me? I'm pretty sure there are laws against that," said Will. Sweat was starting to roll down his temple. His unconscious knew something but was keeping it a secret from his thoughts. The recording churned out something else now. It was Will's voice, slightly tinny due to the quality of the audio, but it was certainly him who was talking. He remembered the conversation. It had been less than a week ago. The day that he considered the chance that the diary may remain in Alex's coffin. Any second now, Eve would reply with her answer: The suggestion of trying the cemetery.

Will waited. He finished talking and Eve was about to answer. Any second. Why wasn't she speaking? The gap was feeling too long—the silence was extending beyond what Will knew it to have been.

"What is this, Dad?" he said, his throat tight. His trembling fingers paused the tape.

"When you mentioned you had met someone… I was curious. We hadn't seen her. You kept on talking about her, but we were never introduced."

"She was busy. Christ, I haven't known Eve for that long. You'll meet her soon."

Frank looked down at his feet. "Just press play."

His fingers didn't want to. The tape was staring at him with blank, hollow eyes. Click.

And there was his own voice. Answering a question that he was certain had come from Eve's lips. "No. No, she just speaks quietly. This is a dodgy recorder; she was too far away to be picked up on it." Will strained his ears, focusing on the words he knew that Eve had said. They didn't come. There was just his own voice. Responding to dialogue that had never been spoken.

"I'm so sorry, son. The girl you met. The girl it seems that you have fallen in love with. She has never existed. She's just a product of the rewind."

CHAPTER TWENTY-TWO: ISOLATION

Breath caught in Will's chest, still painful, although now for an entirely different reason. The room had become engulfed in quivering silence. Frank's chin was down, his eyes searching for some hint of a reaction from Will.

He is lying. This is all just a manipulation trick. I'm not crazy. I'm not… Am I?

"No. This is just like you; you can't handle anyone else being happy so you try to sabotage any chance that they have," Will spat. Frank was looking at him with dead eyes as Will's words bounced from his skin. "Not me. I know you too well to believe a word you say." He picked up the tape recorder, still rolling. "You've edited this somehow. Changed it to make me think I'm losing my mind."

"I don't know much about the ins and outs of the MED. I know it uses DNA somehow. I know that neurons and electrical signals are important too. When you first saw Eve, I assume that you had gone through some kind of trauma."

Will's mouth felt dry. "I had just been beaten… She walked me to the hospital," he said quietly.

Frank nodded. "I assume that she left you before any of the doctors helped you. The mind makes excuses, you see. It knows that some part of what you see isn't real, but it tries to compensate. Anything to convince itself that what you're seeing is really there. She had no house, no real sign of her occupation. If anything, your brain is more adept at creating fiction than any of the FBI boys had been. Stories come naturally to you and you wove this fantasy into reality. You had been through a lot of hardships the day before your first date. If I remember correctly, you had been to see Lenora Brown, and then there were the unfortunate events at the Christmas light turn-on. You found relief in the same way that any human does—in the arms of someone you loved."

There was no way that Frank was right. Everything about Eve was so real, down to her skin under his fingers and her voice—smooth as glass. Then Will remembered, "She made me Christmas dinner. I distinctly remember eating it," he said, almost laughing. "You can ask Wendy, she saw us!" What a horrible joke that Frank was playing. He would have to come clean and admit that he was wrong.

Frank ran his fingers through his hair. "I was the one who made you Christmas dinner. I cooked it here and then took it over for you. The manager allowed me into your room, and I organized it all. I felt bad about what happened on Christmas Eve. Dinner was a way of making it up to you. I considered staying, went as far as bringing an extra chair, but then I figured that you wouldn't want to see me that day, so I left you to it. Of course, that was before I realized what had happened," he said. Shaking, he took another sip of his whiskey.

Will's hands couldn't fit somewhere comfortable. They fluttered around his person before finally settling on the arms of his chair. "I can't do this. Coming back here was a mistake and now you're trying to say that I'm crazy? That I have been talking to a woman who doesn't exist for the past month? This is cruel, even by your standards."

"I am so sorry. It was never my intention for this to happen. I should have worked it out earlier."

Will let out a sharp laugh. "No! It's fine! It's a perfectly normal thing for a dad to force his son into solving a twelve-year-old murder. Everyone does it! Then, when that son is actually happy for once in his stupid, pointless life, they try to pull the rug."

"I won't let you continue to live a lie. That would be far crueler than telling the truth."

"It's not a lie. Ever since I've come home, all you have cared about is me solving your damned case. I was in the hospital for days and you didn't even visit. You're saying this to stop me from leaving. It ends now. I will not let you obsess through me. It's your life and you can waste it catching this ghost yourself."

Frank didn't have the energy left to be angry. Crushed into himself, he took the words without any interruption.

"Eve is the best thing to happen to me in my entire life. I've made up for my sins and I just want to live in peace. No more murders. No more beatings. A sunny beach somewhere is exactly what I need. I love this girl," argued Will, almost out of breath. His body was rising and falling in time with his pulsing chest.

Frank looked up, "you fell in love with her? You only knew her for a month."

"I only needed a day." It was true. Yes, he had enjoyed her attention and her interest in his work. There was more. She calmed him and relaxed his soul. He had known from the start.

"There will be more opportunities. More souls that you can love. This isn't the end, Will. It's the beginning of the next chapter. A chapter that I can assure you will be far more positive," said Frank, trying to sound reassuring.

"I think you're forgetting something," replied Will, coughing into his hand. More blood. "This cancer isn't going anywhere. I am though." He pulled open the door. Marty was outside, having obviously been listening to their conversation. A look of shame was written across his face.

"I tried to convince him to tell you earlier," he croaked.

"Will, please come back," pleaded Frank, getting closer to the pair.

Will turned and let out something that he had been holding back for the past month: "It's not fair that I am the one who gets cancer. I don't smoke. I've not been a heavy drinker in years. You have no excuse. I think we both know that it is you who should have it."

Shadows crossed Frank's face and a hint of a tear formed next to his eye.

"Don't follow me, or I swear I might kill you," added Will, entirely certain that he meant it.

*

There was only one thing that would confirm if Frank was telling the truth. Will would walk to Eve's apartment and find her waiting for him, suitcase in hand, ready to leave Hollyhead in their dust. Maybe a few months down the line, he might find it in his heart to forgive Frank's poor attempt to get him to stay, even if it was fueled by obsession. Just when things were looking up, his father had sucker-punched him in the gut. Again.

Finding Eve's apartment was easy; he had walked her home only a few times, yet the route was carved into his memory. Darkness ate the top floors as he approached, the night creeping down the smoke-stained bricks with a heavy gloom. He trod through the rain and reached the intercom in the corridor on the ground floor, the bulbs above him flickering like warning lights. Thirty-odd names were written on plastic-coated slips of paper.

Louise Scott. Eve said that they hadn't changed the name yet.

He jabbed his finger at the corresponding button, and it lit up with an electric blue glow. There was a crackling ring. It was a few seconds before he got his answer.

"What do you want?" said a voice at the other end. It lacked Eve's softness, instead coming out harsh and gravelly. The woman must be ancient, her vocal cords slowly decaying away after years of abuse. Will put his head to the brick, cold and hard against his skin.

I must have pressed the wrong one. Eve might have given me the wrong number.

He ran his eyes across the various names. There was no Eve Pocock. No one with a name even remotely similar…

Frank was right. You're gone. My God, he was right.

*

The phone line was torn apart until the wires were frayed and scattered across the room. Bedsheets had been left half-off the bed. The pills that had helped dump him in this mess to start with were gone. Five? Ten? Maybe more. He didn't know. They took away his pain, and that was all he wanted. Birds outside had seemed to croak her name and the flashes of sunlight reminded him of her hair, so he crammed his pillows against the closed curtain, shutting out as much of the day as he could. Had Frank been proud? Had his poor attempts at reassurance masked a pride that his son was so fragile? So unhinged?

As much as he had tried to drink the night from his memory, brief flashes kept sneaking up on him. Crushing his face into a pillow hadn't been enough to keep them out. Even with all the evidence that he had been given, he still clutched to the hope that Eve would knock on the door and pull him from his depression.

Pages from *Grimm's* were torn out and thrown across the room. Tiny illustrations of fantastical creatures and unimaginable evil all watched him gleefully. Must they laugh too? As much as it was Frank's fault, the Reaper must take some of the blame. Their disregard for the sanctity of human life had poisoned the town and spread through Will's own veins. There were too many people to blame. Too many had trampled on his life and torn up his sanity. They were knocking now, thundering against the side of his head, desperately scrambling for one last piece of him to carry away. Powerful echoes looped around his ears. There was a voice. Distant and becoming lost through the jeers. Will raised his head from the bed.

Pounding fists hit his door, threatening to take it from its hinges. Why was peace such a stranger to him? The knocks came, and the voice grew louder, overpowering the rest.

"Will, are you there?" it said. A familiar voice. One that didn't fill Will with fear. "Wendy says that you haven't paid for last night. She's given me an hour before she gets her battering ram out. I think she's serious too."

Teddy. Will didn't get up. Was it too much to ask to be left alone? Perhaps if the detective focused more on the murders rather than bothering him then the whole thing could be finished. Despite feeling like his body weighed twice what it had the day before, Will picked himself up and stumbled towards the door, not knowing what he was going to say when he opened it. He slid the chain. The door opened.

"Fucking hell, you look worse than shit," said Teddy, his face repulsed. "I've been knocking for the past ten minutes. Wendy's doing her nut."

Will fished in his pocket and took out a wad of cash. "That'll cover the day. Keep whatever is left," he said, trying to close the door again.

Teddy stuck his boot in and put one hand on the door. "What's happened to you?" he said, now concerned. "Are you hurt?"

"I want to be left alone. Get on with your own thing. In case you've missed it, there's a killer running around out there on your ground and so far, you've done nothing about it." He'd regret the words at some point. Not yet though. He knew just where to do the most damage.

"I'm closer now than ever. I thought you cared about this. Enough to stop wallowing in self-pity and help."

"I write books. I'm not a detective. I'm not one of your cop buddies. I'm not even your friend, Teddy."

"I don't need us to be friends. This is about the Reaper now."

"The town deserves it. Every stinking person here deserves it. After all the glorification of the killer, what else do they expect? We should just let them die."

"Think of the Spark boys and Abigail. Even Meredith Flax. They weren't asking for it."

"It doesn't matter anymore."

Teddy bit his tongue. "Is it such a foreign concept to you that I may actually appreciate you for who you are? Not who you try so hard to be, not who you wish you were, but dull and normal you? Throughout this whole case, you have been trying to come across as someone hard and emotionless. You act like these murders mean nothing to you," he said. "I know that they do."

"Is that right? How do you know?"

"Because you have cancer, because you hardly get any sleep, and you spent Christmas driving around in the dark. You're staying because right now this case is the only thing that does matter to you. I don't know what your motivation is, but a man who doesn't care that he is dying is selfish. He acts for himself because he has no one else left to prove anything to, which means two things. You're a good man, Will, and you don't want to die. Besides, if you did, then you never would have fallen in love," he said, taking the folded note out of his pocket and showing Will's own spidery handwriting. Back when his hopes hadn't been destroyed.

Will allowed himself to see past the point about Eve. It was true. There had been something pushing him to help Mrs. Spark. It had started with Lenora, then evolved into a drive that meant more than his old friend. Even more than Frank. The Reaper was his own obsession and now, the reason for his pain.

If he got the chance, he would gladly tear their throat out. The thought turned into a longing. Feeling the Reaper's throat crush under his hands filled him with a surge of pleasure. Bulging eyes. A large, pink tongue hanging limply as the life drained from their body. Yes, that would do nicely.

"Fine. One more day. Then I'm done." He didn't want to tell Teddy about Eve. Embarrassment being the main motivation.

"We need to go to my house first," said Teddy. Noticing Will's surprised expression, he added: "I called Gillian to no answer about a half hour ago. She must be out somewhere. I'll be in and out before you know it, and then we can head to the station. I'll pick you up some aspirin while I'm there."

*

The car ride fizzed with awkwardness. Will wanted to apologize for his words and once managed to say that he hadn't meant it. Teddy said that he knew and promptly turned the radio up, blasting away any more attempts at conversation. They had even shared a laugh when 'Don't fear the Reaper' started playing. The roads were lined with ice and Teddy drove slower than normal, ensuring the tires didn't lose grip and send the car spinning onto the sidewalk. The vehicle slowed to a halt. They stepped out of the Granada into cold air.

"That's odd," said Teddy. His eyes were directed towards the house. The front door was open just a crack. Will joined him on the path and walked forwards. Teddy put out a tentative hand and creaked it open. As soon as they entered the house, it was clear that something was wrong. Cartoons were still running on the television and a drawing of a cat was left unfinished. A burning smell was wafting from the kitchen so strongly that Will swore he could taste it. Teddy threw his jacket onto the sofa and investigated further. He called out for Gillian and Greta but was answered only with silence. Will passed the chair where he had sat only a day before and walked into the kitchen. A saucepan was bubbling over, sending hot water spitting onto the gas and rising in a torrent of steam. Teddy ran over and switched it off, getting his hand scolded in the process. He whipped it away.

"This isn't right. Gillian would never leave the house and keep the stove on. Not even for a second," said Teddy, eyes wide.

Will's words caught in his mouth. From Teddy's angle, he couldn't see the other side of the counter. Will pointed. Already looking worried, Teddy followed his gaze, and instantly the color left his face. Blood was dripping from the counter onto the floor, forming a pool on the tiles. Teddy's legs gave way, and he buckled to the floor, his eyes not moving from the blood.

"He's taken her. Both of them. The Reaper came for my family," he croaked.

Will wanted to say that there must be a simple explanation, but he couldn't find one himself. All signs indicated a difficult and violent struggle that had only resulted in both Greta and Gillian being taken.

"You need to calm down," said Will to Teddy, who was a strangled mess on the floor.

"Calm down? Calm ain't going to help anyone," he said, getting to his feet, looking like he could snap at any moment. "Why should I be calm?"

"Because if we don't think rationally, then they are as good as dead."

"They are likely dead anyway! Patrols will call in and say they've found two bodies in a ditch. Even worse, they might be strung up like the Spark boys."

"We are onto them this time. Everything the killer does is associated with *Grimm's* fairy tales. There are over a hundred in there. Just gotta find the right one."

Teddy picked up a bowl from the counter and ran a finger across the bottom. "It's *Hansel and Gretel*," he croaked.

"The name is similar, but…"

"Not just her name," he said, turning the bowl around so Will could see. There were a few white and pink mice, one half eaten. "Greta's favorite," he said. A powder had collected on his finger and he dabbed it on his tongue. "Salty… I've tasted it before. On an old case." Before Will could stop him, Teddy hit his temple. "Think. Think. Think," he said, willing the memory into his head.

"Frank will know. The FBI deals with drugs a lot more than you guys do," said Will. He left the room and picked up the telephone, wrapping his sleeve around his fingers. Just in case. He dialed his home, and Frank answered.

"Who's this?" he croaked.

"It's Will. Don't say anything. Just answer some questions." The line went silent and Will continued. "I need the name of a drug. White powder. Something that will make a kid unconscious. Wouldn't take long to work."

"It dissolves," shouted Teddy from the kitchen. "Tell him it dissolves in water."

"It dissolves in water. Any ideas?"

"There are a lot of drugs like that, Will. Anything else?"

"It tastes salty."

Frank took longer to answer. When he did, his voice was lower and knowing: "Gamma hydroxybutyrate. GHB. Dangerous stuff."

"Difficult to get a hold of?"

"Nothing is if you know the right people. It's used medically to treat narcolepsy."

Will missed the rest of Frank's description. His father's voice faltered as the phone fell to the floor, before cracking on the hardwood.

Narcolepsy. Hansel and Gretel. The wicked witch. Car crash. Doctor...

Pieces shifted together. Corners matched up and Will took a step back from the picture forming. Up to this point, he had taken everything at face value. A mistake that could cost Greta and Gillian Ludlow their lives.

"Will?" said Teddy, running into the hallway at the sound of the phone breaking.

"We were looking for a connection between the victims. I know what it is. I think Alex Spark told us the identity of his killer. We just didn't know it at the time."

"Tell me where we need to go."

*

Hollyhead forest. All good fairy tales tell of gnarly trees with thick leaves that shut out the rest of the world. Will and Teddy stood at the mouth of the woods, staring down the path that twisted into the center.

"In *Hansel and Gretel* they laid a trail of breadcrumbs behind them so that they could find their way home," said Will, pointing towards the ground. The Reaper had left them a path, whether intentionally or not.

Only it wasn't breadcrumbs. Drops of blood had soaked into the snow, forming a trail into the shadows.

CHAPTER TWENTY-THREE: THE FINAL ACT

"It makes sense, doesn't it? A house all the way out in the woods. No one would think to check," said Will, his heart starting to race.

Teddy was by his side, loading a handgun with some difficulty—his fingers were trembling and Will was pretty sure that it wasn't due to the cold. Teddy's Granada had taken them up as far through the labyrinth of trees as it could go until the wood narrowed, and it had become obvious that traveling by foot would be a faster option.

"We need to be right. We might not have much time left," said Teddy. The blood drops had become more frequent—the snow hadn't yet erased all traces away. And then there were footprints. A single pair. Snow boots by the look of it, deep into the forest floor. The Reaper had been dragging something by their side, leaving a trench in their wake as it slid across the floor. Time was on their side; there was still enough daylight to allow them to spot the blood. However, it was fading faster than they had anticipated. An unspoken fear between them was that it would grow too dark to see and they would need to resort to their torches, making the walk slower. Each second was valuable, and they were trickling away.

They continued forwards, flinching at any sign of movement among the recesses of the forest. Nerves had taken hold of Teddy, and Will knew that he wouldn't be able to rely on the detective's decision-making skills tonight. Other than the faint trickle of the river running nearby, the woods were silent. All sound had been sucked into the deep snow. Branches had been snapped on their route. The odd twig stuck out from the snow. The serenity of the forest was fresh. It hadn't been long since the Reaper walked their trail.

"I'm right. I know it," said Will, blood pumping in his head. For the first time in days, his body felt awake, buzzing with the kind of electricity that can only be fueled by adrenaline. His mind, however, was still sluggish, and sometimes it seemed like his words were delayed when he spoke, but now was no time for sleep. The suspense was keeping thoughts of Eve from his mind. In the distance, a faint glow weaved through the trees and the pair acknowledged it, deciding that it was the end goal of their journey.

"I didn't mean what I said back at the motel. You're a good man and a good friend, Ted," said Will. He had instantly regretted his words at the motel, only now being able to speak his mind.

"I know. Even if you did hate me, it wouldn't matter. Not now."

Silence. As Will ducked under a branch, a spider-web tore from a tree and bound onto his face. He shuddered and wiped it from his mouth. As the trees became fewer again and the light became wider, he saw the source of the glow. It was a cottage, compact and secluded. On either side, two rows of trees squashed a narrow path that led to the front door. It looked cozy—inviting, even. A white picket fence opened into a front yard covered by a blanket of pristine snow. Small gnomes were dotted around a circular pond of frozen water. The house was made of brown brick, and the frost that had spread across the thatched roof looked like a coating of sugar. It was perfect—like something from a fairy tale. Will allowed Teddy to walk in front, the gun raised at the door in case it opened before they got there. It didn't. The pair split each side of the door.

"Stay there and keep low. We don't know what kind of weapons he might have," said Teddy. Will nodded. A spark of an emotion rose inside him. He wanted to be the one to kill the Reaper.

If only you were here to see this, Dad. It's taken me a month to work out what you couldn't in twelve years, thought Will.

Teddy kicked open the door in one go, causing it to tear from its hinges and fall inwards. He signalled for Will to follow his lead. The hallway was narrow and pitch black, other than the glare from their flashlights. It looked normal, as far as Will could tell. A muggy smell enveloped the scene, like an old book newly opened. Shoes were neatly piled onto a rack by the door and a mahogany chest of drawers was pushed up against the wall, decorated by wilting flowers and a small bowl containing keys and a slightly grubby-looking leather wallet. The carpet at their feet was soaked through; clumps of snow were slowly melting into the faded material. The hallway ran between three rooms. Teddy silently opened one, his gun poised. Bathroom. He shook his head and ventured forwards to the next. In the low light, it was almost impossible to tell what was in there. A piano and desk suggested some kind of study—nowhere that a pair of children could be hidden. It felt oddly familiar as if Will had stepped back into Frank's house. In many ways, he had expected the Reaper's lair to be an imitation of his father's lodging. Their psychology was joined at the hip. As Will crept closer toward the stairs, he heard a faint electric hum. He turned to Teddy and nodded his head towards the next floor.

"Hansel and Gretel were in the oven. That means kitchen," Teddy whispered.

"It sounds like he's upstairs. We can't let him get the jump on us," Will replied, not daring to reply in anything louder than a hiss.

Teddy thought for a second. "You take the gun and check upstairs. Two minutes and I'll come find you. Don't let the fucker get a word in. If you see him, don't hesitate to put a round in his skull. You know how to fire?"

"Point and shoot," said Will.

Teddy nodded. With an unsaid *good luck,* they parted, and Will began to climb the stairs. There was no use treading carefully. Each step creaked as a result of regular use throughout the years. They twisted onto a landing, lit only by the light coming from an overhead window. The light switch was on the far side. Turning it on would only serve to announce his presence. Large wooden beams supported the sloped ceiling. Apart from what looked like a closet, there were only two rooms.

One bathroom, one bedroom.

Will crept forward. Both doors had large bronze knobs and his torchlight reflected slightly as it hit them. He wished that he had covered the torch with some kind of felt, anything to reduce its power. It would be a miracle if the Reaper didn't pounce on him from the shadows. Every few seconds, Will

272

directed the light to the corners, just in case. Slivers of light came from beneath the door on the right, and a throbbing noise pulsed toward him. Trying to steady his hand, Will raised the gun and slowly twisted the door open, expecting a strike to come at any moment. None came.

The bedroom was cold; the walls were lined with air conditioners operating at full capacity—despite the outside temperature. That explained the noise he heard. Moonlight was flooding in through a circular window, filling the room with a silvery lagoon and being the culprit of the light that he had seen in the hallway. A single bed was displayed in the center, covered by a tartan blanket. Will raised his flashlight and it enveloped a figure sitting behind it, just outside the circle of moonlight. Their head lolled forward, staring at the ground. Instinctively, Will brought the gun up.

"Don't move asshole, it's over," he said, rather more bravely than he felt. There was no reply. The person didn't even raise their head. He took another tentative step forward. And another, until he was in touching distance. Hands shaking, he raised the torch. He could have screamed. The body of Meredith Flax was tied to the chair, her neck lined with stitches where her head had been reattached to the body. It was a good job, but not enough to prevent her head from lolling onto her shoulder in a way that wouldn't be possible if she were alive. She had been preserved well. Apart from the fact that her leathery skin had a green tinge, she could have only just died. The Reaper had dressed her in black robes that reached her ankles.

Will stumbled backward in shock, his hand outstretched to stop him from falling. It met something cold and hard, with grooves along the curved edges. He turned. His hand was pressed against a skeleton. It was dressed in blue dungarees, bits of fabric torn and the rest losing its color. Will knew who it was instantly. Gus Spark. The clothes that Lenora had believed to be buried on the Spark's land had finally turned up. All the flesh had decomposed, leaving Gus with a gaping mouth and a bald head. Metal rods connected his arm back to his body—the Reaper had kept it the whole time. Here was the youngest Spark boy, dressed like a mannequin in a stranger's bedroom.

A wave of his torch lit up the other side of the room. Three more skeletons were sitting on chairs, backs straight up against the wall. Alex, Fred, Nigel. Meaning that Gus was joined by Petey and Sam. All were dressed in the same clothes they had worn on the night of their deaths. God, Alex... Preserved forever in the house of his killer...

They must have been brought to the cottage, changed into their iconic gowns and then taken to the billboard. Ed the chef was shackled to the wall, his feet drooping lazily onto the carpet. Most of his flesh still remained clinging to his skin.

Sometimes your brain disconnects from your feet and you can't control your movement. All Will knew was that his unconscious was telling him to walk toward the cupboard beside Petey. Terrified of what he might find, he pulled open the door. Gillian Ludlow fell through the gap. It had taken Will a few seconds to realize who it was. Her face was too mangled to identify her. Her nose was hanging by thin strips of skin and parts of her head were bashed in, with cerebral fluid already drying after having leaked through the cracks in her skull. It was her jumper that gave her away. The flowery jumper that she had been wearing when Will first met her. He fell back. Her injuries were the worst of all; she was too disfigured to recognize from her face alone. Now there was an explanation for the blood back at Teddy's home. The mother was absent in *Hansel and Gretel;* Gillian must have tried to intervene and been killed— whether by accident or on purpose, Will wasn't sure. When coming across a body, humans have the tendency to try to wake the deceased. Although he had only known her for less than a month, Will took hold of her shoulders and shook her, causing her head to roll around erratically on her neck.

She's just passed out. Just passed out.

The way that her head rolled was wrong. Physically wrong. It was tilting back too far, giving her a distinctly doll-like appearance. The shaking subsided, and he let her body relax into the cupboard once again. In his panic, he had opened her eyes. They stared straight through him. Completely devoid of life.

*

Walking down the stairs proved to be a more challenging feat than he expected, largely due to the way they seemed to sway as he walked down. He rubbed his eyes until swirling patterns crossed his vision and told himself to hold it together. Teddy hadn't made a noise since he had entered the kitchen—in his shock, Will had forgotten about his friend. He pushed open the door and was immediately struck with smoke that caused his eyes to water.

Heat was emanating from a room at the back of the kitchen. Acrid black smoke was seeping out from under the door, covering the floor in a dark haze. Teddy was furiously rattling the door with one hand, the other holding keys that he must have taken from a holder by the window.

"My god, he's burning them," gasped Will, before storming towards the door. He didn't need to look closely to tell that it was made of a thick copper-like material. A keyhole was positioned on the right-hand side and there was a small window at the top. Teddy pressed his face to the glass. Inside the room, an iron grating, large enough for multiple people, was stretched across four rods about waist height. Underneath, a roaring fire was burning, turning the bars almost red with heat. On the grating, two small shapes were curled up in fetal positions.

"She's in there! Grets! Grets!" he yelled, as he began kicking the door. It was obvious that it wouldn't work. "We have to find the key, Will. Find him and find the key!" He took another key and forced it into the lock.

"Careful, if it snaps, we won't be able to try another," said Will.

In his attempts to find the key, Teddy had ransacked the kitchen. The countertops were covered in sweet wrappers and cooking utensils. Pans and plates were scattered across the floor and glasses had smashed on the floor. Will opened a window and took a lungful of fresh air that caused him to cough fiercely. Greta could have been in the oven for only a few minutes tops. He didn't want to consider any longer than that. Five was enough.

Teddy tried another key, kicking the door between each attempt. To his credit, he had formed a dent in the copper. But it still wasn't enough.

"What are you doing here?" said a voice coming from behind them. They turned. The Reaper had returned. George Upson, the pathologist—Hollyhead's own master of death. He had entered the room, dressed in a black turtleneck. His face was white yet covered in scratches and blood stains, supposedly from where Gillian had fought back. Flames lit up his face in the darkness. His black clothes caused his head to appear as if it were floating.

Teddy didn't hesitate. Within seconds, he had George by the collar and hurled him against the table, causing an audible crack as his back connected with the wood.

"Give me the fucking key George, or I will pull your heart out through your mouth," snarled Teddy, picking up the pathologist again and shaking him hard.

"No! They must burn," said George, through mouthfuls of blood that dripped from the corner of his mouth. "She sent you here… You're the monsters," he cried, his eyes shut tight.

"We're here for my daughter, you piece of shit."

"I can't… I thought this had all stopped," George whimpered.

"Your stepmom is dead. Or was that not apparent when you butchered her head with a fucking lid? Keep the gun on him, Will. Don't let him move."

Will obliged, his finger trembling on the trigger. He couldn't have shot him if he had wanted to; Teddy was so close that any shot would risk puncturing through him first.

"Tell me how to open it George," said Teddy, slightly quieter. George didn't answer, his eyes frantically flickering from Will to Teddy to the burning oven.

"That won't work…" said Will. George wasn't scared of Teddy. He could be beaten to a pulp and still not give away the information. The Reaper was scared of something much worse than a beating.

It was a mistake to speak. Teddy's attention dropped for a second and George took advantage, bringing his knee up into Teddy's groin. Teddy staggered into the sink, his floundering arm knocking over a stack of dishes. He grunted as his hip connected with the counter and he fell forward. Then George turned to Will. He rushed forwards with outstretched hands and wide eyes. Without thinking, Will pulled the trigger sending a bullet fizzing past George. Tremors were filling Will's hand, and the kitchen was swimming across his vision. Before he could fire again, George was on him. Will fell to the floor, sending the gun flying from his hand and under a gap in the sideboard. Saliva sprayed from George's mouth as he panted, trying to hold down Will's wriggling body. Spindly fingers slapped weakly around Will's neck as he tried to push the pathologist away. Then George had something in his hands. It was the rewind; it must have fallen from Will's pocket as he collapsed. Like a caveman, he brought the rewind down towards Will's head, attempting to crush his face in a flurry of mad strikes. Will grabbed the device, ready to force it away from his eyes. Except he didn't need to. The room started to spin around him, melting George away into the distance. Before he could stop, Will entered the mind of the Grimm Reaper.

*

George Upson had wet the bed again. He could feel it leaking into his bedsheets through the fabric of his pajamas, which he had spent the last month saving up for with his own money. He moved his leg tentatively and a fresh wave of piss washed over him. His new blue and white pajamas would need to be washed again. He bit his lip and scrunched his eyes closed.

Don't cry. Don't cry.

He was so focused on that command that he didn't notice that tears were already trickling down his face and sinking into the pillow in a salty pool. It had been three days since his last accident. He'd managed to clean it up before *she* had seen. Sliding out of bed, George pulled the piss-soaked sheet from his mattress and balled it up as small as it would go. The rest of the house was silent. He stuffed the sheet into a wicker wash basket and walked to his closet, where he had arranged three new ones only a week before. Only one was left. He took it to his bed and stretched it across the mattress.

It was the dream again. Always the same. After the first week of seeing it every night, praying had been the only option he had seen as worthwhile. God hadn't answered him. He hadn't come to save him when the monsters came hunting. Maybe he was busy. Maybe there was no such thing as the creator of all. He had always hoped that if the Devil existed, then God would be around somewhere, too. George wiped a hand across his face, and it came back sticky, whether because of his tears or sweat, he wasn't sure. Hiding didn't work anymore. The dog could smell him. Last time he had hidden in a cupboard, curling his toes so that his wide feet wouldn't stop the door from closing. Then he heard the dog. Its paws tapped on the wooden paneled floor, and he could make out its panting breath behind its fleshy pink tongue. George didn't know how, but it would always find him. Sometimes it would pass his hiding place and George would let out a small whimper of relief. But it always came back. It would paw at his hiding place, its nose pressed at the gap between the wood, letting out angry snorts. He had found that if he held the door shut tight, then the hound couldn't bite at his ankles and drag him out. Then there was the cat. The purring would start, faint at first, but enough to draw his attention. It was a broken sound. He would look up and see two bulbous orange eyes staring at him through the darkness. Before he could run, it would pounce. Its claws sliced at his eyeballs as he tried to throw it away. Once he had been able to make it lose its grip by banging his head against the side of the cupboard. It never worked again. They adapted. They always adapted.

Falling from the cupboard, he met with the clomp of hooves and a strict tapping of heels. The cat would leave one eye partially intact, just enough for him to see the woman coming towards him through the blood and eye fluid. After licking at the congealing blood, the dog would run back to his mistress and sit, still panting heavily, drool pooling in its loose lips. The cat slinked away back into the shadows and George wouldn't see it until his next attempt at evasion. Then there was the donkey. The donkey did nothing, but it gave off the most pungent smell. Its fur was splayed with blood and it brayed similar to the cat—as if it had been dug up and never regained control of its body. George could live with the animals. They only haunted him physically. The witch was the worst. She made no sound. With one hand, she could silence her pets. With the other, she held up a rooster, fat and clumsy. The witch would smile, unveiling a collection of blood-stained teeth, and take a knife from her cloak. Although he wanted to, George could never look away. He had to watch as she dragged the knife along the rooster's neck, causing it to squawk in an unholy manner. Then she would let go, dropping the animal to the floor with a dull thud. Magically, the knife then turned into a wand, and, laughing all the way, the witch aimed it at George. That was when he pissed himself. That was when the boy would wake and cry, holding his breath once again.

The dream had been the same tonight, only he had run. This time, the dog had hunted him down and the cat had thrown itself at him from a long and gnarled tree. It all ended the same.

George dropped the sheets into a small basket and was about to open the door when he heard the clacking of heels. Then the hallway light switched on. He jumped back into bed and pressed his head into his pillow, praying that the clacking didn't stalk him to his door. He didn't see the light creep through the doorway as it opened. He didn't see the shadow. Nor the nails painted blood red. The person sniffed.

"Georgie, you've had an accident again, haven't you?"

No answer.

"I know you're awake. I can hear you skulking away in here."

There was a wash of cold air as George's covers were thrown from him and sharp nails suddenly dug into his arm.

"That's the third time this week," she said, covering him with a voice thick with drink. She had always been a drinker. His real mom hadn't touched the stuff. It hadn't been her fault that she died. A drunk driver had hit the side of her car going twenty above the speed limit. The bend had been tight, and he had tried to overtake. She had swerved until the passenger door was parallel to his truck's grill. George's father said that she hadn't stood a chance. Rumors around the sports field said that her face had been so torn in the accident that they had needed to use her teeth to identify the body.

Another tear slithered down George's face. He had prepared for tonight, even gone to the measures of putting a bucket underneath his bed. It hadn't been enough. And she knew about the other incident.

A scraping noise sounded, followed by a dry sucking sound. Smoke wafted across his skin, slightly hot. The pungent reek of unfiltered tobacco.

"Have you told your father?"

George shook his head, still trying to press it further into his pillow.

"Good, we wouldn't want him knowing. He's already so disappointed in you. Have you told him about what happened at school?"

George remained still, praying in his head that she would leave. All of a sudden, he felt his leg spasm as a burning sensation spread across his nerves, sending them into an electric frenzy. His muscles clenched, and he bit his tongue in shock. He looked up and saw the cigarette planted into his leg, twisting into flesh. The hand that held it was long and bony. It twiddled the cigarette between its thumb and forefinger. The act looked almost gentle, if not for the searing pain in his leg.

The other hand lifted his pajama top and circled the purple bruise he had been trying to hide all day. He'd known she had seen. That day at dinner, his father had ordered him to remove his jumper, the action momentarily revealing his stomach. As soon as she had seen it, George knew that she would visit that night.

"Have the boys been hurting you again? Or was it the girls this time?" she said, gently pressing on the bruise. Her hands were ice-cold.

In truth, it had been both. He hadn't noticed that some pee must have fallen onto the back of his white school shirt. A girl had pointed out the yellow stain and Zach Baker had proceeded to trip him on the school field, before stamping on his stomach.

"You must stand up for yourself one of these days. You can't keep expecting us to pick up the pieces. One day you will have to be the man that your father wants you to be. If not, then we might find that another accident has happened. It might be your fault again. Your father never would have caused something like that to happen."

Her hand dragged lower and another surge of tears gathered behind George's eyes.

She sighed, "if only you hadn't hurt yourself. A broken leg is hardly something to cry about. Your father told me; you see. He said that you cried and cried until the nurse called your mother to take you to the hospital. Why did you do it, Georgie? The other boys in your class would never have cried over something so small. Your bitch of a mother probably would still be here reading you bedtime stories if you hadn't cried that day."

It was true. He had been playing the events over in his mind since the day it had happened. She never would have been in the car if he hadn't cried like a little girl and needed to go to the hospital.

It was that night that he decided it wouldn't happen again. He sat there for the next ten minutes, his mind playing over the events of the dream while the witch stained his body. His soul was already too far gone. When it was over, she took a book from his shelf and opened it. George didn't need to raise his head from his pillow to know what it would be…

"A certain man had a donkey, which had carried the corn sacks to the mill indefatigably for many a long year…"

*

The next day, the farm next door had lost their rooster. It was found a week later, covered in maggots, its neck cut open. The school cat, who roamed so freely about the corridors, was found with its eyes stabbed through and George Upson's neighbors lost their new puppy. It was never found. The farm's donkey was left alive, but they never could remove the red dye from its fur…

CHAPTER TWENTY-FOUR: DEATH

The taste of blood lingered in Will's mouth. Hot sweat clung to his skin all over his body. A part of him felt sorry for George. How long had he been running from the monsters? When did the fictional monsters blend into his own personality? George's stepmother was Meredith Flax. The kill *had* been personal…

Will's senses were overwhelmed, and he coughed onto the floor. The room was a gyrating blur with two figures a few steps away and as the ringing in Will's head stopped, it was replaced by a heart-wrenching sobbing. George was curled in the corner of the kitchen, his hands clutching his head, rocking violently. Teddy was by his side, sending an onslaught of kicks into the side of the pathologist.

"The key! Where is it?" he shouted, firing another strike into George's ribs.

George raised his head. A crimson glaze coated the right side of his face.

"Tell me!" roared Teddy as his victim scrambled on the floor, the tears from his eyes mixing in with the blood.

With a shaking hand, George pointed toward a cookie jar on a shelf above the oven. A porcelain jar in the shape of a gingerbread house. Instantly, Teddy scrambled across to it and smashed it on the ground. A collection of keys fell onto the tiled floor, spinning across the varnish.

"Which one?" he shouted, dropping to his knees. George didn't answer. He coughed, causing a couple of his teeth to fall from his mouth and clatter onto the tiles.

Will pulled himself across the floor, his lungs starting to burn again. "The doors got a copper lock. Look for a key that looks similar," he wheezed, before collapsing onto his back.

Teddy snatched up a key and ran to the door. After a few frantic seconds of rummaging, he wrenched the door open. His arm covering his mouth, he ducked into the smoke. Will didn't have the energy to watch George—he doubted that George had the energy to get up himself. Whatever hadn't been eaten by his psychosis must surely have been beaten from him.

Teddy didn't return for a worrying amount of time. When he eventually did, he was carrying both bodies under his arms. One was Greta, although it was hard to tell due to the soot that covered most of her face. The rest of her body was wrapped inside a grubby brown blanket. Will didn't recognize the other kid. There was little chance anyone would again. His body was so charred that it was only a guess that he was a boy. There was no other way of knowing.

Hansel…

"Hospital, now," coughed Teddy as he stumbled towards the exit. Will followed, the entirety of his chest burning. Then Teddy stopped and nodded towards the gun on the floor. "End him… Let him suffer," he growled.

Seconds expanded into agonizing minutes. Teddy's eyes were pressing on Will, almost pushing him towards the gun. He picked it up, the metal hot against his flesh. This wasn't right. The rewind had shown what created the monster currently crying on the floor.

"We'll arrest him. Get him some psychiatric help," said Will. He picked up George by the collar of his shirt and pulled him towards the door.

"Leave him, Will. Kill him!"

"I can't…"

Teddy's eyes burned with hatred and then shock. Will turned, one hand still on George's sweatshirt. George was holding a burning shard of wood from the oven.

Half snarling, half crying, he smashed it into Will's arm, and Will let go, slapping away the fire that had tried to take over him. He waved it again, and Will's tired eyes watched as the embers chased the swing. They were fireflies dancing in the air.

Will punched him squarely in the mouth, causing him to drop the wood onto the sideboard. Fire spat from the weapon and latched onto the curtains. The flames eagerly jumped to as many targets as they could and before long, one side of the cottage was burning. The ceiling creaked disturbingly, threatening to unleash the top floor onto them. Whatever the interior was laced with, it was highly flammable. Will coughed through the smoke. It would take a miracle for the fire to not leap onto the trees and set the whole forest ablaze.

George was now dazed again, spitting his blood onto the floor. Hopeless. The animal urge that Will had experienced earlier that day had gone. He didn't want the Reaper dead. Not by his own hand, at least. The man had lived his life terrified and acted out of fear. It was no excuse, but Will couldn't kill him. He hauled him up again and pulled him into the hallway.

Teddy was already at the end of the hall. The fire had already spread to the door, lining it in an arch of flames. Teddy wrapped Greta and the boy in his coat and ducked through the fire, managing to escape back outside. It was more difficult with George. He was still crying and kept falling limp onto the floor becoming covered with more ash each time. Each passing second caused more claustrophobia, as the heat pressed in at the pair from either side. The smoke was causing Will's head to pound and he could only pray that they were still moving in the right direction. With immense effort, Will pulled George up. "George! You have gotta keep moving. This whole place is going up!" he shouted, getting another lungful of smoke.

"It's the monsters! They're here for me," cried George, trying to wrench himself away towards the upstairs bedroom. Towards his victims.

"There are no monsters. There's only fire and imminent death!" Will said, his airway closing. With one last tug, George fell away, tumbling onto the floor. He began crawling towards the stairs, keeping his head down. He almost reached the first step when the landing collapsed, showering him with sparks of burning timber and causing the stairs to crash down. George looked back towards Will.

"Oh my god, they're here," he cried, the fire reflecting in his eyes. He was looking around the hallway, his arms outstretched as if he was pushing something away. Will took a step backward and felt his boot crunch into the snow.

The fire curled above George's head and Will could almost swear it contorted into a shape. The shape of a cloaked figure looming over the pathologist. A piece of the ceiling hung loose next to it, forming a hook by the figure's side. The Reaper. Here for its final victim. No one was taking its throne. George screamed as the wall fell onto him, smothering him in a blanket of fire. Then the house fell quiet. The flames had eaten away at the foundations and were quickly making their way to the rest of the cottage, billowing out of the shattered windows into the night sky. A part of Will wanted to step forwards, into the dancing amber and smoke, beckoning him forward with its twisting colors.

Alex. I won't leave you again. Not now.

He took a step forward. Alex was standing where the stairs had been only moments before. He was smiling, the same warm smile that had comforted Will through years of isolation.

"Come with me, Will. It's easier here. It doesn't hurt," Alex said, raising his hand.

"I shouldn't have given up on you. You were my friend…"

Alex tilted his head reassuringly. "It's all forgiven. Just come with me."

One step back into the cottage. Another step.

A hand grabbed Will's shoulder and jerked him away just as the rest of the top floor fell onto the entrance, completely covering Alex. As his face disappeared into the frenzy, it transformed into a skull, the flesh melting from the bone as he screamed. Will shuffled away, feeling the cold seep into his pants. And, at that moment, he felt that his life had gone past its expiration date. Each second following him being pulled from the burning carcass of George's house was a second that he shouldn't have been given.

Freezing air filled his lungs, almost as painful as the smoke. Head swaying, he turned around to see Teddy lurching away from the house, slipping in the snow. He staggered, allowing Will time to catch up.

The detective was mumbling to himself, repeating "hospital" over and over, pushing himself on.

"Teddy, upstairs… I couldn't get her out. He killed Gillian. She was with the others," Will said, still trying to catch his breath. At first, the look on Teddy's face was of unadulterated confusion. He was blinking faster than normal, and the sides of his mouth twitched unnervingly.

"What? No. She can't be," he said before looking at Greta's face buried in his coat. She was stirring, gently. The boy hadn't moved.

"I think it happened at your house. He must have brought her here."

"Why?"

"It was the stepmother who ordered *Hansel and Gretel* to be taken into the woods. It was her fault they were caught by the witch. That's the only reason I can think of. Maybe there wasn't a reason. She might have just fought back."

Then Teddy made a sound that wasn't human—a cracking howl of agony. After he finished, there was nothing but the crackling debris of George's home to fill the night.

*

Hansel was dead. Just like how the witch had planned in the fairy tale, George had placed the boy into the oven first. Poor kid hadn't stood a chance. The charred remains couldn't have belonged to a kid older than five. Teddy held him tightly, determined to get the pair of children into the warm. It was a miracle that Greta hadn't been killed. George had dressed her in some kind of red dress, with a blotchy green ribbon twisted into a bow attached to her hair. Teddy carried her out of the woods. She was close to his chest and screaming now.

"My back, Daddy! My back is burning," she howled, twisting side to side in her father's arms.

"We need to take her to the hospital," said Teddy flatly. It was the first thing he had said since Will had told him of Gillian's fate. With all the information he had taken in that night, his brain had been crushed. Close behind, Will had spent the entire journey staring at the ground, watching the snow fold in around his shoes. Each step ached with fatigue and he had a strong desire to curl up in the frost and sleep.

"Nick King beat up Alex Spark that night. Alex was mumbling about a doctor, and Nick assumed he wanted to go to the hospital. I don't think he was. I believe that he was naming his attacker. Melanie told me that Alex had done work experience at the hospital. What are the chances that he saw George there and recognized him at the fair? He was mistaken about his identity. He thought George was a doctor, not a coroner. Ed had recently been to identify his mother's body. I'm guessing that he must have met George that day. He left the diary in the coffin because he already had Alex. The body was a far better representation of the soul in his eyes."

"I don't care," was all Teddy replied.

They reached the Granada and Teddy placed Greta in the front seat, pulling her seat belt across her chest. He hadn't risked removing any of the clothing, despite Greta's pleas that her back was on fire.

"Will! Get in the car!" he shouted. Will didn't hear; the world had gone muggy, and every sound came through distorted. Abigail was missing. Everything had connected now except for one piece. Teddy swore and got in the car, accelerating away from Will.

"Something on your mind, dear?" said another voice.

Will turned. There was no one there. He knew the voice. If he wasn't mistaken…

"Eve?" he said.

"You know that this isn't the end, right?" said the voice. "A killer doesn't just start again for no good reason. Even a psycho needs a reason."

"Where are you?" asked Will, head snapping left and right.

"You know I'm in your head. What about the rest? Those bodies around George's bed meant something. Trophies?"

"Trophies you want to display. You put them in places where you can see them easily. George positioned the bodies like they were guarding him. They weren't trophies. They were scarecrows…"

"Now we are cooking."

Will's mouth opened in realization. "He was scared of his stepmother coming back. All of those monsters that she said would find him. He was showing that he had killed them. In a *look at me* kind of way. That's why the kills were so public. Except for Meredith, his own stepmother. That one was pure revenge. Displaying his kills scared off the monsters in *Grimm's*."

"All of them except for?"

"Abigail…"

"Which means that George never killed her. He wouldn't show what he didn't kill."

"Quite the pairing, aren't we?" replied Eve. Or the wind. Will wasn't sure. "There was a twelve-year gap between the killings. Why?"

"If George didn't kill Abigail, then it was someone else. George heard about it and thought that the monsters were back. Before there was no need; the death of the Spark boys had kept him safe. He thought the monsters were scared of him. You're not on the lookout if there is no indication that something is out there. It means that whoever killed Abigail is still out there. It's their fault that George started killing again. He wasn't doing the Devil's work; he was already in his own type of Hell, always running from the monsters."

"Do we know who it is?"

"There were only two people in Hollyhead who knew the pattern. Only two knew that George was killing in the style of Grimm. Only they would know to imitate it. Let it seem like George had killed again. Someone who could remember a story from memory and recreate it, making everyone think the deaths were connected. Eve, I think this case has been closer to home than we thought."

There was no reply. Eve's voice had faded into the wind. He was alone once again, except for the chill that had run down his spine.

*

His childhood home sat shrouded in darkness. Will opened the gate and walked through, no longer aware of his aching joints. After a revelation, nothing looks the same. When he was younger, his house was a safe place. True, he had not spent many happy days there, but it was somewhere he could be alone with his thoughts. Now, the cracks in the bricks seemed wider, and it felt distinctly foreign. The front door was unlocked, and he let himself into the blackness of the hallway. He could have thrown up. His heart was threatening to jump out of his mouth.

He knocked on the door and waited for the reply to enter. It came. Will entered the room where it had all begun just a little over a month ago. The room where his father had told him the pattern that he had worked out almost as soon as

George had strung the Spark boys from the billboard. Every clue he had needed was there. How could he have been so blind?

The flicker of a match sparked in the darkness. As the embers burned, the face was revealed. Standing by the window was Marty Goodall.

CHAPTER TWENTY-FIVE:
OLD FRIENDS

"Is Frank not here?" asked Will, closing the door behind him. An icy chill gripped the room. Will's breath curled in the air as he spoke, and each step caused spirals of dust to kick up from the floorboards. It was as if the house had been shut away to rot.

Marty raised his head slowly, seeming like he had just woken from a deep sleep. "No. He's out for the evening," he said. He was wearing a large coat, flecked with mud at the hip. The rings around his eyes appeared darker than ever.

"Out where? He never leaves the house."

"You don't know half of what your old man does."

"I think I'm starting to understand that. Although I sense that is common in Hollyhead. I think if you look far enough into anyone's life here, then you will find something corrupt."

"You can get older, but the town won't ever change," said Marty, taking a draw from his cigarette. His whole body relaxed as he exhaled. "That's the one reliable thing about this place."

"I'm hoping that we will see a change around here now. We found the Reaper."

"You're joking… Who was it?" asked Marty, taking a step forward.

"A pathologist called George Upson. He was the one who conducted the autopsies on all the victims."

"I've known George for years… There must be some mistake. We talked to him a lot in the early days of the Spark inquiry."

"Teddy Ludlow and I went to his house. He has a little cottage in the woods on the West side of town. When we got there, he was trying to kill Teddy's daughter and succeeded in killing a little boy. Greta told me that a boy from her school went missing recently. My bet is that it was him." Will paused. His voice came out in a rasp. "Only there was something we couldn't figure out. I found the bodies of the Spark brothers, Ed the chef, and Meredith Flax in his house. There was no sign of Abigail."

"The bastard most likely hid the body. Poor girl is probably at the bottom of some lake."

"No. George kept all the bodies. I dug up their graves and there was only one coffin that hadn't been disturbed— Abigail's. I found it strange. Why not take hers too? They protected him from the monsters—or at least he thought they did. He had positioned them around his bed. At first, I thought they were trophies. You'll know a lot more about this than me, but I believe some killers keep parts of their victims to remember them by. I got to know George a little better. He is not one to keep trophies. Now I know why they were there. They were scarecrows."

"What happened to him? Have you told Frank?"

"The house caught fire. He was trying to burn Greta Ludlow. I tried to get him out, but the whole building collapsed, and he died. I haven't seen Frank yet."

Marty wiped a hand across his head. "Bloody hell… quite a night."

"There were some things that didn't make sense to me. At first, I put it down to George's insanity. The more I got to know him, the more his thinking came quite sane, as long as you knew the start."

"You should be careful. I've had enough experience with criminals to know how they think. It will change you."

"In the same way it changed you?"

"What do you mean?"

"It was you who killed Abigail."

Marty tilted his head and breathed out sharply. "I know of your actions at the light show. The whole town thinks that you're insane. Is this another one of your delusions or have you actually got some basis for your accusation? You said it yourself, George Upson was the killer."

"When I met you again, you told me that you had changed your name. You said that you used to be called Marty Daniels. I met a girl—a prostitute called Destiny. She told me that Abigail Finsbury had a best friend called Katie. Katie Daniels.

I never put two and two together. There's no reason for her to change her name."

"Daniels. God, I miss that name," said Marty, smiling.

"That was the first hint. Stupidly, I didn't bother to follow the lead. Is that how you met Abigail? She was your daughter's friend? You twisted piece of shit. To think that I actually liked you. You seemed like a good man in this God-forsaken place."

For a second, it seemed like Marty would continue playing innocent. Then he smiled. "Abbie came over almost every day. She was a good girl—kept my Katie on the right path. I waited for a while, but sometimes the urges are too strong." He took another inhale of smoke and blew it onto the window where it pooled into a gray smudge on the glass. "It was completely two-sided. I'm many things, but I am not a rapist. Oh, those were the days. It's always more fun when it's a secret." He started laughing, "I met her old man! He shook my hand and said thanks for taking care of his daughter. If only he had known…"

Will's breathing quickened. "For all these years?"

"Of course not. Like all things, we stopped when she went off to college. I never forgot her. When I thought about everything she would be getting up to there, it made me mad. Who was she with? Whose bed was she waking up in each morning? Then she came back. Katie invited her over for a party last year. The spark hadn't gone; if anything, it was brighter. She told me that there wasn't anyone else. That she had counted down the days until she could see me again."

"You make me sick. A girl forty years younger," said Will, coughing. He staggered over to the couch and slumped onto the seats. The smoke had choked him, badly. Everything ached. Marty took a cushion and held it out. Will slapped it away.

"Fine, just thought you'd rather die in comfort. We can't choose who we fall for, Will. I thought I had that with Clarice. Tricked myself into believing it for twenty-seven god-damn years. Abbie was different. I *knew* that she was the one."

"You don't kill someone you love."

"I had to," Marty said, wincing. "That night. She told me. She told me that it was over. How can it be? I'd loved her since she was sixteen. Do ten years really mean nothing to you kids anymore?" His words were faltering, following the jerking of his head. He raised his cigarette with trembling hands and smoked. "And it was all for another boy? A skinny, acne-riddled germ. She wouldn't have gotten through college without me sending her money every fucking term. What could this guy give her that I couldn't?"

"I don't know. Maybe a night without the help of little blue pills," said Will. His face was dripping with sweat. He wiped his forehead on his sleeve. Marty laughed once and then brought his fist into Will's jaw, sending him crumpling into the seat.

"You've never known when to shut up. I'm telling you what happened. You should have the fucking decency to listen. No wonder your own father hates you. I've gone undercover in gangs and cartels, and that was less painful than having to talk to you. Pretending to like you was the hardest job I have ever had."

Will didn't have any other choice now. His jaw had made a sickening cracking sound when Marty had made the connection and he now felt static crawling across his face.

"Does Frank know?" Marty asked, his voice steadying slightly. Will shook his head, causing another wave of pain to cling to his jaw.

Marty nodded and crushed his cigarette on the windowsill. Will had to be careful. Even without the cancer, Marty would be a good deal stronger. Not to mention his years of combat training from the FBI and the fact that Will was certain his jaw had broken.

"I knew it wasn't a good idea to get you back to work on the case. You should have left when I told you. Frank was only going around in circles. You know, before the Spark boys, Frank would have been on me in an instant. The amount that man has missed due to his obsession is frightening. One time he walked in and Abbie was under my fucking bed!"

Should Frank have known? How badly did the Spark case affect him?

"In the end, I had to. My career could have ended. That wasn't the main reason, however. I simply couldn't bear to have anyone else touch her. Not my Abbie."

"You sawed her arms off, you sick fuck," said Will.

"Your Dad was so obsessed with the Grimm Reaper's return that he never once considered that it was his old pal," criticized Marty, before laughing. "How many people have got away with murder because the detectives were too busy looking for patterns? It's not just me who has slipped through the gaps. Do you think all of those Ripper kills were carried out by Jack? Or do you think that someone saw an opportunity? They made the killers more than human."

"He should have seen through you."

"And he would have if he hadn't drunk himself stupid after he got fired from the Bureau. My fault. In fairness, I told him not to take the case notes home. We were under strict instructions to leave them in the office."

"You were the one who stole the case files. Why?"

"I was angry. Stupid. Frank comes along and instantly becomes the star player. Doesn't leave much room for someone like me."

"You were partners. All those cases you solved were a joint effort."

Marty shook his head. "Nope. I'm not ashamed to say that Frank was always smarter than me. Better with a gun, too. You know how his head works. He notices stuff—patterns that no one else picks up on. He worked out the *Grimm's* link way before I had even considered it."

"You took them to make him look bad?"

"I took them so that he would fall a step or two. Never thought he'd lose his job for it. Admittedly, when he did, I was glad. I didn't work my way from nothing just so he could saunter in and make me look like garbage."

"Frank's not like that."

"Then you really don't know him. It wasn't until the MED came into the equation that he started losing his touch. It affected him worse than the others. I know what the MED can do to a man. Frank never used it as much as I did. He knew how it worked, but never understood its effects. More addictive than crack. It was just my luck to catch you on a day that you had left it behind."

Will thought back to the mugging. He had left the rewind at the motel. Eve had said it was a homeless man who had beaten him.

She was always a figure in my head. She told me what my mind believed.

"It was you? You mugged me on my first day here?"

"I thought you would have the rewind. I knew you would go to the alley first. When I heard you talk down to that hobo scum, I saw a chance. When I found that you didn't have the rewind, I knew I had to make it look like a robbery," he said. He put his hand in his pocket and took out Will's wallet and threw it over. "I didn't need any money. Just a motive."

"Why? What was the point in bringing me here?"

"Frank insisted. I tried to put him off, but he was adamant. He said that you would help us. I knew I would have to keep a close eye on the goings-on once you arrived. When Bruce Fisher arrived, I could only hope that he had seen nothing incriminating."

Will remembered Marty's anxiety when Fisher arrived. Now it was clear. That night could have put him in jail.

"I am a man of justice," Marty continued. "The Billboard Murders have always fascinated me just as much as Frankie. The killer's identity has always been of great interest to me. Now, I know that I should have tried harder to get rid of you, although I confess that the closer you were getting to revealing the Reaper's identity, the more I resisted. His psychological profile told me that he would be charged with Abbie's death either way and then the matter would never be looked into again. By finding the killer, you were putting a stop to the investigation. Any new evidence wouldn't even be glanced at." He paused and looked at Will. Finding it harder and harder to stay conscious, Will matched his stare.

"It's over. Hollyhead will find out what you've done. I'll make sure of it."

"I know you're a writer, but even you should know that is a fantasy. I could kill you just as easily as Abigail; you're dying anyway. I'd be doing you a favor. Cancer and a crippled mind; a combination that means your death would be unquestioned. Running away from his issues for a final period of serenity. You might get a page in the paper. Nothing more. No one cares about a has-been author. You'll be forgotten."

Before Will could step away, Marty was on him, his hands scrabbling for purchase around Will's throat. His strength was overwhelming, powered by raw hatred. The pair toppled over an armchair, collapsing onto the floor. Marty lifted Will's head and slammed it down onto the floor, sending electrical sparks flying through Will's neurons. His jaw screamed in pain as his head was pushed further, enough to cause cracks in the hardwood floor. Through the sparks and glare, Will saw someone. Red dress. Dark hair.

At least I'll be at peace. With you, Eve.

He stopped struggling and allowed Marty to crush his windpipe. As his lungs fought for air, he relaxed, allowing himself to slip into the black stars.

It won't hurt anymore. Wherever you are, it will be home.

As Will took one last breath, there was a thunderous crash, and Marty's hands loosened. A figure had entered the room and Will's vision came back as air infiltrated his system. It was Frank, looking angrier than Will had ever seen him.

In a move that Will had only seen in the movies, Frank darted forwards and lifted Marty off his feet. They crashed into the wall, sending the drinks trolley flying across the room. Marty spluttered as Frank's hand closed around his neck.

"It wasn't just you who wanted to find the killer, Frankie," he wheezed, his eyes starting to bulge in their sockets. Frank's grip tightened and Will heard the rattling attempts of breath twisting through Marty's windpipe.

"You destroyed my life. My reputation was shattered because of you. Everything I ever worked for, gone in a moment."

"I never left you behind, Frankie. I paid your bills! I looked after you. We were in it together!" gasped Marty. His feet were searching for somewhere to push from — anything to release the pressure on his neck.

"You're going to kill him," said Will, his throat still tight.

"Just like he killed Abigail, you mean. Yes, I heard," he said. He turned to Marty. "For once in your life, you should have stopped running your mouth and listened," he said, his hand clenching harder. "Why shouldn't I?"

"Because then you would be what your whole career was built against," choked Marty. After their years together, Marty knew how to get inside Frank's head. Slowly, Frank lowered him down and released his grip. Marty fell to the ground, coughing spittle from his mouth.

"The police are on their way," spat Frank, taking his tape recorder from his pocket and showing it to Marty, whose face sagged into fear. "This will be enough evidence for a start, I think. Then I'll see what else I can dig up on you. Once I'm done, the electric chair can have you."

*

The house was eerily quiet. Frank had escorted Marty to the police station, leaving Will alone in a home that held so many empty memories. He walked into the hallway, not bothering to switch on the light; he knew the way. The wood groaned under his weight as he walked up the stairs, feeling the grooves of the banister beneath his fingers. His other hand ran over the walls that framed photographs had once decorated, now bare except for the chips and stains that had accumulated over the years. And onto the top floor. Three rooms—a bathroom, Frank's bedroom, and Will's. Will moved towards his door and turned the handle. It swung open without a creak, revealing his childhood room. It was exactly how he had left it. A striped blue and black blanket covered his old bed. His guitar, which he had only picked up on a handful of occasions, was standing by his closet, looking as clean as the day he had bought it. Will crouched down by his bookcase. Models of World War 2 planes were arranged on the top, a hobby that had kept him busy during the weeks when Frank was away. An assortment of books still filled the shelves: Dickens, Poe, Lovecraft. Metlocke—*The Death Clock*. The only book he had been proud to write, proud to have seen in bookshops on its release weekend before the reviews came piling in. Will had imagined that Frank would have turned his bedroom into another office, maybe even a gym. No part of him was prepared to see it exactly how it was, with the addition of his own work.

He sat down at the foot of his bed and closed his eyes. The night had passed in a manic rush. If not for the adrenaline, he was sure he would have collapsed. He couldn't help but think of George's demise and how the fire had turned into the figure of the Reaper. How long until it came for him?

"Sometimes it's brave to run away," whispered a soft voice in front of him.

Will gave a pained smile. "You're back," he said, opening his eyes.

There was Eve in front of him, her long hair falling across a scarlet dress. Will didn't think he had ever seen anything entirely pure; this came pretty close.

"You said you would take me dancing. You told me to pick out my favorite dress."

"That was before I found out you aren't real."

"I guess that does put a spanner in the works. I often find that the best things come purely from our own imagination. I guess I am just like someone from your detective book."

"Too perfect to ever actually exist."

"Not perfect. Just perfect for you. Exactly what you wanted me to be."

"I know that you're not real, but we can still talk. You still exist in my mind; I just need to use the rewind," said Will. He could already feel the back of his eyes stinging. "People talk to spirits all the time. It doesn't make them crazy—just religious."

Eve lowered herself to the ground. "I could exist your whole life. I think we both know that's not right."

"Just five more minutes? What are five more minutes compared to the rest of my life?"

"A considerable amount in your current state. If you knew you were going to die tomorrow, then you would want those five minutes."

"I think I have a little longer than a day."

Eve tilted her head in thought. "You could have longer than that. You just need to go back and see Dr. Christensen. These people are here to help you, Will. They don't want to take advantage of you. Besides, five more minutes can turn into a lifetime very easily."

"Would that be so bad?"

"I would love it."

"Just think of it. We could go anywhere. You and me. We can forget all of this. Writing and all this detective crap. I don't want to do it anymore." The words came spilling from his mouth. He wasn't sure if they made sense, but they were real. "I've spent so much time focusing on the dead in my life, I think living is more important right now."

"Will, we can't. You can't."

"You've seen all these people. Dad, Marty, Teddy, and the rest. They're stuck here. It's all fading as we speak. Let's not fade as well," Will took the rewind from his pocket and placed it beside them.

"You could never fade."

The pair looked at the rewind lying in the middle of the floor, its lights still blinking wearily.

"Should I do it?" asked Will.

"I'm only going to tell you what you want to hear."

Will nodded. "You'll leave. I'll never be able to see you again."

Eve kissed his cheek and lowered her head onto his shoulder. He groped for her hand and intertwined his fingers around hers.

"I've only existed in your head. I don't think I'll just disappear. Whenever something was, there will always be something left behind, however small," she said.

Will sighed, still watching the glowing device. "I wouldn't have a career if not for that. We wouldn't have found George."

"I think you don't give yourself enough credit where it is due. The rewind showed you a lot of things, but it was you who remembered that George suffered from narcolepsy. You who found the connection between the victims and why Abigail didn't fit. The rewind didn't help with that. You're a good man, Will Metlocke. You just don't let yourself believe it."

"If you're not here, what is the point?"

"There's always a point. You just need to find it. Lenora is back with her kid. Maybe your story hasn't ended there. All I know is that your life will begin again once that piece of evil is gone," she said, pointing to the rewind.

His whole body shaking, Will stood up, gently pulling Eve up with him. They watched the device for a moment. "Do it for me," whispered Eve.

"Can I ask for one thing first?"

"Anything."

Will drew his hands away from hers and stepped towards his desk. His old record player, dusty and used, still remained next to his stack of vinyls. He picked one up, slid the disc from its sleeve, and placed it below the needle. *Moonlight Serenade,* scratchy but perfect, began to play.

"May I have this dance?"

Eve pretended to be shocked. "Well, this is a fine surprise," she said. She took his hand and they glided into the middle of the room. Placing his fingers on her waist, Will gently pulled her towards him, breathing in the soft fragrance of her skin that he knew could surely not exist. How could something imaginary feel so real?

"I've never danced before," he said.

"Neither have I."

"I guess we just sway a little?"

"I think a general rule is to keep talking to a minimum," Eve laughed.

And they let the music guide them, embraced by the rhythm. Clumsy attempts at spins were made until their wavelengths finally joined, and the steps became fluid. Their laughter only added to their enjoyment of the dance. What felt like the end of the world now seemed a little brighter, and Will reminisced over the events of the past month. The memories made him cry, but they continued to dance until the music began to quiet and the coldness of the night took over his senses once more. He had the feeling of anonymity. He was no longer Will Metlocke, the fraudulent writer, or the detective. The cancer had disappeared and all the depression he had experienced for as long as he could remember was fading with each movement. Now he knew what he wanted: to dance for eternity, listening to Glenn Miller with the girl he loved. There was only one way that could happen.

The pair stopped dancing. Eve looked into his eyes and nodded towards the rewind. "It's time," she said. "No one else needs to suffer as you have."

Will raised his foot, his hand still clasped around Eve's. His body felt like she was controlling it. "I'll see you again."

With that, he brought his boot crashing down onto the rewind. It crunched under the weight, sending bright purple sparks erupting from the interior. When he lifted the leg again, the lights had faded. The rewind was reduced to crumpled machinery. And his hand suddenly felt a little colder.

CHAPTER TWENTY-SIX:
FALLING

The Reaper was dead, and Marty was looking at the chair if the judicial system found him guilty. It was over.

Will followed the trail that twisted into the void. He had kept his promise to Melanie. There was nothing left; nothing, except the cancer slowly eating away at his body until his breathing stopped completely. He took a deep breath in, relishing in the feeling.

The cold had burrowed itself so deep into his skin that he felt numb and certain that he would never feel warmth again. Remains of snowfall were still resting in the crevices of trees and the ice on the forest floor had turned into a thick sludge. Coming here hadn't been a conscious decision. He had left the broken fragments of the rewind on his bedroom floor and walked from the house, forgetting to lock the door behind him. His memory of the walk was a fuzzy blur. For brief moments he had seen Eve. The pinpricks of light reaching through the trees had become her eyes and her voice carried on the wind, seducing his thoughts. Then the trees had fallen away, and the ground became covered in frozen pines on hard rock. At some point, snow had begun to fall again in ugly clumps. Houses in the distance were mostly vacant of life. It seemed that the lights he had seen had come from the Christmas lights in the town square. In a few days, they would be taken down and kept in storage until next winter. Everything has a lifespan; there was no point in prolonging it. With each year, the lights became more disappointing. They had all been seen before and the repetition would continue. Eve had offered something new. A release from the monotony of everyday life.

Underneath his feet, the rock was icy, but he walked forward without caution. Blake's Point. It seemed right. One final chance to show Frank that he had been weak on that night almost three decades ago. Falling had been too much for him. He couldn't solve the Billboard Murders. Will had proved that he was superior and here was the final chance to leave one final cut.

The darkness was calling to him. The bottom of the point was swirling with mist, almost coiling into a beckoning finger. He looked down, branches jutted out from the rock and he imagined himself falling. Air tearing at his face as he fell before colliding with the thick beams of wood, which would undoubtedly break whatever came into contact with it. Maybe he would miss the branches and fall straight down to the rocks below. His head impacting on the jagged edges and splitting into numerous pieces, followed by the rest of his body.

You couldn't do it, Dad. I saw you in exactly this spot, looking down. You wouldn't jump.

He had never been to the Point before. The connection between Frank and himself had been so strong that the path seemed engraved in his memory. It all led here. To a frozen cliff on a cloudless night. Ready to die after so long. Only a step away.

"Will," said a voice behind him. He turned. Frank was standing by the fence, wearing only his white shirt and pants. He hugged himself in the cold. "Would you mind stepping away from the edge? You'd be doing my heart a favor," he said, pulling down the barbed wire with one hand, wincing slightly as it cut into his skin. His eyes stayed fixed on Will.

A tear rolled down Will's cheek before falling onto the rock below. "I don't owe you any more favors," he said. "Go and make sure Marty gets what he deserves."

"I should have stayed with you," said Frank, inching closer. Each step was filled with trepidation—a worry that one wrong move would send Will over the edge.

"You had more important things to deal with."

"Not just now. All your life. I messed up. I couldn't handle watching you grow up without Monica." He hung his head. "We said we would do it together, you see. Your first day of school, first broken bone, first teenage argument. After she passed, I couldn't cope seeing it without her."

Will blinked away the wetness in his eyes. "She's been dead for nearly thirty years, Dad."

"I know. If there was anyone on earth that deserves to fall from that cliff there it's me. It's not the man who just saved a little girl and brought closure to a woman who has been left in the dark for the past twelve years. That man deserves his entire life back. If I could give him that, then I would. Now, the best I can do is give you whatever time I have left. Nothing else matters anymore."

The membrane of fog below seemed to depart slightly; Will could just make out the twisted branches below. "You couldn't jump. When you came up here that night, you couldn't bring yourself to take the leap."

"I don't regret the choice that I made that night. In fact, I think it may have been the only decision that I would make every time."

Will turned. Frank was only a few feet away, his last remaining grey hairs fluttering in the wind. It struck Will just how old his father looked. Frank's outstretched hand was thin and shaking. His body was marked with years of stress.

"How did you know where I was here?"

"Because I think we are a lot more similar than you think."

"It doesn't matter. Your goal is complete. The Grimm Reaper is dead. It's all solved," said Will. "It's what you always wanted."

"Right now, that is the last thing on my mind. Obsession is good for a hobby, but it will make you sick. The Lord knows that's true. I was using it as a distraction. From life. From you…"

"You should have told me about the rewind. For the last month, you have watched me lose my mind over apparitions when you knew that I was completely sane."

"My actions are something I regret greatly. I wish that I could say that the job hardened me to emotion. Although, I consider myself to have never been strong in empathy. As much as you were struggling, you were making progress toward finding the killer. When I realized that Eve Pocock did not exist, I knew that intervention was necessary. I thank you for seeing this through to the end with me."

"Maybe I started doing this for you. Then I made a promise to Melanie Spark. I told her that I would find out who killed her boys. This is for her so that she may finally find closure. And it's for me. The first good thing I've done all my life. Now it's done. That's all I had. A girl and a promise were the only things I had left."

Frank looked at the ground. "There are many reasons to give up. A man with everything he could want will always find a reason to throw it all away. You have more reasons than most. Life is about having one reason not to. I believe you have been thinking about this the wrong way, and a large reason for that is my fault. You were convinced that life was only worth it if you were famous. You thought that would make people interested in you. Fame is too much for anyone. It's the small things that we need to give reason to. Reading a book, smiling at a stranger, or even just getting out of bed. They are all reasons to live. We just need to value them a little more."

"All I had was Eve and she was never even here."

"A formulation of your own mind. Eve was a fragment of your soul and she wanted you to get help. She would never have wanted you to end your life. Considering that she was your own creation, I think that means that *you* were finding a reason to live."

"It doesn't matter what she thought. She was only the fumes from a drug-fueled hallucination."

"She was hope. Hope that this isn't the end for you. She showed you that happiness was not extinct. It's just a little harder to find for some people."

"You haven't been happy for years."

"And all those years were wasted because of that. Since you have come back home, I have found it again—if only briefly."

"When?"

"I showed you what I did on that night. Then we sat on the bench together. Those minutes have done more for me than therapy ever could. You're my son," said Frank, his voice hoarse, "and I love you."

"I'm terrified. I could go through all the treatment and it might not be enough. If I reject it, at least I know what's coming."

"You don't have to decide anything right now. A man should never be ashamed to change his mind. He just needs to face the consequences. After all this, I don't think you have much to be scared of."

"I don't want to lose myself. It's taken me so long to become the character I wanted to play," said Will, choking on his words. His thoughts collided with one another, dissolving into dust in his mind. They reminded him of the snow falling. Dancing in the wind until they settled on the ground and became lost with the rest.

"I don't want fame. I don't even want to be happy; I just want to stop feeling like this."

"I know, son," said Frank, taking the final step. Father and son were now standing side by side, facing their hometown. "The sun is coming up in a couple of hours. We could watch it together if you'd like to."

Will felt Frank's hand on his shoulder. Together, they sat down, and both let out a breath that had been shut away for the past few minutes.

"You know, there is something I don't think you have realized about Eve," said Frank.

"What?"

"Your visions came from that infernal machine. You took that vision and gave it life. Turned it into a character. Still, everything you saw were just images from someone else's memory. It means that Eve exists. Somewhere. I'd say the chance to see her in the flesh is something that is worth holding on to. Hold on to that hope, and then pray that she doesn't find you infuriating," he said, laughing.

And Will laughed too. Frank was right. There was a chance, however small.

The two men dangled their legs off the edge, waiting for the first few rays of the new day, the new year, to warm their skin.

EPILOGUE

Will Metlocke hated hospitals. The lights were too bright, and you could never tell who was ill. He felt himself holding his breath whenever he walked past anyone. Frank was by his side, hands behind his back. The pair walked towards the reception desk, a hollowed circle where a woman was sitting, scribbling into a logbook.

"Will Metlocke is here. He has an appointment for eleven," said Frank, checking his watch. He turned to Will. "Forty minutes to spare. We'll need to leave a little earlier next time," he said.

"Yeah, just in case I need to run a marathon before I get a needle poked in me," murmured Will.

"We might be able to fit you in a little earlier," said the receptionist. She picked up the phone and dialed. "Hi, we have Mr. Metlocke here. Any chance to move his appointment forward?" After a brief pause, she nodded and put the phone down. "Your lucky day. It's all sorted, you can go earlier." She leaned forward over the table and pointed, "down the corridor, first left, second right and you'll be dandy," she said.

Frank bowed his head. "Thank you. Come on Will," he said, pulling on the arm of his son's jacket.

"What does she mean, *lucky day*? I'm having chemo, not choosing a new puppy," said Will, glancing back at the receptionist with confusion. Frank ignored his comment and began muttering the directions under his breath. Will hadn't bothered to listen; he couldn't keep his mind from the anxiety of what was about to become; the long road to recovery, which was far less likely than it had once been.

"This is it," said Frank, pushing open a set of double doors, half burgundy and half a dull brown, with two circular windows at eye level. He stepped aside to let Will in. The room was wide and sparsely decorated. Six emerald green chairs were sitting against the back wall, a window between each with a bright view of the grounds. Will and Frank were alone, except for a woman at the end who was reading a magazine. Will's heart quickened.

He took in three deep breaths before sitting down. Frank looked around for a chair and pulled it close to Will.

"How are you feeling?" he asked.

"Like I'm about to hurl."

"At least you are in an appropriate place for it. I'm sure they have a bucket somewhere," replied Frank, as he pulled a thin curtain around their seats.

"You don't have to stay, you know. The trial will help bring you closure."

Frank waved his hands. "No, no. Marty Daniels is no longer of interest to me. Some things are more important."

Will smiled and the pair waited for a few minutes. He counted his pulse with two fingers. It gently dropped down to a number slightly less worrying.

"Have you heard from Teddy?" Frank asked.

"Greta suffered second-degree burns. She was in the hospital for weeks. I don't know how long she was in that furnace, but she wasn't unconscious for more than a few minutes. They're still testing whether she has any long-term brain damage. She should be OK."

"Physically, perhaps. I fear for her mental health," said Frank. After a few minutes, a nurse entered, her hands full of bags and more medical supplies. Will sat with his eyes closed in an attempt to stop the world from swaying.

"Good morning gentlemen; how are we doing today?" said the nurse.

"I think we're a little nervous," replied Frank.

"Well, you wouldn't be the first." There was something familiar about the voice. It was like a narrator reading a children's book. A voice that felt comfortable. He opened his eyes. The nurse was facing away from him, rummaging inside a brown bag. Her hair was tied into a bun, poking out from a nurse's cap. His heart began to race again, only this time it wasn't due to anxiety.

"When I heard you were coming in today, Mr. Metlocke, I couldn't help but ask if I could tend to you. I've never met anyone famous before and I truly loved your detective book," she said, still not facing him. "I know it's unprofessional and you have a lot on your mind but is there any chance you could sign this?" she asked, taking a large book from her bag. She turned around.

Eve Pocock was typed across her name badge. The smile was the same; the eyes still filled with a kind of naïve optimism. She looked slightly older, but there was no doubt that it was her. Will took the book, and she handed him a red fountain pen.

"Anything in particular?" he asked, flipping it open to the title page.

"Whatever comes to mind," replied Eve, almost buzzing with excitement.

Underneath the title, Will wrote: *Eve, my biggest fan. You've saved my life in so many ways.*

He closed the book and handed it back. She thanked him. Will closed his eyes and felt Eve roll up his sleeve. As the needle entered his arm, he hardly felt a thing.

TOM PRATER

About the author:

Tom Prater was born in Bath and currently resides in Wiltshire. He studies Psychology at the University of Exeter. He hopes to one day write for Doctor Who (being The Doctor is out the window because his acting skills are atrocious). When he is not writing he can often be found listening to The Beatles, daydreaming, or annoying his cat when she is trying to sleep.

This is his first novel, although he has had some short stories published such as 'The Widow's Tale.'

He can be found on various social media pages
@Tompraterbooks
Twitter: Tomprater9

A note to the reader

If you have enjoyed this story, the best way you can help me spread the word is by leaving reviews on Amazon, Goodreads, and Google. Word-of-mouth also goes a long way in helping me. I would also be hugely grateful for any social media posts.

Thank you for reading Grimm's Puppets.

Printed in Great Britain
by Amazon

12629613R00181